THE CAPTAIN WITH THE WHISKERS

THE CAPTAIN
WITH THE WHISKERS

BENEDICT KIELY

With an afterword by Thomas Kilroy

Methuen

Published by Methuen 2005

1 3 5 7 9 10 8 6 4 2

Copyright © 1960 by Benedict Kiely
Afterword copyright © 2004 by Thomas Kilroy

The right of Benedict Kiely to be identified as author of
this work has been asserted by him in accordance with
the Copyright, Designs and Patents Act 1988

First published in 1960

This paperback edition published 2005

Methuen Publishing Ltd
215 Vauxhall Bridge Road, London SW1V 1EJ

Methuen Publishing Limited Reg. No. 3543167

A CIP catalogue record for this book
is available from the British Library

ISBN 0 413 77392 2

Printed and bound in Great Britain by
Cox & Wyman Ltd, Reading, Berkshire

To Frances

One

In winter by the window, in summer by the gate,
His thoughts were all so full of us we never can forget;
And so we think where'er he is he must be watching yet.
In memoriam—Anon.

WHEN THE OLD CAPTAIN DIED THE FAMILY WENT
strange and it wasn't with grief, and if you want to know why,
you should talk to somebody who knew the old captain. He had
soldiered against the Boers and one look at him and your heart
went out with quivering compassion to Kruger, De Wett and all
those pliant, easy-going, gentle, civil, amenable, soft-spoken
half-Hollanders. You couldn't think of anything they or their
forebears had done to draw down on them the punishment of
being matched against the captain.

It wasn't that he had a loud voice or overbearing ways. No, he
had a voice like oil, smooth, almost apologetic. He said his
words slowly as if he was thinking hard all the time and with
great effort trying to avoid even a syllable that would ruffle a
sixteen-year-old girl. You'd see him there on the Diamond Hill
when he'd come in from his big farm to the city, talking to the
priest or the doctor and his little box of a head nodding as if to
say yes, you're quite correct, and I'm only the most abject of men,
and the left thumb hooked in the gold watch-chain on the black
velveteen waistcoat and his right hand on the silver top of his
blackthorn.

1

It was the moustache and the whiskers betrayed him. They made you think twice about all that polite humility. There was something odd too about the flat, flat back of his skull. He had a neck all right in front but no neck that you'd notice behind, and if you study the shapes of most people you'll find something unusual about no neck behind and a neck in front. The whiskers and moustache were as oily as the voice but they were wicked, that's the only word; and I never knew what his eyes were like. I never saw them, for talking to him you kept your eyes all the time on that moustache, feeling that if he made a hostile forward lunge you'd have to grip its points the way you'd grip the horns of a cantankerous gentleman goat.

Talking to a doctor or a priest or a solicitor he was part of every Wednesday and Saturday morning when I had cycled my twelve miles to the city to school. Thumb in watch-chain, hand on blackthorn, moustache erect with wax, he was one with the city monuments, the old hilly streets that rose up, roofs like steps of stairs, to church steeples, for ever and eternally to church steeples. It was a small city of hills, old walls and bells, and he was a monument himself rivalling the winged Virgin Victory on one toe on her pedestal in the Diamond. Wednesday and Saturday were market days. He was an intensely practical man so that nothing less than a market day could bring him from his grey home in Bingen by the sea to the frivolous city.

'Good morning, Captain Chesney.'

My effort to sidestep, to circle him warily and pass on was seldom successful because I was toiling up hill and he was at his ease, majestically overlooking the descending housetops, the sidewalk chestnut trees, the old dark gateway in the seventeenth-century walls, even the brown stones of the Guildhall tower and the funnels and masts of the sparse shipping on the river.

'Ah, here is young Rodgers, the pensive cast of the scholar on his brow. A young man very interested in his books, doctor, unlike my sons, I regret to say.'

'Your boy Frank will do well, captain,' the doctor said.

'He might make a priest. He takes after his mother at the prayers. But I have little hopes of the other two ever making anything.'

'A priest in the family is a great thing, captain.'

'In this country there are too many priests in too many families. More priests in the country than soldiers in the army. If we entered a world war all we could contribute would be a quota of chaplains.'

The points of his moustache vibrated and shone. Mesmerized, I tried to move away, failed, halted with a despondent shuffle after the first step.

'Now, captain,' the doctor laughed uneasily.

The captain was a wit. With all his suavity and pseudo-politeness he was well known to be a man of strong mind and advanced opinions.

'In O'Connell Street in Dublin between the Nelson Pillar and the monument to Parnell I counted on the footwalk on one side of the street only, seventeen priests and two nuns. What would Nelson and Parnell have said?'

It was wellknown that the captain knew his history.

'The Irish vocation, captain, to preach the gospel.'

The doctor, a grown man who had cut people open for cancers and tumours, brought children into the world, saved lives in the Flanders trenches, was as uneasy as myself, a boy not long into long pants, my *Elementa Latina*, dog-eared, among the strapful of books under my oxter. The man never lived except my father, who was at his ease with the captain.

'The Irish vocation, doctor, is to avoid at all costs an honest day's work, and the vocation to the church, as we call it, offers an excellent opportunity.'

'They deny themselves a great deal, captain.'

'Do they deny themselves large brandies in the Dublin hotels or the golfing holidays at Lisdoonvarna or the trips to Rome, to see the Pope of course? Do they give up the motor-cars they never worked to earn?'

'They have to visit the sick, captain, just as I have myself.'

'In the old days the country priests went on horseback or on foot with a bellyful of poteen punch to keep the faith alive in them.'

'You must have priests, captain.'

'We have an exportable surplus. Our only surplus. I'd have them out on the African missions building log churches, or suffering persecution in Mexico. Make front-line soldiers out of them. Give them a chance of martyrdom.'

The slope of the street was against the doctor's chance of escaping as it was against my own. The captain, little box of a head nodding, the waxed tips of his moustache like antennae, his eyes, in hiding under lean-to lashes, swivelling to follow calmly the slow-sailing, swaying masts of a seabound ship, rested on his blackthorn in absolute, unassailable content. Now, long after the event, I can see that it wasn't his opinions that mattered. They were limited and harmless enough and frequently contradicted each other. But the opinions he chose to express at any particular time were always the opinions he knew, with diabolical, uncanny instinct, would offend or hurt his listeners. That doctor was a good church-going man with a brother an archdeacon and a son a curate, and why he, or a dozen others, did not under provocation strike down the diminutive captain was always a mystery to me.

The masts were hidden behind the brown Guildhall tower. The mellow Guildhall clock chimed. I dared to speak.

'Excuse me. I'll be late for school.'

'We mustn't be late, young Rodgers, we mustn't be late for our studies.'

But his dainty hand was on my shoulder detaining me; the gleam from his white cuff irritated my eye.

'The reverend Dr Grierson, that learned man from Louvain, tells me you have thoughts of going for the church yourself.'

There, now, was the poison in the little man, poison, as my father, who seldom spoke to him, said, in the hump; not that the captain was a hunchback, yet although his shoulders were straight and soldierly there was something in him that always watched and crouched. He didn't mean then that somebody had told him my mother was praying that I would become a priest, but that he knew all about the unpleasant, humiliating incident in the parish church on the previous Friday when the boys and girls were assembled for the weekly confession. His own five frightened children had been there and probably he had goaded the story out of them.

The boys were on one side of the nave at the back of the church, the girls on the other side. In a brown, carved confessional box in Saint Patrick's side chapel the learned Dr Grierson listened to the sins of the boys while the girls carried the soft whispers about their misdemeanours to the parish priest who sat, unprotected by any box, in the chill alcove that housed the baptismal font. Unearthly evening quiet, always a little terrifying to me, flowed out from dusky granite and marble corners, along the aisles under leaning, listening oaken angels, out to the churchyard, to long grass and dandelions around graves, to the last feeble chirpings of birds. The sanctuary lamp was one red eye. Swamped light came from a flickering candelabrum before a statue of the mother of God. Coloured light came slanting down on restless, bored boys and girls from the high

5

stained-glass window above the altar. It wasn't very good stained glass: commercial stuff imported from the continent when Irish priests first had full liberty and the means to build churches but no background or knowledge of what was good or mediocre. But it absorbed light beautifully and I loved it, and if it hadn't been for Jim Ball who sat beside me I would have contentedly computed my sins, tholed my boredom, drawn joy from the reds, blues and greens of the figures in that garish copy of da Vinci's last supper. Ball, the born jester, saw those bearded, vitrine faces as the faces of people we knew in the city, in our scimitar-shaped village, in the surrounding countryside, lakeshore, seaside. Judas with his purse was a village grocer; Peter, eyes white and vacuous, was Mickey Alone the tramp with his stump of a clay pipe; and, with ingenuity, Ball was seeking parallels for the sons of thunder when the learned doctor from Louvain struck me from behind on the right ear. Only for our laughter at the twelve apostles we would have noticed that awesome preliminary hush.

'This is a fine carry-on in God's house.'

He was a pale sensitive man with sunken eyes, close-cropped grey hair, a thin Roman nose.

'You, Ball, sit over there alone. You're a notorious troublemaker.'

Ball the hero clumped off to exile several rows of seats away, but bitterly I thought: it's my ear was struck.

'You, Owen Rodgers. What would your mother say? Aren't you supposed to be going on for the priesthood?'

Fearful silence: outside the suffocated birds; in the window the continental reds, blues and greens blindingly mingled, the twelve apostles leaned tipsily over da Vinci's table. But I knew that all the boys and girls in the church would have laughed if they hadn't been afraid, and I, embryo man, was mocked by the manly coarse feel of my first long pants under my sweating, agonised, humiliated palms.

'Speak up. Answer me.'

'I don't know, father.'

'You don't know.'

His precise, cultivated voice went on and Judas grinned at me out of the mess of glassy colour and I was running naked down slippery streets and crawling on my belly to climb impossible wet, boggy, green hills and all the young women from twelve to sixteen in my limited world laughed and pointed at me and said: 'Owen Rodgers is going to be a priest.' His voice, I thought, like the flames of hell will go on for ever and stout Lucy, over-developed physically, will laugh, and gangling Petsie with glasses, under-developed mentally, will laugh. My tears of shame and anger when one day in a scuffle in the tennis pavilion, wrestling Petsie had torn my jacket from the shoulder, flowed down like raindrops from the blue glass eyes of the beardless, nestling John. The voice went on and I was aghast before the un-explained mystery of women in those silent listening figures across the nave. The voice went on and one girl would emerge from and another enter the chill baptismal alcove to whisper what secrets to the parish priest. The voice went on and Lucy and myself, Daphnis and Chloe, out of some half-waking dream skipped white as fish the full length of the rainbow table in the upper room, a summer couple on the secluded sands behind Bingen. The captain's two daughters, Maeve and Greta, never in my agony occurred to me. They never occurred to anybody while the captain was alive.

Some one of the five or two or three or four or all five of them had told the captain about that incident, the lecture from Louvain, my own ignominious flight home when the priest had retreated again into his listening box of brown wood and leaden red curtains. How could I whisper my sins to that then detestable pale face? They couldn't have told the captain, because they couldn't have imagined such a thing possible, that I brought my woes to my father as soon as I was safely home. With his 'cello and piano, his seven violins, the clarinets and glittering brass that belonged to the local band, his shelves of Shaw and Wells and our own revolutionaries from Tone and Fintan Lalor to Davitt and Pearse, my father sat in our drawing-room and listened, and trilled like a troubadour on an ocarina. Then he laid down the ocarina and laughed.

'Poor Dr Grierson has my sympathy.'

From the wide bay window we could look over our crescent village, the round tower, the square Norman keep, the church steeple, to the sharp cut of the Gortin gap and the jagged heights that circled Bingen.

'Sympathy?'

'Take it from me, boy, he needs it.'

Because you could talk to him and trust him, because he knew about music and books and people, because he had been a famous centre-half and behind his rimless glasses had vague kind eyes, I took it from him without query or question. When Dr Grierson met me again he took me gently by the elbow and we walked as friends all along the crescent street. Lucy peered out at us from behind the hand-painted platters in the window of the shop where her father sold glass, china, hardware and earthenware; and which of the four was Lucy? Although I cringed then with gooseflesh because that friendly walk made it certainly look as if I was the makings of Melchisedek yet I knew the learned man meant well and I forgave him from my heart, and in time I found out, as lucky people who had fathers like mine always find out, that father knew what he was talking about. Learned Louvain and France and better living and per-

8

fume on Parisian boulevards were memories behind that pallid clerical forehead. The glass of wine glistens aloft in evening light in our odd drawing-room.

'But on the Continent, Mrs Rodgers, people don't drink as they drink here. Wine has a social function.'

Too social for the learned doctor, as whiskey was too strong. I saw the tray myself late at night passed mysteriously into the bar of a certain hotel, passed out again, to a private snug, with its grinning glass of Jameson's social malt, passed in and out, in and out. The men drinking after hours at the bar-counter pretended not to see, not to know nor pity, not to prophesy, with foreboding eyes and lulls in the murmured talk, the *dies irae* of episcopal censure and demotion. Alone in the snug, the reverend doctor was sociable with his memories, in conflict with the cabining present, wrestling with his dark angel: to carry God's body with a shaking hand from mouth to mouth along the perspiring marble rails; to read the long Palm Sunday gospel with heavy eyes and uncertain voice; to sit, closed in red curtain and brown wood, with chalky palate, remembering Paris, listening to little boys' stories about apple-stealing and self-abuse.

High above the Guildhall tower the captain breathed salt air as if like Bingen it belonged to him alone.

'The learned cleric in his less convivial moments has some interesting theological conundrums. This one should interest you, young Rodgers: Is it better to be born and damned than not to be born at all?'

'I couldn't say, captain.'

'You haven't considered the matter, yet. But you will. You'll get plenty of the like when you go to Maynooth.'

The medical man fussed and looked at his watch.

'The hospital's waiting, captain. I must be off.'

'We mustn't hold up the hospital routine, doctor.'

'I'll see you at the trials, captain.'

'You'll be welcome, doctor. It will be a big day at Bingen. Perhaps young Rodgers would care to come. He could talk theology with my son Francis.'

He never said simply Francis or Edmund or Alfred or Greta or Maeve but always my son this or my daughter that, and marked thus his ownership and power.

'Is it better to be born and damned than not to be born at all?'

His smooth, well-shaven skin crinkled momentarily, then was smooth again with noiseless laughter at the thought of that hopeless choice between hellfire and dark neance, the predicament of something less than man and subject to absolute power or blind, groping, thrusting vegetable chance. The glossy moustache tips, the hairs of his whiskers were electric and alive.

'Yes, captain, I'd be glad to go.'

I knew what he meant. His hand released my shoulder.

'Off to school then. Good-bye, doctor.'

But we didn't leave him, he left us, left the doctor, tall, decent, ashamed before my young gaze that he hadn't exploded like a man and assisted the captain's triumphant departure with a dynamic downward push. The doctor mumbled something, uttered nothing articulate, went off uphill towards the winged Victory toe-balanced on her Diamond pedestal and, like every female on every monument in every town in the world, the butt of broad jokes about her singular intactability. Fascinated, I watched the captain descend from chestnut tree to chestnut tree along the steep footwalk, his small feet, polished shoes glittering, tight pants, good tweeds, neat, small shoulders, tweed cap topped by a button, down and down and down, swinging his stick, stepping smartly, growing smaller and receding into history as he descended, oh, they marched through the town and their banners were so gay, Red Coats, Boer war drums, Martini Henrys, Kipling, Dolly Gray, Mafeking and inflated talk, down past shops and a cinema and pubs and offices. The cave of a gate in the old walls received him and the world was normal again. The Guildhall clock marked another quarter. Far down the river the Glasgow-bound ship hooted derisively. I was late for class and mutely took my punishment, for under God what was the point in telling anyone that I had been detained by Captain Conway Chesney's dissertation on the benefits of creation?

There is a grove in Haemonia, a fine name for the part of the country I come from, shut in on every side by steep white hills of granite. Its name is Magheracolton but men call it Bingen because the captain renamed it as an echoing memory of his travels along the Rhine, and who could gainsay the captain? Through this grove flows the foaming water of the Gortin river gushing out from the bottom of the Gortin range. The noise of the water wearies the ear far beyond its own neighbourhood. This was the home, the most secret haunt, of the great captain. Sitting here in a grey-white house cut out of the local stone, he dispensed justice to his sons and his two nymphs of daughters, Jove himself protect them.

That, as you can see, is a slightly altered passage from one of the books of Ovid they never gave me to read in school, that diverting book about animals turning to stone, men and women to trees or animals or stones or stars, seduced Io to a sleek heifer, and of genial Jove trying his luck with a Grecian nymph every time Juno turned her broad back; and it's my way of introducing you to the sheep-dog trials on the greensward before the captain's house in Bingen.

From our drawing-room window and even from our garden gate where I swung my leg on my bicycle you could look over our crescent village to the sharp cut of Gortin gap and the jagged heights that circled Bingen. To the right, beyond the village, the first glimpse of sea was a long tongue of silver water narrowing to a point, lapped between fields. It shone like a vision the morning I set out for Bingen. It was a silver tongue in the green mouth of God, it was a sword restless in a green scabbard, and the village, clean, quiet, still asleep, was a new village. Our own bungalow, all squares and inexplicable curves and painted a vivid orange, had been modelled by a half-demented local contractor on something my father had seen in a book about new building in Germany. It squatted incongruously, mockingly, like a yellow God with a curved green eye, on its superior height above aged, whitewashed houses and a few mansions of grey, weathered granite. Portly and warm with red brick was the easily identifiable house where the parish priest lived, then a monumental works with crude crosses and pious, expressionless statues, then four red petrol pumps, the first pub, two grinning, satiated dogs meditating on the previous night, then the half-mile sweep of the crescent street as far as the Big Oak, the pub and the actual tree, where roads went east and west along the sea. But my short cut curved left around the crosses and statues, uphill through narrow lanes of tiny, whitewashed cottages with loitering greyhounds and dishwater marks like the tracks of giant snails. My road passed the church, the door still closed, the dew bright on the deep churchyard grass that seemed to have dandelions all the year round because, Alfred Chesney said, dandelions grew better out of dead men. The thing suppressed by terror of the captain in Alfred when he was at home broke out, wild-eyed and hunchbacked, as the most outrageous whoppers, when he escaped to the relative liberty of school. My road passed the round tower that had no top on it (an American tourist once asked what firm made it, was solemnly given the name of a Dublin printing firm, solemnly wrote it down), passed the bridge, the old churchyard where the poet was buried, the square Norman tower. My road wallowed for five miles in fat well-watered farmland, then climbed in curves up Gortin Gap, brown and bare in those days before the orderly ranks of afforestation took possession of the hills. My road paused for rest on the crest of the Gap by a cool spring with a stone seat beside it. The inscription cut on the seat told you to rest and be thankful and the same words, it was said, with what truth I know not, were stamped on the back of a certain light lady once the popular toast in those mountainy places. Sitting on the stone, so cold in the morning that it must long have forgotten the light lady, I looked back beyond the village to the big lake and the far smoke of the city, and forward and down on Bingen, crystalline white hills guarding it, beyond it the wide rolling Atlantic.

Like the Elizabethan land-grabbers who came, uneasy in cod-pieces on awkward saddles, to conquer and possess, the captain knew how to pick a good place for a permanent abode. You could damn near reach out of a window in Bingen and take a salmon by the gills. The Gortin river, fed by rain-swollen streams that came cataracting down the high rocks, curved like love around the green ground on which Bingen House stood, spread out then over sand, narrowed again for thrust and penetrated the sea under Bingen Head. The granite house was two storeys tall and seven windows wide and behind it the barns, byres, stables, carhouses and haysheds were like a fortified town. Curved backs to the prevailing wind, a semicircle of sycamores and hazels shaped by wild air but still resisting it, guarded the place like a palisade. Far away along the sand a man and a horse were motion-less, the life drained out of them by distance. To the right the rich bottom land of Bingen went winding on for two miles under the mountains, every acre the captain's, and the sheep on the grazeable foothills and the four white, thatched cottier houses and the men and women who lived in them. A Rhinelander would have been surprised to hear the name of his steepled town echoing under those mountains. But he would have admired the man who renamed the place so thoroughly that even the old people no longer used the traditional Gaelic name, Magheracolton. He would have admired the German efficiency of the farming.

One of those cataracting streams began in the rest-and-be-thankful spring, crossed the road, took its first daredevil, musical plunge. As if it were a living companion I followed its descent with joy, stopped now and again over steep glens to look down on its body growing full and sinuous; and the sun came up warm. Even in summer the leaves on the Bingen trees were dry and brittle. They crackled like tinfoil as I walked my bicycle not on the long, unbordered avenue but directly across the flat grass, past the pen from which thrawn, blackfaced mountain sheep would be released in sets of four to test the wisdom of the dogs. I was first on the field and alone except for the distant man and horse and the morning rooks. By the wooden platform built for the judges I leaned my bicycle and, opening the small gate in the low wall that surrounded the house, tiptoed, I don't know why, up the path to the door and knocked, not too loudly, three times and in vain on the grained wood of the captain's Schloss. Two rows of tall Michaelmas daisies swayed from the waist and laughed at me. The ramblers were red and wet over my head. Terrifyingly, because they had seemed to be motionless the man and horse had vanished. Had a quicksand sucked them down or the sea or a sea-monster swallowed them? Utterly alone, rooks being little company, I was the victim of the feeling

14

that somebody from somewhere was watching me. It was poor policy to come so early to a strange house. There was a whisper within, I could have sworn, a light step on a stairway, a creak of a board as if someone had paused breathless, poised on one foot. But the whisper might have been the sea or the river and the creak the wind in a branch.

Then and there the house captured me like an incurable disease or a shady past or a drug habit or a perverted love. It was so totally different from anything I had ever known. There was love in my eyes, I fear, as I looked at it, and to circle slowly around it at a safe distance from the meaning and heart of it was to fondle flesh obscenely. No smoke from a chimney. The captain would be canny about fuel. I was the medieval traveller guessing at unseen beauties rising warm and alluringly dishevelled to lean out over casements while his horse pawed ground and he waited for bugles to say morning, drawbridges to descend, pennants to run out on the wind. Or in some alchemic cellar a black hunchbacked dwarf might follow the ways of evil. These coloured ideas came later with reading and reflection. When I climbed the oak tree behind the stables I was not then Kojja Nasreddin scaling his way into the harems of Bokhara but any boy climbing a tree as naturally as a cat or a monkey. Protected from birth by the high stable wall, the oak had grown as an oak should, an erect, legitimate child of good earth, no bastard of the seawind like the sycamores and hazels. As any boy would, I meditated sitting in a wide fork of the tree in preference to walking prosaically on the ground beneath, and then walked from that fork along a strong branch, leaped a few feet into the long loft above the stables. From low rafters drying onions dangled in string bags and the floor was wisped with hay. Down below, horses moved, iron shoes scraped cobbles, and through a trap-door I could see the shining black back of one of the chasers the captain kept. The smell of the loft, the smell of Fuenterabbia in lazy heat with garlic and onion and cattle odour deadening the air, drugged me. The black gloss of the animal's back dazzled me and I breathed in a trance with the deep breathing of the horses. The captain's voice alone might never have recalled me if the words he said hadn't been like gunshot in a family vault.

'Slope arms! Right wheel! Quick march! 'Eft right, 'Eft right, 'Eft right, 'Eft right. Halt! 'Tenshun! Alfred, you clumsy fool, lift your feet, they'll fall themselves. Gravity will bring them back to earth. Mark time. Lift. Lift. Lift. Up. Up. 'Eft right. . . .'

The words of a military instructor, obscenities excluded, and the captain was not in language obscene, are necessarily limited. But if Demosthenes had spoken down there in the farmyard or John McCormack sung by Bingen in the morning I couldn't have been more startled. For five minutes I sat there petrified while, matching his instructions, feet marched or slammed to rest on the cobbles. When I was able to move and had tiptoed to the far side of the loft to peer through swinging wooden doors down on the yard, I was just in time to see the captain strike Alfred heavily on the ear. The blow cracked like the snap of a strong ash branch breaking. To reach to the ear of his shambling, stoop-shouldered son the little monster had to go up on his tiptoes. Their big nailed army boots I noticed, oddly enough, before anything else, before the army caps and uniforms, puttees and all, the pipeclayed belts and shining buckles, before the clumsy, antiquated Martini-Henry rifles, a man's work to lift one, that they so laboriously carried. The windows of Aylmer's army and navy store, that grandiloquently named pawnshop, were interesting with such relics of ancient wars. But you never associated them, stuffed and immobile, with human beings, and only a madman would guy his sons in such regalia. Fascinated, I watched while they marched and counter-marched, wheeled, swung sharply at right angles, shouldered arms, presented arms, carried the ton-weight rifles at the slope (Edmund, no taller than the captain, stepped in perpetual danger of tripping over his), swung them to their shoulders (Alfred was the only one strong enough to balance his, straight and steady), sighted them on imaginary men of the African veldt, did everything but fire a shot or form fours. Fascinated I was, but ashamed too, knowing what it was to gloat and to pity simultaneously, to be in agony for friends in disgrace and to be unable to tear myself away from the absorbing spectacle, to wish to share my own kind father with them and to thank God fervently I wasn't the captain's son. Their faces were comic ciphers under the peaks of the caps: Alfred pale-skinned, the lower half of his face all chin; Edmund round-faced and olive-skinned; Francis thin and ascetic, with burning brown eyes that looked up suddenly and saw me, Peeping Tom Rodgers, at the red-leaded wings of the loft window. He made no sign. His face was unchanged. But he shook me so with fear and startled shame that I leapt away from the window, tottered and swayed on the edge of the trapdoor, saw below me the shining black back of the thoroughbred, had a mad vision of myself landing straddle like the hero of a cowboy film, galloping out of the stable, trampling the captain to death in my course and ridding the earth of a proven demon. But, thoroughly frightened, I staggered away from the trapdoor and fell on the floor. Sensing instinctively the struggle between myself and the law of gravity, the noble animal whinnied and stamped, battered wild, shod feet against the wood of his stall and made enough din to cover my fall and retreat. Ever since, I have had a warm spot for stallions. Back along the branch and down the oak like Kojja Nasreddin routed from a harem, Sultan's men in hot pursuit, castrating knives in their hands. Then away like an athlete across the grass to the edge of the

17

persistent river, not caring what woman's eye might look on me from a house window. My hands and wrists in the cold brown water, I lay on my belly on the bank cleansing myself, I hoped, from the sin of gazing at somebody else's disgrace, a desert father who had luxuriated with his phantom temptations, or Gyges who conspired with King Candaules to look on the naked beauty of the Queen. But an unlettered boy was unable to find refuge from ignominy in classical analogies. Because I had looked with half-amused curiosity I knew I was as wicked as the captain, and Candaules was only a name in a book. I'm looking for salmon, I said, the salmon are running now, the men will be netting them today, and I fooled myself that in the brown turbulent twists of the water I could see a flashing fish belly. But I knew in my soul I was just staring, dulling my eyes and the image in my memory until the look in Frank Chesney's brown eyes would fade. This was a haunted house and I was unhappy because I had seen one shameful ghost. I lay there until Frank, no longer dressed in that hideous, ill-fitting pawnshop uniform, touched me with his swordstick on the right shoulder-blade and said: 'Owen, we didn't know you were here. The people are beginning to arrive.'

Two hours later the first four scrawny, unbiddable black-faced mountain sheep were on the field and the first entrant, a sensitive, golden collie was at work.

'Release four sheep,' called the judges.

They stood with their broad tweed backs to the semi-circle of silent, tense spectators, and far away across the grass a man pulled a rope, a pen gate swung open, the mountainy four stepped out, suspicious even of the easy, carpet-like ground. This was a test of skill as old as time but I felt the house behind me and my heart wasn't in the ancient game. Close to the judges and myself the shepherd leaned against a post, whistled, spoke soft words that were shaped like the sounds of a shallow, summery river, and away went the lovely dog. He circled widely, out to the domino phalanx of parked cars. He closed in like a tiptoeing nurse on the sheep. He crouched like a kitten on the grass at the first sign they might bolt in alarm. He urged them gently on, nosed them towards the shepherd, responded delicately to every word and whistle from his master, curved the sheep slowly home to the pen, leaped up forepaws on the shepherd's shoulders to kiss the beloved face and take like a prima donna the cheers of the simple people. There was such understanding and love between men and dogs that it was difficult to imagine how the captain tolerated the exhibition on the green before his castle. The judging of rams in the rows of pens between the estuary and the west gable of the house was more in keeping with the spirit of the place. Fearless among those truculent brutes, he was the coolest, most appraising, most deliberate, the wisest, one felt, of all the judges. He knew the signs of value in their blunt, dangerous faces, wicked curving horns, broad backs and those other gentlemanly appurtenances which, rams being rams, a judge must take into consideration.

'The proboscis of the sheep-tick,' he said, 'is used for sucking blood. The Latin name is *Melophagus Ovinus*.'

A cynical dark ram excreted but nobody laughed. On the lips of the captain the name of *Melophagus Ovinus* was not to be treated lightly.

'My little daughter,' said Lucy's hardware father, 'was bitten by a hard, black, shiny bug-like insect. Do you know, captain, I couldn't squeeze it out of her skin. Not a squeeze. I had to burn it out with a cigarette butt.'

So that, I thought, seeing for the first time into the secretiveness of womanhood, was where Lucy got the blister, a boy
would have boasted of it, on her dimpled arm.

'Paraffin oil would have been better. A little dab.'

The captain dabbed imaginary paraffin oil towards the left
eye of the ill-mannered disrespectful ram, but, unmoved, the
ram stared back at him and bartered his chances of a red rosette
in the day's manly contest.

'You should have enough paraffin in your shop to bathe your
daughter twice over.'

There was laughter, in which the victim joined, at the expense of
Lucy's father, for Captain Conway Chesney was a recognised
wit.

'I never knew why,' said a farmer, 'a sheep louse would bite
a human.'

'Females of the species,' said the wise man of Bingen, 'have
been known to attack humans and after engorging for about
eleven days go through the act of fertilization within a period of
from two to three weeks.'

'They lay their eggs,' some daring noman translated.

The smooth-shaven skin tightened, the moustache tips
vibrated, but there on his own ground, master of men and of
rams, his horn-handled shepherd's crook above him like an
episcopal crozier, the captain was too self-possessed to show
annoyance at the unasked-for annotation.

'Without a blood bath the eggs remain barren and the young
could not be extruded from the mother just as their skin is
hardening into the puparium stage.'

This time nobody translated and even the rams behaved
themselves like house-trained poodles. Captain Conway Chesney
ended his discourse on the Sheep Ked, Sheep Tick or Sheep
Louse, called *Sciortán* in the native Irish but known to the

learned, and for ever after to Owen Rodgers, as *Melophagus Ovinus* the Lesbian lover of Lucy.

Tying rosettes for services rendered on the black brows of those arrogant, stinking males, the master of Bingen was at home among his brethren. His small feet were secure from damp in boots of good leather, for him no vulgar rubber, that laced up to his knees to meet breeches of corduroy. He wore no jacket, but outside a high-necked Aran island jersey of white wool, he wore a loose tweed waistcoat to carry his pipe, matches and heavy bemedalled watch-chain. Victoria's dew-lapped face shone from the central medal to remind us of valour displayed against biblical voortrekkers, and his skin shone with superfluous health, his whiskers with oil, his moustache with wax. The brass button on the top of his tweed cap shone back at the sun. The ramshorn handle of the crook, twisted and coloured by a craftsman in Scotland, did its part and likewise shone.

'A lost art in Ireland,' he said that day, 'the making of a crook like this. The Irish are too slovenly to preserve things as the Scots do.'

He was apart as the rams were, like a ruler, from the wise, affectionate dogs, from the dealers selling fruit and lemonade at stalls he graciously permitted them to erect. He was apart from the children of the countryside whom he allowed to play on the far side of the river while his men swept the water for his salmon. He was far, far superior to the big-booted farmers wasting their money on whiskey in the jovial tent or the cadgers, drovers, hangers-on, slinging the dregs of their beer into the river. I was apart from them myself. They were all fantasy to me after my vision that morning from the loft, after the uncanny feeling of being watched from behind still curtains, after the welcome the captain had given me in the vast, over-cluttered drawing-room of Bingen House.

Frank left me suddenly in the wide hallway where worn, uneven tiles were still wet from morning scrubbing. He was gone like a shadow down stone stairs to a basement. Until the captain's voice called me, I stood there puzzled, hesitating, staring at a picture called *The Tale of a Glorious End*. A tall, bewhiskered captain back from the wars with his arm in a sling, gave the news of a comrade's death to the stricken mother, quivering sister and upright tight-lipped father of the comrade. He raised his good arm and prepared to speak. But just as I prepared to listen, silence and gloom all around me, the real captain spoke instead and called me to him. Strange sounds have drawn men to drown in marshes. This was the bad enchanter of these black back-lands giving his commands; and the effect was all the more uncanny because when I stepped over the drawing-room threshold I could see no man at all. The glassy head of the shepherd's crook led me to him. It looked at me, from two mongol eyes the craftsman had cut in the dyed ramshorn material, over the backward-curving top of the high back of a low-seated armchair; and down low there the captain was hidden, an open book on his little corduroy lap. His capless head showed a bald circle four inches wide. He looked out at his land and I looked down at a baldness I had never suspected. Without turning around, without saying welcome, he tapped with a forefinger on the open book and straightway talked black magic to me.

'This book, young Rodgers, should interest you. A clever young man like you.'

'What is it, captain?'

'It's about necromancy, the black art, you know. It says here there's no reckoning how many children Gilles de Rais, the wizard, devoted to death in his orgies. More than two hundred corpses were found in the latrines of Paris.'

The tallest, widest whatnot I had ever seen in my life rose up like the Empire State Building in one corner of the room. It held, not tinkling trinkets or gewgaws, but tusks and horns and twisted knives and on the top shelf a brown shrunken skull.

'Have you read of Gilles de Rais?'

'No, captain.'

'Now I'm disappointed. Those good brothers aren't too strong on history.'

'They teach us all about wars, captain.'

'Because they've never been to war. Wizards are more famous than wars. There was a wizard once lived up there in the mountains.'

He point slowly, exactly, he was never the man for the vague wave of the hand, to a rugged corner between the Gap and the ocean. There was a stuffed snake on the wide marble mantelpiece and above it a portrait of the captain in red coat, gold epaulettes, a high helmet: as gallant a shape as Sir John Moore. They marched through the town and their banners were so gay that I ran swift to the casement to hear the drums play.

'Wasn't it Micky Doran, captain?'

For the first time he looked at me, almost with joy, assuredly with interest.

'Ah, young Rodgers, come to the top of the class.'

With a small dry hand he caught my wrist and led me around until I stood between himself and the light of the window.

'At least you know your local history, but then you heard your learned father talk about him.'

'He was at the black art.'

'Up in mountainy Segully where the fleas ate the man, as the proverb says. Your father was a great friend of his.'

'Once with a pitchfork Doran drove the four police out of the barracks in the village.'

'It was a graip. Your father misinformed you. I was a witness of the incident. Mr Doran was clad in long white underpants and a frieze overcoat, the last of its kind I've seen. What else did your father tell you?'

'He chopped the finger off a rate collector.'

'Hiding in his cabin, talking baby-talk like a child. He said: "My daddy always opens the door by putting his finger through the hole under the latch." The rate collector was idiot enough to oblige. Did your father tell you he was the only welcome visitor to the Doran cabin?'

'No, captain.'

'Ah, you should ask him. Not that I'd suggest your father dabbled in black art.'

Ashamed in the loft, I had clutched a net of onions so tightly that my right hand still smelt sour.

'Mr Doran had his sombre side. When his old sister died he kept her corpse in the house for a month so that he could profit by her old age pension. He went to prison for twelve months.'

'I never heard that.'

'No doubt your father spared you the sordid side. Could you reach the bell pull, my young friend?'

The little legs were crossed, his right foot in its good leather twinkled in mid-air following a perpetual motion figure of eight. The easy, sinuous movement, the twiddle of the shining toe absorbed me.

'I said, could you reach the bell pull, young Rodgers?'

'The what, captain?'

We had no bell pulls in our happy, crooked, musical bunga-low. You could talk easily from room to room. The bright air willingly conducted sound. At important moments like meal-times a half shout served for a summons.

'That white enamelled knob to the right of the fireplace. My

24

two daughters must have gone to China for our morning cup of tea.'

Warily I circled his living foot. It darted like the fang of a snake excised from the monster on the marble mantelpiece. The marble was as cold as they say a corpse is, when my left palm rested on it. The grate looked as cold as if it had never known a fire. Peeping over the brass firescreen I could see that it was filled with fragments of white paper frilled like fans, the handiwork of some lonely fanciful woman on dark afternoons of weariness when sycamores and hazels wrestled madly with the wind and the black horses stamped in the stables. Through long corridors of gloomy air the sound of the bell returned to me. My face was as hot as the grate was cold. Following the sound of the bell and carrying each a tray came Maeve and Greta; brown hair and dark hair and plain grey aprons were all I noticed.

'Supply and demand. Sit down, young Rodgers. Solve the problems of supply and demand and the world would be a simpler place.'

I agreed.

'To get the goods that are wanted to the place in which they are wanted. To get tea from the kitchen to yourself and myself who want it here in this room.'

The people were gathering on the green outside and soon, praise God, he would have to take his crook and walk out among them to show he was the master.

'My daughters, as you see, have solved haulage and transport problems and here is the tea. Do you use sugar, Mr Rodgers?'

I did, but I said no because I didn't feel like sugar.

'Two spoons for me, Greta.'

She bent over his cup and although I looked at her I didn't see her then nor for a long time afterwards.

'Supply and demand sum up everything. Food and famine. Men and women all the world over.'

He smiled sweetly over the steaming cup. He tinkled the spoon, as if it was a tuning fork, against the china and listened appreciatively to the tiny bell-like sound. The solvers of the haulage and transport problem were whatnots in the background and to humiliate them still further, I felt, he treated me as an adult equal, a person who knew about supply and demand, necromancy, the benefits of being born even if only to be damned. Supply and demand kept him talking until somebody tapped on the door, whispered to Greta who whispered to the captain that the judges were on the green.

Outside, apart from the captain, it was a Fenian day, a Homeric day: trials of skill, weather-beaten men with long crooks, shouts from the estuary where the nets came up showing living silver. Young couples rambled off across the narrow, swaying footbridge, stepping warily over gaps left by missing planks. For young lovers it could have been a thrill to cross that bridge because it had no handrail and they could arm each other across, together above swift water, to vanish into the warm security of the dunes. Myself, I was then more interested in the skill of the dogs or the salmon in the net than in the skirts of girls. The sun shone. The clouds that swung inland over Bingen Head were high and snow-white. Out in the air Alfred, Edmund and Frank enjoyed themselves as well as they could in the neighbourhood of their father. But the evening came when the Fenian games were over and the people on the road home. In the drawing-room the captain entertained the judges and a few special visitors. In the basement kitchen, where I ate with the family, gloom settled round us like clay round a new coffin.

Alfred was older than myself. He was tall, long-faced, pallid, prognathous. He sprayed minutely when he talked so that the schoolwits, on the odd occasions when he became vehemently eloquent, raised before his face imaginary umbrellas. The nickname we gave him, with the kindness so marked in young boys, was Slobber. His back to the kitchen's barred window, he ate morosely, his face in the shadow. Now and again he felt his right ear, recalling morning drill and the captain's disciplinary measures. He favoured the dreary company with none of the whoppers or wild imaginings he had become famous for since the morning of the Austrian dog.

'It's an Austrian dog,' he said. 'They get bandy-legged from walking through deep snow.'

It was a fox-terrier with curved, deformed forelegs coming to meet us as Alfred and myself ascended the Diamond Hill to school. From my knowledge of dogs I ridiculed Alfred, passed the story on to the class and bitterly regretted my nastiness afterwards when he sat pale, wet-lipped, silent, an Austrian dog himself, unable to reply to the repartee. But that evening I would have welcomed an Austrian dog, an Australian dingo, a Bactrian camel, some amiable, shuffling, comical creature to woof or bray into the silence, to set us talking and laughing like young people, after an exciting day, in any normal house in any country in the world. Edmund, of an age with myself, bright brown eyes darting upwards from under a low fringe of curly hair that would never lie back straight as he wanted it to do, did try to talk.

'That was one good day.'

Frank, silent since the door of the house had closed behind him, agreed that it had been one good day. Apart, eating at a small table of their own, the girls said nothing.

'There was a man today,' said Edmund, 'had a black and white dog answered only to Irish.'

No response. In the yard three feet above the level of the damp kitchen floor one of the men was exercising a horse, and man's legs and horse's legs passed and repassed the window.

'Up by Segully he lives where the magic man Micky Doran lived, and pays no licence for the dog. When the time comes for the police inspection he says to the dog, " *Siúd an Péas,* " and the animal runs up the mountain to hide until the police are gone.'

A very Irish dog, I thought, but said nothing and knew they were waiting for some further humiliation before my eyes. The prisoners were dead quiet in the cells just before their fellow was haled out for flogging. As eight o'clock chimed I heard the sharp, neat steps descending the stone stairs and knew the monster with the cat-o'-nine-tails was on the way.

'Here he comes,' said Edmund.

The others looked at him silently as if he had betrayed their dearest secret. Unable to run, wanting to say it was time for me to go home, I sat chewing chalk while the rhythmical steps, they marched through the town, came on and down. When the door opened the five of them stood up and faced it as if a band was about to play an anthem and honour compelled them to look towards the flag. By the living God, they stood to attention like statues in the great shadowy kitchen with the rough, black brace around the grey, red-and-yellow smouldering hearth. It could have been a cave out of a wonder story, so unlike it was to my father's fey bungalow. I stood up with them. What could I do? I was swayed as the undecided, the undetermined are always swayed when a tyrant takes control. What will he do? Will he flog them all, myself included? What sort of a house is this? I knew a moment of clammy terror. To be back and happy with the bass fiddle and the ocarina and the boys of the village band dropping in of an evening for chat and practice. In the stables across the yard the horses now and then clinked hooves on the cobbles. The sound was distinct as the chiming of clocks in a monastery. But when, for self-protection, I turned to face the fear, he was simply standing inside the door, a stiff-backed note-book in his hand, preparing to read. He looked at me and at his five puppets of children, and he may have smiled a different smile from his customary, taut grimace or it may only have been that the shadows tricked my eyes until I thought he looked human. I was too young then to know that the grey juice of the barley could make beasts human and turn decent men into beasts.

'I think our guest could sit down. I hope, Owen, you enjoyed your day.'

'Yes, captain.'

The guest sat down, his back to the window and the horse and man passing and repassing, and from the notebook the captain read out in a voice almost merry what he called the orders for tomorrow.

'Rise,' he said, 'at five-thirty.'

'Greta and Maeve,' he said, 'will in the usual way supervise the cleaning of the house from top to bottom. The silver, Greta, needs particular attention.'

Greta said: 'Yes father,' but she said it, as I remember, without any voice.

'Alfred,' he said, 'will be in charge in the stables. The bedding was disgraceful in the black stallion's stall this morning.'

'Edmund,' he said, 'will see to the cattle and the carhouses. You have plenty of help. I pay good money for it.'

'Francis,' he said, 'because of your delicate state of health you can take the air tidying up the green. The people around here aren't civilized enough to leave a place the way they found it.'

'For the boys,' he said, 'parade will be at seven sharp. After breakfast, since there is no school tomorrow, we'll walk the land.'

He closed the book with a snap.

'Dismiss,' he said.

They sat down. He clicked his heels and bowed to me like a German.

'Good night, Owen,' he said, 'my respects to your harmonious father.'

He was drunk, I decided, and mad and bad.

'Ask him more,' he said, 'about Doran the wizard. Your father is a mine of information.'

'Francis,' he said, 'you will walk to the gate with Mr Rodgers, junior.'

He went back up the stairs and only in hellish irony could pipes have played to the precise snapping of his feet. Mutely I shook hands with Alfred and Edmund, and Greta and Maeve moved their lips to whisper some farewell but they did not reach their hands to me.

The light was still white on the granite of Bingen headland but the sky in the vee of the Gap was red with sunset. We walked silently across the cool grey grass. Half-way to the gate the wind swept around our feet a fleet of orange papers that during the day had wrapped golden spheres of Spanish joy for the children of Bingen valley and beyond. They danced on past us in a widening semi-circle. From the spokes of my bicycle Frank rescued two fluttering captives, sniffed them for the odour of Iberian groves or warehouses like the cave of Ali Baba, released them to follow their companions.

'I could give you a hand cleaning the place now, Frank.'

Then he laughed at me, real amused laughter, and I knew for

the first time that he was growing up to be a strange, sallow man indeed. He clicked the catch at the head of the sword stick, speared a lonely fragment of newspaper on the six inches of blade that shot out.

'We could stab them,' he said, 'the way Hughie Heron stabs the flounders when the tide takes them up the estuary.'

Then he balanced the stick on his shoulder as if it was a rifle; he paced backwards and forwards, clicked his heels, right-about-turned as if he was a sentry at Buckingham Palace.

'It'll be easier work by morning light, Owen. The wind will blow them all away. Thanks for the offer all the same. But it might even be against army regulations to clean the place now.'

He rushed round and round in a circle, heading a bayonet charge, stabbing shadowy enemies with the little blade, the pinned piece of newspaper fluttering. He lay down on the grass near the gate and laughed and laughed. Knowing nothing better to do, I leaped on my bike, switched on my lamp, rayed it at the hills ahead. His laughter and his merry farewell followed me for fifty yards of the road.

The noise of the falling rivers was brittle, more distinct than it had been in the morning. All the stones were moving, chains and chains of stones at the bottom of the rivers, long ranks of stones by the edge of the sea.

The village band had been and gone. Jim MacElhatton's French horn was an uncovered Buddhist image on the drawing-room table.

'How did you like the barracks?' my father asked me.

He took off his glasses, rubbed his tired, near-sighted eyes.

'John. Please,' my mother said.

'That's what it is, isn't it? A barracks run by a perverted sergeant-major. He blows them out of bed with a bugle in the morning. Ask Hughie Heron or Fee the jockey.'

'I'd look well talking to Fee the jockey. A wee man with no nose.'

'The loss of a nose could happen to a bishop.'

'It would be more likely to happen to a drunk jockey who slept in a piggery on the night of Mountfield races and had his nose chewed by a sow.'

'He thought the sow was somebody else . . .'

'I dare say,' said my mother.

They laughed. I drank my cocoa. He put on his glasses and walked over to the naked French horn.

'The bugler of Bingen. The captain with the whiskers. We could offer him a place in the band. Jimmy MacElhatton's wind is failing since he took to county football.'

'I peeped through the blind,' he hummed, 'very cautiously in, lest the neighbours they might think that I was looking at the men.'

'Owen,' said my mother, 'is the schoolmate of those poor children.'

'For the band's troops were the finest I did see,' he hummed, 'and the captain with the whiskers cast a sly glance at me.'

'John, you shouldn't go on like that before Owen.'

'He'll know it sooner or later. The whole country knows it.'

'Did you see his poor wife?' my mother asked.

For the first time I realized I hadn't even expected to see a mother in that house. My father looked thoughtfully at my silence.

'She was a domestic servant,' he said, 'before she saw the

captain's brass buttons. To her face and before the family he advises them never to marry beneath them as he did.'

My mother bit the thread, tweaked the shirt button to test its firmness. Red hair had gone grey gently over a plump, contented face.

'Ten years ago,' she said, 'I saw her at Mass.'

'She's supposed to be an invalid,' he said.

Lovingly he drew its white garment around the shining brass of the French horn.

'Jimmy could have put the night shift on this monster before he went home. I suppose in a way she is an invalid. Sick in the mind and persecuted and buried down there in a dungeon.'

'That Sunday at Mass she had on an old shiny black coat that would disgrace a pauper.'

'Shane O'Neill, the history books say, used to keep a lady of his, the Countess of Argyle, chained in a dungeon until he felt like having her up for wine and supper.'

'John. Please,' she said.

I finished my cocoa.

'Go to bed and sleep now,' he said, and patted the cover of the French horn.

'Is it true,' I asked, 'that Doran the wizard of Segully where the fleas ate the man kept his deceased sister in the house drawing the pension on her?'

'It happened that way,' said my father. 'Michael Doran had advanced views on social welfare.'

Two

IT SEEMS UNNECESSARY TO SAY SO, BUT WE GREW UP.
Frank went off, as his wise father had prophesied, to become a
priest. Edmund took to his heels and fled to find a job in England. My father sent me to Dublin to study medicine and
Alfred went to prison for twelve months for a sexual offence;
and the captain died. The rivers raced down from the hills and
the winds blew over Bingen.

Alfred, the imaginative, the Austrian dog, began his adult life
by falling in love.

At a corner of the lake on the road from our village to the
city there was another village, a statue to a martyred patriot, an
eel weir, a big bridge with a clanking, movable, metal centrepiece, and a big house. The colours of the wide lake changed
with wind and sunshine. Clouds curtained and revealed far-shore
mountains. A river burst out from the lake, a bloated sullen
river with reedy banks, no relation to the wild tributaries of the
Gortin river, curved round the big house with its pines and
sloping lawns and Australian terriers and Alsatians, all female,
playing on the grass, passed under the bridge, through the eel-
weir, under the presented pike of the hero, went on unwillingly
to help ships from the Guildhall dock to the open sea. That lakeshore country was a green undulating land of small fields, long,
thatched, whitewashed houses fronted by flowering hedges and

well-kept gardens. Behind the houses were stacks of barrels and white packing-cases that brought the fish, in ice and salt, on their travels to Dublin and London. Every rise in the road along that shore showed infinities of blue lake and a boat here and there on the tossing water. Well-trodden footpaths or boreens under high hedges crossed the fields to the shore, the moored boats, the square, tarred sheds where the gear was kept. It was a land that prospered on and smelt of fish. On the islands in the lake and all along the flourishing shore the people thought of eels when they weren't thinking of bream, pike, salmon or freshwater herring, so that Alfred's true love once said, with the vehemence of a girl who came from the mountains and didn't like the odour of fish, that it was a wonder to God the lakeshore women didn't grow tails instead of legs, like the mermaids in the story books.

The Eel Queen of the Land of Fish was the widow woman who lived in the big house and owned the weir and the lives of the men who worked the weir and fished on the lake with miles of line and millions of hooks. Alfred's beloved was a kitchen-maid in the house of that powerful woman.

The veil fell from the patriot and his pike, and the eyes of Alfred being opened he saw a woman for the first time. She came from the mountains and danced and sang before him and, if she had been left in peace, could have made a happy man of the captain's eldest son. He saw her and he knew that he had found the long-awaited, long-expected spring, he knew his heart had found a time to sing, the strength to soar was in his spirit's wing, and the captain, who didn't believe in patriots, was far away at Bingen fishing with Hughie Heron, one of his four cottiers.

'Owen,' said Slobber the great lover, 'that's a nice wee girl standing over there on the grassy hummock behind the platform.'

The crowd cheered at that exact moment for Dr Grierson,

intoxicated only with the social wine of patriotism, had ended a thundering speech about rack and rope, the penal laws and the rebellion of 1798. The sullen river, tormented to energy by the will of the Eel Queen, gushed through the vee-shaped weir. Across the water, men loaded a lorry with white wooden cases packed with live eels for the London market, where the people would eat anything that didn't bite them first. Chains shrieked on pulleys as the cheering faded and, dripping out of the water, rose one of the huge storage tanks where eels were kept fresh but captive, ambushed by conical nets on their way from the lake's mud and weeds to the dark womb of the Sargasso deeps. The unveiled patriot, pike in hand, looked eagerly at the ascending eels as if, like ourselves, he was anxious for his food; or menacingly as if, remembering rack and rope, he was furious to see Irish food on the way to English bellies; and we looked in consternation at Alfred Conway Chesney.

'Over there,' he said eagerly, his lower lip glistening. 'On the hummock.'

'There are twenty girls over there,' said Jim Kinnear.

'At least twenty,' said Jeff Macsorley. 'We'll count them if you like.'

None of them, I thought, to be compared with Lucy of the house of glass, china, hardware and earthenware. Edmund said nothing and Frank, on college holidays like myself, was fishing with his father and Hughie Heron. Under the grey eye of my father and the baroque baton of Jim MacElhatton our village band let fly.

'They should play a wedding march,' said Jeff Macsorley.

'Or "Put your arms around me honey",' said Kinnear, waggling his hips. '"Hold me tight, huddle up, cuddle up."'

Edmund laughed suddenly, stopped laughing just as suddenly and looked over his shoulder at the eels.

'The little girl,' said Alfred, paying scant attention to us. 'With the blue coat, the brown hair, the blue handkerchief on her hair and the freckled face.'

'How much more of her can you see?' I said.

'Go on. Tell us. Tell us,' said Macsorley and Kinnear.

We all laughed except Edmund who went on looking at the eels as if he hadn't stopped every day on the way to school to look into the writhing horror of the tanks, and Alfred who went on staring at the vision, the sun woman on the green mound. Cracked shafts of sunlight made the spray below the weir and the packing-cases shine like fresh snow.

Two men in brown dungarees bent down with a net and out of the raised tank ladled eels that would be wriggling still on the pan in London. The wind was heavy with their sticky odour and, ever since, when I've remembered Alfred's first love it was only to smell eels and feel ill. Headed by the band the procession formed to march through the village on the route the hero had walked once with the halter around his neck, and in young men's wonder we tried to see the first woman to attract the pale, blue eyes of shambling Alfred. His long trousers were too long, his jacket tail was short enough to show a shiny patched seat. I walked behind him in the procession.

'Slobber Valentino,' whispered handsome, athletic Kinnear. 'Isn't he God's gift to the sex?'

'She'll need her *parapluie*,' whispered Macsorley who stuttered and talked French and meant to write books when he grew up.

So for my own credit let me put on record my words of mercy. Unlike Jeff and Jim I had been in Bingen.

'We'll catch her for you, Alfred. We'll catch her for you, never fear.'

Remembering 1798, the procession swung left from the river bank to inundate the village street.

'There she goes again,' said Alfred.

He pointed, like a huntsman who had seen a hare legging it around the shoulder of a mountain, to the crowd gathered outside the hotel, but when I looked I had lost sight of the blue handkerchief and brown hair, saw nine hundred coloured handkerchiefs on the heads of nine hundred country girls with the intimate reek of peat smoke from their pores.

'To hell with the hero,' I said, taking Alfred by the greasy elbow, making for the heart of the crowd.

'Wait for me,' said Kinnear. 'I'm good at this sort of thing. I caught eight seventeen-pounders last season.'

So Kinnear joined the love chase, and stuttering Macsorley, but, small and neat, brown-faced and smiling, Edmund followed the band. Kinnear had more reason than any of us for saying that he was good at that ancient game of chasing women. He was good at every game, a county footballer equal in strength and skill to the best and most experienced while he was still a boy at school. He was handsome, with delicate, girlish features that grew paler when he was angry; he didn't flush or bluster like the commonalty of men. He had stiff, dark, curling hair that sloped up at a steep angle towards the left, and a wasp waist and a dainty way of walking that disguised his brute strength. Even in his schooldays he could punish a whiskey with equanimity and had had an affair with a lady hair stylist in the city, a woman of liberal ways and splendid platinum blonde coiffure, beautiful as a film actress, to our eyes, against her background of chromium fittings, and perfumed, as she always was, most delectably. Afterwards she had a child by and, in that order, a marriage with a particularly obnoxious member of the police force but that only added to the status of Kinnear as pioneer, explorer and, cuter than the cops, adroit getaway man. In there among the lamps, bottles, mudpacks and setting devices, in a room perfumed like the boudoir of Cleopatra, a million miles from the shelter of a ditch or the railway bank or the black shed at the bottom of the market yard, those usual sweet beds for budding sex in our village, he was the first of us to lose his virginity. That wasn't our way of saying it. He never seemed to suffer any pain of loss. His football was unaffected and he was more popular than ever with the girls. Macsorley too, asthmatic, gaptoothed, crew-cut, voluble, was attractive to girls just because of his wheezing, stuttering oddity, his daring volubility. I looked as well as my father's son should, I had been to college dances in Dublin, and Lucy, much sought after, made no secret of her love for me; so that all together we felt when we tracked the shy fawn through the forest of rural girls, round the corner at the hotel, along a hustling side-road to the fair-green, in among the chairaplanes, hobby-horses and switch-back railways, that that ugly duckling Alfred couldn't have had better allies. For brotherly mercy we would find the woman of his choice. Her face, which we hadn't yet seen, would be as weird as his own. We would talk to her, turn her simple head with our condescension, captivate her with our wit, give her to think that Alfred was a fine fellow because he had such friends. We would turn her over to him, bound and his slave for ever, and go our way to our own superior women and ways of life: to medicine, literature and the law. But when in the dusk and the rising hurdy-gurdy noise, with the showmen switching on their glaring lights one by one, we ran her to earth on the hobby-horses she came, drawn magnetically, not to Kinnear nor myself nor the eloquence of Macsorley, but to Alfred Chesney. Even in that place she was gentle and lovely. She scarcely saw us. She had eyes only for one man.

'Hallo, Mister Chesney,' she said.

She could have been waiting for him from the time of Lilith.

Flabbergasted, we walked respectfully behind them along the badly-lighted village street.

'Mister,' said Kinnear. 'Holy God.'

'Do you think he knew her before?' I said. 'On the sly?'

'No,' said Jeff.

He was never less eloquent, never more wise.

'If they knew each other before,' he said, 'it wasn't in this life.'

'She knew his name.'

'He's the captain's son. He's known.'

The thought chilled us. We saw them ahead in the light that came from the crowded singing hotel. His arm was around her. She was close to him. He leaned over her. It was love.

'Your bad example, Kinnear,' said Jeff. 'Everybody wants a woman now.'

'My foot, my bad example. After this I'll take lessons. I'll go to night school.'

'She's pretty too,' I said.

'I wouldn't charge her,' said Kinnear. 'I positively wouldn't charge her one copper ha'penny.'

She was a small, snub-nosed, brown-haired girl, freckles inlaid to fair skin, and she stooped a little when she walked as if she was hungry, or cold in the stomach with momentary, delicious fear. The hobby-horse hurdy-gurdy noises were far behind. The patriot was the grey ghost of all the rebel men who had died on sodden hillsides. The full, sullen river crushed down on and smothered the irrelevant noises of the weir. God give me always the leaping water in the Gortin hills. The lake wind was cold, but clammy and viscous, with no blue-green, purifying tang of salt sea.

'We'll walk no farther,' Kinnear said.

We leaned on the bridge.

'What would we go farther for?' he said.

'Except to see Alfred happy,' said Jeff. 'It's funny to think of Alfred at it.'

'It's funny to think of anyone at it,' said Kinnear. 'It's a funny business.'

'It would be a change to see him happy,' I said.

'Tell us about that house, Owen,' said Jeff.

'I will. Some day.'

'When you do, I'll write a book about it. A deep south novel, suh. *The Book of Bingen* or *The Monster of Magheracolton* by Geoffrey Austin Macsorley. Best seller. Film rights. Alfred and Maureen O'Hara meet in typical Irish village, all fights, poteen and shamrocks. Victor McLaglen, shrunk a bit, could be the captain.'

'You're a sinister, secretive bastard, Owen,' said Kinnear. 'Like your father.'

'Thanks.'

'No offence. But he knew all about the mad Dorans. You know all about the Chesneys. Some day for hellery I'll get myself invited to Bingen. One of the girls will ask me.'

'Those girls,' said Jeff. 'Phew!'

'Give those girls a chance,' Kinnear said. 'You'll see wonders. Trust uncle who knows.'

'They'll never get a chance,' I said.

'That brown-faced Edmund I don't like,' Jeff said. 'Poor old Alfred's like something you'd keep in a cage feeding nuts and sugar lumps to.'

He spat into the deep, sliding water and we heard light steps, her steps, running from the darkness beyond us and around the pine-encircled château of Dame de Nesle, Queen of the yellow-bellied and silver eels.

'Jasus, he's raped her or something,' Jeff stuttered.

'Alfred the raper,' said Kinnear.

We gripped the bridge in glorious, cramping laughter, and then she was beside us speaking so gently, so softly, no smell of peat smoke from her pores, no smell that came out of a chemist's bottle, but the smell of tall, fresh flowers as if she had walked all day in a garden. For the first and last time in my life I envied Alfred the Austrian dog.

'I asked Alfred,' she said, 'to come up to the kitchen for a cup of tea. The mistress is out. There's nobody there except old Sarah the housekeeper. We could have a dance.'

'Is it me,' said Macsorley, 'to dance with Sarah?'

She laughed, very pleasantly indeed.

'I know you,' she said, 'Jeff Macsorley.'

'You know a lot of people.'

'I come from near Bingen. Hughie Heron's my uncle. Are you coming or not? Don't keep Alfred waiting in the dark.'

We followed her as, out that day fishing on the Gortin river, Frank and the captain had followed the long, springy strides of her tall, red uncle, Hughie Heron.

'Alfred's fun,' she said. 'He was too shy to ask you himself.'

We couldn't believe that Alfred could be fun, not at his own expense, to anybody, but we agreed in polite stupefaction, marvelled at the blindness of love, and followed her light feet to find her lover loitering in the shadows of the trees by the gateway of the Big House—like a policeman, Jeff said, lying in wait for a housebreaker. We walked on the grass to avoid the noise of grinding feet on the gravelled avenue, but Rose (for that, as the old novelists would have said, was her name) walked boldly in the centre of the way, linked lovingly with Alfred. How happy the captain would be to see his son chained arm in arm to the niece of his cottier, Hughie Heron. The idea inspired glee and terror.

'Sarah likes a tune,' she said. 'She likes company.'

'She's going to get it,' said Jeff.

'You'll mind yourselves and no bad language. Sarah's very holy.'

'We'll join her at prayers,' Jeff said, 'while Alfred and yourself indulge in sinful dances.'

We were just a little late to join Sarah at prayers, for on the floor of the great kitchen, brightly tiled in black and white, she was rising from her knees as we entered, and rattling her rosary beads back into the pocket of her apron. She was the tallest old woman I had ever seen. She was infinity in a dark woollen dress and white shining apron. She stood like a pillar by the Aga cooker, her hand on the regulator, her neck twisted to turn her long yellow face towards us. She had the face and eyes of a kind old witch but she made us welcome to one of the rarest evenings I remember. The tea was hot and strong, the griddle bread was tasty, the music, made like the tea and bread, by Rose, was unique; for Rose danced and simultaneously played on the mouth-organ, an achievement, I've always felt, fit for any circus. Faultlessly she danced, a hornpipe, a jig, a reel, her feet neat and accurate, her breathing unperturbed. She danced a two-hand reel with Jeff who belied his odd, asthmatic appearance by being an excellent dancer. She danced a four-hand reel with Jeff and James and Owen, your informant, and Alfred, sitting beside Sarah, tapped his big feet on the floor and smiled, as if God had suddenly endowed him with beauty, brains, happiness and a thousand pounds in the bank. He couldn't dance. The gunnery and drill lessons at Bingen in the morning had taught him never a dance step. With bright eyes and her brown hair loose she was dancing a two-hand reel with Owen when the devil it seemed came into the kitchen and said, in accents of the lanes of Dublin: 'She's back again. Break it up, dancing Rosie.'

'Who are you to order, Jim Gilbert? And my name's not Rosie.'

'I'm only telling you she's back. She's drunk.'

'You helped her. You're drunk yourself.'

'Would you blame me, when I get it free?'

My back was to the door and I had to turn to see him: a well-built man in chauffeur's uniform, sallow-faced, with narrow, brown eyes, a thin line of moustache, a scar on his right cheek.

'Sorry to spoil the sport, boys,' he said. 'But Rose and Sarah know there'll be hell if she hears the music. She hates music.'

'Except corks popping and glasses jingling,' said Sarah.

'And drunk men whispering nice things to her,' said Rose.

'She's the mistress,' he said. 'There'll be hell.'

'There will and all,' said Sarah with resignation. 'There's always hell where there's drink and badness.'

She rose stiffly, her hand on Alfred's heavy bottle-shoulder.

'Run boys, run,' she said.

'Hands to yourself, Jim Gilbert,' Rose said.

There was fire in her face and something sharp and nervous in her voice although the yellow man had done nothing I could see but gently brush her shoulders as he passed towards the pantry, and on the pantry's threshold he turned around, laughed, with very white teeth, not at Rose but at the four of us, measuring us up, asking himself which was which, and said he was sorry. Kinnear, very white in the face, looked back at him meditatively; so for the sake of peace I led the way out and we ran, James and Jeff and Owen. Whispering in the shadows by the gateway, we waited while Alfred cuddled or whispered or kissed good-night, or whatever the like of Alfred would do, to

44

his dancing girl. Rapidly, mechanically the shadow of a woman passed and re-passed across an upstairs, uncurtained window.

'This place I've heard about,' said Jeff. 'About that woman and the driver from Dublin.'

'Tell us, tell us all,' we said.

'He does more than drive,' said Jeff.

'He drinks a little,' Kinnear said.

'All that and heaven too,' said Jeff, 'or so the people say.'

'A man has to do something for his living,' James said with charity. 'But if I was in love, I wouldn't have my girl under that roof.'

'It's a queer house,' said Jeff. 'Sarah would need to pray a lot.'

'Sarah's safe at her age,' James said.

'The whole place stinks of fish,' I said. 'Everywhere I go I meet queer houses. I'll soon be master of queer houses. I'll be the greatest living authority.'

'So long,' said Jeff, 'as it's not bad houses.'

Because we were still more or less boys we laughed at that until Alfred, his arms long as an ape's arms in the shadows, came down the gravel. He didn't run lightly as a fellow might who had just kissed the fresh lips of his girl good-night and *auf wiedersehn*, but one big foot went down dully after the other as if he was weary or had parcelled his boots in potato sacking. Behind him the Eel Queen pulled down the blind, or somebody more sober pulled it down for her, and that night there was no more music.

A cylindrical glass jar that had once held acid drops was, by general consensus of opinion in the parlour behind the hotel bar, no fitting home for a cobalt-and-crimson spiny-backed fish whose breed was native to Japan but who, with five relatives recently deceased, had been purchased by the hotel proprietor in an aquarium in Dublin. At an angle of forty-five with the crumb-littered floor of the jar, nose down, feebly twittering tail up, it stared morosely through a double wall of glass at Dr Grierson's whiskey.

'Those straight sides like glass precipices must be frustrating for a fish,' my father said. 'He wants weeds and rocks, places to hide. Even a Japanese fish.'

'In a department store once, I heard,' said the doctor, 'that an old lady brought an action because the goldfish on show in a bowl hadn't had their water changed often enough.'

'The Society for the Prevention of Cruelty to Goldfish,' said pert Edmund.

'I'd marry that girl,' whispered Alfred to Jeff and myself. 'I'd marry her like a shot.'

The sibilant in the last word shot a globule of spittle on to Jeff's right nostril, but scholar, gentleman and saint as he had suddenly decided to be, he restrained himself from wiping it away.

'Ask your father first,' whispered Kinnear.

Immediately we regretted the words, but they were spoken, reality was around us, the captain was as tangible as the glass-topped tables in the parlour, the November gloom was down.

'Nevertheless,' said Dr Grierson, 'in spite of their environment five of those six Japanese fish lived happily in that jar until the visiting Americans came.'

'They bet money that the fish would die,' said the girl through the service hatch. 'And five of them did.'

'Fed them gin most likely,' my father said. 'Time for home now, boys. Where were you four?'

'Best not ask them, John,' said Dr Grierson. 'Young blood. Young blood.'

46

The rims of his bright eyes were moist, his thin patrician face was unusually flushed. With the sweet suction of an Irishman who liked malt, with none of the savouring and sipping meet for the contents of cobwebbed, continental bottles, he drained his glass. The girl behind the hatch turned her eyes away in embarrassment and was frantically busy upsetting and rearranging rows of coloured miniature monsters filled with liqueurs. By the way my father tilted his chin and indicated the door I knew he was glad there were only a select few in the parlour and that he wanted me to lead the way to the car. He drove us home in the big seven-seater that was half-ways between a hearse and a four-poster bed. The patriot's ghost shook his pike after us as we clanked, the car outdoing even the noise of the metal centrepiece, over the bridge.

'It was a great day,' said Dr Grierson. 'He was a great, young man. Those were harsh, terrible times of persecution.'

He sat beside my father; and Jeff and I, our backs to them, sat on the subsidiary tip-up seats facing Edmund, James and Alfred. One lighted window above the trees marked the walls and roof that contained praying Sarah, dancing Rose, and what else we feared to imagine.

'The hero that I now speak of,' said my father, 'was proper tall and straight. Unto the lofty poplar his body was complate.'

'The image of our Alfred,' said Jeff.

'The old islandman sang that song well today,' Dr Grierson said.

'His growth was like the tufted fir that does ascend the air,' sang my father.

Lightly he mocked the balladman's ullagone, but he was a sincere gatherer of country ballads and years ahead of the fashion that set people at smart parties on both sides of the Atlantic wailing like keening women at a Connacht burial.

'Alfred rides again,' said Jeff. 'The trail of the tufted fir.'

But Alfred, crumpled in silence, did not respond to this gentle, well-intentioned gibing, for how could he tell the captain how a kitchen-maid who danced hornpipes and simultaneously played the mouth-organ could be as lovely as a fire-tried virgin before the throne of God.

'Wonderful,' whispered Kinnear. 'You don't know what you missed, Edmund. A willing woman sitting straddle on every separate hobby-horse.'

With occult, obscene gestures he passed his twitching, experienced fingers before the nose of Edmund.

'Edmund's a good little boy,' Jeff whispered.

Fearful of my father and Dr Grierson, I tried to telepathize Jeff and James into decent silence.

'Edmund doesn't know what you mean,' Jeff said.

There was no need to make things worse, I felt then, by taunting Edmund with tall tales of sins that had never happened, by sitting between him and his brother and making it so obvious that our allegiance was to awkward Alfred.

'And waving o'er his shoulders broad,' whined my father, 'the locks of yellow hair.'

'A sinister, secretive bastard, Owen,' Kinnear said, 'like your father.'

So, secretively and alone, and in sinister fashion selecting a dark day of low sky and moist wind, I cycled up to Segully mountain to meditate on the shell of the house where the magic man had once lived. They called it a mountain but it wasn't a mountain. It was a triangle of brown spurs of moorland, lost and forgotten between two main roads. Every crevice of a glen that day had a full stream screaming on its own note, forcing a way between green, slimy, uncomfortable rocks to add to the force of the Gortin river. In the Lammas floods those torrents could tumble bridges. One rough road straddled all the moorland spurs, shot down steep slopes all dangerous with loose stones, humped over little bridges with parapets gapped and broken. Rutted lanes, half rivulets, clambered up to square, white, shelterless farmhouses. Higher up there were tracks for sheep and, on the fringe of floating mist, cairns of stones piled up before roads were invented. It was a pitiful, pathetic land and not in the least sinister. It had ruins of houses by the dozen, thatch rotten and sagging or completely collapsed, smoke-darkened walls bared to wind and rain and falling stone by stone, skid-row nettles whistling wearily above cracked, abandoned floors.

'They were happy here once,' I said to the mountain sheep. 'But they closed the doors for the last time with relief. They fled to the towns or to Britain or the States. They had the sense to admit this moorland was no place for Christians to survive in. This was Segully where the fleas ate the man. This was every sodden Irish mountainside. This could have been the door where the rate collector lost his finger. Here, in this damp corner smelling of weeds and decayed plaster, the dead Doran sister may have rotted slowly while Michael, the wizard, benefited by her old age pension.'

But try as I would, even with the help of dusk and mist, mizzling rain, the monotone of a torrent in the glen below, I couldn't see the shell of the Doran cabin as a place of perverted horror. It was comic, almost. It was a place for tumbling country girls on a warm, sunny day. Michael Doran had never been a wizard and Kinnear was an ass to imagine it was anything other than friendship or the curiosity of a travelled, thoughtful man that had made my father the only honoured guest under the roof that had once been here. Just as it was friendship that brought me to Bingen. But cycling down rough hills and wheeling my bike up rough hills on the road home I was foolish enough to ask myself: friendship for whom? There was nobody in Bingen I could call a friend as Kinnear and Macsorley were friends. A rabbit trapper walked home in the dusk, long iron in one hand, five dead rabbits in the other, a dismal hound sloshing at his heels, an Austrian dog. My laughter to the moorland at the instantaneous realization that Alfred could never be a friend, nor sallow, reserved Frank, nor Edmund. A woman's torso was silhouetted in amber lamplight above a half door, and one quick squint at her through thickening rain had more revelation in it than X-ray photographs of the Bingen sisters. They could no more be friends of mine than the shadows on the wall, and I lived again through one odd half-hour in the back row of seats in the dark cinema at the Guildhall gate during my last year at school. Complacent beside Lucy I listened with little attention to Jeannette Macdonald. Greta Chesney sat at my left, a negative quantity in blue school gaberdine, pigtails, blue school beret as flat as a pancake; and high on the ecstasy of one Macdonald trill and tra-la-la-la-la-la I found to my horror that Greta's hand was in mine. So close to the curved, developing warmth of Lucy, it was sacrilege and a denial of life to touch those cold, lonely fingers. Greta Conway Chesney was a ghost. She wasn't really there in the cinema. She was supposed to be in the convent at a music lesson. Round the bole of a Canadian tree, Mounted Policeman Nelson Eddy bayed his Indian mating call at the celebrated soprano. To my right, Lucy swooned with delight. To my left, sharp fingernails dug into my palm: my first disconcerting experience of *ménage à trois*. Greta would not have been there deep in Canadian woods if she hadn't borrowed the shilling from Lucy who, wonderful girl for a pauper of a schoolboy to know, had abstracted that and more besides from her father's till. Shame seeped from my hand into that gripping hand, those stabbing fingers. What she thought when I snatched my hand away before the lights betrayed me to opulent Lucy, I had no means of knowing. She thanked Lucy quietly for the money. Then, sullen-faced, shoulders hunched with bad temper or to crush down tears, one black school stocking wrinkled on her calf, she ascended before us to the bus-stop in the Diamond. The chestnut candles were bright above her. They mocked her shabby shadow. She was a shadow creeping back beaten to the dog's lair of shadows in the big basement kitchen at Bingen. Was it better for her to be born and damned in Bingen than not to be born at all? She could never be friend or beloved to Owen Rodgers. She wasn't real.

But her father was real. The shock of a truth I was reluctant to accept set my bicycle skidding on the wet road. Even in the strengthening rain I slowed up to think: If I have a friend in Bingen it is the captain with the whiskers. What have we in common? He talks. I listen. He is always glad to see me under his roof, welcomes me, treats me as an intellectual equal and so flatters me. Why? To annoy his own sad, subdued offspring. To be revenged in some perverted way on my father who will never stop to listen to him as other men do. If the son stands mute in his presence is he, the captain, requited for the way the father contemns him? Why does he fascinate me, or is it him or the place: the sweep of river, the strand, the black horses, the hard white hills, the sycamores and hazels twisted before constant wind? Was the fascination Bingen or its owner had for me just the fascination the perverted thing has for the normal, curious, thoughtful, travelled man like my father? Was the marching captain just the leader of a line of grotesques that were to make mockery for me of all ballads about drums and brave men marching normally to war? After him go all my nightmares, their banners never gay: the complacent pederast telling me with joy about the gyrations of his squirming love with a West Indian boy; the elderly man who said his mistress would lose all attraction for him if he thought she was faithful and unpolluted; the businessman who borrowed and never returned Jeff Macsorley's copy of *Bel Ami* because of his unholy liking for the episode about the old lady and the boots; the twin-pinnacled girl who danced with me in Dublin, fainted with hunger on the ballroom floor, and whose pointed breasts proved to be the heels of two Vienna loaves, scooped out. Perversion? Poverty? Pride? Is blackavised, thoughtful detachment the worst perversion of all?

Her dark hair enhaloed by a sweet pea advertisement her father had pasted on the glass inner door of the shop, Lucy might have been Madame Butterfly. She was pleasingly sallow too, her eyes slanted, her cheeks plumped out smoothly, so that Kinnear said some wandering Punjab pedlar, satchel crammed with coloured combs and scarves and beads of horn (as the Monaghan poet sang) had touched her mother with a tarbrush behind the rolls of lino in the dark at the back of the shop while her oblivious father was out in the daylight of the front window adding up the price of crockery. He had indeed the hangdog appearance of a little man who might have been cuckolded. He walked in the dusk, shunning company, on the road past the two towers and the churchyard wall, holding on to the lead of a somnolent Great Dane that slavered. He never left the house on Sundays except to go to Mass. But every Saturday night he had carried into the house, discreetly by the back way, two dozen of stout, and after Sunday dinner (it was said) he sat by the kitchen range, on his head the bowler hat he wore to church, reading cowboy stories until he had consumed the two dozen. His wife and daughter, to my knowledge and by no hearsay, treated him as they'd treat a yard brush, and added strength to the tale of cuckoldry by a traveller from an antique land. But, considering the captain, I was never inclined to think small men so easily befooled.

To her right the window was sensible, blue-and-white kitchen delf. To her left the window was garden tools, rakes, hoes, clippers, straw mats draped from the handles of lawn-mowers. Dry between them, Madame Butterfly waved to me as I dripped my way home from the dismal ruins of Segully. She pulled back the iron grille she had been closing and I stooped and stepped in beside her, between china and tools, forgetting ruins to embrace the warmth of growing things.

'Those Nosy Parkers across the street will see us. You're soaking. Where under God were you, Owen?'

'Cycling.'

'So I see.'

She wore a tight-fitting, spotted, satin dress.

'Keep your secrets so. Take away your wet hands.'

'No secrets.'

You could never be certain with her whether her pouts were planned to make her more endearing or whether they were the natural outcome of a spoiled child's nastiness. She stooped to padlock the grille, her satin bottom pushing back the shop door with the sweet pea halo so that the shop's warning bell tinkled. Pneumatic olive breasts rose and fell, the shadowy split appearing and disappearing.

'In Segully I was. Sightseeing.'

'Seeing what? Stones and mud? Heather and mountain sheep? Is the man mad? My da owns a farm up there but even he hires a man to go up and look at it.'

She wiped rain from my forehead with a dry, good-smelling forearm. She could be motherly.

'Come in and dry yourself, Owen. I want a cup of tea myself.'

Her father, in his box counting the day's gain, doffed his spectacles and donned them again to salute young Rodgers who had gone to the university, which was imprudent, but who some day, being the son of a clever man, might be a doctor, which was something. Her mother, she said, had lain down with a sick headache. Above our heads, axes and saws dangled from a low ceiling, and how could any man, big or little, be cuckolded if he had so many sharp weapons within easy reach? In the kitchen behind the shop the Great Dane slavered and slept by the red, bubbling range. His obese body intruded on the space available to Lucy and myself for sipping tea and enjoying the fumblings of a half-innocent attraction. It was fear kept one right, Lucy argued, and what would you do in our village if anything went wrong? Torn between poltroonery and the inspiring vision of Kinnear's hairdresser, aloft and beacon-bearing like the statue of liberty, Owen Rodgers with reluctance and relief agreed with Lucy. What could you do in our village if anything went wrong, short of marrying Lucy and that, in spite of her warmth and comfort, was a thought to run away from? I was too young to want or value comfort. So we kissed, we glawmed, we tiptoed on the fringe of the forest. Knowledge like the brute of a Great Dane was asleep at our feet. Her arms I think I always loved, the deep dimples at the elbows when she stretched them luxuriously, the cleft of soft flesh at the elbow, parodying the deep, mysterious cleft between her breasts, when she bent her arm to raise the teacup to pouting lips. Two arms alone are not enough to love. Her pouting lips were cushions comic enough to be pricked with schoolboy pins. But she warmed me because she was Woman, welcoming, embracing, but still enigmatic, intangible. She was wisdom and revelation and growing up, and destined, happy girl, to grow further and wiser with me. One wet day while we were still at school—why are all the days of Lucy remembered wet?—she had been Aphrodite, the first wriggle of sap and flicker of fancy, teaching me in one glance more than a dozen smutty schoolboy stories. She had worn a pink and white dress and wine-coloured school blazer with insignia already curved by her precocious development. Her bare legs were blue and pink, colours not favoured by the best fashion models but liable to catch man's eye at any age. Toenails peeping from sandals were illuminatingly crimson and from breast-pocket school insignia to toenails she revealed continents. Her seat was creased alluringly by the wooden sill of the shop window. Her back was to a series of coloured picture-plates. Her hair was crudely bobbed. As if she had given it great thought she smiled at me.

In the kitchen, greedy of warmth and Lucy and strong tea, I moved warily to avoid the slavering monster.

'He's harmless, Owen. You could walk on him like an old rug.'

'Oh, lovely Lucy who would make the world your rug.'

'Owen Rodgers, you say the cutest things.'

Her intonation echoed the goddesses of the cinema by the Guildhall Gate. She was probably right about the passivity of the brute but I was too young yet to awaken monsters and, stepping two paces back, I took no chances with a Dane of his size.

'Owen? Is the man afraid?'

But she took two paces with me and we glawmed and kissed and kissed and glawmed. The monster snorted in his sleep. Saws and axes to guard honour swung and shone from the shop ceiling. Lovingly in the distance the little father tinkled his cash.

'If I could go with you to Dublin,' she sighed. 'And see life. And leave this dull place.

'Life,' she said again.

We glawmed. We grated our cheeks together. A kiss skidded sideways and I looked over her shoulder into the opened, lurid eyes of the monster. They squinted.

'Away from this dull place,' she said.

'Dublin,' I said.

'And be a doctor's wife,' she said.

'Do you want a wife?' asked the eye that squinted at the range.

'Will you ever be a doctor?' taunted the eye that squinted towards the shop.

'When I crossed the wild,' said Jim MacElhatton, 'I chanced to see at break of day the solitary child.'

The band laughed. They waited for my father who had gone to the attic for clarinet reeds.

'Her name is Lucy,' sang Barney Quigley, the big drummer. 'And everywhere we go . . .'

'Bowls he was buying,' said Jim MacElhatton. 'For the Saturday haircut of the seventeen sons of Paddy Macillion, the captain's cottier.'

'One of the seventeen MacElhattons could do with his tongue cut,' I said.

The band laughed. Bob Lowthers blew the cornet. In two minutes the band could reduce the tortures of young love or curiosity or what you will to unimportant comedy.

'Seventeen elephants in one bird's nest,' I said, pressing home my advantage.

Led by Jim himself the band laughed at my bucolic repartee

for Jim was proud of being one of a family of seventeen tall men and women, athletes, footballers, dancers, singers, musicians, reared in one small, five-roomed house.

'Roosts their mother must have put them on to sleep,' my mother said. 'Roosts. Seventeen jersey-black giants in one wee coop.'

'Mrs Rodgers,' Jim asked, 'did you send Owen to the hardware shop to buy saucepans?'

The cornet blared again. The laughter of the band shook the house. Above us the sound of my father's footsteps drummed in the attic.

'Or some monkey brand soap,' the big drummer said. 'First class for the complexion.'

'Your girl-friends in Bingen will be jealous,' Jim MacElhatton said when the door had closed behind my mother.

'He goes there, I think,' said the cornetist, 'to make love to Hughie Heron's wife, Lizzie.'

Because my mother was in the kitchen and my father in the attic and Dr Grierson had not yet arrived, they could lapse and relax easily into the intimate bawdry of country places: how Lizzie Heron, it was well known, had a child by Hughie and a child by another man before she was married; how Hughie on the morning after the bridal night had said: 'Boys, there's nothing like matrimony; last night I heard Lizzie's maidenhead cracking like a lath'; how the captain had recently routed the warble fly inspector from his land, saying: 'By God, sir, there are more warble flies on your private parts than there ever were on my cattle'; how the captain was so greedy of the land he owned he wouldn't let a rook alight to rest its wings.

'I'm going there tomorrow to fish,' I said.

But nobody heeded me. They talked about how the captain boasted of his days in the Boer War which they held was no war at all but only walking forever around South Africa; how the captain had told a crowd in the bar of Grainger's hotel in the city that his name was Conway Chesney because his grandfather hailed from Conway in Wales, and how a rude stranger, a commercial traveller, had said it was God's mercy his grandfather hadn't first seen the light of day in Hackballscross in the County Armagh.

'He put down his drink unfinished,' said Barney the big drummer. 'He walked out of the bar. He's a ball of temper.'

'Won't he throw the sweet fit,' said Jim MacElhatton, 'when he hears his heir's courting a skivvy at the eel weir at Redmond's Bridge?'

'Courting a what?' I said.

For that slighting word, skivvy, had no relation to Rose who danced and sang, who had such clear skin, innocent freckles, glossy brown hair.

'Owen wouldn't know what a skivvy is,' said the cornet.

'Thinks it's a centre-forward in a hockey team,' said Jim the French horn.

The room glistened and grunted with brass instruments being raised, lowered, caressed, puffed into, tested, for my father would soon be among them.

'A lovely girl she is,' said one clarinet.

'But the captain is a hoor for social distinction,' said another clarinet.

They waited, holding the clear seductive pipes of Pan, for new reeds and my father.

'The misfortune is,' said the trombone, 'she's nothing but a niece of Hughie Heron. The captain will never have that.'

'He married a maid himself,' said the big drum.

'We all did, we hope, even Hughie Heron,' said the piccolo.

'He never allowed her to forget it,' said French horn Jim.

'That house at the bridge's a sordid place to find a sweetheart,' the cornet said, and went like a golden goat up and down the scales.

'A bad house, that woman, the drink, the Dublin driver,' said all the instruments in various notes.

Alfred, I saw, long hair curled, wide-brimmed hat with jaunty feather, hawk on wrist, bells on the palfrey's bridle, a cavalier, a troubadour, ever since the day of vision and the patriot's unveiling, a young lover buoyant with first knowledge, the happy holder of an angelic secret that sadly, because of the nature of our small society, couldn't long remain a secret.

'Here we are. The reeds,' my father said.

In his left hand he held the reeds, in his right hand he held a bottle of whiskey which he put in the bottom of the sideboard to await the coming of the Louvain doctor. A social nip in a musical home was a better thing than secretive large ones passed rhythmically into the snug behind the hotel bar.

'First that medley of Irish marches,' my father said.

The rain was persistent on the curtained window. Irishmen all we marched away to brave brass notes. Far away rock torrents roared, rain eroded the drear, deserted stones of Michael Doran's Segully. What would happen when the captain found love growing fair in the midden he had made himself? Far away the gulls driven inland called round Bingen, trees swayed and bent, the river meeting salt water made the rain trivial, the black horses stamped. Somnolent, warm, dry, among the bright marching brass, I was the normal son of a normal man.

Stonecutters' chisels giggled in the monumental works but the solemn, pious, expressionless statues did not smile. Away from the intoxication of the big drum Barney Quigley cut an urn draped with cerement cloths for a big Presbyterian farmer who didn't hold with statues of saints or Christs on the Cross, and whose wife had passed over.

'Good fishing,' Barney called. 'Give Lizzie my love.'

Face grey with dust among memorials of death, he grinned in the sunlight, and it was a pet of a morning, the sun bright as Jamaica even if the clay was squelchy after the night's rain. Every stream in the world was in brown-and-white spate and it was heaven for lazy fishermen and the big hook baited with blue-headed worms. Clustered, intimate rooks collogued around towers and church-yard trees. Ballet-dancing starlings were in session in giant whitethorns by the captain's rickety footbridge, raindrops flashing in the sun as they fluttered and pirouetted from bush to bush. Standing by the gate, I watched Frank, in black clerical clothes and rubber knee-boots, walk towards me, his head un-covered, his fishing-rod quivering above him like an aerial, and I had the feeling that rooks and towers, starlings, bushes, wet grass, the great roar of the river, the distant, chastened sound of the sea, were perfect and unalterable. Never since have I trusted that feeling. Thick smoke ascended, a warning signal and most unusual in the early morning, from one chimney of the house. We followed a field-path west towards the last landward spur of Bingen Head, glistening with cataracts, capped with mist, towards the serrated greenery of Drumard Wood where Hughie and Lizzie had their innocent love-bower.

'He's in Drumard meadow,' Frank said. 'He's with Macillion cutting out two bullocks for beef.'

For the captain killed his own bullocks and bacon, bulled his own cows, fulfilled the final requirement of the Irish strong farmer by having a son studying for the priesthood in May-nooth. Rigidly the sallow makings of a priest paced beside me. The wild, salt air of Bingen had cleaned from his thin face a colony of carbuncles, product of college mass-cooking, that had disfigured him four weeks previously when we met in Dublin on the way home: budding doctor, budding priest, heal their bodies, heal their souls. In the train, in a rare, weak loquacious moment he had talked about our vocations.

The kind, wild air of Bingen beat his hair against the oblong, sharp-boned top of his head. After the barbarous college coiffure his hair had recovered and grown again to conceal prematurely-thinning patches. He had lost, too, the odour of the cold college —it had been noticeable on our train journey—out of which the odour of priesthood, vestments, candles, altar wine, would develop. But the air of Bingen could do nothing to the unsmiling muscles of his face, taut and rigid even when one of the doomed bullocks raced back again to his worried, watchful brethren, and Hughie Heron, attempting to turn him, fell, smacking his rump on a loose stone, rising with a blast of profanity that was snatched away blessedly from clerical ears by the angel wind.

'Hughie's vexed,' Macillion said.

He held Hughie's stout bait rod and gaff and net. He was a small man but as deft, it would seem, as Big MacElhatton in begetting children: children like himself, small, dark-haired, vivacious, the girls neatly aproned, the boys always needing or getting haircuts and sitting, bowls like Turkish hats on their heads, while the father snipped simply around the delf circle.

'Wonderful,' my mother would say truly, 'how well those Macillions and MacElhattons did for themselves in life. Seventeen of each.

'Wonderful,' she would laugh at me. 'Your father and I could only manage one son between us. And look at him.'

'He's vexed,' Macillion said to the fishing-rod. 'The trouble's on his mind. He hates trouble.'

'What trouble?' I asked.

Frank looked ahead as if there was nothing in the world but long Hughie, his red, untidy, drooping moustache, the sou'-wester he waved in his hand, the running bullock.

'Up at the university, Owen,' Macillion said, 'you'd read more Irish history than ever.'

'Not a lot, Paddy. Books about diseases. Doctors' books.'

'God save us. Still, somebody has to know these things. The old people were content with herbs. They'd die rather than be opened.'

'They died too often,' I said.

My voice, I fear, had not the conviction of the born medicine man for the thought of operating or being operated on filled me with horror. But, quite content with the way he had switched the topic of talk away from the trouble that had vexed Hughie, Macillion rambled on about my early schooldays when a lust for patriotic reading had stuffed me with guff about the great O'Neill who fought Elizabeth the First, about Tyrell of Tyrell's Pass and Brian who beat the Danes at Clontarf. Frank ticked his reel. The bullock accepted his doom, lowed piteously, continued his eight-o'clock walk.

'I'll take the beasts now and leave him free,' Macillion said. 'Good luck with the fishing.'

Walking away from us he mimicked the bandiness of Fee the jockey but Frank did not laugh and, now that I think of it, did I ever see him laugh except that evening in the dusk when he speared the flying paper on his swordstick; and was that sound the best he could do in the way of laughter?

'The trouble,' he said.

It was an apology for Macillion's discretion. It meant: You are one of us, Owen, and should know.

I accepted the revelation as my right.

'My father found out about Alfred and that girl at the bridge.'

Who told, I wondered? The evil chauffeur? The drunken Eel Queen? Praying Sarah? The tongues of the townlands?

'There was hell on earth all day here yesterday.'

His voice was cold and precise, already a little like the voice of Dr Grierson.

'This place was always unhappy,' he said. 'It was never hell until yesterday.'

The distant trees swayed and bent. Smoke from the chimney of the house leaped away towards Bingen Head. Starlings shook flashes of mercury from whitethorns. The herd of bullocks took a few truculent forward paces as if meditating a smashing-of-the-van rescue attack on the two patchwork cottiers.

'Owen, will you pray for my father?' Frank said. 'He doesn't know what to do with himself.'

His hand on the reel trembled like the hand of a man in the horrors of drink but his voice when he told me about the end of Alfred's one and only true love was as cool and steady as Barney Quigley's chisel.

His sparse, agonized words told me only part of the story.

We crossed the river by the shaky footbridge and went inland over sandy, hillocky ground, following tall Hughie who had a springy stride as long as three steps of an ordinary man. Under a bank that overhung like a drooping lip Frank raised and lost the first fish of the day. We saw the white flash even in the muddy fresh. We heard the splash even above the noise of the wild river.

'That was a big one,' Hughie said.

'To miss the first rise is bad luck for a fisherman,' Frank said.

'Pishrogue and nonsense,' said Hughie.

He dipped his bait in the same run of water. He watched his line tighten where Frank had missed his rise, and the fish that day were so mad for worms that he brought out from under the lip of the bank ten ounces of fighting mountain trout, a black bullhead on him, a cannibal trout.

'You taught me that nonsense, Hughie.'

'When you were a child, master Frank. You're half-ways to a bishop now. Don't you see this cannibal was sorry for being rude to the clergy and he came back to apologize.'

He wrapped the still-kicking trout in a handful of grass and dropped it into Frank's bag and, as he stooped, I was fascinated by the thought that to kiss Lizzie, if mountainy men took time to kiss, he would have to clear his lips of a curtain of red hair. But underneath the curtain there was a gentle musical mouth that a woman could love, for he was a piper of a long race of pipers and a renowned lilter, in the old style, of mouth music, when there was no instrument to make music at the country dances. His long back went on ahead of us and when we struck a stretch of sunken rushy ground where the river was sleek and dangerous his big hobnails sprang with goat-sureness from one turtoge of dry footing to the next. We moved more slowly.

'It was Edmund let the cat out of the bag,' Frank said. 'To save his own skin.'

Little brown Edmund. Plump smooth skin.

'My father beat Alfred like a cur dog. He locked him in the stable with the stallion.'

The day's first quick shower rolled like snow down a mountain, polished every angle of rock until it shone, licked us as a kind dog would and went on towards Bingen and the sea.

'He struck my mother,' Frank said. 'She tried to save Alfred. He said things shouldn't be spoken or written down.'

That was all he told me then or ever after and all I wanted to hear. The rest of it came to me, unbidden and uninvited, over the years and from various tongues: Fee the jockey, little black Paddy, long red Hughie, from Kate Carr, the other cottier and diabetic old charwoman who could dispose of a turkey egg, boiled in a black tin, as rapidly as any other old spaewife could take a pinch of snuff. It came to me too from Maeve and Greta who were not, you might say, even born when it happened.

The previous day, it seemed, Edmund had tried, not for the first time, to run away. The other four never ran away. They dug their heels in and suffered. They had courage. They accepted the dreadful truth that they belonged to Bingen. But Edmund was the will-o'-the-wisp of a coward without loyalty to place or person. He was also a fool, for if he had wanted to run away he could have done so successfully any one of a hundred days when he was in the city at school. But only immediate peril and panic could send him scampering, always at the wrong moment, always towards the deep, dark turbary to the east of Drumard Wood and Hughie Heron's cabin. For up the wooded slope beyond the turbary, with its mud-fringed, pear-shaped bog pool that the local children called Thread the Needle, was the direct road to the city, ships, freedom. A small farmer's son from that slope had set all prisoners an example by running away to the British Merchant Navy and coming home on furlough to enchant the ears of his stick-in-the-mud contemporaries with the names of Singapore, Yokohama, Valparaiso and the physical attributes of their female inhabitants.

'Edmund took with him once on one of his canters (Hughie Heron told me) a pan loaf as provender, and a pound of butter.'

'Provisions for a long sea voyage,' said little black Paddy.

'And once,' said Hughie, 'he stole a hot griddle cake that Lizzie had left to cool on the stone slab outside the window.'

'And once the captain rode after him on horseback, on the black stallion.'

Simon Legree, I thought, wasn't a patch on the seat of the captain's pants.

'And caught him weltering in the black mud at the edge of Thread the Needle.'

'And took him home,' said Kate the diabetic, 'and roped him to a post in the byre and threshed him with a bog birch-rod until Hughie there, risking life, livelihood and the roof over his head, interfered and snapped the rod out of the captain's hand.'

On the famous occasion of that penultimate runaway the captain again struck the recaptured Edmund, struck him on the face with his fist, in the kitchen in the presence of his mother, brothers and sisters. Edmund whimpered, pleaded for mercy, then to save his skin said that Alfred had done worse than he had ever done. Between blows he whimpered out the idyll of the eel weir and the dancing maiden, and had the reward of being forgotten in the storm that burst over Bingen. The most dreadful detail of the scene came to me from Greta to make me wonder about the awful secret moments of men when they are seen only by people completely in their power and by the God who made them.

'He ran up and down the stairs,' she said, 'waving his fists, shouting again and again: "My son and a skivvy, my son and a skivvy." My mother stood silent in the corner of the kitchen. She never spoke to him again after he struck her when she tried to protect Alfred.'

All that day while we fished the Gortin river Alfred was bolted, trouserless, in a stable, and Edmund, whether by good luck or cunning, had won for himself a temporary, valuable oblivion.

★   ★   ★

Where Frank fell into the water there were stepping-stones across a brook and a high-hedged shelter belt for cattle. He was right all the way about fisherman's luck: miss the first rise and you miss the lot, and get soaked to the skin into the bargain. If the trout had leaped out on the bank before him and begged for mercy he couldn't have caught one of them, and to make matters worse Hughie and myself between us could have filled a creel. To give us something to laugh at and to help Frank to mask his chagrin Hughie drew our attention to the line of tall whitethorns grown on a plan to break the wind for winter cattle. He told us how a mad major from London, on a fishing holiday in the County Mayo, had hired a man to chop down a shelter belt because he hadn't room on the bank to cast his dry fly, and the furious Mayo farmer who owned the land heaved the major into the Moy river. Listening to Hughie, Frank set out to cross the tributary brook on the just-visible stepping-stones, stepped carelessly on an unsteady stone and sat down in two feet of water.

The sight of his surprised face above the brown surface set us laughing until he clambered out on the far side and we joined him. Water bubbled up from his knee-boots. He stepped out of them, not angry, not smiling, and drained them patiently on the grass.

'You're soaked to the skin,' Hughie said.

'It'll dry off. There's sun and wind.'

'It'll dry off better at Kate Carr's hearth,' Hughie said.

There, behind us, by God's grace and the kind twists of the river, was Kate Carr's cottage tucked into the corner of a hazel wood like the cottage of the witch in *Hansel and Gretel*. Her old blind collie barked in two cracked notes as we approached up the flagged pathway. Hens squawked and fluttered under fruited, gnarled apple trees. Frank walked ahead of us leaving a track behind him like a shower of rain. Two turkeys tweeped by the well with the beehive-shaped, whitewashed roof.

'Sore asses they have,' Hughie whispered to me. 'Laying eggs for Kate. She could eat a man off his horse.'

From the thatched lean-to at one gable end of the cabin a chewing goat, body in darkness, old bearded head in evening light, eyed us sceptically.

'Kate's boy-friend,' said Hughie.

Staring back at the goat, seeing a vision of himself and Kate who was not a woman at all but a shuffling ant-hill of grey shawl and red flannel, thinking too of the troubled, over-worked turkeys, Hughie and myself suffocated with laughter we couldn't explain to Frank. Under the sopping clothes the body that was half the captain's body and would be the Lord's body stiffened with indifference that drove him away from us. He was already by the fire in shirt and trousers, his dripping jacket and pullover in Kate's hands, when we stooped over the threshold into the dark, little, one-roomed house. It smelled of turf smoke and meal food mixed for hens. But the fire was a high red pyramid, glowing with welcome, and Frank and Kate were two silhouettes against it, Kate cone-shaped, Frank a thin, rubber cylinder as he bent to slip braces off his shoulders. Then he looked at me because of my unexplained laughter, as he had looked at me that morning when I played Peeping Tom on the drill exhibition. There was no false modesty about him as he undressed, but there was no reason for being modest before Kate who had nursed him and looked like a blossomless whinbush, and who said again and again in an old voice as brown as hazel nuts: 'Dear goodness, dear goodness, you'll get your death.'

'The bottle, Hughie,' she said. 'It's behind the dresser.'

Stooping into darkness, rattling among pots and pans, dis-turbing an old clucking hen who had sought refuge there for

68

her uneasy, late-in-life folly and who walked indignantly away from us, one wing drooping, to rejoin her untrodden sisters under the apple trees, Hughie brought to the light a bottle of white spirits that had never known gauger or the yellow deception of burnt sugar. Watching him as he bent forwards to uncork it, I saw Frank's narrow, naked, bony, yellow shoulders and, to my own surprise, turned my eyes away. The seasoned medico who had kissed and fondled Lucy was afflicted with the seminarian's inverted modesty that Frank should have possessed. With shame I thought of convents where (I was told) nuns had baths with their night shifts on, as if that made it any better. With merriment, to crush that shame, I remembered a tale told me by an ex-member of a religious order about his novitiate days when the novices bathing in Dublin Bay were instructed while undressing to keep their eyes not on their own bodies but on Howth Head, lying like a great whale on the far side of the water: a warning that had its comic aspects because at that time Howth was experiencing an unpleasant outbreak of pederasty. Nuns in sopping nightdresses, novices half in and out of bathing suits, all vanished in smoke when Hughie pulled the cork. Poteen was poteen, and far from my father in flat, dirty Dublin I had already acquired a tongue for whiskey. Frank, crouched on a low stool, was wrapped in a blanket. His dark hair, rubbed dry by Kate, stood up straight, and between that and his bright eyes and bony, sallow face he might have been a Comanche Indian, medicine man before his time. His clothes steamed before the blaze. When Kate stooped to kiss him as she shuffled forwards to swing her soup pot on to the crane and over the fire, Hughie and myself roared with laughter, but because he smiled with us my mind was clean again. Even if he was reared in that sad, wind-surrounded house he was still innocent and didn't know as we knew that Kate when young had enjoyed a reputation for excessive amorousness.

Over the cups of poteen, partially reduced to civilization by the addition of goat's milk, Hughie sang to her, to her old wrinkled face and meal-mumbling, toothless mouth half-hidden under a dusty hat the shape of a German helmet, to her grey shawl, to her red petticoat that spread out queenly when she sat down on a chair with short-sawed legs.

'With my dog and gun o'er the moorland heather,' he sang. 'To search for pastime I took my way. It was there I spied a lovely fair one. Her charms invited me awhile to stay. I said, My darling, should you find I love you, tell me your dwelling and your name also . . .'

Then, in a voice of unbelievable sweetness, the lonely, contented voice of a self-absorbed child, Kate answered him and sang:

'My name excuse, but you'll find my dwelling near the mountain streams where the moorcocks crow.'

'You didn't lick it off the grass, Owen Rodgers,' Hughie said.

He watched me pour poteen into my cup.

'There was your uncle Peter, the horsey man.'

'My uncle Peter, I'm told, is a living man far away in the U.S.A. He's only a legend in this part of Ireland.'

'Port wine mostly he went in for,' Hughie said. 'It was a great drink with the quality in those days.'

'He told my mother that any Rodgers who ever took to drink became a victim. So she says, for my benefit.'

Mountain dew and goat's milk had made me eloquent and wise.

'Everywhere I go I meet old men who remember my uncle Peter.'

'I said, My darling, would you wed a rover,' he sang, 'my former raking I would leave aside. Here is my hand and we will

70

pledge each other. If you prove constant I'll make you my bride. . . .'

He had the longest arms I ever saw until I saw the mummified arm of Donnelly the bare-knuckle boxer in a glass case in a pub in the County Kildare. He reached past Frank and myself to clasp Kate's right hand.

'We're a pair of old fools,' she said.

With a bunched, begrimed left hand she wiped moisture from the red lower rims of her eyes. But she sang her response as if she was eighteen and ready to elope with a soldier.

'If my parents knew that I'd wed a rover, great affliction I would undergo. I'll stop at home for another season near the mountain streams where the moorcocks crow.'

'The Lord forgive you, Frank Chesney,' said Hughie. 'Spitting out the good poteen.'

He was more familiar in drink with the makings of a priest than he would have dared to be in sobriety or perhaps it was that the river water had washed off and Kate's holy shroud of a blanket had wiped away the sacrosanct odour, and the captain's son was again completely part of the privileged earth of Bingen. Alfred in the stable about that moment had, although I was unaware of it then, wrapped his trouserless legs for warmth in a piece of sacking found in a manger.

'Spitting out the good poteen,' said Hughie. 'You won't be like the old-time priests at all. They could take it out of an old sock.'

'There's one in the village,' I said, 'does his best. He studied the art in Louvain.'

'Speak with respect,' said Kate, 'of the Lord's anointed. Even if they like the drop, what else consolation have they?'

The right arms of Kate and Hughie rocked like a swing before the fire. The soup pot gurgled with laughter. It was possible to forget that the cabin and the ground it stood on belonged to Captain Conway Chesney.

'So farewell darling for another season,' sang Hughie. 'I hope we'll meet in yon woodland vale. And when we meet we will embrace each other, and you'll pay attention to my lovesick tale . . .'

Their four hands were now joined tightly. The beast no longer squinting stared meaningfully at me over Lucy's rounded shoulder, and with poteen-glow and fire-radiance and the meaty smell of the soup my mind filled languidly with fancy; warm, moon-ruled tidal water stayed, then swallowed the thrust of the river. That comic Red Indian in the blanket would one day consecrate the Lord. Alfred had no longer a sweetheart, the rivers wriggled like eels, and the Boer War captain had seen the ghost of a skivvy peeping cautiously at his crimson splendour as the troops marched through the town. Young lovers on a morning moorland, Kate and Hughie joined their voices. . . .

'It is hand in hand we will join together and I'll escort you to yon valley low where the linnet sings his sweet notes so pleasing near the mountain streams where the moorcocks crow.'

When the song ended there was only the sound of the Gortin river, a rush, a lull, a rush, a lull and again a rush, and high above us on the rain-sleek mountains all the tributaries sang.

'My life on you, Kate. You'll have the six best fish of the day's catch.'

'There's luck in odd numbers, Hughie.'

'The seven best, so.'

'The stomach isn't so good now,' she said. 'My appetite isn't what it was.'

Her hands caressed protuberant red flannel.

'The trout is tasty, Kate.'

Their smooth bellies marred by clinging blades of grass were rose-red in the firelight.

'They'll be appetizing,' she said.

Behind her back as she stirred the soup Hughie grinned at us. He was as happy as a child at her comic simulation of lack of appetite. Her soups were famous. They were grey in colour and glutinous, and everything went into them: bones, giblets, pieces of meat that rejected the teeth and skidded round the mouth as if they were alive and (said Fee, the jockey) dead men's thumbs, bulls' pizzles, and frogs and newts from the dark depths of Thread the Needle. Minestrone was mere water to those soups.

'Your clothes are dry, Frank.'

Hidden behind the curtain of the outshot bed he re-attired himself. There was eating and drinking in the grey soup that day, and afterwards we had a trout each, cleaned by Hughie and myself, cooked by Kate. It was food that would satisfy even a chronic diabetic and in all my years since in the hotel business, I never found a chef could make a soup to steady a man after poteen and goat's milk. Frank, his clothes crumpled but dry, sat silently by the fire as if he didn't want to go home.

The evening sky was high and cold and grey. Hughie, walking away from us into the shadows, was the good giant lumbering home to his castle, his glorious deeds done. The house showed no light. Frank looked at it steadily while I leaned my bicycle against the gate to harden the tyres.

'I won't ask you in, Owen. You know how it is.'

I didn't know then. Nobody could have imagined it.

'Get to bed quick and warm,' I said.

Frank, I felt, was denying me a right when he closed the door, however politely, between myself and whatever was going on in Bingen.

'You'll be hungry, Owen.'

He was pitiably apologetic, and mercilessly I met his unspoken apology with easy laughter.

'Not after Kate's soup. And fresh trout. And poteen and goat's milk.'

With no answering laughter, he solemnly shook hands with me. The poteen, still alive with seeds of energy under the heavy topsoil of soup, took me as light as a lark over the mountains.

Doctor Grierson was still at his ease in the drawing-room, a whiskey glass in his hand. The ends of his trousers were half-ways to his knees to show silk socks, suspenders, sections of long woollen underpants, as he sat cross-legged and talked about Lourdes.

'The river Gave is as grey as my hair,' he said. 'It rushes down in pointed elbows and in one of those elbows is the grotto.

'The *pernod* is very good,' he said.

'In the topmost church of the basilica,' he said, 'at two in the morning there were Belgian pilgrims. All the women, young and old, dressed in black and wore veils. They held out their arms cruciformly . . .'

The whiskey in his right hand, as he demonstrated, came within smelling distance of me.

'They sang, magnificently in unison, a haunting hymn called *Chez Nous*.'

'In my youth,' said my father, 'there was a coffee shop of that name on the Diamond Hill.'

He refilled the doctor's glass while the doctor, politely inattentive, turned towards my mother and searched in his pocket diary for the date the Bishop had tentatively fixed for the diocesan pilgrimage to Fatima, Lourdes, Lisieux and the Rue du Bac.

'Rome will be next year,' he said. 'You'll love Italy, Mrs Rodgers.'

At the door he was eloquent but a little unsteady on his feet and my father said: 'Take my torch from the kitchen, Owen, and light the doctor as far as the first lamp.' The semi-circle of village street lights, a recently-installed system, was below us down the slope, and I walked with him as far as Lucy's door where we stood talking, wise, cultured men of the world, about wine and France and the city of Dublin. It was aeons away back through dark tunnels of time to that confessional evening when he slapped my face in front of Christ, the twelve feasting apostles and the assembled maidens of the village. Being a man now, I wanted Lucy, warm under blankets, to know it, so I kept my voice unnaturally loud, and if the doctor noticed my cockerel folly he was too wise and sympathetic to comment on it. The face of Mr Pickwick, visible in the new street-lighting system, winked at me from a painted plate but I didn't know then that it took a good forty-eight hours, as well as Kate Carr's soup, to dull the sabre-swinging buoyancy of illegal, mountain whiskey. Since then, in the course of my business, I have watched goatish men and women drinking for a purpose and have often thought of patenting, to save them time and imagination and to make money for myself, that cocktail of poteen and the satyr-juice of mountain goats. Oh, the doctor's step as he went away from me was neat, feat and delicate, the step of a man of Paris on the Avenue Montaigne, not of an Irish curate on a village street. He was a man of civilization who, under the balcony of the desired one, had talked to me like an equal. His odour was warm with good cigar smoke and ten-year-old Jameson, good shaving soap and a little hair-cream for his thinning thatch. It was a great contrast to the odour of yellow, cold Francis in the captain's unhappy castle. To Lucy between the sheets, between sleeping and waking, I willed with Lovelace grace my gallant thoughts, and walked up the hill to my father.

'He's a very civilized man,' the doctor had said. 'A father you should be proud of. Eccentric, but eminently civilized.'

'The doctor is a very civilized man,' said my father. 'But God help him, he's in a predicament.'

Meditatively, as if he was about to offer me some, he held the dwindled bottle of ten-year-old in his hand, then changed his mind, smiled wryly, drained it himself. My father, I regret to say, was tight.

'Let loose to Louvain and Paris,' he said, 'to learn and look about him and never able to get over the fact he had to come back to Ireland.'

'When a clergyman here,' he said, 'is overfond of the skirts, it's easier for him to get his paws on a bottle of malt. Anaesthetic.'

I was shocked. I thanked God my mother wasn't in the room. I was ashamed of my loud-talking under fair Lucy's casement.

'I shouldn't feed him the whiskey, I suppose,' he said. 'But then he'd better have it here in private than in a public house or in Grainger's hotel in the city. We've no neat girls here in glass boxes, have we? No temptations with black dresses, white collars and long red fingernails. You haven't seen any, have you, Owen?'

'No, father.'

He laughed a long, grey, gentle laugh. I never knew a man could laugh more intricate wrinkles into the corners of his eyes. He looked over his shoulder as if he half expected to see a neat temptation in a glass box hidden between the 'cello and the old upright piano with the bust of Beethoven on top.

'No, not one. And I'm told if there was one here you'd be the first to notice it.'

My mother came in softly then, her hair bundled for repose in a blue night-cap.

'Are you looking for something, John?'

'Oh, no, no. Just something I thought for a moment the doctor might have forgotten.'

She was puzzled by our laughter, a little vexed, too, at being shut out from our secret. She sat down with us at the dying fire and our laughter died away into a world that belonged only to men.

'I'll never understand you two,' she said.

But her face and voice were again content. My father finished his whiskey.

'One of the boys from Bingen was here tonight,' he said.

He had to repeat himself before the news registered.

'Who? Alfred?'

'No. I gather the great lover is under lock and key. More unlucky in love than his school-friends. It was Edmund. He wanted his fare to England. I gave it to him. It's no secret, if you're talking to the captain.'

'Was it wise,' my mother said, 'to interfere?'

'He showed me his bona fides. He has a job there. Dr Grierson will write to the parish priest in the place he's going to, to see he doesn't lose his faith when he gets there.'

'That's the main thing,' my mother said.

'We Irish are lucky to have the faith,' he said. 'Otherwise we'd have nothing to lose.'

'John,' she said.

I laughed.

'Owen,' she said.

'The captain will go on fire, da.'

'He'll burn sooner or later.'

'John,' she said.

His unusual bitterness startled me. It was abnormal in such a well-known, friendly man.

'It was time somebody saved something from that wreck,' he said.

He looked at his watch.

'The boat's cleared the loch by now,' he said. '*Bon voyage* to Edmund Conway Chesney.'

Three

THE WETTING AND THE GENERAL HELLERY OF THE
captain were between them the cause of the illness that came
close to killing Frank Conway Chesney.

'Greta,' said the captain, 'have you brought me the vinegar?'

The sunlight sloping across the drawing-room from the
window behind me brightened the green bottle and her bare
right forearm. With revulsion, because I was still young enough
to think of Psyche as completely smooth-skinned, like Lucy,
I saw the faintest down of hair just below the elbow.

'The specimen is here,' he said. 'You can withdraw now,
Greta.'

He stood with his back to the mantelpiece serpent and looked
now at me, now at his opened notebook. As medical orderly
while there was illness in Bingen he wore a spotless white,
starched-linen jacket. From the breast pocket protruded a silvery,
cylindrical thermometer case. His face, what of it was visible,
was flushed a hectic, unusual red and the points of his vital
moustache had faded to a weary yellow; but those odd colour
effects may have been caused by the sunlight shining on him—
there was autumn in its afternoon—or they may simply have
been a contrast to the whiteness of his jacket. He held the test-
tube of urine up to the light, added a drop of vinegar, circled

the tube in tongs over a spirit-lamp set on the cold fireside tiles. The lamp roared nastily.

'The patient is well,' he said, 'all things considered. In these cases there is often an excess of albumen in the urine.'

'Yes, captain.'

'I almost forgot, Owen, you know more about these things now than I do.'

'I don't know much yet, captain. I've only finished my pre-medical.'

'You're modest, Master Rodgers.'

As he stooped, heating the tube, I tried, without success, to read the hieroglyphics written on the notebook left open beside the serpent.

'The specimen's turning cloudy,' he said. 'There is an excess of albumen. Now what does that mean to you?'

On his hunkers beside an argent Nevada river the old prospector flashed the pan, asked the opinion of the young prospector.

'Would it be rheumatic fever, captain?'

'Brilliant. Brilliant diagnosis.'

He stood up. Whiskers and moustache bristled and glistened from the heat or from enthusiasm about the accuracy of my wild guess.

'It could be rheumatic fever. But I don't think it is. Not yet. It was stopped in time. Greta!'

She must have been waiting outside the door. She was in the room again instantly.

'Greta. You could take this away. Tell your sister Maeve to bring me the disinfectant.'

Before the door had closed behind her he was again absorbed in his notebook.

'Greta,' he said (not to me but to the serpent), 'might make a good nurse. The symptoms,' he said (turning again to the sunlight and speaking to me), 'are all here, written down.'

He ran his right little finger, wax-like and delicate in the sunshine, down the page.

'Thought to be a hypersensitive response to previous infection by group A.B. haemolitic streptococcus,' he said. 'Great words, Owen. But the medical terms would present no difficulty to your father's son.'

'I'm not so certain, captain.'

'Therefore the patient,' he read, 'will have previous history of one of the following.'

He ticked them off cheerfully.

'One, scarlet fever. Two, tonsilitis. My son, Francis, never had scarlet fever but much against my will he had his tonsils removed in that seminary. Three, naso pharyngitis or rhinitis. Construe, young Rodgers.'

'Nose infections,' I said.

'You have chosen the right profession, Owen. Although once I thought you had a predisposition to theology.'

'Not me, captain.'

'You never solved the gay doctor's conundrum: Is it better to be born and damned than not to be born at all?'

'No, captain.'

'A fine conundrum. Hughie Heron, whose education isn't the best, was told by a man in a public house on a fair day that he would give Hughie a conundrum, and Hughie answered that a man he heard tell of had died of a conundrum.'

He folded the notebook, marked the place with that little finger, and laughed his dry metronomical ha-ha-ha.

'He died of a conundrum,' he said.

Sweet words about moorland lovers flowed out from the curtain of Hughie's red moustache. The captain, eyes again on the opened notebook, sang, while his haunted, sallow son lay sweating upstairs, of pyrexia, increased respiratory rate, of large joints, red, swollen and tender, of erythema nodosum or red blotches on the shins, of chorea or generalized twitching of muscles, of deafness, rapid breathing, mental confusion, multiple skin haemorrhages, dizziness and vomiting, of toxic dose and sodium salicylate. It was the devil's dark hymn, a paean of praise to all the ills the flesh is heir to. Beauty withered. Love decayed. Noses collapsed into pestiferous black pits like rat holes. Fair living breasts softened to crawling pulp. Only the serpent remained immune, singing of death with the voice of the Bingen captain. At that moment, perversely, I knew I would never be a doctor, that I had no faith in healing, no sanative power in me, that before illness and misery I would be aghast and helpless.

'What did the doctor say, captain?'

He looked at me sadly. The cuffs of my jacket, I saw, were frayed. He closed the book slowly, slowly withdrew the indicative little finger, looking all the time not at the book but at me. He closed the holy gates on the ignominious one who had revealed by five fatal words his turd-befouled unworthiness to look any longer on the mysteries. Bearing a basin in which Dettol was wreathing squid-like vapours in cold spring water, Maeve came to my rescue, and in embarrassed delirium I saw sunlight deep and molten in her warm, brown hair. Shame, and the sun, for the first time opened my eyes to the loveliness of the hair on the head of a girl who hardly as yet existed.

'Can I see the patient, captain?'

He dipped his hands in the basin. Lavabo, I almost said. He washed them with the intensity of Lady Macbeth. He was heroically trying to avoid speaking harshly to me. He payed particular attention to each fingernail. He dried his little hands and reached the towel to me to signify absolution and forgiveness and I knew that if it hadn't been for my foolish betraying of the understanding there was between us when I asked him about the doctor's opinion he would even have led me upstairs to the sickroom.

'I have decided,' he said, 'to admit no visitors yet for a while. Quiet is of the essence.'

For me, too, after that fearful *faux pas*, quiet was of the essence, and I kept as quiet as I could while I backed across the uneven tiles of the wide hallway to the door which Maeve held open for us. Did I imagine it, or did she really smile when I stumbled over the badger-skin rug that lay across the threshold? How could you know if a woman smiled or not when all you could see was sunlight sinking into brown hair?

He walked with me across the grass, an unusual condescension. Out in the yellow sunlight he was again faded, the brassy healthy glow no longer in his hide or hair.

'The young recover quickly,' he said. 'Time is the only thing can't be cured.'

'Doctors know nothing,' he said. 'Don't let them drill you. Read the books but form your own opinions. Your learned father should have told you that.'

Lifelessly, without gripping me, he held out to me the coldest hand I have ever touched and I said I would come again soon, early next week, before my studies took me back to Dublin.

In his sweating illness, Frank told me years afterwards, great white birds flew towards him from the sands beyond the estuary where the man and horse had seemed to vanish on the first morning I visited Bingen. The birds swooped in and down and away, he said, to the rhythm of the Yeats poem that says, I would that we were, my beloved, white birds on the foam of the sea.

'Do you remember once,' he said, 'that Alfred swore birds in their graves turned white and we buried a dead bird and dug it up again and for once Alfred was right? It was white.'

Through hours of rhythmical, feverish heat the white birds followed him and the lilt of the long lines of the poem swung him somewhere in the air, half-ways between the bed and the high ceiling lemon with sunlight: he was haunted then, he said, by numberless islands and many a Danaan shore where time would surely forget him and sorrow come near him no more. Then, after a long time the white-winged rhythm ceased, he dropped into desolation and black loneliness. All the beloved, numberless islands of Bingen, sheltered corners of fields, smooth-grassed places under trees, drifted before him like lighted pictures and away from him into shadows. He knew then, he said, that he was Gainsborough, the painter, who had loved so much his own English land around Sudbury that there was not a picturesque clump of trees, nor even a single tree of any beauty, which was not from his earliest years treasured in his memory.

'All that,' Frank said, 'was precognition, because at the time of my illness I had never read Yeats or heard of Gainsborough. How could I have foreseen that I would one day be on the mission near Sudbury?'

Not one word of that rigmarole, with all due respect to the clerical cloth, did I believe. On the mission, as the Irish complacently call it, in England, Frank had learned to drink good wines and take an interest in the occult. When he talked that claptrap about his precognition we were holidaying together in a golfing hotel on a green sea-surrounded headland not far from the Yeats country and the sands of Lissadell. He was far from his ecclesiastical superiors. He was as full of wine as Dr Grierson. When he gabbed about precognition he was an echo of his father on creation, nothingness, damnation. But I feared that

from the day of Alfred's humiliation on the score of the melodious, dancing girl, from the day of his own tumble into the
water and the love-singing of Kate and Hughie in the cave of a
cabin, Francis Conway Chesney had ringed himself against
reality with a baying, invisible pack of Austrian dogs whelped in
the stable where his elder brother, trouserless, was exposed to the
humiliating draughts of truth.

'We can foresee things, Owen,' he said. 'The white birds
flew in over the estuary and down around the house. They
roosted by the footbridge. Birds have foretold death.'

But I swear there were no white birds hovering in the air that
evening when I shook the captain's hand—cold, was it from
Dettol or urine testing?—and cycled home through the familiar
Gortin Gap. There was a furnace redness on the sparse mountain
gorse, a blanched mist above the bottom land, a callous rattle in
the falling streams. Long before the ridge of the Gap, where
Lucy, who had cycled to meet me, was waiting by the rest-and-
be-thankful spring, I had forgotten how sunlight soaked into
Maeve's brown hair, I had forgotten the faint frost of hair on
Greta's forearms. As a macabre medical I knew that hair grew
not only on the living but on the dead. Lucy was as smooth as
cream, and even if the squinting monster was still asleep, the
dusk was warm.

My mother said to my father: 'Didn't he deny them the milk
that would have put bone and tissue into them and it leaking from
the cows in the fields? Who can he blame if Francis is delicate?'

My father said to my mother: 'He has ideas on health would
have terrified Bernarr MacFadden. He abominates doctors.'

My father said to me: 'How does he tolerate you, the makings,
God help us, of a general practitioner?'

It couldn't be possible that my wise, grey, kind father knew less about anything, the present, the future, the heart of his own son, than the cold little monster of Bingen?

Early next week, then, before my studies took me back to Dublin I cycled again to Bingen. It was a sunny, windy, showery day. The river was as red as claret with the juice of the peat. On the green before the house I counted sixty-seven sheep gathered together as if for some momentous convention. Stranger still, the front door of the house was open, swinging to and fro in the wind, and red petals of the strongest, most durable ramblers had been blown in along the hall floor. But even though I was the one favoured stranger allowed across that threshold I took no advantage of the open door and waited and knocked again and picked up rambler petals and crushed them idly between my fingers and thought of silk-white Lucy, and in the end Frank Chesney came towards me down the stairs, along the hall, over the scattered petals. He wore an untidy brown dressing-gown, belted with the sort of tri-coloured, snake-hooked belt that schoolboys wear. His unkempt hair was lustreless from days in bed and the sour sweat of illness. His face was pale and pimply, his forehead perspiring.

'I'm glad to see you back on your feet, Frank.'

Without any noticeable emotion he pointed across the green to the footbridge.

'My father dropped dead this morning, Owen. Over there. He fell into the river from the bridge. He was washed nearly to the head before they got him. Hughie Heron and the men had to take him out in a salmon net.'

Before God, I almost said, 'He died of a conundrum.' Then something like panic before mystery made me want to laugh.

All those white, laughing cataracts had conspired together. God and the Gortin river, and the old gods of rock and water, grass and bush, who, before Bingen, had answered to the name of Magheracolton, had watched the captain for years, waiting for this ultimate, ludicrous moment. The little tyrant of his fields had tumbled down. Death had taken him like a fish in a net, whiskers and moustache, perhaps, protruding through the mesh, the funniest sight until the professor caught the coelacanth. I knew, but could not feel, that I had lost a friend, or someone who saw through me, which might be the same thing. In spite of Frank's lifeless, pallid face I might have disgraced myself by hysterical laughter if I had not glanced beyond him to the far end of the hallway to see Alfred with his trousers on, to see also for the first time, leaning on Alfred, mother supported by son, the once beloved bride of Captain Conway Chesney, man of Mafeking like Baden Powell, now bereft and a widow.

Four

Oh, father dear, you left us,
Which made us weep and sigh.
But, oh, the saddest part of all
You didn't say good-bye.
                          In memoriam—Anon.

'BE GREGARIOUS!' THUNDERED THE REDEMPTORIST preacher.

In Newman's church, in Stephen's green, in Dublin, he preached an Advent triduum to a congregation of university undergraduates. Newman's head in marble looked out, from his niche in the wall, past James Kinnear, student of law, Geoffrey Austin Macsorley, student of the arts and aspiring creative writer, and Owen Rodgers, reluctant and disgruntled student of medicine.

'Be gregarious,' he said, and waved his right hand at the male students on the gospel side of the nave and at the segregated, ghettoed females on the epistle side.

'On walks or picnics,' he said (to the epistle side), 'never be alone with a young man nor' (to the gospel side) 'with a young woman.'

On the epistle side one entire pew-full of bras and girdles strained with suppressed laughter, touched off possibly by that unctuous, reverberant use of the word picnics.

'On cycling expeditions in the Dublin hills,' he said, 'be

gregarious. Stay with the flock. Play safe. When boy and girl wander off alone together there is always danger.'

'Mother of Christ,' muttered Kinnear.

'Three hundred days plenary indulgence,' whispered Jeff.

'I want to be alone,' Kinnear whispered. 'Oh, I want to be alone. Yes I want to be alone with Mary Brown.'

'Seven years and seven quarantines,' Jeff said too loudly and too hoarsely.

An apostolic student in the pew ahead of us slowly swivelled his neck to look sideways disapprovingly at Cardinal Newman. Uneasily, drowsily remembering past guilt and flippant whispers in the Holy of Holies I saw da Vinci's figures in gaudy stained glass, heard Dr Grierson and fluty Lucy, saw Maeve Conway Chesney attentive to her quiet, white mother on the day they interred the captain.

'In the days that were,' said the thundering son of Saint Alphonsus Ligouri, 'the vice of the Irish people was drunkenness. Then came Father Theobald Mathew who said, "Here goes, in the name of God . . ."'

'Down the hatch,' Jeff whispered.

'And set Ireland on the path to sobriety, temperance and self-respect. But temperance was not enough. Total abstinence was the only safeguard and God sent Father Cullen, the great Jesuit, to found the pioneer league of total abstinence. The members wear pins in their coats to show to the world their heroic resolve to abstain from intoxicating stimulants in reparation for the drunkenness of others.'

Two nights before, at a party in a coloured student's flat, in a crisis caused by the lack of a corkscrew, Kinnear had adroitly levered corks out of beer bottles with a total abstinence pin gladly loaned for the purpose by an intoxicated student of engineering.

'Today,' said the man in the pulpit, 'the besetting vice is impurity. It confronts you wherever you go.'

'Alas, no,' Kinnear whispered. 'Or so I fear.'

He contemplated the coloured coats on the epistle side. The slavering monster squinted at me over Lucy's shoulder.

'Why not then have a pin for those who have banded themselves against this vice, to wear in their coats?'

'A safety-pin,' Jeff moaned.

'A league of purity,' said the preacher.

'Ireland for ever' Kinnear whispered.

'Let us pray,' said the preacher.

'By all means,' said Jeff.

In the crowd crushing towards the door an apostolic student with two pins in his lapel, one to show he didn't touch alcohol, another to show he didn't take the name of God in vain and was pledged to make spiritual reparation for the blasphemies of those who did, said: 'He's as up-to-date as Fulton Sheen. He knows the young.'

A second apostolic student, a mere man of one pin, said: 'His article on grace in last Sunday's paper was very practical.'

'Bridget,' said a neat little Dublin girl (round posterior in a tight-fitting crimson coat), 'Bridget, remember never to be alone with a young man.'

Daintily-fingered, she flicked holy water from the font to the forehead of her plump, bucolic companion.

'Would he have us,' said Bridget, 'buy a pig in a poke?'

All the easy music of Munster was in her voice.

'Where's your purity pin, Molly?' Kinnear said.

He was arm-in-arm with little, round, red-bottom. Thick rain in Saint Stephen's Green made amends to Lord Ardilaun, benefactor of Dubliners by a grant of land for park, pleasaunce, flower-bed and lake, for the outrages of the pigeons.

'Pinning her unmentionables,' said Munster Bridget. 'Something slipped at dissections.'

'Be gregarious, James,' said Molly.

'With you anytime I'll gregariate.'

Bronze and unbending, the generous Lord looked at us from ground where an Archbishop in different, distant times had been hanged. Winter earth was dark under bare trees.

'Let us be gregarious in the Red Bear,' said Jeff.

'Let us walk,' he said, embracing Bridget, 'by the trees on the canal bank to the Red Bear and be intemperate if not impure.'

Arm-in-arm five of us walked by sluggish water under ancient, dripping branches. Ahead the lock thundered, the lights of the Red Bear shone.

'The trees on the canal bank,' said Jeff, 'are more sinned against than sinning.'

Dead water came to life at the straining vee-shaped lockgate, and nostalgic Owen saw from the ground of Bingen the vee of sky reddening behind the Gortin Gap. All things reminded me. Shadows nudged me. Voices spoke to me but the words were shapeless mockeries, meaning nothing but inexplicable loneliness. We crossed by the lockgate's shaky catwalk, holding, with laughter and exaggerated care, to wet chains. Below us white breasts of water curved down into a booming stone prison, curving and falling to the rhythm of marching pipe music echoing in my head at that exact moment for no reason I could think of. Afterwards, when we had circled our way around the fallen trunk of a monster tree torn down by last week's tempest, around the ungainly tripod crane erected by workmen to swing the brute to the saw, I knew why white breasts of water, parabolas of water, had reminded me of pipe music. That particular pipe tune, I knew, would never leave my ears while I lived. In a pub, slightly tipsy with Jim and Jeff, walking to the gents, fumbling with my fly, whistling automatically as men do at such moments of truth, it was always that tune I whistled.

Linked between Molly and Bridget, being gregarious according to the advice of the ghostly father ('I knew a man,' said Kinnear, 'slept with two sisters'), I whistled: 'They marched through the town and their banners were so gay.

'That I ran quick to the casement,' I sang, 'to hear the drums play.'

'Owen,' said Molly, 'has a sweet voice.'

On the slippery, grimy, green terazzo floor of the porch of the Red Bear we shook the rain from our coats.

'Our theme song,' Jeff said. 'A chant about a great soldier no longer with us. I'll write a book about him when Owen tells me the secret.'

'The captain with the whiskers,' I sang, 'cast a sly glance at me.'

Then the white breasts, white birds on the foam of the sea, were no longer canal water. They were silk and white, late-autumn roses. The noise of the Red Bear was the rush of the Bingen sea, The voice I heard was not Molly's Dublin lilt nor Bridget's easy, coaxing Munster music, but the assured voice of Maeve Conway Chesney. For when the captain, like the male lamprey consummating his act of procreation, died and gave her life, she revealed herself as the most capable, most confident woman I have ever known. The nondescript covering, the shell, the case in which the captain's life had kept her locked, cracked wide open.

'In Würzburg museum,' said the captain with reflective, scientific appreciation. 'In Würzburg a learned German doctor showed me an odd iron harness. Possessive, medieval men locked up the nether parts of their ladies to preserve them, while their lords were absent, from rape or foolishness. Practical people the Germans, Owen.'

Dying, his hand unlocked the harness. She stepped out new, beautiful, part owner of the world and Lucy was only the queen of the many women who are curves fore and curves aft. Maeve bent down over her mother in the great bedroom above the drawing-room where the captain's corpse, netted at the confluence of fresh and salt water, dried and dealt with appropriately by the undertaker, had lain, and where, after the burial, the ailing widow (no death could give to her frail, pale body life abounding) spent most of her days of lonely dreams.

'Comfy, mother?'

She fixed an armchair cushion behind the old head. She combed the scant silver hair, her right arm arching with the style of a trained hairdresser, the comb gently distributing comfort and order. With a damp cloth she cooled the luminous white skin over the distinct, prominent forehead bones.

'You won't talk too long, Owen.'

'No,' I said.

She was an intimidating stranger who had once been a shadow. In her presence I found it difficult to sit down, impossible to say her name, was tongue-tied as once I had been before her father. She wheeled the armchair around so that the widow could look out through the window over the green to the river and the sea, but not to the bridge where the captain fell. The pantomimic ocean rose blue and fell blue, swung white in long parabolas and breasts over tongues of Bingen rock, fell spent and made no sound. For the window was closed, the wind for once blowing away from the house as if with the captain conquered it had rested for a while its attack. The only sounds in the bright, newly-papered buttercup-and-pale-rose room were the ticking of the glass-domed clock, the soothing words of the girl. When she walked past me towards the door the white rose on her blouse disintegrated, petals showering on the carpet and, like an omadhaun in a love poem, I stooped to gather them, fumbling clumsily, hearing above my head her soft laughter.

'It's not worth while, Owen. You can't stick them on again.'

But she held out her hand, small, strong, with stumpy, square-topped fingers, and took them from me. She had the oddest wristlet of brown freckles. She could have had it, too, when she was lost in the shadows of the great basement kitchen, listening to the hooves in the yard outside, saying yes father to the order of the day.

'Let the wise old people talk together now,' she said. 'I've work to do.'

'Mother wanted to talk to you,' she whispered, 'but not too long.'

'No,' I said.

'She's not over the shock,' she said.

'I'm going to Dublin tomorrow.'

'It was good of you to stay on for a few weeks,' she said.

Opening and closing her fingers, she crushed the petals.

'Your mother and yourself, Owen, were a great help.'

She touched my hand and walked to the door but she was a bodiless, superior spirit, most unlike Lucy, and I could smell only rose petals. The clock ticked. One giant wave, repelled by wind and shore, reared up, turned white, fell slowly. We did not even hear the noise of its despair. The door closed.

'Sit close beside me, Owen Rodgers,' said the widow in the chair.

Those were the first words the captain's widow ever spoke to me. Through the crowded two nights of her husband's wake she had sat tearless in the corner of the drawing-room, between the snake and the wide front window, mutely shaking hands with sympathisers, a pale statue, speaking only to my mother, Lizzie Heron, Maeve and Greta, and to Kate Carr who came now and again, curtsied to her, carried her cups of hot tea.

'I heard so much about you, Owen,' she said. 'You're a good friend to my children.'

The hand she held out to me was cold and deeply hollowed between thin brittle bones.

'My late husband always had great praise for you.'

'I'm sorry, Mrs Rodgers,' I blundered, 'for your trouble.'

It was the countryman's stock phrase of sympathy, but only God or the spirit of the dear departed could have known why I used the name of my blonde, hearth-ripened contented mother to this shadow of a woman. She didn't, as far as I could see, notice the slip.

'Yes, dear, yes,' she said.

She looked at me and smiled without meaning. Her pale eyes were loose in their sockets.

'He was strict,' she said.

Seven spouts of white broken water I counted, silently hovering above and silently falling on the rocks. This frail body lost in stiff, shiny, black bombazine had once stirred desire in the captain's small, neat limbs. Fair limbs, said Saint Augustine, whose embraces were pleasant to the flesh. Or once had she been, like her daughter Maeve, a remote, untouchable queen, an Easter morning vision fresh risen from the tomb?

'I said so often to him,' she said, 'they're girls and you should let them out to dances. But he was strict.'

She leaned towards me. She whispered. She glanced nervously at the walls, as if to redecorate them so soon (Maeve's idea) after the tragedy was an impious outrage the dead might well avenge.

I wanted to open the window. In the silence of that room the noise of the waves would have been as heartsome as the laughter of children.

'Do you dance, Owen?'

'In Dublin I dance.'

'I was never in Dublin. I wanted a honeymoon, but he was full of cares and buying this place and I forbore to ask.'

The waves mesmerized me. I rocked with them. I rose and fell. The little opulent bastard who had seen Table Mountain, who had talked as if he had owned the Rhine hadn't the time to take his bride the length of Dublin.

'I wasn't much,' she said. 'I was a maid in a kitchen when he came to me.'

She had peeped through the blinds, very cautiously in, and the scarlet coat had seared her eyes with love. As a confused, exhausted escape from silence and her sad voice I imagined my ears humming with pipe music.

'We could have a dance here,' she said. 'If he wasn't dead so shortly.'

'We could dance at Christmas,' I said desperately.

'I was fond of dancing once myself. The sets and the lancers. Not so much the waltz. There was more company in the sets and lancers.'

One small foot in a patent-leather buttoned boot drummed rhythmically on the carpet. It held my eyes and my attention, drew me away from the freedom of the waves, and it was then in the still room that the movement of the captain's pipe tune and the words that went with it in our corner of the country became part of me for ever. She talked as her foot tapped. The pipes, the bandleader a giant under his busby, swinging his staff, the swaying sporrans of the kilties, the drunken ecstasy of the big drums and kettle-drums, the marching troops home from hanging Kruger on a sour apple tree, came towards me down long roads and through a hundred towns.

'It was a big house I worked in,' she said. 'Bigger than this. They had two dozen servants if they had one. But they were considerate people if you did your work well. They had a music box.'

'Like a gramophone,' I (to say something) said.

'When they played the music box it went tinkle, tinkle, and they were good enough to ask us, all the help you know, to come in and stand in a row to listen to it. Even when there were visitors.'

'Even then,' I said.

I shivered. The free waves mocked me. The servants in a grateful subservient row listened to the music box.

'He came there visiting. Home from the war. The music box played . . .'

Her small foot for a moment ceased tapping, but the rhythm of the lost tune the music box had played could not be recaptured. The foot resumed its march. Pipes and troops advanced.

'He looked at me. I looked back as well as I could. The mistress didn't like us looking at the men. Then he came to me in the kitchen and put his hand on my shoulder and whatever came over me, I struck him with the saucepan I was cleaning and the sauce out of it dribbled down the front of his lovely uniform coat.'

She was laughing softly at the memory.

'Whatever came over me. Maybe it was the smell of drink off him. But he was good as well as strict, Owen Rodgers, for he told the mistress he stumbled and fell, and saved me my job and married me a year later. It was a good house to work in.'

If I could only have relieved my feelings in filth and blasphemy the way Kinnear so obviously could do. This was how love began: sauce spilt on a soldier's coat after a drunken grab at a girl working in a kitchen. It wouldn't have seemed so damnable if he had been seven feet high with some inches to spare, looking like a king in command, lurching in liquor between the pots and pans to find the skivvy he had selected from the disciplined music-box parade, foul, lecherous, red-faced, ready to ruffle the skirts from any knees that would stay long enough in the same place. But Captain Conway Chesney, as well organized as Germany, had picked his victim with deliberation, and the blow with the saucepan was all that was needed to harden his resolution.

'I was a complete stranger to him,' she said. 'Wasn't it kind of him not to complain of me?'

'Small men,' said my father when I mentioned the matter to him, 'are said to be wonderful. Like widows.'

'It was the whiskers,' Kinnear said. 'It's written in the best books that at the time of the Boer War whiskers were a sexual symbol. Think of King Edward and the dolls in Paris.'

'It's true to this day,' said Jeff. 'Whiskers or moustache. Look at Hughie Heron. Ask Lizzie. A kiss without hair is an egg without salt.'

She was humming to the tapping rhythm of her foot. She was standing up, her back to the window, shutting off the waves from me. She was tiny, frail, tottering, and I half-rose to steady her but, smiling like a confident young girl, she waved me away and, to my consternation, sang. Her eyes closed tightly. Her wrinkled face tilted upwards. Her hands were clasped behind her back. Her quavering voice was a tragic parody on the way my father, mocking Captain Conway Chesney with the whiskers, used to sing the same song. Oom Paul high among the sour apples, she sang as the troops marched jauntily through the town of that remembered meeting and thrilled skivvies peeped out from behind the curtains.

'Next we met,' the words went, 'at a grand ball and of course I thought it right to pretend that we had never met before that same night. But he knew me at once, I could tell by his glance, and I hung my head and blushed when he asked me to dance.'

The door opened behind me but either through embarrassment or timidity I didn't turn around. Maeve, I knew, would disapprove. Then a low, slow voice, a girl's voice that never, I could have sworn, had I heard before said: 'Mother, you should be resting.'

It was my cue to arm the widow back to her chair, smelling as I did so a faint odour of illness and decay from the cushions Maeve had planned to make the chair comfortable, seeing so close to me the wrinkled, almost transparent skin of her right cheek, hearing the end of the verse die away into a faint whisper from past, lost times: 'My heart it is enlisted and will never more be free, since the captain with the whiskers cast a sly glance at me.'

The only sly glance I possessed I cast sideways to see Greta, white-aproned like a nurse, crossing to the window.

'We could do with air,' she said.

Seeing and hearing her at the same time, I knew I had heard her voice before. She opened the window. Her crisp, curling black hair was as untidily cut as if she had attended a home-barbering session in Macillion's kitchen.

'This window's sheltered,' she said. 'There won't be a draught, mother.'

The waves stood up high and fell forward. Even though the wind blew against their advance and away from us we could hear whiplashes of water laid along the rocks, we could hear the endless moan of the breakers, shrill gull cries on the long sand. Without dread I stood by Greta at the window and looked at the sea. Far out a long, black pencil-line would suddenly appear, magically drawn, evenly advancing towards the shore, rising easily, changing colour to shining white, trampling, falling in abasement.

'The sea's wonderful today,' Greta said.

She might have been inland-reared and looking at the ocean for the first time.

'It's the offshore wind,' I said.

'Hasn't Greta grown tall, Owen?' the widow said. 'She'll be as tall as Alfred. My people were tall people. Edmund will be tiny like his father.'

Without dread I could look at Greta and see that she had grown but not grown startlingly into life as Maeve had done. The shadows, in her odd quietness which was more by far than the lack of intensity in her sparse words, still held her. Yet I was glad it was Greta not Maeve who had interrupted the song and discovered me a careless nurse, for I felt about her then, as the captain may once have felt about her mother who was the daughter of tall, unterrifying people, that she could do me no harm.

Greta, knitting something in cyclamen wool, stayed quietly with her mother, and I walked through the house, through the kitchen to the wide cobbled yard. His precise steps would never again tap down those stairs as he descended for morning drill or in the evening to issue the orders for the next day. The yard was no longer a drill square or an exercise square for prisoners, but in windy, yellow light (a startled chestnut tree pushed by contrary air against its customary slant stood by the corner of the stables) it was one of those sporting prints, supplements to magazines defunct a century since, that one can still see, framed and grown venerable, in hotels in old market towns. Noseless, intent on his task, a wizened leprecaun of a man, arms holding reins aloft, hands wide apart, Fee the jockey slowly paced and circled a bay mare. Once in every circle he stopped to flute words from his oddly-orificed face to Hughie Heron and Maeve, in white shirt, man's riding breeches, yellow leather boots. They bent over the red setter bitch that that day had come out of nowhere and followed me to Bingen. The glistening red body, the kindly eye, the sensitive, twitching right forepaw seeking friendship in the air as she lay on her side to allow Hughie and Maeve to probe her belly, was an instructive contrast to the grossness of the squinting mastiff in the room behind the hardware shop. She was at home at Maeve's feet. She was already in love with those squat fingers.

'Thanks, Owen, oh, thanks for bringing her to me. We'll call her Gortin Lass.'

'Gortin Lady,' Fee whistled. 'She'll never be a lass again.'

Surrendering the discovery to Maeve I felt that the animal had followed me only because she knew where and to whom I was going. Owen Rodgers never had much of a way with dogs. She had come startled to the Gap road down a boreen that no longer led to any house. She had stood watching me, head on one side, friendly, lonely, as I wheeled my bicycle up the slope. There had been no sound of guns on the mountain that morning. She led the way back up the boreen and I followed but there was nothing to see, no searching shooting-party, no huntsman ditched with a broken leg and waiting for his faithful setter to return to him with aid. There was only a wet valley, a cabin now used for cattle, a faraway waterfall, low mist in wisps over the damp ground; and where the wandering red setter came from was and was to remain a mystery.

'She's fretting,' Maeve said. 'I'll swear she's had little setters.'

With gentleness and purity her stumpy, square-topped fingers caressed grey nipples that were spent and miserable as if the glossy red body had been sucked dry by some dog of a mountain demon, the ghost of a dog of the necromantic Dorans. She raised her red head, signalled friendship with rattling ears, twitched her mouth in a dog-smile.

'She has a lovely temperament,' said Hughie.

Expectant calves, ears alert for the rattle of buckets of warm swill, closed in together in the field behind the hayshed and, led by Alfred, three of the young Macillion boys, all needing haircuts, all bearing two buckets apiece, paraded across the farmyard from the boiler house.

'The pied piper,' said Fee as he circled.

He still shambled, he was still Slobber, but his crisp curling hair had been treated by the best barber in the city, he wore a strong tweed suit, trousers and all, and a pair of fine leather boots laced to the knees; he was son and heir and, damnation to the powerless and dead, the owner of Bingen.

'Would you give her to me, Miss Maeve?' Hughie said.

She shook her head and laughed and said: 'Owen gave her to me, Hughie. I couldn't give away a gift.'

The nape of her neck was broad and strongly built into her shoulders, and below the upward twist of her bobbed brown hair her skin was clean from any rough disfigurement of stubble.

'What use could she be to you, Maeve, except as a pet?'

'I like pets, Hughie.'

'I dare say.'

He palmed his moustache upwards with his broad left hand and his face, brown as old oak, wrinkled with laughter. His eyes like my own were on her brown hair and the clean skin of her neck. With imaginary gun to shoulder he covered and followed the swift, circling soaring of a grey gull.

'But think, Miss Maeve, of me and the boys out with the guns on the mountain. This could be a good gun-dog.'

'How do you know?'

'I know. I watched her an hour since running wild across the green after seagulls and hoody crows, leaping ten feet in the air. Then I clapped my hands like the shot of a gun . . .'

The big hands clashed. The sound echoed back from the high gable of the house, from the barns and stables, and beyond the hayshed Alfred was rigid for a moment, turning towards us his broad-chinned flabby white face, startled, I'll swear, by that handclap into memories of brittle orders at morning drill.

'She stopped dead, one forepaw in the air, her leg lifted on the crook, her head straight to the wind, rigid, not moving a muscle, tail high behind her. She has the instincts.'

'Poor Gortin Lass,' she said. 'Afraid of guns and bad men.'

Her arms protected the beast. A grateful tongue licked the wristlet of freckles. Hughie bent down above her, the heavy right-hand pocket of his long-tailed jacket swinging west to touch her shoulder, and, recalling the bandsmen's crude talk of Hughie and Lizzie, the sour laughter about vanished virginity, I felt indignantly that something was being defiled. Gently I wanted to manœuvre Hughie to the east and myself to stand protectively above the bending woman and the bitch, and I was so new to the sensations of idyllic and distantly-worshipping love (no talk I had heard or jokes I had laughed at had prepared me for them) that I didn't know I was jealous of old, singing Hughie and jealous even of the liberties of the offshore wind.

Hughie's fingers toyed with and parted the animal's black moist lips.

'She's not a pure bred but she's a thoroughbred, Miss Maeve.'

'She's my Gortin Lass. Owen gave her to me.'

'She has these white hairs around the mouth.'

'I saw a lovely setter,' I said. 'In the city. With white paws. On the Diamond Hill.'

'A crooked dealer,' said Hughie, 'would treat those hairs with dye or boot polish.'

'Nobody will polish my Gortin Lass. Has she had puppies, Hughie?'

His great right hand gently rolled the bitch over and inspected the teats while Maeve rhythmically shook hands with the quivering right paw.

'She has had puppies.'

'Poor orphans,' she said.

'That's us, the five Chesneys,' said, behind me, the pert voice of Edmund, and there he was in all the glory of plus-fours and silent soft-soled shoes that he had brought back with him from England when he returned, late and with no signs of mourning, for his father's funeral. They were plus-fours of a bright grey check tweed and there were classy flashes of green ribbon where the breeches joined his socks. He wore new horn-rimmed spectacles and his crimped hair (Kinnear, who was an authority on hairdressers, said the waves and undulations were the work of skilful tongs) reeked of perfumed oil, and never before had I noticed it but there was a black offensive mole to the left of his nose and he had cauliflower, negroid nostrils. He rubbed his hands. He was brisk. He was business.

'Great flesh on those bones,' whistled Fee. 'Good eating in England.'

He stooped as he circled, his malformed, devastated features endeavouring possibly to express irony, and lightly tapped Edmund's artificially-padded left shoulder. For a flash the pudgy olive face went grey with anger and then Edmund laughed, insincerely.

'I have the shop, Maeve,' he said.

'Rockefeller. Congratulations.'

She didn't look at him. She continued to fondle the belly of Gortin Lass.

'You didn't know, Owen, I was after a shop in the city.'

'I heard rumours.'

'In Columba Street it is. By the Guildhall Gate.'

'It's a good stand,' I said.

'I'll make it hum. Confectionery etcetera. Drug-store style. Stacks of money in it. Watch me flying from the land.'

'You'd be a lovely bird,' she said. 'A game bird.'

'I've seen things in England, Owen.'

His appeal was to me as to the oracle and repository for all the voices of Bingen. Hughie and Maeve whispered together over the dog. Alfred, leaning on the gate behind the hayshed, admired his young stock, and the three Macillions walked back with empty buckets to the boiler house.

'There's money in business, Owen. Buying and selling. Refrigeration's the thing.'

'Try it on yourself,' she said.

'You must sell people what they haven't got,' he said.

'Supply and demand,' I said.

I saw the bald crown of the captain's head.

'Sell Fee a nose,' said Hughie.

Edmund stretched his arms, breathing deeply. He said, 'It's good to be home again.'

'It's good to see you, Edmund,' I said.

Somebody had to welcome him.

'But, God, this place is small, Owen. Even the city looks small after London.'

'It's small even after Dublin. It's a small city.'

'But it's slow, too. It's dead.'

'Tell them about Killeter,' whistled Fee. 'Tell them, Hughie, how Jim Macenhill, the returned American, came home drunk to Killeter.'

Startled, possibly, by the radiance of Edmund, the bay mare waltzed sideways and Fee's curses, then his soothing words, were like the wind playing scales on a winter's night in the frame of an old window.

'He came drunk all the way from Boston,' Hughie said. 'He leaned drunk on a tree on a hill above Killeter.'

He stood up huge above Maeve and the setter, above Edmund and myself. He spread his great arms. A length of rope trailed from one of the hanging pockets of his long jacket. His red moustache was stained with the blood of twist tobacco. He was Magheracolton. He was a great sycamore that had grown on that ground before any imported weed like the captain had come from foreign parts and taken fibrous, insidious root there, and Fee was the twisted, whistling thorn-bush that would last as long as rocks and sea.

'He looked down the hill,' said Hughie. 'He saw the bridge and the river with less water in it in the June drought than there was beer at that instant pressing on his bladder. He saw the three houses, the closed, bleached door of the one pub, the shafts of an idle cart pointed to the sky. There was one sow sucking the cart chains for nourishment. He heard hens somewhere but he could see no human being.'

'He cried,' whistled Fee. 'He cried, Hughie.'

'He cried against the tree like a child. He was lonely for Boston. He was lost for Killeter the way it was before he knew

Boston. He said: "Killeter, you're done. Not a dog to bark at me. Not a wee boy to throw stones." He went back to Boston and never came home again.'

'Killeter, you see, was small after Boston,' Fee whistled.

In his circle he leaned low and again touched Edmund's left shoulder, lifting the padding, letting it fall again, exposing the falsity. That was when the captain or something that was vicious came uppermost in pert little Edmund, man of business, for he turned on Fee with a whitefaced gasp of anger, struck upwards at the shell-holed features, missed, and blindly tried to grasp the saddle girth on the mare, was adroitly fended off by the jockey's boot on Fee's bandy root of a leg. If I hadn't grabbed Edmund as he came staggering back he would have gone heavily to the ground. He said: 'Thanks, Owen.' He ran sobbing towards the house. Looking after him I saw Greta, her mother's tea-tray in her hands, pause by a window in an upstairs corridor to look down on the painted scene, the sporting print. Then Alfred came towards us, a laugh on his wide face, a dribble from that laughter on his square level chin.

'You shouldn't torment him,' I said.

'The pimple,' Hughie said. 'You'd think he was away from us for ninety years.'

Easing the nervousness of the mare, Fee gently gave her her head, went rocking at a canter twice round the farmyard, then, leaping her beautifully over the low gate behind the hayshed, he was gone beyond the scattering calves. Maeve followed him, clambering over the gate. Her loosely-belted white shirt ballooned behind her as she climbed and bent and balanced and leaped. There was a slight stiffness that was graceful not crippled in her left hip as she ran across the grass. The setter, barking baritone, ran round her in circles, leaped up every time she raised her right hand, fingers clicking, in the air.

'We should by rights put an advert in *The Courier* about that bitch,' Hughie said. 'Some decent man has lost the makings of a gun-dog.'

'Maeve will never part with her,' I said.

She would keep me in Maeve's mind, was my hope, when I was far away in Dublin.

'You could phone an advert from the village, Owen. There's no phone here.'

'Not yet,' said Alfred.

'Miss Maeve will have a phone,' said Hughie, thoughtfully. 'Edmund will have a sweetie shop. What do you want, Alfred?'

But Alfred just smiled at Hughie's question. He rubbed his chin dry with a long, bony forefinger. As a horse would, he rubbed and felt the ground of Bingen with his right foot. He said: 'I have what I want.'

In a far field Lizzie Heron was throwing a halter on a piebald horse. In widening circles Fee trotted the mare, and once again in pursuit of gulls and hoody crows and followed by Maeve, the red bitch headed for the sea. Maeve was fifty yards from me. But I felt I could see that wide base of her neck and the fair skin delicately stretched over filigree bones.

Three students, flatulent with Red Bear beer, fitted with drunken discomfort into the one big bed in the basement flat Jeff had, inaccurately, called Sodomy Hall. The flagged floor was, winter and summer, hoar-frosted with ground-damp corroding enough to rot linoleum. The fireplace was half-ways up one wall and the fire's heat, when there was a fire, vanished with a chilling, derisive whistle up the cavernous chimney. There, was the centre for the carefree student life of Rodgers, Macsorley and Kinnear.

Still booming in my ears the voice of the preacher said Be gregarious, and, without a woman in the bed to share between us, we were as gregarious as three normal young men could be. Commend me for ever for nightmares to the black beer milked pint by pint from the coppery udders of the Red Bear. In his sleep, beyond Kinnear and at the far side of the bed, Jeffrey Austin Macsorley (the beginnings of his book about Bingen and the captain lay on the table in the far corner) broke barley wind.

It was the hind end of Hennigan's hayshed by the roadside on the village end of the Gortin Gap on the evening of the mysterious materialization of Gortin Lass. As big beside me as the fat woman in the Fun Palace, who slapped her autobahn thigh and said Ain't I a dainty lass, Lucy lay in the hay. She wore crimson slacks. She mottled her face with tears as big as glassy marbles. On Hennigan's seasoned grass she rolled away from me and said: 'That's why you don't love me any more, Owen. Him. Those girls. You've always gone there without me.'

Is a distorted memory a nightmare? I suppose it is. Kinnear in his sleep flung out one wild arm. I told Lucy I loved her dearly.

'You don't want to kiss me.'

To my surprise I kissed her vast red posterior. It hadn't happened that way nor had she been so monstrously dropsical the evening we argued in Hennigan's hay, and over low hedges watched Frank Conway Chesney, black and thin, wheeling his bicycle homewards up the slope. I went ahead of him to sunlight and Maeve, to beauty always dazzling with halo and nimbus around it, beauty's outline lost in its own light, never quite human, never quite clear to the eyes. What's beauty anyway?

'What's beauty anyway?' roared the drunken poet in the Red Bear.

'Is beauty,' he asked, 'a flight of city cyclists, a funeral at a church gate, a swan shape hatching out new swan shapes on a shapeless mound of twigs, rubble and excrement, or tulips, trees, or the soft inside of the thigh of a virgin girl?'

'Beauty,' said Jeff (who disliked the loud poet), 'is a fat servant girl in a new red coat on a sunny May day.'

'That all depends,' said Kinnear (who knew), 'on the way you feel on a sunny May day.'

Asleep or awake, in the hay or in the triple bed, I knew that the point was not that I didn't love Lucy any more. Only her arms I had always loved. My mind, fair enough, went back before Frank to Bingen to the holy presence of his sister Maeve. But I was only experiencing the revulsion from the unexplored body (still virgin Lucy) that makes most males on the experimental verge of manhood Puritans for a while. In Catholic countries it helps to fill the seminaries with young men captured at the right impressionable age. In Protestant places it sets young fellows with earnest faces singing solemn hymns at street corners to the accompaniment of miniature harmoniums. It made me love's own sweet troubadour. I had felt the Lord in no symbolic, sensuous, snake-handling fashion. The Lord was light, and brown hair, and I was saved, and flat, dirty Dublin built by a stinking river on a lazar's marsh, and the unlaundered hold-all bed of Sodomy Hall (one night Kinnear who always, he said, wanted an orgy, slept in it with two half-whores) and the knives and dead guts of the medical school were the flames of damnation from which I must escape. Sordid Dublin, the wrath-to-come, had frightened me away from Lucy. She, all warm, all woman, became because of Dublin a freak, a fat woman on show in the Fun Palace, in nightmare moments a slavering, squinting monster like her father's mastiff. I couldn't heal or soothe one scab away from the world's body, so I had to cut and run for refuge to old ballads of a pure world, to the captain's honeyed daughter and the hills round Bingen. How was I to know that I was as noxious a prig as the most gregarious preacher that ever pounded a pulpit or compiled a prayer manual telling Catholic women how to examine their consciences on the sixth (adultery) commandment, or the ninth (neighbour's husband) prohibition.

On the quays of Dublin, once, a cultured Irishman, half-Parisian, friend of Joyce, Eliot and Pound, looked up the river Liffey towards the westering sun, the way Jack Yeats looked when he painted the woman dropping flowers for the dead (murdered on Bachelor's Walk in 1916 by the King's Own Scottish Borderers), indicated the red-and-brown, tottering, Georgian tenements and said: 'Dublin is very beautiful.' Beside and beneath us flowed Anna Livia Plurabelle, a dirty old woman, rotten weeds disfiguring her stone thighs. Nobody, not the Dublin Corporation, not the Port and Docks Board, would undertake to scrape her clean.

'Last cleaned,' said Jeff (a grown man and a writer), 'in nineteen thirty-two for the Eucharistic Congress. We'll dredge the Liffey again for the Second Coming.'

But the cultured man, his nose obviously away in perfumed Paris, cast his eyes westwards as far as Connemara and the red Atlantic sunset, cleansed with salt, and saw beauty. From the triple couch in Sodomy Hall the view was otherwise. Atlantic salt might have helped our sheets. On the night of the gregarious preacher the mark of Kinnear's orgy still stained the undersheet, the more so as one of his lady visitors had not been in her best health. Worse still, it was befouled for me by the memory of the nightmare night Owen Rodgers out of curiosity became a man.

Beginning in charity, that night went on to curiosity, then to heat, disgust and a colony of persistent body lice.

'There are no prostitutes in this city,' the decent Dublin citizen roared down the stairs of the old Abbey at Sean O'Casey.

That was the night they fought about the Plough and the Stars.

She was belated, locked-out for the night from the dubious hostelry where she eased insteps and other parts weary from the pavements. She was Dublin Lass appearing mysteriously on the homeward path of Owen Rodgers, throwing pebbles at a blank, unanswering window, half-cursing, half-sobbing, homeless, smelling of cheap red wine. Benefactor to all lost females, Owen Rodgers offered her a roof to cover her head and, honestly, meant no more. She was dark and not beautiful.

'She's all yours,' Kinnear said, making with the instantaneous acceleration of an adept county footballer for the distant couch by Jeff's writing-table.

Jeff, at a party in the flat of a coloured student from Fernando Po, was, he said, acquiring universal experience. My need of somewhere to lie down, and curiosity and pity (I flatter myself), for how could you ignore a woman so ugly and so alone, did the rest.

'Darlint, darlint,' sobbed Dublin Lass.

In the morning she took, under protest, a little money and sat unconcernedly on the lavatory seat while Kinnear shaved at the bathroom mirror. Oh, far away it was to the chromium fittings, the perfume, the blonde head of the hair-stylist who eventually succumbed to the policeman. Being a medical student did at least teach one how to get rid quickly of the clinging friends she left behind her. Dublin, said the man of culture, is very beautiful and so, in many ways, it is and, as Jeff said, dirt is everywhere and the Liffey not the only river that breeds slime. On far, green fields the saintly Maeve ran behind golden Gortin Lass. Fun is everywhere, too, and happy parties, pure girl students and college societies, antiseptic but playful nurses ('The nurses,' said Kinnear, 'are the worst'), and trips into the Wicklow hills and hortatory talks from holy men who advise parties of people in cars to pass the time in prayer and saying the rosary in order to make reparation for the sins committed, as everyone knows, in the backs of cars. Everything is everywhere. But for Owen Rodgers everything was not enough unless it was crystalline mountains guarding green Bingen, or the rush of all the streams to make the Gortin river, or the ballads of Hughie Heron, or the old city with grey walls and brown Guildhall and hilly streets ascending ever and always to chiming steeples, and the winged Victory in the Diamond holding a wreath above the head of the captain, and Dr Grierson holding aloft the good drop to the light as reverently as on the altar he would raise the Lord's blood, and my father pausing to look meditatively at him and to tap moisture out of the ocarina. Everything was nothing unless it was Maeve. I was a man now. It was a painful thing to be. I was unwilling to accept sadness, sordidness, the sweat of a city, the knives in the medical school probing to find the rotten thing, the meaning of death, the secret of the snake.

It is curious to meet the dead in dreams. He stood straight and still and white and dry. His left arm was raised and bent, the fingers crooked as if they rested on the cane a soldier would carry, walking out in dress uniform. Only his eyes moved. They were crimson. They flickered so rapidly I could hear them crackle.

'Is it better to be born and damned,' he said, 'than not to be born at all?'

'I died of a conundrum,' he said. 'I died of a conundrum.'

He went on repeating that until I woke up and padded across the damp, flagged floor to the damper bathroom to ease my belly of Dublin and the black blood of the Red Bear.

Four strong parish priests, strong farmers reinforced by the Grace of State, drank four large whiskies in the lounge of a Dublin hotel frequented mostly by the clergy. Warming their souls against cold rural journeys back to advent presbyteries, they sat content, oblivious of December and sleet on Christmas shoppers on the streets outside. Wisely, in a place where, among stronger colleagues in Christ, men who could punish their malt or leave it alone, his compulsive weakness might be too well known, Dr Grierson ostentatiously drank coffee, discreetly laced for him by an understanding waitress in some arcane adytum or sacristy behind the public bar. Those white, delicate hands, that precise, gentle voice could not but stir sympathy in the heart of any woman. His high forehead perspired. The thin tissue of hair on the high-domed head became transparent as he leaned towards me to add milk to my unlaced coffee.

'Francis is late, Owen. Francis is late.'

'The Maynooth bus may be late. The crowds. The roads must be bad with the storm.'

'You're calm, Owen. Your father's son. You're a calm, blackavised man.'

Envying him the secret ministrations of the devoted waitress I was everything but calm. Adding to agitation, or aggravation, two aspiring curates, little older than myself and at a table close to the sturdy parish priests, tried out their fledgling strength on two small brandies laced with ginger ale. With a Red Bear hangover and nothing in my cup but coffee I eyed their drinks as

Judas eyed the spikenard that should have been sold, said he, for the benefit of the poor. Judas had, after all these years, stepped down out of the Munich stained glass and into me. Judas was a shadow soul repossessing a body. Judas, I thought with agony, as the spiritless coffee scalded my upper lip, Judas was me.

'You will not then, Owen, come back for another term of medicine?'

'No, father.'

'You find you haven't the vocation for it?'

'Yes, father.'

My back was to a radiator. The room was an oven. The room with hoops of Roman collars and sombre black coats was a synod.

'Our only exportable surplus,' the captain leered at me.

Like a djinn he wreathed upwards from the curate's ginger ale.

'In O'Connell Street in Dublin,' he repeated, 'between the Nelson Pillar and the monument to Parnell, I counted on the footwalk, on one side of the street only, seventeen priests and two nuns. What would Nelson and Parnell have said?'

The sleet was on the streets (I shook my head and blinked my eyes and to myself execrated Red Bear porter), drenching the lust out of Nelson and Parnell, impeding Christmas shoppers and the progress towards us of the captain's clerical son. The sleet was on the big windows in blobs like salted snails and the exportable surplus had wisely run for comfort and cover. Once again I shook and blinked and the wreathing vision vanished. The radiator attacked me from behind, suffocated me with warmth.

Savagely, aware that I wasn't at my most eloquent, I complained: 'I couldn't help people. I couldn't make them better.'

'It's a good reason, Owen. A humble reason.'

I couldn't say: 'I don't even want to.' For where would be the point in telling this remote, dreaming man, already half-ways to nirvana with the whiskey savour on his palate, that I wasn't trying to be humble?

'Often, even when we want to help people, we find it impossible. We fail them. They don't come to meet us. Pure spirits, the books say, you'll find it in Lepicier, *Il Mondo Invisibile*, can communicate knowledge if one wishes to send and the other to receive. Radio sets. All that is needed is that a spirit should be prepared to reveal its thoughts to another spirit and that that other spirit should give its attention to them.'

He closed his eyes as if he was quoting. He leaned back his head and leaned back his body and balanced, upheld by Grace of State, on the two hind legs of his cane chair. His housekeeper could have made a cleaner job of his stock and collar. The two brandy boys were better cared for. Even as I contrasted my frayed doctor and their glistening laundery a flunkey, exemplifying the age-old respect of the Irish for their clergy, came to tell them that their car, fathers, was ready when they were ready and that the sleet, obedient as the sun to Joshua, was lifting. So were the doctor's eyelids. He looked sadly at his dwindling coffee.

'We're not pure spirits,' he said.

The way his pale thin lips moved (the upper lip had a prominent, clearly marked filtrum) wasn't a smile but it was pathetic and kind. It drew me to him sadly and warmly. He called his waitress. Ignoring brandy neophytes and the four malt whiskey evangelists, he said: 'My young friend, too, would like some aid. Study is very exacting.'

She was a bony, faded blonde with pointed elbows, but I'd swear she looked down on him like love itself, the starved elderly aunt of the two blonde angels I had once seen, in a gaudy

Latin American print, beaming in with goblets of aid to a brutally bleeding crucified.

'It would be bad if you continued and became a doctor and only then discovered you had no healing power.'

Enjoying my laced whiskey, I agreed. The two curates went off to their chariot and left half their ginger ale behind them untasted. But now that I was looked after myself they had no power to unsettle me.

'A priest is supposed to be a healer,' he said, 'and too often I find myself an interfering fool. I had trouble recently about a marriage case, a separation dispute, I tried to settle. Poked in my nose under orders from higher up.'

Our village parish priest was a carbuncled dictator who raised cattle.

'Net result, Owen. The woman almost went daft with frustration. You were a medical. You're a man. You know what I mean.'

'Yes, father.'

'The legal costs came twice as heavy on the man. I should have left the laymen, the lawyers, alone to settle it. They had no law of God to satisfy. That couple weren't interested in any law higher than the law that sharpens claws and fangs in the jungle.

'Or the law,' he said, 'that makes the tom-cat's first love-move a bite in the back of the lady's neck.'

That talk made me sweat.

'Darlint, darlint,' sobbed Dublin Lass.

For a moment I was glad because I thought he was smiling and I hastened to smile with him and to sip my second reinforced coffee. As it happened he wasn't smiling. The four strong men called for four more large ones. Were these the confidences my father listened to night after night? The sky was whitening, the windows clear of sleet. Frank, thank heaven, would soon be here.

'I failed,' he said. 'I didn't heal them.'

'That wasn't your fault, father.'

'My surgery is the confessional,' he said. 'The decent people say their sins, sniff my breath through the grille. They tell each other in holy charity: The doctor's at it again.'

'No, doctor,' I said.

'On their death-beds the old mountainy men think I'm there because I want to be remembered in their wills.'

'The dying need the priest,' I said.

Where did I hear that? My own voice, the voice of Owen Rodgers, counsellor, consoler, startled me.

'Captain Chesney needed the priest badly,' he said. 'He didn't get one. He could have done with vats of oil and all he got was the river water.'

'God only knows the heart,' I said.

That was Kate Carr's apothegm.

'Did you know he left me money in his will? Not for masses. Just money. A hundred pounds. No stipulations. He must have hoped I'd drink myself to death the quicker.'

'He couldn't be that bad,' I said.

'He was the devil incarnate, Owen. He was ruin. But he got his money's worth of masses. Your father keeps me in whiskey.

'Your father,' he said. 'Your father, Owen. If it wasn't for that civilized man, his music and his company, I'd go mad. Then I have my boat on the lake and a day now and again with the yachtsmen or the mayfly men. You know the colony of old British colonels in the fishing hotel at Tower Bay. You must come out with me some day on the lake.'

He whispered again to the waitress. Striking what you might call a jarring note, two red-faced country shopkeepers, fingers crooked from the greasy till, came in with their wives and mountains of Christmas parcels.

'The boat and the open lake are good for sanity,' he said. 'There was a man in my year in Maynooth who got a curacy on an island off the west coast. When the deadly monotony and the lack of company got too much for him he used to go out riding his currach over the wild Atlantic billows . . .'

The coffee cup in his hand was a soaring, descending currach.

'There was another man I heard of, a curate in Connemara, who would swim away from the shore to the full extent of his powers. Until he was utterly exhausted. Then he'd turn to the land and fight for his life all the way back.'

The currach was a bird alive on laced coffee. The semi-suicidal Connemara curate, far from the land, was drowning pleasantly in vats of oily malt. Owen Rodgers was happy. He was for home and the brown-haired primeval land of Maeve.

'That man,' said Dr Grierson, 'lived to be ninety. He died in bed. He died a bishop.'

He focused his swimming eyes on me. Around pale pupils the wriggling, wormlike flecks of crimson were living and distinct.

'Have you any notion what you'll do now?'

'Not a notion, father.'

'I'll think,' he said. 'I'll think. I'll talk with your father. We must help each other.'

'You're wise not to be a doctor,' he said, 'if you feel that way about it. You're no thaumaturgist, Owen. The born healers are few and they kill themselves. Virtue goes out from them like the Son of God until they're spent and dead on the cross. The rest of us are parasites. We suck the healers dry. We eat them alive. Pinheads of lice on cockchafers.

'But a medical doctor, at least,' he said, 'doesn't know what loneliness is.'

Another woman and two overdressed, fat-faced children

119

joined the party. I was on my seventh whiskeyed coffee, and when Frank Conway Chesney came, unkempt again and spotted with college pimples, he was a piece of comic driftwood on a warm sea as my westering currach undulated nobly towards Hy-Breasil Bingen, the isle of the blest.

'The ancient yew tree at Maynooth,' asked Dr Grierson, 'the great ancient yew tree that Silken Thomas, the Geraldine, slept under on the night before a battle, does it still stand?'

'It still stands, father,' said Frank.

The train raced homewards. He was the captain's son. He would sleep under the same roof as Maeve. He spoke precisely. He eyed Dr Grierson nervously.

'I bought this book, father,' he proffered, 'in Burns, Oates and Washbourne.'

It was a blue book. It had to do with the Lord's passion, death and glorious resurrection. The name on the spine told me it was by the gregarious preacher. The doctor opened it, adjusted his reading glasses, looked at it with sustained hauteur. Two lamps in a tiny, unroofed station that flicked past us showed drifts of sodden, grey sleet. The country was drowned for Christmas.

'They were thinking once of pruning that yew tree,' the doctor said. 'It grew out, Owen, and down and into the ground again. It was a cathedral. It was a banyan tree.'

Frank asked: 'Do you like his work, doctor?'

'Piffle,' said the doctor. 'A prig. A pain in the face.'

Darkness over drenched, desolate Ireland absorbed me, one lone, outnumbered layman locked in a box with twice his weight of clerics.

'When I went to Maynooth,' said the doctor, 'when I walked by that ancient yew I thought I would be a writer. Apostolate of the pen, no less. I would be Fénélon. I would preach like Lacordaire. Preach about what? The stipends? Peter's pence? Impurity, the only Irish sin? Pay up, pay up and play the game. Write about what?'

I couldn't bear to look even at Frank's reflection in the carriage window because I felt that his face aghast, his lack of knowledge of the strong spirit related to the coffee as the soul to the body, would have broken me down with undignified, unexplainable laughter.

'Rehash Fouard? Rehash Le Breton? Write like this? *Absit*. God forbid. Far be it from me.'

With mock unction he read from the blue book: 'Pilate was quite unprepared for the fanatical outburst which greeted the Nazarene as he emerged bloodstained, crowned in purple cape. . . .'

He flicked over pages.

'The order for scourging an innocent man will arouse doubt and astonishment only in those who do not know what the Romans called the disciplinary powers (*coercitio*) of a magistrate. . . .'

'He does not doubt,' said the doctor. 'Nor is he astonished. Unlike the rest of us he knows about the Romans. What do you think of that, Owen?'

'He shows an interest in corporal punishment, doctor.'

'Over Christmas, Francis, you can learn all about *coercitio*.'

He handed back the blue, rejected book. Whiskey was, in the eyes of God and men, the only excuse for our callousness, and it was less so for me than for the doctor who was old and embittered. It never dawned on him that, without reading books at all, Frank would be an authority on *coercitio*. For a few, awful minutes the captain travelled with us through the deadly sleet.

'I wanted to teach the people about art,' the doctor said. 'I used to read articles in magazines about what priests were doing in France and the Rhineland. Your father knew the Rhineland well, Frank.'

When the man was mentioned the spell was broken and the captain vanished.

'Yes, doctor.'

Was Frank a subdued, restrained saint or just a ranker showing respect for lofty regimental markings?

'In our village church you may have noticed, if you craned your neck, high up in the shadows on the east wall, an old crucifix belonging to the penal days. Some loving, primitive craftsman cut it out of black bog oak, risking his life, perhaps. Faith guided his hand. I said to Higher Authority: Suppose we take it down to the light? Let the people see it. Do you know what Higher Authority said to me?'

'That his prize bull,' I said, 'would take the red rosette.'

The doctor leaned forward. In the train's light his skin was tight and yellow. He gripped Frank's knee and the poor creature, God help us, quivered at the touch like a nervous horse.

'Do you know what Higher Authority, the pastor of the parish, said to me?'

'No, doctor.'

Around the rocks of pimples the red blood washed slowly.

'In his best behind-the-mountain English, Higher Authority said: Haven't they the crucifixes on their rosary beads? And the penny catechism? That up there's a quare botch of a thing anyway. If it were coloured, itself.'

'But we have Saint Dominic,' the doctor said, 'on one side of the pulpit. With a face and figure like a dummy in a shop window. We have Saint John the evangelist on the other side of the pulpit. Identifiable by his eagle and his hermaphroditical face and dressed in a red Dior creation. All the old women think he's Saint Philomena.'

'Art,' he said.

'Far away is France,' he said.

'But I always have my boat on the lake,' he said, 'and mellifluous John Rodgers.'

'Owen,' he said, 'you're the child of kindness and music. Live up to it.'

Then he rested his head and closed his eyes and far away in time and space the merciful music of the waves of a summer lake gave him peace and sleep.

Once only Frank spoke to me on the rest of that homeward journey. His brown eyes burned. His unhealthy face was drawn and pitiable. The doctor had gone to the lavatory.

'Owen,' he said, 'don't tell anybody about this. It isn't right the laity should see a priest like that.'

Peeping Tom Rodgers had once again looked through the red-leaded windows of the stable loft and a guardsman on parade had fallen flat on his face. But I couldn't resent Frank's admonition about secrecy. He knew so little. He had gone straight from Bingen prison to the cold college and never known the educative kindness of the village band, the trill of the ocarina, or heard the happy doctor talk of the *téléférique* on Pibeste mountain or of the elbows of the grey Gave river.

That was how, in the sleet before Christmas, I came to my own city for the greatest love of my life.

Lucy, enduring some passing glandular phase, was plump enough to be comic.

'The Lord,' said Jim MacElhatton, 'has been generous to that girl.'

With subtle gestures he disrobed the French horn.

'A guarantee of comfort this cold December,' said Barney the big drum.

Owen Rodgers, as yet unsure of manhood and worse than ever with prickly heat after the revelations of Dublin Lass, was too embarrassed to answer back. Lucy was soft and stout, but strong, and liable to pull one off balance by the concentration of her embraces. She made me at such moments feel like a medium-sized host I once saw raised high on his own hearthrug and carried, kicking, red-faced, pretending to take the joke, around his roomful of guests by one of those jovial, bearded giants who are occasionally allowed into even the best parties. But Lucy, to my increasing regret, was my woman. She sat by my side when I drove my father's hearse of a car to Bingen the Sunday before that Christmas. There was snow drifted deep in the Gap. The previous Thursday a breadman from the city had walked down to Hennigan's for help when his motor-van lodged in the snow. He and the help returned with ropes, shovels and chains and the van was still there but the bread was all gone.

'Fairies,' said my father. 'The Gortin fairies.'

'The ghosts of your friends, the Dorans of Segully,' said my mother.

'Where Micky Doran is tonight he needs no bread,' said Dr Grierson.

'He knows it all now,' said my father.

'As the poet remarked to me in Dublin,' I said, 'when the cardinal died, he's gone now and he knows what I knew long ago, that there's no God.'

'Owen,' said my mother.

So, happily, I would have jammed the car in snow in the Gap to give the mountain goblins or the ghosts of the Dorans opportunity to purloin Lucy. But we travelled instead the long way round by the snowless coast road. Lucy sat close to me. In the back of the car bespectacled Petsie, elongated, under-developed mentally, and the first woman in our parts to wear trousers all the time, was mauled alternately by James and Jeff. In the occasional lulls we talked of the wonder of a Christmas party in Bingen.

'The captain,' said James, 'will arise in wrath.'

'Speak well of the dead,' said Jeff. 'Even his own family are revising their opinion.'

'Greta told me,' said Petsie, 'they were broken-hearted when he died.'

Greta, I knew, would never to a Lesbian fool like Petsie, would-be successor to the *Melophagus Ovinus,* Sheep Ked, Sheep Louse, Sheep Tick or *Sciortán,* have used an unbalanced, extravagant word like broken-hearted.

'He was their father,' I said.

'What a father!' said Lucy.

'How would you know?' I asked.

Those days I was always ready to pick a quarrel with Lucy and to grow hot with bottled-up rage when she retreated into the sullen silence she mistook for dignity.

'No matter what he was,' said Jeff, 'they have to imagine they had a human being for a father.'

Petsie said: 'They'll never convince anybody else. Stop it, Jim.'

With malice I abstained from contradicting Petsie and could feel Lucy withdrawing from me the folds of her garment and her stout thigh.

'Even Hughie Heron,' said Jeff, 'told me the captain wasn't the worst. He generated contention, Hughie said, but he was a decent man at heart.'

I said: 'You all know a lot about the captain.'

'I'm studying,' Jeff said. 'He's part of my Ireland. So are you, Owen.'

In angry silence I drove the rest of the way to Bingen, and my anger grew worse as the night went on. What right had Kinnear to whistle with appreciation when he saw Maeve in an emerald taffeta frock (he could rattle off that it was figure-fitting, bell-skirted, and with diamanté clip close to the round brown shoulder that was almost bare), and what right had he to grab her for the first dance of the night in the great kitchen where one hundred mad, shockheaded Macillions were parading in sets and lancers with Hughie at the pipes and noseless Fee at the melodeon? What right had asthmatic Jeff with his long, hooked nose, blackheaded skin and two prominent teeth, to lean like a squire on the drawing-room mantelpiece, toasting himself by the blazing log-fire, fondling the captain's snake and making succulent, soothing noises?

'That scar, Owen,' said Lucy, 'on Greta's arm. They say it was with a rope or a burn the captain did it.'

'Your own father once burned your arm to rid you of a sheep tick.'

She drooped her eyelids gently while we danced, and said contritely, maddening me even more with the thought that she thought her contrition should move me: 'The things, Owen Rodgers, you remember.'

No ghost of the captain rose up to reserve Maeve for me, to reprimand Jeff, to burn a derisive brand on Lucy's plump bottom; and, black with hatred in the middle of all the brightness, I was mournful with regret for the lost exclusive darkness of my wizard's cave. Death and the river for ever had swept away my rights. To the mouth music of Hughie, four of the Macillions danced a four-hand reel. To the fiddling of Edmund, dressed in his English best, Maeve and Kinnear maddened me further by dancing a polka. Edmund, the gay blade, was already fiddler and singer and a droll card at dances in the country, dances by the lake, dances in the city.

'The shop,' said he as he fiddled, 'goes famously.'

My eyes on Maeve, I said I was glad to hear it. Like a bronze helmet her hair, undisturbed even by the liveliness of the dance, gathered around her head. The disconcerting thing about her was that she always seemed on the verge of smiling at some joke that only she saw. Once, leaning on the metal bridge, spitting down into the sullen water of the Eel river, Kinnear, I remembered, had said: 'Some day for hellery I'll get myself invited to Bingen. One of the girls will ask me.'

'Those girls,' Jeff had said. 'Phew!'

'Give those girls a chance,' Kinnear had said. 'You'll see wonders. Trust uncle who knows.'

The things, Owen Rodgers, I remembered. Uncle James danced beautifully, his pale, well-cut face unsmiling, the sharp delicate nostrils twitching a little. Uncle, like a thoroughbred dog, knew a good scent and I hated Kinnear that night but fortunately for that night only.

'England taught me to be wise,' said Edmund, when his fiddling stopped and he rested and the dancers moved from room to room.

What could one do but look in amazement at the wise brown man and realize that when it came to making money on confectionery and ice-cream he was probably as wise as he claimed to be?

'Irishmen learn to go ahead in England,' he said. 'The first question an Irishman asks when he gets there is where can he get Mass on Sunday. A month later he wants to know where he can get overtime on Sunday. . . .'

I stopped listening to him for they had vanished together,

bronze head and the head with that slanted mountain of dark curled hair. Maeve and Kinnear were somewhere together, talking to each other, talking about me, laughing at me, saying: 'Poor stick-in-the-mud Owen who can't escape from Lucy.' I showed them. I fled from Edmund's wisdom and from Lucy's jealous love. Behind me, as I ascended, the music began again. I was alone in the wide hallway and the captain in the picture, one arm in a sling, his good arm extended, still stood ready to recite the tale of a glorious end. If the real captain, my captain, had been alive, his daughter wouldn't like this be hiding in corners with young men. In jealous madness it never occurred to me that if the captain were alive Maeve would only be a shadow in a corner and for the first of a harrowing series of occasions I set out to search for her. It was a windless, moonless night, bright because of frozen snow on the ground, but no night for lovers to be abroad. There were no foot-tracks to be seen before the house. For a moment I was almost demented enough to sniff at the ground like a dog, but the clean, steadying cut of the frosty air gave me back enough sense to realize that if they were anywhere together they must be inside the house. So I went up to the first floor, the music from the lively basement still mocking me, and walked from end to end of the ell-shaped corridor and stood at the window where Greta had stood the day Fee had fended off Edmund with his foot. The farmyard below was white like a Christmas card and completely deserted. The whiteness went on into the grey vague mystery of pasture and mountains, visible only because it was known they were there. The long corridor was lined with closed, expressionless doors that I was afraid to open because, jealous already, I was afraid of what I might find. Only one door, close to the stairhead, was ajar. Since there was little space behind it for the romantic celebration of the mystery I dreaded to unveil, I tiptoed into the smallest room. Then, with the door of the water-closet held a little ajar, I could command a view of the main arm of the corridor. Hughie Heron was singing now a ballad about a witless sailor who, walking down London Street, purchased a basket from a strange woman to find on closer examination that the basket contained a baby.

'Be aware of false women where them you may meet. Be aware of false women going down London Street.'

Uneasy on the lavatory seat, the old-fashioned chain swinging like a pendulum at my left ear, I considered the words suited the occasion.

'If they proffer a basket make sure you don't buy, for fear that you'd purchase a big bungereye.'

Bungereye, whatever it meant, seemed a perfect word for a bad bargain in love. Every voice in the kitchen uproariously and thrice repeated: 'A big bungereye.'

'Ladilee whack,' roared Hughie. 'Foll the diddle eye doh. Stryangle, Stryane.'

All the voices thrice repeated the mystic refrain and then, in the lull before the dance music began again, a door in the corridor clicked open and Peeping Tom had his just reward. I could see them clearly: Frank and Alfred, one neat, small and thin, the other high as the sycamores and bent like them almost from birth. They stepped out of the widow's room and to my surprise Frank locked the door behind him. They walked towards me along the corridor and stood to talk at the stairhead a few feet from my undignified hiding-place.

'Your mother's afraid, Alfred. You must humour her.'

'She's your mother too, your reverence. I don't want to be a keeper.'

'You'll do what I say.'

'Who's the eldest?'

'If you don't do as I tell you and as she wants I'll find out, even when I'm not here. You'll pay for it.'

'What's she afraid of? We won't eat her.'

'She's not afraid of the living.'

'A locked door won't keep out the dead.'

Coming from Alfred that was sheer ratiocination. I couldn't close the door because the click of the catch would betray me. If they opened the door and found me there I would be disgraced. Never eavesdrop from a water-closet. French comedy always provided a decent ornamental screen to shelter listening husband or surprised lover. There was a little Englishman once who hid under a bed in order to find a direct way to the heart of the plump lady he loved, but the bed was a low-slung divan bed and the lady was heavier on the horizontal than she had looked on the hoof, and when she sank into her heavenly nest above him she pinned him to the floor in peril of suffocation. There he was for the night, the mattress muffling his cries, while his beloved snored and eructated and, if scandalous rumour is to be believed, did worse in his hearing. By morning he was no longer in love, but then the English are unstable and sentimental in matters of the heart. With more freedom of movement than the prisoner under the divan had enjoyed I made the *de more* crinkling with paper('*Courage, mon ami,*' as one waiting Frenchman said to another, '*j'entends le papier*') and then demonstratively pulled the chain, waited for a while and brazenly stepped out. They were still together, Frank whispering, Alfred sullen, at the head of the stairs.

'We didn't know you were there, Owen.'

'It's a place,' I said, 'we all come to sooner or later.'

I was angry and ashamed at myself for my slavish pursuit of his lovely, undefinable, light-surrounded sister, I was weary of his sallow reproving face and so, it seemed, was Alfred, for the laugh that pickled spittle on my face was genuine relief spiced with malice at Frank's expense. The music below stopped.

'It was a good night,' Frank said. 'I hope you enjoyed it.'

'Fine. But a little satisfies me. It's time we went home. How's your mother?'

'Fine, fine,' he said and his face was quivering with misery.

'I'll go to bed, Alfred,' he said. 'Say good-night to the visitors for me.'

He watched the elder brother, the owner of Bingen, descend the stairs, and Alfred was one of those men who couldn't walk downstairs without appearing as if he would trip and fall over his own wattle-toed feet. The good dark suit with the divided tail fitted him in so far as the ingenuity of tailor could persuade any fabric to fit him. Gone was the jacket with the short, tight sleeves and the malformed trousers with shiny, patched seat dangling behind his knees like a dewlap. But no cloth could conceal the fact that he was a misshapen creature who had once, walking barefoot and trouserless in a byre, bade good-bye to love. That same thought I knew trebled the misery of the lonely man by my side, a lonely son of a monster who had taken on himself the supreme isolation of dry celibacy and priesthood.

'Owen,' he said, 'I'm sorry I was rude. I was worried.'

I didn't help him out. Let him talk. Let her damned-well dance with Kinnear until her insteps fell.

'My mother's poorly. She's not well in her mind.'

The crowd were coming laughing into the hallway. Bingen's first festivity was over.

'My father, Owen, left an awful mark on us. On that Alfred. On this whole house.'

Maeve's voice called: 'Owen. Where's Owen?' Lucy was coming up the stairs with the prim step of a plump female intent on private business and seeing, to her embarrassment, two males, one consecrated, one beloved, on the threshold of the holy of holies.

'You knew him well, Owen. You listened to him. You saw him. We can talk to you. You're one of us.'

With a smile and a mow and a coy 'Excuse-me' Lucy passed and locked herself in. Maeve again called: 'Owen. Where's Owen?'

'They want you below,' he said. 'I won't go down. Parties are not for me.'

'I'm here,' I called. 'I'm coming.'

Then Lucy applied the chain and wild water, a Wordsworthian mountain rill, went off not to the Gortin river but to the captain's specially constructed septic tank.

In Germany, the captain told me, they are finding industrial uses for sludge.

'I pray that God will forgive him,' Frank said, 'and forgive us all. If God wills me to be an ordained priest he'll always be mentioned in my masses.'

'Mention me too,' I said.

'He was a strange man, Owen. He would hurt himself so that he could hurt others. He was his own enemy. I wonder often what was in his mind when he fell into the river.'

'Thinking,' I said, 'what he would do to Hughie for not keeping the bridge in repair.'

It was my feeble, ill-timed effort to be light-hearted.

'He thought a lot about death, Owen.'

'Is it better to be born and damned,' I said, 'than not to be born at all?'

'He was a disappointed man, Owen. I don't know why.'

Lucy was between us. So, leaving Frank in the shadows, I walked, embracing Lucy, down the stairs. There was no odour from her, neither of body nor perfume. She was just soft and warm.

'What a party!' Jeff, who was tight, said again and again.

'Edmund,' he said, 'is a pimple but he had a lavish hand with the malt that, I suppose, Alfred paid for.'

'Petsie, I love you,' he said. 'Long pants and all. But quite against my natural inclinations. Lucy, there, is really my type. The complete woman. But she loves the unworthy Owen. My thousand pities. My sorrow deep as the salt sea.'

Petsie said: 'Shut up.'

Lucy, silent, sat far away from me, for the peace-making effect of my embrace on the stairs had been more than nullified by the fond farewell I had from the Bingen sisters. Kinnear too was silent all the way home.

We were alone, Lucy and Owen, before her father's shop. My father's car, for the sake of quiet, was parked fifty yards away with Jeff and Petsie squabbling and Kinnear saying nothing.

'My father is buying the public house at the Big Tree,' Lucy said.

'Is that so?'

'Not that you care. Your thoughts are far away.'

'What's wrong now, Lucy?'

'Now? It was then. You dropped me like a hot coal at the foot of the stairs when that pair ran to kiss you good-night.'

'That was only friendship, Lucy.'

'Big brother Owen. Smirking between them like a cat with cream when they licked you on each cheek.'

'What did you want me to do? Hit them? Bite them?'

Standing between the two sisters, an arm around each waist, I had been conscious only that the fabric of their frocks felt differently under my fingers and that Petsie in the background had moved protectively towards the abandoned Lucy.

'Want you to do? Nothing. Anything. Go to Dublin. Drown yourself in Thread the Needle. Oh, Owen.'

To my shame and amazement I heard myself say: 'Oh, Lucy.'

But my touch on her soft warm shoulder stirred her to fury.

'I know. I know. I'm fat and she has a lovely figure. I hate her. I hate her. I hate her sister Maeve too.'

'Her sister Maeve too,' I repeated.

I knew confusion.

'Her sister Maeve too,' Lucy repeated and repeated and (believe it or not) stamped her foot and turned and tugged away from me.

'You can have her, Owen. You can have both of them chopped up on a butcher's board.'

She scratched my face and ran, like so many plump women, amazingly light on her feet, amazingly agile from the waist down. The bell on the shop door rang, then rang again as she popped out her head, her hair dishevelled. Her hair grips had come unstuck and by the aid of our efficient street-lighting system I saw, for the first time, that she had abundant, beautiful hair. She was weeping. She said: 'I never want to see you again. You brute.' She held the door open expectantly but, fearful that she would arouse the whole village and that the bandsmen would have a topic of talk for ever, Lothario Rodgers took like a hero to his heels. Behind him the shop bell tolled the ending of one phase of love.

★   ★   ★

'Women,' said my father as he eyed with Olympian detachment my scratched face, 'are incalculable.'

He laughed quietly for, I'd say, five long minutes.

'Dr Grierson has plans for you,' he said. 'Talk to him.'

He finished his whiskey. The smart of Lucy's fingernails salted by his laughter, I plotted reprisals.

'Tell me,' said I, 'as man to man, why you hated Captain Conway Chesney.'

He studied his empty glass. His lips moved silently. He was whispering to the past, consulting the oracle of Segully.

'Hard to say,' he said. 'He was a reorganizer. That's a destroyer. He changed the old name of Magheracolton to Bingen. There was a good song about the hills above Magheracolton. Would that be a good enough reason for hating a man like the captain?'

Five

TWO NESTING SWANS, IMMOBILE ON THE PILES OF RUBBLE
that swans call nests, warmed their eggs into life by the fringe of
Thread the Needle. Their watchful, jealous mates cruised, admiring their reflections in the ebony water. It was, as you may guess,
April. The fender in the residents' drawing-room in Grainger's
hotel on the river-front near the Guildhall, the select, secluded
room where the clergy did not have to disguise their whiskey as
Irish coffee, was made of tubular steel that swept soaring up at the
ends in delicate swan shapes. Two mallards tame as kittens shared
the love nest of Thread the Needle with the swans. With Hughie
Heron and Maeve and Gortin Lass I watched for the coming of
the spring mackerel. The sun warm on us, we lay in a sheltered
corner fifty feet up on Bingen Head, the rocking sea directly
below, seven of the Macillions scattered at distances on the low
rocks between ourselves and Bingen House.

'They come all the way from the deep middle of the Atlantic,'
Hughie said.

His great-veined hand held Gortin Lass quiet.

'They come in blind,' he said. 'Each fish with a skin over its
eyes. That's the pishrogue. From here up to the Point Lighthouse
they'll tell you that's why mackerel take no bait before July.
They can't see it. That's the fable.'

He waved his hat and shouted down at the shore. The shout
was relayed from one wild Macillion to the next until Alfred,
on the green by the river, waved his white, wide-brimmed,

rancher's hat in answer to Hughie, in salute to the spring and the mackerel who were back in the Bingen sea. Out there the calm water ruffled, then spurted white and swished and churned. The little pear-shaped bay between the head and the estuary and the start of the long strand was living with fish. Excitedly, lovingly reaching out for Gortin Lass, my gift, Maeve's hand was intercepted by mine.

'A pishrogue,' I said. 'A fisherman's fable. Like the day Frank fell into the river.'

Her grip responded. The mackerel a second time riddled and whitened the water. My thumb clingingly rubbed the fortune-telling palm of her hand.

'My own opinion,' said Hughie, 'backed up by what I heard a trawlerman say, and he went often as far as the Fareos on a boat out of Grimsby, 'is the male and female are so itchy in the spring they take no time to eat.'

The Macillion boys, six of them, and for luck one bare-footed, bare-legged sister, went clambering over rocks, racing along sand towards the master of Bingen to claim the present of silver that came by custom to the watchers when the incoming mackerel were seen. Far beyond them, on the road sloping down from the Gap, there was a black speck that was Greta cycling home from the city. Maeve's slacks were belted with a man's tie that looked oddly familiar.

'They say the skin falls off in June,' Hughie said. 'Their eyes will be open and their bellies empty by June.'

Like two eels entangled in a tank at the patriot's bridge Maeve's hand and mine entwined and twisted. The Gortin river, deep and quiet, rocked backwards inland, cradle after cradle, with the first flow of the tide. I thought as we walked: if the river had been like that when the captain fell, would it have nursed him landwards gently and lulled him to sleep in the deep right-angled bend below Kate Carr's cottage? Edmund, now an athlete, wanted to fix a diving-board above that pool. But the mood of the river and the ground of Magheracolton was all for rejection and denial, voiding and spitting out, on the day the captain's heart stopped and his body became garbage. In bottom ground below Drumard a tractor scratched at the corner of a spongy field. The rooks were always so low around the Gap that they looked as if they were fluttering to climb the brown-grey, razor-cut edge of the captain's private quarry. Pink blossoms snowed round the stable doors at Bingen, and Greta, crossing to the kitchen door, carrying chemist's parcels for her bed-ridden mother, walking away from Maeve and myself as once she had walked away upwards and under chestnut candles from Lucy and myself, was a dark shadow in a lighted shower: but tall and strong now, no humility, no wrinkled, bedraggled stockings. Swans were nesting by the water, hatching beauty on reeds and rubble, blind fish were in the bay and Owen, the blackavised, was blind and demented with love for Maeve Conway Chesney.

Dr Grierson said to me: 'Come with me, Owen. I have a future for you.'

'Praise God,' said my father. 'What is it? The lay apostolate?'

'In a sense,' said the doctor. 'Leave it to me, John Rodgers.'

'Drive me to the city, Owen,' he said. 'Drive to your manifest destiny.'

Then, a secretive shadow of a smile on his thin pale lips, he settled down beside me in the hearse of a car. Under chestnut candles on the bright Diamond Hill whom should we see but Maeve Conway Chesney. She stood on one of the flights of steps necessary in that steep street to provide level footing before the doors of shops. To my momentary annoyance she was laughing with and talking to a red-faced, heavily-built young man with bulging, enormous shoulders and biceps, a broad, hooked nose, and yellow hair with a water-sleek curl on a narrow forehead.

'Molphy the boxer,' said the doctor. 'Brake the car.'

My annoyance was gone for what merit, under God, could there be in a shuffling scuffler from the back lanes, a booth-boxer who would never even reach eminence in his own brutal business. Then annoyance was washed away by joy when the shifty fellow, the seat of his blue suit shiny, vanished up a side-street and Maeve waved and came towards us, not running as she would with Gortin Lass but walking sedately, her small lips apart with her own particular smile that never seemed to affect her deep blue eyes. She was no longer an unfettered, capable, dextrous half-of-a-boy reared between mountains with three brothers and men who knew about animals. She was no longer dressed in men's flannels upheld by some man's necktie. She was a real woman with a red head-scarf and a red skirt enscrolled in black-and-white characters with magic names of French wines. Her blouse was white with large red buttons. Her bag was white with red trimmings. Her bare legs were tinted with the faintest blush of golden down.

'Come with us,' the doctor said.

He stepped out, bare-headed, a fine tall man. He held the door while she stooped in sideways and slithered over close to me. In a sunny angle of the side-street the boxer halted under an overhanging tassel of ivy to light a cigarette and look back enviously, to my ecstasy, out of gimlet eyes. Monstrous spectres shrank back to their caverns when my love walked in the sunlight. She was firm and fresh between us. Her perfume reminded me of flowerless, strong, green, edible plants and then of crushed strawberry beds on a broiling day. The car dropped as if we were in a lift down the steep hill, and the abruptness of the descent accentuated unbearably the cold-and-hot, painful expectancy in the pit of my stomach. My hands on the wheel were unsteady. The cave of a gate in the old walls swallowed us as once on a memorable morning it had swallowed her father, but the sunlight pursued us to glint on immemorial stalactites under the arch. Then we were out into the full-blooded traffic of the Guildhall Square, four-wheeler horse-drays clattering from the docks, long-distance buses lined up below the walls and under the muzzles of guns silent since sturdy men had shut another gate in the face of the plumed and belted lover, James Stuart. Against him the maiden city had crossed her legs and remained aloof. No evocative names of French hillsides, bleeding with vineyards, had robed those frigid Protestant limbs.

'You choose elegant company for a young lady of your station,' the doctor said.

He was sharp. He was proprietorial. He was the curate of the parish speaking in a voice I hadn't heard since the evening he struck me on the left ear.

'He spoke to me, father. I couldn't pretend he wasn't there.'

But her voice, always so firm and confident, faltered as if she knew she was rightly rebuked, and I was angry with the Louvain doctor. Where the way narrowed beyond the Guildhall Square a procession with drums and banners had blocked the traffic. Drumming and piping and followed by solemn-faced demonstrators, the bandsmen cornered around the base of the brown tower, mellow in the sun, and high up in the air the lovely clock chimed eleven to recall again the captain and the derisive whistle of the departing Glasgow boat. One should, I suppose, have whispered an aspiration, Lord Jesus have mercy on his soul, for the eternal repose of the man who needed vats of oil, who out of his evil had begotten beauty, who received only as his reward the chill slap of the Gortin river. The beauty, the reward, was mine. Reaching across the wine-emblazoned skirt the doctor handed me a lighted cigarette and she, non-smoker, absently watching the banners and drums, intercepted it, pulled on it, placed it, reddened with her lipstick, in my mouth. For the first time I tasted her lipstick and thought, deliciously ill, every bite she eats and swallows goes flavoured thus into her body.

'Beaune,' he said.

He touched the B with the tip of his finger.

'St. Emilion,' he said, and drew the finger lingeringly around the curves of the M.

'Beau . . .' he said, and stopped.

The . . . jolais was hidden under her left thigh.

'Haut Médoc,' he said, grasping the second challenging word between finger and thumb, lifting the smooth cloth an inch away from the limb it covered.

'My two Alsatians,' he said, 'are called Pétain and Foch. They sleep at the foot of my bed and the housekeeper who is old and ugly objects. France, Owen, is the land to live in.'

When his delicate hand released the Médoc, the cloth settled back again with a rustle, and guiltily, for the first time, waves of wine flooding between two smooth ridges, I thought of Maeve as a woman with two legs. French girls with skirts kilted high trod the wine-presses, thighs splotched with burgundy. A particularly resonant pipe drone startled me. It was the voice of conscience rebuking me for my impure betrayal of my dream. My face was as hot as if from far sweltering Pau or Brabantane a wind, oily with leaves and clusters of fruit, had blown across the crowded square of a rough, northern city where men's palates, calloused by sour heavy beer and burning spirits, were insensitive to the rich blood of the earth and the sun. The white hand that held aloft the altar wine (cheaper to buy than wines for the table and in greater demand in Ireland) that would be the blood of God, had toyed with bounding, spurting life of satyrs.

Slowly the procession went, banners tilted, through the Guildhall Gate. Children, straddled on the ancient guns, cheered.

'Ahead now, Owen,' he said as the traffic moved. 'We're bound for Grainger's hotel.'

'Temptations in glass boxes,' my father said.

'You're just her fit, Miss Chesney. You're just her size,' old George Grainger said to Maeve.

The old man (he was past seventy but he looked a florid over-blooded fifty) was not quite sober. He had been sad when we came to him, but now, it seemed miraculously, he was elated. Both the learned doctor and Owen, his young socius, were non-plussed by his offer, but Maeve, comfortable in a low arm-chair, one leg tucked underneath her, Haut-Brion scrawled across a suspension bridge of flimsy skirt, looked complacently out of one of the windows of the high room and smiled and said: 'Thank you, Mr Grainger. But you're too good. It's too much. I couldn't possibly.'

'But I know they would fit you,' the old man said. 'It dawned on me like an inspiration when we were coming up in the lift, the doctor, Mr Rodgers, yourself and myself. You have what she had, the heavens be her bed. You have it all.'

He curved his hands. He outlined what had once been the shape of his young, lately-deceased wife, the third wife at whose funeral he had solemnly assisted.

'The hair plastered in waves on his head at his age,' said Jim MacElhatton. 'Old soldiers never die.'

'A wig,' said Barney the big drum.

'No wig,' said Jim. 'Dyed brown, but no wig. The size of him. The big hands. The red face.'

'Three wives under the clay,' said the piccolo, 'and nothing to show for the tricks he played on any of them except one worthless sot of a son.'

Now he stood above Maeve, he poured whiskey from a decanter for the doctor, he looked down at Maeve, he considered perhaps the possibility of a fourth life, he was warmed with a passion to see a dead wife's clothes moving again on a lovely, young, living woman.

'They're in the next room,' he said, 'hanging useless in the wardrobe.'

He looked as seemly-sad as a redfaced man with brown wavy hair, who was over seventy and seemed a healthy fifty, could look.

'When the deceased was alive,' he said, 'these rooms, as the doctor knows, were our private apartments. I haven't used them much since.'

The hotel's main entrance was on the waterfront. Leaning on the back of her chair, looking over her coppery head (she had shampooed her hair and every strong strand shone with auburn light), I watched ragged children attentive like limpets on the river wall. Their more active, daring comrades played from gunwale to gunwale and brass wheel to brass wheel of a quivering, queasy block of moored ferry-boats. One slow, filthy collier, engines reversed, arsed her way apologetically to sea, her black smoke blown inland and bowing and scraping to the lofty, maiden city. Streets of workers' houses went step-by-step up the steep, far shore in a part of the city where, said Jeff, the people in one street could and often did spit or worse down the chimneys of their neighbours in the street immediately below.

'This is an excellent drop of fifteen-year-old, doctor,' old George said. 'For the connoisseur. The clothes are hanging there going to waste, Miss Chesney. It would give me great pleasure.'

In chill, shrill wind across French skies the banner of Haut Brion rippled, collapsed, reshaped itself as she stood up. She followed the triple widower to the door of the bedroom and I followed, and the doctor. His composure restored by the whiskey's penetration to his palate, he gave the clothing ceremony his *nihil obstat*: 'It's a generous offer.'

What less or more could even the most learned doctor say when a man offered the robes of his buried beloved to another woman?

Aloof as a galleon in the middle of the bedroom stood the tall mahogany bed in which three wives had lived and, for all I knew, died: had been enjoyed and cried darlint, darlint, or perhaps mutely submitted to duty and the inexplicable male, as so many good Irishwomen are taught to do. Married and trapped in a bed it is difficult for even the most pure to be gregarious. Their lover and survivor walked across the carpet, reverently raised two Venetian blinds, and, a brisk if aged *maître d'hôtel*, dusted his fingers in that dusty museum of a room. Then, sliding aside the door of a huge, built-in, floor-level wardrobe, he displayed coats and coloured dresses, stooped down and thoughtfully fingered cold, deserted shoes. His decorous dark suit was clerical. His old-fashioned collar was turned down at the points. He was never seen in public without a white carnation in his buttonhole.

'What size are your feet?' he said.

'My shoes,' she said, 'are large four and a half or five.' She studied her raised right foot. Though humbly I would have measured the arch, heel and toes, it still shocked me a little, even if in a way I was proud of her wickedness, to know that she was mocking this kind, old, amorous, uxorious fool. Except when she talked to Hughie Heron it always seemed by the hint of a ripple around her fine, wide mouth that she knew some comic, half-disgraceful secret about the person she was talking to.

He said sadly: 'I have no daughter. My son has no wife.'

'We can leave you now, Maeve,' said the doctor. 'We have a little business.'

She swivelled from the hips, reluctantly taking her eyes from the treasures in the wardrobe, and stretched herself lazily and said: 'You'd better leave me. I must change.'

We left her. Old George closed the door reverently enough to satisfy even me. In a younger man his reverence would have made me jealous. He said: 'Is Mr Rodgers interested, doctor?'

'So far I haven't mentioned our plans. I was as reticent as the sphinx.'

'What plans?' I said.

'Mr Grainger will tell you, Owen.'

Detaching himself, the doctor at the sideboard refilled his glass.

'Does Mr Rodgers take a drop, doctor?'

The doctor didn't look round. He said: 'Very seldom. Only on special occasions.'

In ironical comment the humble, departing collier hooted.

'A young man,' old Grainger said, 'is as well without it. God knows, I should know. My son's a great trouble to me, Mr Rodgers. Do you know him?'

Everybody knew him. Everybody knew him so well they crossed the street when they saw him coming, and in bars, where he was a familiar, unwanted figure, he could clear customers from a counter quicker than a pestilence. His red face, protruding eyes, clammy alcoholic handgrip, were more dreaded than the insidious advances of process-servers. He started fights and left anyone foolish enough to be caught in his company to extricate themselves as well as they could from the ensuing maelstrom. One sad night I had seen him come perilously close to sudden death when, in the presence of a huge, intoxicated Irish army officer whose two rebel uncles had been murdered in 1920 by the Black and Tans in the neighbourhood of Clonakilty, County Cork, he had raised his glass and toasted His Majesty's forces. On some impulse of charity Kinnear had dragged him to safety.

'He never took too well to his second mother,' old Grainger said piously.

There were even nasty rumours which, to do myself justice, I never believed, that Grainger Junior, in the best corncob-country fashion, had taken only too well to his third mother whose clothes were now borrowing new life from the warm, fair form of my Maeve. Behind that closed door she was standing brightening the dead room, reflectively fingering dress after dress, choosing, disrobing, glimmering at herself from the wardrobe mirror. Out of reverence, out of fear, I tried not to but could not help seeing her. She should have had her bevy of mute Nubian eunuchs bowing and kneeling around her as if for some rite around a goddess or a consecrated queen.

'What I could to teach him the business, I did,' George Grainger said.

'Thrown out of the best training hotel in Dublin he was,' said Jim MacElhatton, 'for notorious misbehaviour with the female staff. . . .'

'But I had to expel him. My only son. He would have ruined this hotel. It humbles me, doctor, to have to say it. My own flesh and blood. He did mountains to destroy the goodwill I built up over the years. Colonel Goldsmith and his whole connection left me because of him.'

He bowed his head on his hands, running his fingers (they were puffed and swollen rather than abnormally big) up around his ears. It was a wig. He said: 'To make a long story short . . .'

Then the door opened and Maeve, sweeping in like an actress, was with us, walking close to the old man and causing him to glance up joyfully, turning around slowly before us for admiration with the stylized glide of a mannequin.

'There are two of these,' she said. 'Oh, they're lovely. Mr Grainger, I couldn't possibly.'

'You do them credit,' he said.

Shedding wine from her limbs she had been naked and now she was clothed again, more beautiful than ever.

'There's this one in peacock,' she said. 'Dancing dresses. And one in black and both beautifully boned in the bodice. And look, just look, doctor, at this matching stole.'

'I am an authority on stoles,' he said. 'Purple stoles.'

One end of the peacock stole held to her waist (when she doffed it her shoulders were bare), she backed with tiny jigging steps to the bedroom door, bright cloth dipping as she retreated.

'And underneath, a stiff petticoat,' she said. 'You can hear it rustle.'

We listened. Distinctly we could hear it rustle.

'But I'm in the way,' she said. 'What do you men care about fashions?'

Smiling, old George flashed white natural teeth he was rightly proud of and said: 'We couldn't, doctor, could we, have a handsomer teacher? Could we, Mr Rodgers?'

'Owen looks so serious,' she said: and, taking her curtain, was gone into the bedroom, leaving the door slightly ajar behind her so that I felt excitingly that we shared one room and could hear, as George Grainger revealed his sorrows and his plans, the rustle of rich clothing that she, and, I recalled, the expert lawyer Kinnear, would know by name in the lingo of *haute couture*. The only woman, too, who had ever undressed in the room with me was Dublin Lass, and she, with a modesty then inexplicable to me in a sad soul who looked (said James) like the last of the old-fashioned whores renowned in balladry, had fortified herself behind an armchair and switched off the light.

'To make a long story short,' George Grainger said, 'he drove away patrons with his drunken bad manners.'

It was a ballad of dirty Dublin in my head distracting me as I tried to keep my eyes from the slit between door and jamb. It was no relation to the ballads of love and the old times, or even to the happy lilts about unwise sailors, that crossed the melodious lips of Hughie Heron. In the Red Bear the loud poet recited: 'The dean of Saint Patrick's Cathedral flung open his old-fashioned dhures.'

'He costs me money on every front,' said George, 'in wrecked cars and fines and drink. A boy that went to the best Jesuit college with the cream of the country.'

'The cream of the country,' said the doctor, 'rich and thick.'

'And the ghost of Dean Swift,' recited the poet.

'But it was the end for ever when he insulted Colonel Goldsmith.'

'Toddled forth in his shift,' said the poet, 'to the last of the old-fashioned hoors.'

'On the occasion of the colonel's last visit I was in bed with the bronchitis.'

'Unusual for you, George,' said the doctor.

Glass in hand he walked across the room to the window, stood tall and dignified, an Abelard on a rostrum, possibly meditating on the professorship he never got, stooping a little to look down on the river and the children monkeying around the moored ferry-boats.

'The weather, doctor. This climate would kill a horse. But it can't harm the tourist business if we know how to treat our guests. This country, doctor, has a great tourist future. The type of Colonel Goldsmith now, with more acres than you could count in Pembrokeshire. Inquired after my health like the gentleman he is. "How is Mr Grainger?" he said to the son. Son . . .'

It seemed cruel to allow him to continue with the narrative. What colours would she wear when once again she walked before us?

'". . . Very well, thank you, never better," he snapped back at the colonel. "I was asking you about Mr Grainger, sir," says the colonel. "I am Mr Grainger, sir," was the answer, turning his back on some of the best business ever crossed my threshold. He moved, the colonel did, himself and his whole party and one titled gentleman in the company, down to Tower Bay. He didn't even finish the large brandy that was before him. He wrote to me, nicely enough, to say he only moved because the lord wanted to be closer to the lake when the mayfly rose, and to inquire about my health and condole about my dear wife. What do you think of that for a son?'

'He was hardly meant for the hotel business, George.'

'Under God, what business was he meant for? Explain to me, doctor, how a man could get a son like that.'

The doctor said simply and kindly: 'You did your best, George.'

'The custom will come back when they know he's gone. Goodwill, cleanliness, service and efficiency. But I'm not as young as I was, doctor. I need youth to help me.'

He looked at me and I was looking at the opening door,

because for her second advent and visitation to mere mortal men she stood lightly on the threshold, saying she knew she was a nuisance but she had to show us this, and held out her skirt fanwise and curtsied like a coy girl at a school concert. It was a gentle jersey, she told us, bowed with black velvet ribbon and worn with a velvet-ribbed skirt, and look, she said, look at this satin cummerbund. She had forgotten—or was it forgetfulness? —to rearrange the hair tousled by changing and that was the way, I knew, her hair would be in the morning when she woke smiling and flushed, the corners of her eyes moist with sleep. Curtsying in the doorway, distracting George from his aged sorrow and the doctor from his drink, she was so completely relevant that I saw myself in time to come living in these rooms, practising cleanliness, service, efficiency and other beloved, ravishing things, creating good will. When she bowed her way backwards from the door my mind was made up. When George turned towards me to say there was an opening for a young man and would I be interested, and the doctor, finishing his drink, marking finality, said that Owen would be the right man in the right place, who was I, since she had decided, to gainsay them? At your service: Owen Rodgers, hotelier. We shook hands all round and summoned her from fashions to the celebrating of the beginning of a new life. She came as herself, dressed in wine, and hugged me and said: 'Owen, how wonderful. I'm happy.' She whispered: 'You should see me in some of the clothes that are in there. One dress is lurex lamé, shining like gold with a butterfly bow over my middle.

'It would blind you,' she whispered (her mouth to my left ear). 'The old fellow must have spent millions on her.'

Then George Grainger admired her skirt and the doctor said we should have a similar one praising Irish whiskey, designed for our air hostesses of the future to help the export trade and attract the eyes of rich Americans to our most marketable commodity. But George cried: 'No,' and, 'Wine,' he said, 'only wine for a lady,' and picking up the house phone (gallant, by God, thought Owen) he ordered wine from cellar cool to match the skirt of a beauty. When the champagne was poured he said: 'And to welcome you, Owen. I'll call you Owen.'

She sipped the wine. She rested in the crook of my left arm.

'Let us drink,' said the reverend doctor, 'to France, to Louvain, to Salamanca that the bishops of Ireland stabbed in the back. Let us drink, my friends; as Costafreda the Barcelona poet said, death does not exist, the wheat will have its crop, the woman will wait.

'Gentlemen and Maeve,' he said, 'this is a very special occasion.'

His pale eyes were kindly and at ease, no red wriggling flecks of weariness showing.

'This is the third time,' she said, 'I drank champagne. Once at the Christmas party . . .

'I'd flatten the world,' she whispered, 'in that gold dress.'

Old George and the doctor were talking about the caves of the Dordogne 'and,' said Old George, 'one thing I could never understand about the French, my goodness, for such a civilized people who know all courtesy and cuisine, was the terrible state of their conveniences.

'What you want, Miss Chesney,' he said, 'I'll have packed and sent to you. It would give me pleasure and herself that's gone pleasure if you wore them.'

The doctor said again that it was a generous offer and, watching from the window a spotless white corvette slicing her way to port, we drank more champagne.

★   ★   ★

'Thank God you're settled,' my mother said.

She was resting in bed and the medical man who once on the Diamond Hill had helped me to listen to the captain, had been attending her.

'So you'll never make a doctor,' my father said. 'You're squeamish about blood and indolent about facts. George Grainger will teach you well. You can dress to kill and chat to people and manage the whimsies of the female staff and count spoons.'

Jim MacElhatton said: 'Don't do what young Grainger did in the Dublin hotel.'

'There's money in it,' my father said.

Then followed the idyllic days. Where Maeve went I went, and merely to be with her and with Gortin Lass was heaven. Everything in our small city became intimate and beautiful then as I learned how to count spoons and in my spare moments walked with her in holy purity, far from the sweat and sighs of Dublin Lass, far from the fancies with which Lucy's presence used to fill my mind. This truly was laburnum and lilac love. We were as pure, believe it or not, as any ideal the gregarious preacher could hold before the young men and women of Ireland.

Everything, I said, in our small city became intimate and beautiful then, and one noticed with a stab of affection, like someone seeing the gestures of his father in his son or the deepening of lines on a known face, even the bright saddles on low window-sills in by-streets where lazy men sat and spat and sharpened clasp-knives. In the drowsy lunch-time lull old people that one never saw at any other hour of the day rested without words, under the protection of the Virgin Victory, on seats in the

Diamond. The uncanny comparative silence of that hour seemed broken only by the voice of the man selling apples near the arch of the Guildhall Gate (the old walls still preserved rings to which marketing men had once hitched horses) or the limping, peg-legged rattle of looms from a small shirt factory. A few sailors, early on shore, peacocks in bright, ill-creased, foreign suits, looked speculatively at everything in skirts, took a solemn, academic interest in the protruding balloons of bums of the afternoon's young matrons gabbling on circular swivel stools in the hotel bar. Brown eyes in lean, tanned faces were the eyes of children wondering about toys in shop windows. It was a religious little city just as Ireland is a religious little country. Those hilly streets ascended always to steeples and bells, and most of us climbed up to pray whether we meant it or not. But, being a seaport and a garrison town, it had for centuries its proud tradition of depravity, and reckless soldiers and sailors sought fun, and fought, in the pubs of the Fountain Lane grid-iron under one corner of the walls, where even the white-putteed shore police, by gentlemanly agreement, left them to their recreations. On the walls and along the docks, dying slowly because it was a small, decaying port, Maeve and myself found two favourite places in the city for hand-in-hand walks.

This (I read from a plaque in a corner of the walls sheltered by a high, brown-brick gable) was Cowards' Bastion.

'Being most out of danger,' said the plaque in the grave tones of the seventeenth century, 'cowards resorted here.'

She sat on the butt of a siege gun, wearing the wine skirt to please me, and, her toes straining towards the sandy ground, bent herself at right angles, her shoulders on the barrel, her coppery head towards the embrasure. Bending down quickly, Owen Rodgers, *trouvère*, kissed her lightly on the forehead, then on her warm, dry lips. To preserve us from temptation and recall us to time, the Guildhall clock chimed the quarter. She leaped up laughing, hugged me, danced around me in that corner where cowards had gathered to be away from cannon balls. Cowards in congress, what could their talk possibly have been about?

This was a busy place once in the days of small ships and tall sails, creaked the wooden planks of the dockside as they moved uneasily under our loitering feet.

Through cracks in the timber we saw yellow water glazed over speckled mud. The malty smell of two mills was strong around us and one solitary outlaw of a jackdaw plotted and thieved for God knew what. Ahead of us and high up, traffic passed east and west behind the steel trellis of the one big bridge, and underneath, ten feet above the sweep of the spreading water, railway trucks were lined like chests of booty in a Cyclops' cave, and from the shadows bogeymen chatting around a brazier waved greetings to the familiar young couple. Beyond the bridge and the bogeymen there was a wilderness of rough grass and rusted, disused railway tracks and then a steep ridge, now coated with grass and flowers, that had once been slag shovelled and scraped out of exhausted engines that through seven radiant counties had chugged and pulled all the way from Dublin. Over that ridge, our lovers' bastion, we were cut off from everything except the broad movement of the water, gull cries, a car or a bus seen, but diminutive and unheard, on the southward road on the far bank, a stately sail or the humble chugging of an outboard engine. On a seat the bogeymen had made for themselves out of discarded sleepers and then, reverencing our dream, had abandoned to us, we sat side by side and hand in hand, and sometimes, in a way she had, her head rested sideways on my shoulder, close to my neck, and every hair and every breath was a sign of God. There was no dirty danger in our being alone together far away from the bulls and cows in the champing, grazing, butting, rutting herd.

That was our city and that was our dry, tender love. Yet the great joys were not when she came to me in the city but when I cycled or drove by the patriot's bridge, by our crescent village and the Gortin Gap to visit her in Bingen. For in a city, no matter how small it is, you grow away from silence, from the mystery of a solitary morning walk, the freedom of a child dancing across an empty road, the noise of brimming roadside runnels, the heavy complaint of the corncrake, his wings wet with dew, the triumphant indignation of hens on nests behind cottages. From Grainger's hotel the homeward Bingen road went up with early morning worshippers past the cathedral. Shop-keepers, or their assistants, gave their tiny premises the morning cleaning, corrugating the dust with clogged brushes over sticky pavements. Odours of breakfast, and chimney smoke unable to rise against the steep slope and catch the clean wind, fell back heavily against the face. A few, half-clothed toddlers played at ease in the path of the scant traffic and the dogs were always asleep in those high streets of kitchen houses. Husbands left early to work in the mills and the docks. An insurance agent, book in hand, gossiped with two fat, greasy-aproned matrons, and the milkman, like milkmen in every town in the world, had his own secrets.

Over the ridge and free of the houses there was a bridge I always stopped at, to look back at smoke, to look ahead at a golden world that had begun before I was born. Out there the music of the ocarina melted into the lilts and songs of Hughie Heron; the shadow of Doran the wizard, on some winding road on a May evening, could have been mistaken for a wandering harper. A hill stream, churning out of a high wood on the left, sluiced under the bridge, shot down the hill at an odd angle on a terraced, concreted course designed to control its spate. Birds chirped in the wood and there were innumerable wagtails on the water and for a whole six months, securely held in a concrete corner, a retired tin kettle was becalmed far down the terraces of the stream. It became part of my journey to paradise and every time I passed I looked to see if it was there. With eyes closed then, on the bridge I was listening to the Gortin river, and, slowly opening my eyes, I could see, far away, white rocks like remote Himalayan snow, the outline of Bingen Head. It was no longer the precipice that guarded the dragon's cave. It was a shining mountain, musical with streams, musical with the sea at its base, and happy above the home of the ringleted love of my youth. Wagtails and old tin kettle and Bingen Head meant more to me than all the money minted or all the words in books. Among the strawberry beds at Bingen the quiet, methodical Greta had placed saucers of milk so that the household cats, claws among soft, red sweetness, quenching their thirst, could frighten away the marauding blackbirds; and that spring and into summer, the soft turbary warm under us where we lay by Thread the Needle, Maeve and I studied the devotion of the swans and watched the cygnets growing and whitening into beauty.

'They always come in odd numbers,' said Hughie.

'That's another pishrogue,' Maeve said. 'Four years ago the swans here had two cygnets. Ask Greta.'

It was incredible to me, but a matter for joy, that the mute, shoddy-brown girls in the captain's cave could have paid attention to or talked of the swans.

'I wonder,' she said, 'is it the same two swans, year after year?'

'Try putting rings on them,' said Hughie. 'The captain did once but the birds he ringed never returned.'

Feeding by the margin of black mud the swans hissed savagely at floundering Gortin Lass. Then, tail in the air, the mother dived for food for the family, her long neck wriggling and refracted under the water. Flocks of sparrows grubbed around the deserted nest, and Gortin Lass, daunted by the swans, stupidly chased the sparrows, barking underneath them as they flew with full beaks towards the river. The breathless heat, early that year, was around us on the river bank. The river asleep was a blue-black cloth ripped now and again by the movement of a lazy salmon bass. Far away on the wooded slope beyond Thread the Needle the call of the younger brothers and sisters of the small farmer's son who had run away to sea rose shrill and clear from hazel woods that were to be momentous in the love life of Alfred Conway Chesney. We lay in the shadow of a sloping river bank, smelled the good grass and held hands, and across the water the sunlight was as unreal as a painting. Lizzie Heron, carrying a milking stool, followed by two collie dogs, crossed pasture to squat and squeeze juice out of contented Jersey cows. Edmund, the athlete, might suddenly upset our heaven by trotting past in a track suit, attended by two hirsute Macillions. As he did, they also wiggled arms, flexed legs, shook hips, like four-minute-mile heroes relaxing between lunatic sprints. Sometimes the athletes went in bathing suits, dripping with water from the pool below Kate Carr's cottage where Edmund had at last fixed the diving-board, and once the three of them, not knowing we were there, ran past stark naked. Maeve lay flat, face down on the grass, and choked with laughter. Greta, with us for once, sat as pale as Kinnear and said nothing.

Those then were the idyllic days. One evening behind our lovers' bastion she leaned her head sideways on my shoulder in that way she had and said: 'Owen, can I look at the world from a new angle?'

She wore tartan slacks and an expensive sweater that had once belonged to the third Mrs Grainger, but try my best, I cannot remember the colour or the material of that sweater. There are so many things I cannot remember about her and so many things I never knew. The river that evening was very busy with pleasure boats.

We, Maeve and I, were invited to go with the doctor by the water all the way from the Guildhall dock to Tower Bay the day he took his new boat to the lake. About that time we were seeing a great deal of Dr Grierson.

'If you get too close to Maeve,' Kinnear said, 'you always have a padre to splice you. Beware of getting too close to her.'

But when I, without meaning the inquiry or caring about the answer, asked him why, he laughed and said no wise man stayed too close for longer than was necessary to any woman, that the padre himself, who was known to have a weakness that way, looked with kindly eyes on the captain's daughter and might, in friendly rivalry, strike a goat's horned head on Owen Rodgers, son of John. Echoing Hughie Heron, Jeff sang: 'There's an alehouse near by and we'll sit there till morning comes, if you are satisfied we will agree that early next morning we'll send for the clergyman to bind us as close as the bark to the tree.' Then, since old Grainger was off on his annual pilgrimage to Lourdes, once a year for thirty-nine years, and we could drink undisturbed by his ullagoning about his graceless son, we drank in the hotel bar the health of Maeve, the Louvain doctor and the new boat, and Jeff, but not Kinnear, consented to travel as a distinguished observer on the maiden voyage.

'Give me a country tavern,' said Jeff (when we could see, rocking towards us across the water, the old Norman tower with the cluster of hotel buildings at its foot), 'with a goose to kick away and the son of the sod to sing Boolavogue.'

'Owen could do with a drink too,' said Maeve. 'He looks cold.'

She sat in the stern with the doctor and they had their hands together on the tiller. Although the wind had been cold enough on the lake, on our day-long journey, to chap lips and set noses dripping, she was not cold or red-nosed or absurd. The day on the lake had tousled her hair and strengthened her skin the way wind and water would shape sand, foam and clear stone into beauty. More than any of us, and none of us were pampered or city reared, she belonged to mountain, lake and sea and to the enigmatical rhythm of wind and rocking boat. The lake was shadowy in evening, tossing away from us towards a far shore already sinking backwards into a fumy, oozy night of eels and pike. Wooded islands were black, floating bundles. West of the tower a flat, sleek tributary river, dark as tar, writhed through reedy fields, and, sheltered by low trees, was the hotel, the colonel's corner, the place of refuge sought by Colonel Goldsmith and the titled gentleman, a noble lord. Before the two huge boathouses some boats still rocked on the water, the ribs of a grounded decayed barge were gaunt in the reeds, the windows of the hotel bar were already lighted. It was by no means the type of Irish country tavern that Jeff's words would have led one to expect, for within the bar all the retired colonels in the world, all as colourful as the walls around them, were deployed in full force. The man of the house was himself a retired colonel, finding rest, his warfare o'er, far away from the guns of the Huns and the much more formidable taxes of the Britons. Colonel Goldsmith was there and the noble lord, with the telescope under his oxter, and it was my job, with the help of the gracious presence of the padre who was popular, to be ingratiating to them and woo them back to George Grainger. The

Wiltshires were there too, and the Beverleys and the drunken Beverley son with his handlebar moustache.

'Should we sit,' said Jeff into his first whiskey, 'with the gillies on the bench in the corner where, with cunning humility, they keep their distance, mumble to each other, move only to nod at nobody in particular when the foaming free pints are sent over by the beneficent breed of the Beverleys?'

The doctor was deep in discussion with the tall, noble lord whose long face was puce with alcohol. They inspected the telescope. Maeve was suddenly surrounded by tweedy men, mostly old, and Jeff and Owen were an island.

'For centuries, Owen, the gillies have known their place. Their forebears in the days of good Queen Bess trotted, glibs of hanging hair blinding them, by noble stirrups over mountain and morass. If the man in the moon farted at them and they thought he was a lord they'd off with caubeens and crook their knee and say "yis, yer hanner".'

The Fortescues were there too and the Kilgobbins and the O'Mahony-Featherstones and the American woman that Colonel Simpkin-Braddon had married for her money.

'Very compact, Owen. Suppose we squeeze over to the corner under the perpetual dapping cup.'

She was chatting cheerfully to young Beverley. She looked up at his eyes or was it his noble growth of a moustache? He bent down to her and talked drunkenly and to emphasize a point laid a hand on her left shoulder and together they laughed like clowns. I didn't like young Beverley, yet how could I be jealous because she talked and laughed with a comparative stranger in a crowded bar where the walls were festive with the covers cut from coloured magazines? There was a Frenchman called Lanoux there, a colonel in appearance, who had captivated in the heat of the Riviera a big-boned, horsey woman of the

Piddington-MacCarthys. The blackfaced gillies despised him because he spoke more like a travelling bagman of a Punjab Indian than like one of the real gentry. Gesticulating, he talked to the padre and the long puce lord who again unslung his telescope, pointed it at one of the well-built cover-girls who made the walls radiant, and lord and Lanoux roared with laughter so loud that even the gillies looked up suspiciously from their pints. Meditatively the padre turned his glass of brandy, a chalice, in his two hands. In a lull Maeve could be heard saying: 'What a wonderful idea in wallpaper!'

'Luscious girls,' said Jeff, 'wheat plains in Canada, temples in Tibet, the Rocky Mountains, Cologne Cathedral, Copacabana beach, all the things the poor can't have and the places they never see. I groan, Owen, for the gillies. Sad Firbolgs.'

'She was quite extraordinary,' said the lord. 'She was Greek. That was nineteen seventeen. The month of May, if I remember rightly.'

'What do you think, sir,' asked young Beverley, 'of the debutante who swam the Serpentine in her underwear? Cheered by officers of the Horse Guards.'

'The officers of the Horse Guards, sir, are gentlemen.'

'The Sunday papers say she did it for a fiver.'

'Quite frequently girls in their underwear in London do things for fivers.'

'Hush,' said a voice. 'Padre present.'

'Ladies present,' said the padre.

The general tumult arising again almost drowned his voice but I could see his lost, disconcerted smile and realize that here, among these people who by tradition regarded clergymen as comedy or as menials who sat below the salt, he was out of place even if he was popular, he lacked his customary masterful composure. Drinking mechanically, Jeff and myself were well on the road to happiness. Beverley and Maeve touched glasses. The swaying of the crowd sent them swinging around in a slow circle, facing each other, glasses raised, like a cock and hen in a mating dance in a Disney film about wild life on the prairie. Sullenly, mysteriously unwilling to go to her, angry with my own sullenness, I watched her full left cheek, the dark shadows under her brown eyes, her opening mouth, the teeth bright and strong. She was mine, it seemed, but it occurred to me then that she never laughed with me as she was laughing with young Beverley. What part of her did I own except an adolescent embrace, a dry kiss, a few words spoken as if she and I moved in a dream?

Then the lord in another lull spoke and said: 'You should be here when the mayfly rise. Crawl over your boots here, by Jove, on the floor of the pub.'

Pints purchased by the O'Mahony-Featherstones were carried over to the monkey-house of the gillies and from the lion-house the colonels roared under moustaches tawny as manes, their leather-faced mates snarled back at them, and sinister in glass cases the heaviest captured trout of past dapping seasons fixed baleful, glassy eyes on their captors. Weary with the long day on the lake, hungry after insufficient snacks of sandwiches eaten in the boat, weary inexplicably of my holy love for the unholy captain's daughter, weary of brandy and Jeff's incessant talk, I turned my back to the crowd and studied a twelve-pound trout that the year before last had posthumously been awarded the dapping cup.

'Brandy,' said the girl behind the bar, 'is great for sad hearts.'

So we drank more and more brandy and I turned around, my head buzzing, to see that she wasn't there, nor Beverley. The mating dance, I thought, was over and the birds had winged to find a nest.

'With that glass,' said the lord, 'I can see the grass growing on the far shore.'

'What the butler saw,' Jeff lisped. 'Lord Peeping Tom. Vicomte Voyeur.'

Indicating that I was adjourning for natural causes and asking Jeff to set them up again, I squeezed my way, drunkenly glaring at colonels and gillies, through the crowd to the damp, fresh air outside, feeling that if one man queried my movements or followed me murder would be done and damn the doctor, damn George Grainger and his courtesy, cleanliness and service. But to my deeper humiliation nobody paid the least attention to me. Outside the darkness was a descending wave, a roaring in the ears, and the wind from the restless, crisply-washing lake carried a mizzle of rain. She was mine because I knew the fountain she came from, because her father had favoured me before she was born. Even if I turned my back perversely on her in a crowd she had no right to go anywhere without my permission. It was so dark now I couldn't see the old tower or the handle of the gate at the end of the path. With the sticky rain even the road wasn't white underfoot and for a while I moved uncertainly like a man suddenly blinded. Stumbling once over a grass margin, I made my way around to the front of the hotel. A lighted basement window showed me twelve inches or so of white apron tightly tied around a stout body and two strong forearms washing dishes, but even the lord's Peeping Tom telescope couldn't have told me whether the washing woman was young or old. Teetering on the gravel I laughed alone at Jeff's brandy vision, what the butler saw, of the lord, eye to his glass, playing *voyeur* to the fair women of the lake's far shore.

'Working in Doncaster,' said Jim MacElhatton, 'I knew a man who was a born Peeping Tom, couldn't help himself, hiding behind hedges in parks, crawling like a commando on his belly when the loving couples would be too busy to pay much attention to their surroundings.'

'In Dublin, in the Phoenix Park,' said Barney Quigley, 'the bright boys used to nip in at the critical moment and make off with the handbags.'

'Late at night,' said Jim, 'this fellow in Doncaster would go on his knees in side-streets to peep under blinds into strange rooms. Better a bush to hide behind, he said to me once, than the best woman ever built.'

'Great sense there,' said Barney the big drum. 'One glance and away.'

'No responsibilities,' said the piccolo. 'Everything in the imagination.'

The back seats of all the parked cars were empty. Except for the lighted basement kitchen and a dim, coloured light in the entrance hall, the front of the hotel was in darkness. All the life was away at the back in the bar. Down a sloping lane towards the sound of the lake and the boathouses I staggered. Wisps of weed and bundles of broken twig littered the concrete slips and, in the season, the short-lived mayflies would crawl up in hundreds out of the water on to those twigs and weeds. Behind me the boathouses were dark caves, and above them the clubhouse the yachtsmen used sheltered me from wind and rain, from the bellowing in the hotel bar, but not from my own insensate jealousy, or the booming of brandy in my brain, or in my ears enchanted humming noises. Then through the noises I heard the whisper of a woman's voice, the mumble of a man's voice. They were behind me in the dark cavern of one of the boathouses. Standing at the entrance, my back to the lake, I could see nothing, yet drunkenly I knew the obscure, mocking joy of Peeping Tom, eyes to the slit under the window blind, like God himself seeing people when they thought they were unseen.

'There was a big farmer from Fintona,' said Hughie Heron, 'who suspected on the way home from the Lammas Fair that his wife was behind the hedge with a tea traveller. In the heat of the moment he watered over the hedge and the joke was it turned out to be another couple altogether.'

Should I peep and peer until shapes grew out of the shadows? Should I block the door and stand until they had to face me and walk out? Or should I emulate the feat and risk repeating the error of the Fintona farmer? Brandy on an empty stomach made up my mind for me and forty yards away, having covered the space in three antelope bounds, leaning into some unfortunate man's boat I relieved my head of noises, my stomach of vapours and my soul of hate. The lake was a dance behind me. The wind was a shouting high up in the sky. The boathouses looked blank as Egyptian pyramids. The rain was heavier, so I tottered back to the bar, wiping cold sweat off my forehead, saw the welcoming red-curtained window, saw, to my stupefaction, my lady Maeve in the corner under the perpetual dapping cup, talking, not now to Beverley, but to Jeff, the doctor and the lord. Dry as bone she was, dry as snuff, dry as the Sahara desert. She hadn't been out in the rain. Then I thought of the Fintona farmer and laughed until I cried, and she said: 'Where were you, Owen? We were worried.'

'For a stroll to stretch my legs. To the Tower.'

'The brandy,' said Jeff, 'came back with a bang.'

Jeff was bleary drunk.

'Oh, Owen,' she said. 'You were ill.'

She put her hand on my forehead. I was a flat balloon. Who had owned the voices in the boathouse?

'One more brandy to settle it,' said the doctor. 'Then we'll eat.'

He was grave and alone and very sober, a dark, learned man in the middle of all that tawny jollity.

'Every one in this home for old colonels,' said Jeff, 'is as drunk as owls. In among the gillies, Owen, in the heart of the deep, dark forest, there's a postman with a bag on him singing songs.'

His long nose swept down like a sickle towards his brandy. He said sadly: 'A postman with a bag on him singing songs was never seen before. Catch me a gilly,' he said, 'catch me a stuffed trout.'

His elbows were slipping slowly off the edge of the counter, so, the doctor and Maeve leading the way, Owen Rodgers, aided by the noble lord and sane and sound again after his recent indisposition, armed his old comrade, the man of letters, to a bedroom. While Jeff slept it off, the doctor, the lord, my love and I and Colonel Goldsmith, ate well in a private dining-room. Away from the tumult the doctor was himself again and, due to his Louvain eloquence, the courteous bearing of Mr Rodgers and the winning beauty of the captain's daughter, Colonel Goldsmith, the lord and the telescope spent the last month of their holidays in Grainger's hotel and were introduced by the suave Owen and Hughie Heron to the wonders of the Gortin river. Young Beverley, a decent fellow at heart except that his father treated him rather stingily, joined in one or two of those fishing expeditions.

Outside, the night in the bar went on to acquire a legendary reputation. It went down in tradition that young Beverley even bought a round of drinks when he won a fiver from the hapless Lanoux on a wager over the weight of the brown trout that Mrs Piddington-MacCarthy had taken second place with in the dapping contest three years previously. When he said: 'I say, this is on me,' even the gillies stood up and showed the world they had legs like real men.

Feeling fine after food I drove our party home in a hired car.

The Louvain doctor was at his most eloquent. Maeve sat beside me. Jeff alternately slept and sang. For the development of the hotel business and the progress of the tourist industry it was a night to remember.

In lucid, waking moments in this dream of love and fair, shadowy women, the escapades of Edmund kept us laughing and excited. Looking on life from a new angle, I spent leisure moments at the front window of George Grainger's high room and realized how different people looked from above. There, striding with a flourish on the footwalk by the river wall, went Edmund Conway Chesney. He had grown a brown beard. He wore a grey linen summer jacket. His left foot turned noticeably inwards. No fond father had ever been solicitous that he should startrite and walk straight. In those glad days he was trigger-happy in everything he did. In a seaside resort sixty miles away, he, in his sober senses, and young Grainger, in his customary horrors of drink, wrecked a restaurant, hired a hackney the sixty miles home, refused to pay the fare, assaulted the driver and by bribery and corruption, Kinnear mediating, got away with it. Surprisingly, his shop prospered, well-stocked, glittering, crowded with customers catered for by Edmund himself and four white-coated female assistants. Surprisingly, for one Saturday night I saw him desert a customer, a fine, befurred lady, and leave her with cash in hand and her parcel half-wrapped and with the staggering explanation: 'Excuse me, madam, I must see this fight.' The glorious young Grainger had just staggered into the shop to announce that Maggie Patterson, the fiddler's daughter from the Fountain Lane recreation area, a lady known to her acquaintances as the Jennet, a title which she could not, because of one unwanted child, honestly claim, had encountered at the Guildhall Gate the fusilier father of her child in the company of another woman. To be fair to Edmund, though, half the customers in the shop followed him, for the encounter, by the standards of our city, was a considerable social occasion, and his charm was so compelling that the lady in furs waited until The Jennet had adjusted her affairs, the interloper was routed and Edmund's curiosity satiated.

Kinnear was the unwilling witness of another escapade when Edmund, to settle a wager with young Beverley who now and again came on his own to fish the Gortin river, climbed out on to the roof of an excursion train, debagged and rebagged himself and then danced a hornpipe as deftly as Mouth-organ Rosie of the house of the Eel Queen ever did. Employing his whetted legal acumen, and not for the last time on behalf of the brood of Captain Conway Chesney, Kinnear settled the rumpus with the railway company. In plus-fours, and in the odd company of young Beverley, young Grainger and the boxer Molphy, with Jeff present, as he said, as a political observer, Edmund, it would seem, made dabbling movements towards devil worship in the storeroom at the back of the shop. They began simply enough: splitting a bible with a knife, tying a huge, old-fashioned door-key to a prayer-book, holding the shank of the key while the prayer-book revolved, making the sign of the cross backwards, invoking the dead and judging whether the invocation was heard or not by the direction, number and speed of the revolutions the book made. They proceeded to table tapping and the mystic circle of bodies linked by gripping hands in the darkness. Nothing worthy of the attention of the Society for Psychical Research happened until one night the boxer, either for fun or because his simple mind had had enough of the arcane or because there really was something in the room, roared: 'Mother of Jasus, let me outa here!' Panic ensued. In the crisis, and to prove the reality of diabolic intervention, the electric light fused. In the scuffle at the doorway of escape young Grainger was pushed down the thirteen steps from the store to the shop-level and dislocated his shoulder.

'All of a sudden,' Jeff said, 'they were like wild animals and myself in the middle of them like an ancient Christian. Alas for science, I observed nothing, and the Adversary himself or the captain with the whiskers could have been in the room.'

Ever afterwards Edmund's sallow face would redden and the wide nostrils twitch at any reference to the esoteric and he confined himself to more extrovert activities. He put the night-watchman on a road repair job drunk, tossed the red lamps over a wall into a meadow, and Lucy's father, driving home, bogged his new car in a trench two feet deep. Edmund had to pay for that caper for although Lucy's father may have been cuckolded and was ruled by his wife and daughter he was no dozer in money matters.

'I'll never regret loaning him his fare to England,' my father said. 'With what delight he dances on the grave of his dear father.'

Down under the mendacious tombstone which Greta and Francis had had erected in the name of the family, down under the artificial wreaths and the white doves of peace in bowler-hat glass cases, the captain could, for all Edmund seemed to care, have been turning like a carcass on a spit. Observing with distaste his adolescent antics, his beard, his glittering shop, his horn-rimmed spectacles and crimped hair, the black mole to the left of his nose, I knew the revulsion of the ordered mind in an age of anarchy and dissolution. Then he accepted the challenge of a travelling circus man who was offering twenty pounds to anyone who would emulate his reckless riders and seven times circle the wall of death. The place where the challenge was given and accepted was the fairground in the patriot's village where Alfred had first met his Rose.

Rose, by the way, was gone from the house of the Eel Queen. When Alfred, liberated by his father's death, went to find her she had vanished, taking her music with her, it would seem, into sad lands.

'Under a cloud,' Kinnear told me. 'The kind, decent people say she left under a cloud.'

'Innocence,' said Jeff, 'survives by luck and circumstance. The world turned wrong for Rosie.'

From the gallery of the wall of death on the fairground we could look over the village to the house, on sloping grass and in its circle of conifers, where the lake ended and the river began. Jeff and Kinnear were on my left, Maeve on my right, Alfred farther around the gallery railed for spectators at the top of the quivering cylinder where men on motor-bikes defied the law of gravity by centrifugal motion, and exactly across the circle from us was the boxer Molphy, a high-necked sweater curving up like yellow petals to the bizarre red blossom of his muscular, heavy face. Maeve was unusually quiet. Alfred was not with us for he had taken of late to secretiveness and keeping his own company. We had left Edmund outside the hollow cylinder testing the machine he was to use, watched by the showman, a harelipped Saxon who smiled with cunning and contempt and with just a little foreboding because his twenty-pound challenge had been accepted. On pedestals to each side of the entrance two of his men in jack-boots, helmets and leather zipper jackets (the posters described them as hell-riders) revved their engines hideously, sending the wheels spinning on rollers spinning contrariwise, to draw to the exhibition the curiosity and cash of lakeside and countryside. In a lull in the horrible din we could hear the Cockney voice of the showman, sharp and clear enough to carry across the lake to the colonels and the stuffed fish in the Tower Hotel: 'Here beside me stands a courageous man ready and willing to accept a fair challenge. Can he or can he not do even one part of what the hell-riders do? Can he circle seven times around the wall of death? Come and see, folks. Come and see for yourself. Performance is proof and proof needs performance.'

Two other hell-riders did a preliminary performance, warming engines, gathering speed, oscillating easily on the straining planks as if some unseen hand was swinging them at the ends of ropes, passing in front of each other and behind each other, taking their hands off the handlebars, demonstrating their skill in one of the most idiotic occupations known to man. One of them as he passed waved to Maeve but she was looking straight ahead and did not answer the salutation of the flying cavalier. Their circling ceased. Their engines purred to silence. The moment of truth was at hand. Petrol fumes ascended the hollow cylinder like decayed odours from a drying well. Then the red curtain over the entrance was drawn aside, a small boy wheeling a motor-cycle entered, led by the showman, followed by what could have been Edmund Conway Chesney, a small figure disguised for space travel. I knew him by his beard and his turned-in left foot. The gallery was full. The people were scarcely breathing. The showman drew the curtain close, pawed the sawdust, bowed to the appreciative, expectant public, and in the silence Jeff's voice could be heard: 'Edmund the hell-rider. I never thought I'd live to see it.'

Across the circle from us Red Molphy the boxer smiled, to my amazement, for I had never credited that face with such genial pliability of muscle. Maeve giggled, but the generality, interested only in the Martian now settling himself in the saddle, gave him the tribute of respectful silence the chosen people must have given David as he stepped out blithely with staff and stone and sling.

He took an eternity warming his engine. It roared and purred, roared and purred, occasionally screamed, puffed, and backfired with the rattle of a Bren gun until it was obvious from the sagging bucolic jaws around us that the eel fishermen and farmers were afraid that the captain's son would turn tail, prove recreant and bring dishonour on us in the eyes of all nations. He shot off at last with staccato acceleration, jumping like a grass-hopper, bouncing back from his first address at the sloping ramp, sending the showman scuttling for shelter, bouncing back twice, three, four times, then slowly gaining wheel-grip on the planks of the ramp, rapidly gathering speed, attaining the per-pendicular wooden wall, rising half-ways up the cylinder, circling once, twice, thrice, four times, five times, six times, seven times. The cheers and the speed must have urged him on to lunacy and beyond. There he was, half ways between earth and heaven, the conqueror who had accepted a challenge, and why, Edmund and many another man might have reasoned, should he stop now? He was at home on the wall of death. He was the captain's son. He was a natural hell-rider. He accelerated. He circled again and again. The showman ran out shouting and gesticulating like an indignant husbandman execrating ravening birds. Swooping suddenly, Edmund skimmed by, a foot above the man's bald head, and the gallery quaked with laughter as the defeated challenger scuttled back behind the red curtain. There was no stopping Edmund. Jeff referred the matter to Jesus, Mary and Joseph and implored them to see that Edmund at least had the wit to keep a grip on the handlebars. Two of the leather jackets peeped out through the curtain, studied the meteorological phenomenon, made eloquent gestures of helplessness and withdrew to safety. Farmers and fishermen roared with delight. Maeve was laughing with hysterical excitement, running her hands through her glowing hair and, short-sleeved, showing a fragment of an inch of clean, soft armpit. Skimming the rim of the well, now blue with petrol fumes, the back wheel of the bicycle smashed a fragment of the protecting railing but, wild with enthusiasm, the people had no terror for themselves or the rotating lunatic and they scrambled for the fragments that landed in the gallery as if they were sacred relics or priceless portions of the hangman's rope. Owen Rodgers, when Edmund was lapping for about the seventieth time, closed his eyes and waited for the second sudden death in the house of Conway Chesney. But, wonder of wonders, Edmund got himself and the bicycle under control, slowly descended, inch by inch and circle by circle, touched the ramp, touched the sawdust, cut off the sizzling engine, opened his visor, stood up stiffly. The cheer that greeted him could have set the grey patriot by the bridge brandishing his limestone pike and crying out for vengeance on the perfidious Saxon for the broken treaty of Limerick and the martyrs of 1798. What followed was inextricable confusion. It would seem that the showman, facing Edmund and backed up by his jack-booted troopers, refused to part with the twenty pounds because Edmund, he said, had been guilty of breach of contract in exceeding the mystic number of seven anticlockwise circles. I missed that part of the performance because I was taking a lover's advantage of the crowd to whisper something to Maeve, my lips oh so close to her pure, pearly ear. But I did see Edmund swing at the showman and I did see two of the jack-boot brigade pinioning his arms and I did see Kinnear scrambling over the railings, dropping down to the sawdust, flooring the showman with as neat a right swing as ever came from a county Gaelic footballer in a moment of goalmouth aggravation. Jeff and myself followed, as became gentlemen and sworn comrades, and had the welcome support of two long-line fishermen and the boxer Molphy. The cheers that greeted Edmund's triumph were nothing to the cheers that cracked the sky for this second, unexpected, free-gratis-and-for-nothing part of the programme. Having missed the major engagements of World War II and being too young to be in an army canteen when the Dublin fusiliers came looking for beer, the battle of the wall of death must rank as the greatest engagement that Owen Rodgers, shouldering his crutch, can boast about to his children's children. My wounds were a black eye, skinned knuckles, a bruised thigh when I fell on a jack-boot boy and he kicked me, and a perfectly good jacket split up the back. The black eye was an asset in the hotel business in which physical or moral blemishes do not drive away customers and in which a good story from a daredevil of a man can attract them.

Then, as is the way with fights, it ended as suddenly as it had commenced. Kinnear with a bloody mouth and a ripped shirt front was standing in the centre of the arena like a sculptor's effort to symbolize the noble art of self-defence. Before the shoulders and science and the terrifying professional taciturnity of the boxer Molphy flanked by the hard knuckles of the two fishermen, the four leather jackets had broken and fled. One of them summoned the police who tactfully lingered until the victors had abandoned the well-fought field. On behalf of Edmund, Jeff was accepting payment from the showman and, with the most elaborate gestures, was insisting on single notes counted out one by one to the applause of the gallery. When the red curtain parted and Maeve, wildly laughing, came into the

174

bull-ring I moved two paces to go to meet her and then halted as if the one good blow a leather jacket had caught me on the side of the head, had stunned me and set my brain buzzing. For between me and my Queen stood the Red Boxer mopping his nose on his sleeve with a gesture I once saw Jack Dempsey use in a newsreel.

'Red's a hero,' she said. 'Red's my hero.'

The hero, I thought, is grey stone by the river. But her squat hands I could see on his slow, silent shoulders and I could hear her half-laughing and half sobbing and saying again and again 'Red's a hero. Red's my hero.'

'We all helped,' said one of the fishermen.

'It was a right fight,' said the second fisherman.

'Strategy,' said Jeff. 'And numbers.'

'Red's a hero,' she said. 'Red's my hero.'

'The struggle is over,' said Jeff. 'The foe is defeated. The day is ours. Beautiful Edmund's heart is so full of emotion he forgot to say thanks.'

'He wouldn't know how,' said Kinnear.

'Red's a hero,' she said.

Her squat fingers rose and fell on those motionless shoulders. They were fungoid growths on rounded Segully rocks.

'It was all for the old land,' said Jeff, 'and not for gain or the praise of men.'

'Red's my boy,' she said.

The Red Boxer, without turning towards us, mumbled something and clumsily disembarrassed himself of her hands and of her face, the proud face of my Bingen queen, which must have been nesting somewhere on the broad savannahs of that fantastic yellow sweater. He moved stiffly as Frankenstein's monster towards the curtained entrance.

'Oh, Owen,' she said.

She came towards us, excited, laughing, her hair tousled and not tousled.

'Oh, Jeff,' said Jeff. 'Oh, James.'

'A drink,' said James.

Rudely he spat blood. He turned his back on Maeve.

In the hotel bar when she had excused herself and headed for the powder-room he rinsed blood out of his mouth with water, then drank his large whiskey in one slow sliding draught. Jeff surveyed the sole sad survivor, now advanced in years and infinitely lugubrious, of the colony of cobalt-and-crimson spiny-backed Japanese fish.

'The soulful expression,' he said, 'of the boxer Molphy.'

'The boxer,' he said, 'would have been bashful in our elegant society.'

Kinnear said nothing.

'Edmund's an ungrateful, bearded bastard,' Jeff said.

I said nothing.

'No comment,' said Jeff.

'I'll have another drink,' said Kinnear.

'She drinks gin and orange,' I said.

'So be it,' said Jeff. 'A gin and orange and three large whiskies.'

Edmund without doubt was an ungrateful, bearded bastard but he had behind him the sympathy of lakeside and countryside, of the city and the two villages, when he returned early one morning, bearing a shotgun, to the patriot's village and expended seven cartridges in the air over the wall of death. The showman, sunning himself in the delusively peaceful air of our hospitable land, saw the bearded vision in linen jacket approaching with the measured step of his father combined with the menacing step of the Ringo Kid. He leaped to conclusions about the gun, rabbited up the steps into his caravan where his lady companion, in *déshabille*, was wiping the sleep from her eyes, and cried out: 'My God, that lunatic is going to shoot me.' (The circumstances of that morning and those dramatic words were later reported in full in our two local newspapers.) The showman phoned the police and since the matter had been taken to the arbitrament of the gun the police were forced to act.

In court Edmund swore he was shooting at rooks and three villagers swore with him, adding a rider to the effect that the rooks were particularly rapacious that year and a menace to the crops. Three other villagers, with what might have seemed to the showman a lack of relevance, swore that the hurdy-gurdy noises were a disturbance to the peace of the village and that an octogenarian, bedridden widow hadn't closed an eye in sleep since the erection of the death wall. It was also proved, and here the showman must have experienced a vertigo that never afflicted him when he himself was a hell-rider, that he had imperilled the peace by trying to welsh on a money agreement and that Edmund was the son of a lamented father and a member of a respectable family. To give the matter ecclesiastical sanction the local parish priest testified that the showpeople were a disturbing influence in the locality. He based his testimony on the fact, not stated in court, that the showman's lady companion wore tight red trousers, looked like a holiday friendship in the Isle of Man, and was not legally or sacramentally united with the showman.

The case was dismissed. In Irish legal annals it was never, even in Kinnear's expert knowledge, again equalled, until in the County Clare two members of Judge Rutherford's overzealous witnesses were bound to the peace for being assaulted. The showman departed for England possibly with a lifelong doubt about the efficacy of law. A sub-editor on one of our local papers wrote as a heading: 'Scion of noted family shoots over showground with shotgun.' To this day, I am told, Edmund Conway Chesney is known as The Scion.

Francis Conway Chesney, taller, more thin, hollow-jawed, more pimpled, nervous from constraint, promising well in the strictly delimited world of Irish clerical scholarship, was not amused. In the sultry dusk, the whatnot hidden in shadows, Fee with a hammer tinkling like a leprechaun in the captain's private smithy, the sounds of the river and sea two contrasting, metallic monotones, he leaned his elbow on the marble mantelpiece, slightly displacing the serpent, and disapproved. To Alfred, to Edmund, to Maeve and myself he said: 'I could be told about all this in Dublin when Doctor Grierson and myself were returning from Lourdes.'

With dubious and gloomy pride Alfred said: 'We were the talk of the country.'

'What will my classmates say,' said Frank, 'when I go back to Maynooth?'

Edmund, a Cistercian with beard and white linen, intoned: '*Per omnia saecula saeculorum.*'

Frank's pale, bony brow was moist with perspiration. Behind the ridge of Segully there was a rumble and a purple sky and thunder in the air. Frank touched the snake. He said: 'It doesn't help a clerical student to have relatives appearing in the police court.'

'The Court acquitted me,' said Edmund. 'Neither should thou nor any man condemn me.'

Maeve giggled. She said: 'Go thy way and shoot no more.'

'That's no way to abuse the scriptures,' Frank said.

For the first and last time I saw the hot flush of blood in his sallow cheeks.

'Oh, Frank,' she said, 'for goodness' sake. It was all fun. Ask Owen. You'll believe Owen. Owen was in it. Owen got a shiner. He's boasting about it since to the customers in Grainger's. It's as good as a bathroom to every bedroom.'

She tightened her arms around her stomach and, her legs wide on the low end of a couch where she sat, bent in no lady's laughter. Then Francis cracked in hysteria and all the years of abasement in that kitchen, all the rigid listening for the approaching, metronomical steps and the orders of the day, all the horror of saying 'Yes, father' to a dragon, all the tension of the cold college, came out in a scream: 'Fun! Fun! Fun! I'll be the laughing stock. Fun! Fun! What would our father say if he was alive?'

'Attenshun!' said Edmund.

He stood up and clicked his heels. He paced up and down the room. He was General Gordon surveying the Chinese. He was the captain as I had seen him the morning I peered peeping down from the loft above the black stallion.

'That's what our father would say,' said Edmund. 'Attenshun. Form fours. Slope arms.'

'That's enough,' growled Alfred.

Low in the armchair, in which so long ago the captain had discussed the Dorans and necromancy, the new master of Bingen uneasily moved his ungainly limbs and growled like a grizzly.

'"My son and a skivvy,"' said Edmund. '"My son and a skivvy." That's what he would say. "Out to the stable, Alfred. If you want to live like an animal live with the animals."'

'That's enough,' said Alfred.

'Look at him,' said Edmund. 'Look at the heir and the eldest.'

He pointed at Alfred. His beard was aggressive. Maeve laughed.

'Creeping about,' said Edmund, 'like a weasel in the woods above, after a country whore isn't in her right wits.'

'Edmund,' said Francis, 'your sister is present. Stop that language.'

'Stop your holy mouth. She hears worse from the boxer Molphy, that is if he's able to talk at all.'

'That's enough,' said Alfred.

'You,' said Edmund. 'Your father's son in the gripe with the sailor Brannigan's sister who hasn't come to the use of reason or the age of consent.'

'No more of that,' Frank said.

'Attenshun,' said Edmund. 'Form fours. No one will ever say attention to me again, your reverence. Not you or the President of Maynooth or the Archbishop of Dublin or the Pope of Rome. Not king, kaiser or cardinal.'

Slowly Alfred sat up straight in his chair, his great clumsy hands on his knees, and Edmund, I knew, was the nasty, cowardly boy who, on one horrible day, had blurted out, in order to save his own hide, the springtime secret of dancing Rosie.

'If our good father,' he said, 'had let him marry the skivvy he might be a normal human being . . .'

Then in fear he stepped back a pace, for Alfred had stood up, huge and stooped against the window and the last light. His voice shook and, God help us, there were tears in his eyes. He said: 'Edmund, if you had kept your rotten mouth shut I might never have lost Rosie.

'And listen to me,' he said, 'no hairy molly like you' (and with his two hands he gripped Edmund by the blond beard) 'is going to talk like that to me in my own house.'

The scream of pain and anger that came from Edmund must have penetrated to the stableyard and the smithy for I remember as I moved in to separate them and, alas, to collect a second shiner about which I could not boast, that the leprechaun tinkling of Fee abruptly ceased. There were four of us, three lay and one cleric, struggling like madmen before the baleful serpent's gaze, and the captain's ghost darting in and out among us like a diabolized Ariel, and Alfred shaking Edmund by the beard until flesh, blood and hair could stand no more and the bulk of its blond beauty came unstuck in his hands, and Edmund screaming and cursing blue and flailing at Alfred with hands and feet, and Frank, like a hapless Christ before whom the waves would not be stilled, commanding his brothers to cease from strife, and Maeve flat on her back on the couch pealing laughter at the high ceiling, and the door suddenly opening and Greta standing there in dark frock and nurse's white apron, and Edmund's chin like a war-devastated wheat-field splotched with the blood of uprooted heroes. She made no comment on the odd tableau she witnessed. She said: 'It's time, isn't it, to light the lamp? There's thunder.'

'I'm sorry, Owen,' Frank said, 'you had to witness this.'

'Owen doesn't mind,' Maeve said. 'Owen's one of us.'

'The boxer Molphy,' I said, 'would be more use in a crisis.'

She stopped laughing. Greta said: 'Owen, my mother would like to see you before you go.'

By the old woman's babbling bed Greta, sitting close to me, placed her hand on my arm. It was an olive hand, slender and beautiful. Her wrist was delicate and light. Never before, although I had touched it that day in the cinema with Lucy, had I noticed that hand. On her white apron there were a few strands of her dark hair fallen like rich, strong shreds of metal. She whispered: 'She's very failed, Owen.'

An old mountainy man, a friend of my father, had once boasted that he would defy death until he was no bigger than a rook with old age, and in that hardy land of sea, mountain and lake where men and women lived long, I had seen old people still active but shrunk by age to half their size, and I was accustomed to dead, placid, yellow faces in the candle-light of wake-houses. But that fragment of a woman, pale as silver, sunk in deep pillows, her withered limbs not even rumpling the covers, terrified me at first. Momentarily, to reassure myself that flesh was solid and real, I touched the lovely, olive hand that rested on my arm. Pale eyes, no colour any longer discernible in their pupils, turned towards me and Greta whispered: 'Sometimes, Owen, she doesn't recognize people any more. She rambles. Yesterday she thought Edmund was our father.

'Sometimes,' she whispered, 'she totters downstairs and wants tea and then changes her mind and wants milk and refuses to go to bed. Two nights ago Alfred had to carry her back to her room.'

From the hollow of the pillows an old weary voice spoke and, our heads together, we bent to listen.

'Are you talking about him, Greta?'

'No, mother.'

'None of you liked him. None of you knew him.'

'This is Owen, mother. He came to see you.'

By the warmth of her blushing face I knew that the old woman had not asked to see me, that apart from milk or tea or death she would never again ask for anybody or anything.

'Owen,' she said. 'Is that Owen Rodgers you mean?'

'Yes, mother.'

'He's a good boy. He was always a good friend to my children.'

'He still is, mother.'

'I'm told he's doing well in the hotel business.'

'Yes, mother.'

'They say his father's very severe on him. It isn't good when the father's too severe.'

Her eyes closed again. She sank deeper into the pillows. We sat close together until the room was in warm summer darkness. We had nothing to say to each other. She was only a white glimmer of linen even when we rose and I followed her out of the room, along the dark corridor and down the stairs to the hallway where the lamp was lighted. The tale of a glorious end was gone from the wall. In some shadowy corner of an attic or stable loft the officer with the wounded arm would, wordless, tell his epic forever to the weeping mother, the tremulous sister, the fine old father with the stiff upper lip. Until Bingen fell, the dead hero's sword, dusty, rusty and forgotten, would lie across the table between his portrait and a vase of flowers.

'Maeve's taken a cleaning fit,' Greta said. 'She says she'll brighten this place or die.'

'She brightens the place.'

'She wanted to get rid of the snake and the whatnot, but Alfred stopped her.'

'Alfred's a powerful man.'

Francis was somewhere at his prayers. Edmund, smarting in beardless wrath, had gone back on his motor-bicycle to the city. Alfred was sulking somewhere in the farmyard and Maeve was nowhere to be seen.

'I'll walk to the car with you, Owen,' Greta said.

'No, Greta. Your mother needs you.'

The night was sultry. West of Segully on the dark hills there was the glow of a heather fire, the long red line stabbed now and again by black shadows as if the Dorans and all the dead and the ancient, long-suppressed, elemental spirits of Magheracolton were dancing in malevolence around a Sabbath fire above the chaos that had descended on the captain's too-well-ordered house. My mind was agonized by the absence and strangeness of Maeve, by wonder at her unreasonable hysterical laughter. I wasn't considering the old woman or Greta. I didn't want Greta with me. She was in the background, a white-aproned hospital nurse saying meaningless, routine words as you walked back down the interminable, heartless ward in which your best friend had just died.

Six

A HOT JUNE IS A BAD MONTH FOR JEALOUSY, BECAUSE
jealousy is death and in a hot June life is everywhere. The
green scum on the fringe of Thread the Needle, pulled up
and tousled by the sun, burst into flower. Wide, pulpy pads
of water-lilies appeared mysteriously on the black water. The
two cygnets grew proudly and were proudly attended. The
wild ducks and their brood vanished magically to some open
sunny lake. Thread the Needle drew me then as the dank
bog lake near our village drew the occasional sad people who
decided to drown themselves. You can see life better in a
swamp than in a clear running river, for life grows out of
refuse and dirt, out of matter ejected and rejected by the
perspiring body. Over gin in the city's one little select lounge
bar, as far away as I could get from Grainger's and sober
responsibility, Jeff laughed and coughed as if he had the croup
and said: 'Well, love's wonderful. Owen, you're transformed.
Philosophy in the shape of Owen Rodgers has followed re-
ligion in the shape of George Brownwig Grainger into the
hotel business.'

'Plankton,' I said, 'is the dirt of the sea, and sour youghourt
and all the curds and wheys and crawling cheeses are dearly
bought to varnish the walls of rich bellies. To nourish the beef
tapeworm. Shall I tell you about the beef tapeworm?'

'By no means.'

He raised his glass.

'Among the rampant weeds,' he said, 'according to the Japanese poet, the elegant is smothered.'

Among the rampant weeds, God knows, my elegant dream was smothered and the horror was that I had nothing tangible to protest about, could not even say exactly why or where jealousy had begun. In a moment of hysteria she had been kind to the red boxer Molphy. Twice she had not been where I had expected her to be, yet my mad suspicions had collapsed from lack of proof. But the devil helped me to feel something, to hear something. A shadow, inexplicable in the universal sunlight, came over her. She looked east when she should have looked west and hell was between us. In the city shops the young women bought by the score coloured dresses and yards and yards of coloured cloth. They washed themselves in the sea and soaked in the sun. They showed brown shoulders in buses or on the Diamond Hill, and I looked at them with as much indifference as if they were roast pork which I've always disliked since I read of Grossman, the Berlin murderer, who sold hot-dogs outside a railway station, chose as his victims fresh servant-girls newly arrived from rural Germany and, waste not, want not ('Practical people the Germans, Owen,' said the captain), baked them into material for more than usually phallic hot-dogs.

Miserable over my drink in that same select lounge bar, I hid myself in a corner and waited, hoping that she might enter with someone else and give me reason for my inexplicable agony. Once, when she rang me at the hotel, failed to find me and left a number for me to ring back, I went feverishly from number to number in the book, a man lost in a jungle, hoping to find that she was ringing me from some incriminating place, thinking I should bribe the exchange operator to tell me where it was. In a celebrated crim. con. case a husband in our city had once used bribery in order to interrupt a telephone conversation not meant for his ears. After thirty minutes of that lunacy it dawned on me from an inspection of the digits that it was a public call-box. She was standing somewhere on the street, waiting, and when I rang, there she was and oh, so sweetly reminded me I was to be in Bingen next Saturday. But when I cycled, taking the June air, to Bingen, the great house was empty: no Maeve or Greta, no servant, male or female. Alfred was probably in the hazel woods and Edmund had not revisited the place since his drastic depilation. The June grass on the great green burned my feet. How I was mocked by the warm content of calves in the right-angled nook of a colony of haystacks. The river and the sea were asleep and the dazzle of the sun from a sky of lead was painful. I fingered the footbridge that betrayed the only friend I had had in that house, crossed it, hoping it would crack under me, walked upstream the way Frank, Hughie and myself had walked on a famous day, and looked uncomprehendingly at the bare back of a woman, naked to the waist, who lay face down, sunbathing in the long grass by Edmund's diving-board.

She said: 'I know it's you, Owen. I know your step.'

Her voice was muffled by grass and earth.

'If you're looking for Maeve,' she said, 'she's not here. She was called away. Suddenly.'

'Who called her?'

It seemed the most natural thing in the world to sit down be-side her.

'Nine men,' she said, 'or maybe it was only three. They had hair enough on their faces to do for nine.'

'Beverley was one,' I said.

At least I had a clue.

'Wasn't she expecting me?'

'She didn't say.'

'It wasn't only Beverley,' she said. 'He was there but there were others.'

Sitting and smoking I saw vaguely the curl of the soft cloth of underwear around her naked waist above the loosened band of her skirt. Across the river the whiteness of Kate Carr's cottage leaped at me from the hazel wood.

'Owen,' she said, 'don't blame Maeve. She'll go anywhere she's asked to go.'

Across the river on a living day of wild showers, wind and leaping trout, Kate and Hughie had sung about mountain lovers.

'Owen,' she said, 'I like your company but my shoulders are beginning to roast. My mother'll be awake soon and needing her medicine. If you wait for me at the footbridge I'll dress.'

Together, her breasts covered that had been naked in the late June grass, we crossed the fatal footbridge. Through long dusky corridors in a ghostly house I carried the tray for her, stood at the door of the sickroom while she spooned medicine to her murmuring mother, drank with her in the basement kitchen, and noseless Fee the jockey came in from somewhere and drank tea with us; and I was back in my father's house (where I was stopping for the night) by my own sick mother's bedside before I fully realized that that voice from the grass and those lovely brown shoulders were Greta Conway Chesney.

Two days later it was July. The weather cracked in rain and thunder. The river steamed. The little boys with patched pants were listless on the river wall. In the haze shabby tramp-steamers came and went like lugubrious ghosts. In the dusk the trees along the river rustled like silk and from the two high rooms old George had left to me when he moved out to a new house in the suburbs, I could hear the noise of the little city like the faraway mumur of the Bingen sea. The lights in the step-by-step streets across the river were lines of rising stars. But up in those rooms I was as lonely as a lighthouse-keeper, and Jeff and James were always to be found in some dockside pub carousing, until all was blue, as a preliminary to their return, without me, to Dublin and study. Then one foul night, unnaturally dark because of the low sky, Jeff said with the decision of the surgeon who has decided to operate and have done with it: 'If you want to find her, Owen, she's gone to take a boxing lesson.'

Kinnear sucked his thin lips, looked at his pale face in the fly-spotted mirror behind the bar, said nothing, and because I was drunk I went searching for her for the last time. The city was hunchbacked above me to the left. It was a night for monsters and deformity. From the city end of the big bridge I could see that tide and brown flood-water, meeting and quarrelling, had seeped up into the abandoned grass before Lovers' Bastion. A train whistled in from the south and for a while the crowd debouching from the railway station absorbed and comforted me. Then I was a dreary pilgrim in a long street of half-empty warehouses and, under my feet, the muddy, slippery stone sets were criss-crossed with dockside railway tracks and pitted with viscous puddles. Down in that swamp, in a warehouse left empty as the port decayed, was the gym where the boxer Molphy and his colleagues skipped, pushed, pranced, feinted, shadow-boxed, deep-breathed, sparred and hammered the heads off each other. Because the boxer's hopes and the city's pride in him were rising for the coming competition ('Red's my hero,' said the maiden city, 'Red's my boy') the shabby place had become sacrosanct in the eyes of the followers of the noble game. To add to the difficulty of gaining admission a flock of dung-tartled bleating sheep on the way to the boats and slaughter and a state of mutton in the English Midlands blocked my way for a full five minutes while I stood under the rusted framework of an idle crane and the rain from its desolate, unwanted arm dropped red on my hat. You went up a steep stair-way, dirt grinding underfoot, the jumps and bumps and punch-ball blows of men in training resounding overhead. You hammered for eternity at a closed door and when at last it opened an embrocated, bald, toothless doorman, towel around his neck, bare forearms tattooed, said: 'No admission except Press or on business. What do you want, mister?'

'A message,' I said, 'for Miss Chesney.'

The door slammed in my face. The metronomical bumping continued. Five minutes later a small boy with a shock of brick-red hair opened the door and said: 'You're allowed in, mister.'

There was my queen, in slacks and rainproof and a wine scarf like the wine skirt on her head, waiting for me in a vestibule illustrated with crouching pictures of every monster from Corbett to Carnera.

'Oh, Owen,' she said, 'I was hoping you'd come. Come in and see the fun.'

Outside, in mud and warm rain, bleating sheep went docilely to the slaughter. She linked her arm in mine and led me on, the French perfume I had given her struggling with rank odours of sweat and embrocation. There, red as Jezebel before my eyes, was the great arse of the boxer Molphy, straining fit to burst his silken, crimson knickers, his leg muscles standing out like steel ropes, his bare torso bent down at right angles and steaming like the river as shoulder-to-shoulder he and a sallow, wiry training partner pushed and grunted like bulls with locked horns deciding a gentleman's claim to the most delectable cow. One light featherweight of a fellow made shapes at himself before a long mirror. Far away in shadows, out of the blazing ring of billiard-saloon lights, four or five athletes rhythmically skipped and addressed punchballs. But the other thirty or forty men in the place, in various stages of dress and undress, stood in a semi-circle and watched as devotees might watch the showing-forth of a god. She held my arm tightly and pulled me closer to her, but since every fool must come at some time or other to the first glimmerings of bitter wisdom, I was afraid to look at her face. Anyway the scarlet monster fascinated me, if not, perhaps, exactly as he fascinated her or his male admirers. That stiff body, that bullish head and slow, uncomprehending face had suddenly assumed beauty, speed, wisdom and mastery. He ceased pushing, stood up, extended his arms. Two acolytes tied on his gloves. Two more mopped him with towels. A fifth inserted a gum-shield. I waited for the watching semi-circle to burst into a Latin chant. For five minutes he inhaled and exhaled.

'Watch him,' said one of the worshippers.

He gripped my free arm but he was talking ecstatically to the world.

'Just watch him. Red's a beauty. He breathes,' said the worshipper, 'with his brain. Red's our boy.'

So this was where she had learned her phrases. She held my arm as if it was the only arm in the world and there was no denying that sparring with three partners, one after the other and once with two together, hissing through his gum-shield, exercising attack and defence, light as air on his toes and long in his flexible arms, he was a beauty, a ram worthy of any rosette that the dead captain, a judge of rams, could have pinned on him.

'He'll win,' she said. 'He's certain to win. I'm so glad you came, Owen. I want you to drive me home.'

'Good-night, Red,' she said. 'Keep it up. Be a champ.'

'Best of luck, Red,' said another worshipper. 'The city's proud of you.'

Reverent hands draped his body, glowing and giving out heat like a watchman's brazier, with a dressing-gown. In the crowd she was suddenly torn away from me or she slackened her hold and the Red boxer, moving towards his sacristy of a dressing-room while the devotees stood around to touch the hem of his vestment, kissed her as he passed full on the lips, and the tattooed man with the bald head said: 'Training, Red, training, there's a time and place for everything.'

At the bottom of the stairs, the wet street before me, I heard her steps rapidly descending and following, her voice calling: 'Owen, wait, wait.' But I walked on, not turning my head, for twenty yards before she overtook me.

'What's wrong, Owen? Don't you want to drive me home?'

'Yourself and your elegant friends. I was in the way.'

'Don't be a boy, Owen. You're never in the way. You were always with us.'

'I'm not always with you.'

'Do you want to be? Don't mind the boys in there,' she said. 'They mean no harm.'

'Bloody shower of thugs.'

'Language, Owen, dearest. Oh, they're not clever like Jeff Macsorley and yourself. They don't read books. Don't walk so fast, Owen. You'll pull my arm out of its socket. I wouldn't marry one of them. But they're good fun. If you walk on like that with a long face I'll think you don't want to leave me home. And I love you, Owen. Really I do.'

'What about Beverley?'

'Oh, he's just fun. But you're always there, Owen.'

'Like the snake and the skull and the whatnot, you can't get rid of me.'

'That snake it gives me the creeps. There's something not nice about snakes. But you're nice, Owen, and if I was as nice as you and owned a whole hotel I'd ask a girl in for a cup of tea before driving her all that cold way home. Old George would offer me champagne.'

'It's very late. Alfred will be worried about you.'

'Alfred? Oh, Owen, you kill me.'

Her laughter had the sound it had the day of the hellish scuffle in Bingen. She swung round to face me, held me by both arms, kissed me with the lips the boxer had kissed and said twice over: 'Poor worried Alfred. Oh, Owen.'

The joke was still living, although her laughter was the silent laughter that made her bite her lips and set her shoulders shaking, as we went up in the lift. We walked along corridors with shoes, disembodied feet, outside doorways, a feature of the hotel business that has always seemed to me uncanny, to the upper room. The fire burned bright. The light slanted gently from two shaded table-lamps. The bottles were in the sideboard and the night porter ready and willing to carry up tea for two and to see that my car was waiting at the door below. With curtains drawn, glasses, china, and cutlery catching the glint of the firelight, Jimmy the night porter who came from near Bingen stopping a while to chat, the incoming tide rhythmically lapping the river wall, that room was a pleasant place. Owen Rodgers who was a hotelier just because at a crucial moment he had seen this woman seeming relevant at the doorway into that bedroom, should have been a happy man. Yet although I had known her since she was a shadow in a cave, although I loved her and she said she loved me, there was a painful silence between us when Jimmy had descended to his duties. After the last cry, the last struggle on the surface, it must be that drowning people go to death in silence, clutching at phantasms, grasping only yielding water. For five minutes in that deformed night she was water in my hands, yielding and opening out so easily that modest Owen, the prig, who had never seen himself as the masterful lover, knew such sweet consent was not for him, or not for him alone. She said: 'Are you afraid, Owen? What could you be afraid of?'

Safe on the surface, at the far side of the fire, rescued from the last fatal immersion, my hands around my glass were sweating, but how could I tell her I was afraid she would cry out: 'Darlint, darlint.'

'You don't want me, Maeve. You want other people.'

'What must I do? Send you a gilt invitation card?'

'Why do you go to a place like that gym?'

'Why shouldn't I?'

'It's no place for the like of you.'

'What am I like?'

'It's no place for a woman.'

'Oh, Owen, stop talking. Come here.'

But I swam away from her towards the shore.

'That tie,' I said.

My glass, with a life of its own, like the water diviner's hazel rod, twisted in my hands.

'That necktie you used to tie your slacks with, it belonged to Kinnear.'

'So what? Kinnear's nice. He's your friend.'

'In this room before old George moved out I found a scarf that belonged to you.'

Her Bingen laughter mocked me.

'The boy's jealous,' she said. 'Whip the wig off old George and you'll find the marks of my lipstick on his bald pate. Hughie Heron will be my next love. Hughie does love me in a nice way. Old George just likes the way I smell.'

'The boxer kissed you. You went with Beverley when you were to wait for me. Paradise,' I said grandly, 'was made for one man.'

For one shivering moment the water and death by drowning almost tempted me from my safety on the far shore but that was the moment that she, or the powers of hell, picked for her to throw her drink in my face, to struggle into her coat while I sat cold and motionless, to say to me, almost to scream: 'On my hands and knees I'd walk home, Owen Rodgers, before I'd take a lift from you.'

From her slamming of my door to the ringing of my telephone a half-hour must have passed. The drink had dried on my face. I sat where she had left me. I thought: 'If it's that woman on the phone I'll cut her off. I'm a fool no longer.'

It was her brother, Alfred. He said: 'Is Maeve with you, Owen? I'm ringing from home.

'Frank's here,' he said, 'and Edmund. Everybody but Maeve. Is she with you?'

I lied that she was with me. I said: 'What's wrong?'

'Her mother's dying, Owen. Bring her home quickly.'

'I will,' I said. 'This instant.'

'Edmund,' he said, 'is to drive over the mountain for Dr Grierson. You may meet him in the village.'

She was waiting alone and silently in the lounge. She was, even in her fury, too shrewd to go trudging the twelve miles home to Bingen. Silently we drove up the empty streets past the cathedral, on into the dark countryside, then by the eel weir and the patriot's bridge with the vast lake spreading restless and unseen away to the west. When the lights of my own village were visible a mile ahead I rested my hand on her arm. But she was motionless, unresponsive, no longer weak water. She was frozen to ice. She was stone. The lips that a while ago had opened as if she was tormented by hunger were clipped together in a hard, loveless line. When I told her her mother was dying she only said: 'She's been dying for a long time. Longer than you know. Before you ever saw her. When we used to watch you like an old, wise man listening to our father.'

'I never felt wise.'

'She had Greta to nurse her,' she said.

Then she was silent again, ignoring me.

There were six or seven people huddled together at our gate, gossiping around Edmund's car, as we came down the slope into the village, and in the drawing-room, surrounded by the band, silent and sympathetic, the bright instruments discarded and grotesque, Edmund, his beard rehabilitated, was delivering his message to Dr Grierson and my father. The doctor travelled with me to Bingen, stopping at his house to collect the viaticum and holy oils, but Maeve went ahead with her brother. Lucy, as far as I remember, was one of the gossiping group at the gate. The bronze head of Maeve, my dream, was reduced to a dark silhouette picked out by the headlights of my car as we mounted the Gap road to the Rest and be Thankful Spring.

'You young people, I suppose,' said the doctor, 'were happily dancing?'

He had been long enough with the band and my father's bottle to be at his most talkative.

'We were at the pictures,' I said. 'A boxing picture.'

'In the midst of life we are in death,' he said. 'It seems the old woman wandered out of the house when Greta, that good girl, was attending Lizzie Heron who's ill.'

Alfred, he told me, had come running to Hughie Heron's cottage in the murk of the late afternoon and wailed like a child: 'She's gone, she's gone, my mother's gone.'

With Hughie and Gortin Lass and black Macillion he searched the paths and fields around the place, looked with dread on the high river, found her gathering brambles, like any old cottier's wife or woman of the roads, in a deep meadow that was still uncut because of the wet weather. She was on her way, she said, to see Kate Carr, and, wet and shivering and talking nonsense to herself, they brought her home and Greta vainly tried to hoard the frail little spark of life that remained to her.

'In the midst of life,' the doctor repeated, 'we are in death. This country, Owen, is much possessed by death. The dark days. The rain. The funereal black beer. The cheerless, hopeless Sunday sermons.

'On the question of death and sermons,' he said, 'I had a set-to this week with Higher Authority.'

'I heard that sermon.'

'On a Sunday morning of rain and offshore wind,' he said, 'which is unpleasant in these parts. You can't even smell the clean sea. And style. Have you studied Higher Authority's inimitable style?'

'A little, father.'

'Bourdaloue. With perhaps a soupçon of Lacordaire. "As the great Newman says," is his favourite opening phrase, and then he emits a noise like one of his own prize bulls bellowing. Do I disedify you, Owen?'

'No, doctor.'

'In our student days we are taught to edify the laity.

'Offshore wind,' he said, 'and rain, wet coats, dripping noses, Irish misery on every face among the faithful, myself eaves-dropping in the sacristy, and the topic of the day is the miracu-lous raising of the daughter of Jairus. That, dear brethren, says Higher Authority, was a great miracle. I imitate his style, Owen, to the best of my ability. The like of that miracle, says he, doesn't happen nowadays because none of you have the faith of Jairus. And there's another great miracle in the gospel: the raising of the widow's son of Naim. A poor widow like any of you with the pension, and the Lord listened to her because she had faith. And there's a third great miracle: the raising of Lazarus who was already four days dead and, according to the words of holy writ, stinking.

'Now, thought I in the sacristy, this is his chance to talk to wet coats and watery noses about life and hope and resurrection. Does he do it?'

'I was there,' I said.

'You'll all die, Higher Authority said. Whether you know it or not, you'll all die. That's the one thing you're sure of. How many of you sat there in those seats fifty years ago when I came to this parish as a curate? Death is certain. And after death, the judgement. So, lay not up for yourselves treasures. The collection today will be for the new chapel of ease in the townland of Killeter. And when, Owen, I argued with him about life, death, resurrection and the state of this rain-soaked island he said to me: Grierson, with your foreign notions, are you a Catholic curate or a Protestant heretic or a freethinker? The craze for pleasure has this country ruined.

'Death, Owen,' said the doctor, 'is all around us.

'Ahead of us and under the mountains the woman was dying who had spattered red sauce like thick blood on the Boer War captain and who for nine months had carried my lost Maeve in the security of her womb.

'Even over my beloved lake,' he said, 'the pall of death has fallen since those four young people were drowned in the hired pleasure boat. Foolish, inexpert young people who didn't know one end of a boat from the other, or the wind or the moods of the lake. In any other country in the world they'd get better boats

198

and teach young people how to handle them. Here, the man who hires out the boats won't hire them out any more. Young people no longer go boating on the lake. No more picnics on the islands. Barring the colonels and the long-line fishermen and myself, the silence of dust and ashes is even over my lake.'

By the time we rattled over the grid of the cowgate the whiskey talkativeness had gone from him. All the windows in the house were lighted. The door was open as it had been the day the river took the captain. The old woman died quietly, the doctor and Greta by her bedside, the blessed candle in her hand, her senses soothed with holy oil, the rest of us silent in the background in the musty room. The only one of that strange quintet who showed the conventional signs of sorrow was Alfred. There were tears on his face when he shook hands with me and thanked me for my friendship over the years. Edmund, man of business, had gone back to the city while the doctor and myself were refreshing ourselves by the drawing-room snake. By candlelight Frank prayed quietly by the bedside, his sallow, pimply face almost as thin and hollow-jawed as the dead face of the captain's wife. In eternity would they ever meet? Was it better for her to to be born and damned to meet the captain than not to be born at all? From Greta and Maeve I had the cold, wordless handshakes they had given me in the basement kitchen that evening long ago of the sheep dog trials.

That wet July, too, with the rain steady on the moored desolate boats that, because of tragic death, were no longer hired out for pleasure, my own mother died. One midnight she said to me: 'Leave my bedroom door open, Owen, so I can hear the chiming clock tell the quarters.'

The familiar, mellow clock chimed away time. The breast

cancer ate away her life. I motored back through wet darkness to the two high rooms I had grown so morosely to hate.

To Dr Grierson the day before she died, she said, in one lucid, undrugged interval: 'Should we call you doctor or father?'

'After all these years,' he said, 'of calling me both. Said as you say it, Mrs Rodgers, father means a priest of God. A doctor is just a man who has read too many books. Call me anything, Mrs Rodgers. But count me a friend and pray for me.'

Lucy cried in our house and at the funeral as normal women cry at funerals, as if she had lost her own mother, but neither in the house nor the church nor the graveyard do I remember seeing any of the Chesneys. Ever afterwards the band practised in MacElhatton's crowded house and sometimes my father went to join them. But mostly he sat alone drinking, or with Dr Grierson drinking, and played few tunes, and dust gathered on the ocarina. That's one way for love to end.

Lucy's tears over my mother's coffin had no power to draw me into community with her, to hale me back out of loneliness. Lucy, even in tears and even at such a time, was still half comic, half repellent. When the skies cleared again and we returned to the interrupted summer, and bare brown shoulders were visible again in the city, I saw her one day on the Diamond Hill. She didn't see me. North to south, I was descending from the Virgin Victory to the Guildhall Gate. East to west, she sailed past under my bows. She wore a summer frock so revealing that from my superior altitude a considerable portion of her soft, ample breasts was visible. The vision in my black mood reminded me of nothing. On her dimpled face was the strangest, most childish, self-absorbed smile. Viciously I thought that in her peahen mind was the idea: 'Everybody's looking at me and I'm lovely.' To stir such stupid unconcern into the basic animal life, the customary twitches, sighs, terms of endearment sobbed upwards since time began to plunging, sweating males, would—or would it be?—to know power. That was the state of mind of Owen Rodgers recently curdled by the deceits of love. Lucy walked by so close to him that he could have stuck out his tongue and touched her plump, rose-petal cheek, or shouted in her ear or patted her bottom as the daemon of the dead captain prompted him to do.

'In one of the houses of the Reeperbahn of Hamburg, Owen. Where the sailors go for amusement. You'll see the place when you travel. Beautifully organized like everything in Germany. The waitresses have square low cuts in the front of their frocks to show their breasts.'

The waxed points of his moustache were gleeful as goat's horns at my virgin, pre-Dublin Lass embarrassment.

'Spherical cuts in the rear,' he said, 'to show their bee oh tee toms. Occasionally a customer, you know what sailors are, pats a behind and the girl cries, all in fun of course: 'die Raub'. That's the German, Owen, for assault. It's part of the service, like the table napkins and the cutlery. Elegant and highly organized.'

Comic as a Reeperbahn waitress with her tail-end on view, Lucy sailed on like Columbus towards the west. Owen descended to the south alone, and cold, even in August sunshine, as a pinnacle or crevasse in the vastness of Antarctica. Whether to try to annoy me or to assuage some loneliness of her own, Lucy had actually gone so far, Petsie told me, as to keep company for a while with the young master of Bingen, but that brief affair ended, as you would expect an affair between the bandy-legged Austrian dog and the plump daughter of bowls, kettles and hacksaws to end, in ludicrous comedy. The memory of Petsie's

narrative had me laughing in no kind way—what reason had I
to be kind?—as I went up in the lift to my eyrie, looked across
the summer river at two visiting warships. Already in the bar
below there were three seagulls, bright-plumaged hens who
followed the big ships from port to port, knowing by some
instinct when the men roll ashore with full pockets and fresh
ideas. Over the house phone I advised the chief barman to keep a
particular watch on the propriety of his customers for the wig of
old George would follow his hair at the faintest suggestion of
accosting, even high-priced accosting, on his premises. Courtesy
had limits.

'The day romance ended,' Petsie told me, 'Alfred insisted on
driving the two of us to the glens and lakes away beyond
Segully. At least he insisted on driving Lucy but she wouldn't
go without me.'

Petsie now had long dark hair, a nervous, melancholy face
with cheeks inclined to splotch red and she was beautiful in a
sad, sensible sort of way.

'I'll never forget that day,' she said mournfully. 'It was
hilarious. We drove up and we drove down. We swam in the
lakes. We cut off the engine and free-wheeled down the corkscrew slope to Killeter. We picnicked in the heather and Alfred
chased the two of us as if we were rabbits. He couldn't catch me
but he rugby-tackled Lucy and burst the placket of her skirt as
she fell. It was hilarious. We stayed up there the livelong day.
He had drink in the car too, a French liqueur with slippy bubbles
in it that I've never seen before. Nothing would satisfy him on
the road home but for Lucy to drive and me to sit with him in
the back. Then for me to drive and Lucy to sit in the back.
He's harmless but he's a grizzly bear. The laughs of us in the
evening and the hooting of the horn set the farm dogs barking
around the haysheds. The people at the milking peeped out at

the byre doors. I had the foot down and Lucy was spluttering "Hands off, Alfred", and without thinking I said: "Alfred, if your old father could only see us now." Lucy went on laughing. But Alfred said: "Give me the wheel, I'll drive." He didn't speak from that minute until he left us at home in the village. He left us there on the pavement and barely said good-night. We didn't see him for a full week after that. Never again, not once, did he ask us out in the car with him. He even had the nerve to tell his stiff big sister, Greta, that I couldn't keep my mouth shut for five consecutive seconds.'

Brazen above the laughter of women, the hum of the engine, the barking of dogs from peaceful farms in the August evening, Alfred, haunted man, had heard the early morning bugle at Bingen, the voice of the captain: 'Attenshun, halt, eyes front, hands off Lucy, back to the stable, if you must live like an animal live with the animals.'

'If our good father,' Edmund said, 'had let him marry the skivvy he might be a normal human being.'

Edmund, informer that he was, always the first possessor and willing disseminator of ill news, was willing if called upon to tell clergy and laity about whatever it was that Alfred, like a weasel, was pursuing in the hazel woods beyond Thread the Needle. Indeed, apart from that one comic episode with Lucy and Petsie, Alfred was a slinking creature, a furtive shadow, lurking like a satyr in the trees around the sailor Brannigan's house or haunting like a ghost the patriot's bridge and the vicinity of the mansion where the dancing girl was no longer. There I found him once in the dusk as I drove to see my father. The noise of the weir and the restless lake all around us, we talked uneasily about cattle and crops. He stood stooped by the car when I had cut off the engine. His arms hung down by his sides. He shifted from foot to foot and desperately licked wet lips before every remark.

He was the only contact I had with Bingen for several weeks until Greta, in mourning clothes, trouble in her pale face and dark eyes, a new hair-style with dark fringe hiding her strong brow and giving her head a comically dome-like appearance, came to me in the hotel.

'We haven't seen you in ages, Owen,' she said.

'Work, Greta. I've been very busy.'

'Don't let anything anybody does keep you away from us.'

'Nobody did anything.'

'It was mean of none of us to show up at your mother's funeral. But I was ill. And Frank was away. And the others.'

'I know,' I said. 'Frank sent a telegram of sympathy. When he came back he called to see my father.'

'We need your help, Owen,' she said. 'Alfred's missing for the last two days. Frank's gone back to college. Edmund and Maeve don't care if Alfred was at the bottom of the sea.'

'You mean *you* need my help.'

'Alfred and me,' she said.

Then, high in the upper room, where her gay sister had modelled in a dead woman's clothes and later assaulted the virtue and the dreams of Owen Rodgers, she crumpled, face in hands, in an armchair, sobbed while I stood helpless above her, and said: 'I want a job in the city, Owen. Since my mother died that house is driving me mad. While she lived I had something to do, a reason for staying there. But now. The wind at night and the loneliness. Alfred coming and going like a wild thing out of the jungle. He never speaks to me. Just looks at me and eats so slowly I could scream. The country's talking about him.'

'What about?'

'I thought the world knew. Edmund knows and jeers at it.'

'At what?'

'There's a Brannigan girl that's simple. She's only fourteen but she has a name already. Young Brannigan threatened Alfred the last time he was home from sea. He could as easily threaten a dozen other men but Alfred has money.'

'And Maeve,' I said.

'She's no company for me. She's not often at home in the evenings. I'm sorry, Owen.'

'Rest here,' I said, 'and eat. We'll find Alfred.'

In a bar by the Guildhall Gate the Red boxer told James and Jeff and myself where exactly we would find the vagrant master of Magheracolton.

'If you want to live like an animal,' shouted the captain, 'live with the animals.'

'Boxer,' Jeff said, 'this is no place for you to be in. You're in training. The pride of the city depends on you.'

'I'm drinking orange crush.'

He held up the sickly drink. It was the same colour as his high-necked sweater.

'Shaka, the great Zulu,' said Jeff, 'trained his warriors for battle by enforced chastity and by making them jump bare-footed on thorns. When they stamped their feet the earth shook.'

'You know it all, Mister Macsorley.'

There was an uncanny, underground intimacy between asthmatic Jeff with the hooked nose, sparse sound teeth, lisp and croup-like cough and the stolid, unsmiling, red-faced boxer whose yellow hair, for battle, had been cut in a close prison crop.

'You don't stamp on thorns, boxer?'

'No reason to.'

'But you practise chastity. No visits to Fountain Lane while you're under starter's orders.'

'I live up that way, Mr Macsorley. A lot of decent people do. You'll find a pal of yours there now. Drunk as a lord.'

'Mr Chesney, no less?'

'No names, no pack-drill, Mr Macsorley. He asked me the way to where Maggie the Jennet lives.'

'Zulus,' said Jeff as we climbed the Diamond Hill, 'were a curious people. The boxer's bald head reminded me of them.'

'You shouldn't fool with a boy like that,' James said. 'He might misunderstand you.'

'Not me. He respects intellect, James, my dear.'

With the forceful stride of explorers James and myself swung west out of the Diamond, passed the jail, swung north-west out of a wide, well-lighted main street, strode, our heels echoing metallically, under the dark arch of a narrow gateway, followed the curve of the walls down thin alleys steep enough at times to need steps. In soft soles, stooped, trotting with shorter paces and talking all the time, Jeff travelled with us.

'They had one most interesting custom,' he said. 'The Zulus, I mean. They had many interesting customs. They impaled their enemies, for instance, anus foremost on high, sharp-pointed stakes and allowed them to settle down at leisure.'

From the lighted streets on the slopes beyond, where the happy road ascended towards the past and Bingen, the cathedral bells chimed Ave, Ave to Maria our Lady of Lourdes. Below us in the dusky, dimly-lighted grid-iron of lanes, a pub at each corner vociferous with singing sailors and soldiers, Alfred was with the animals. Or he was deep down among the wriggling eels, the only sexual symbols left in the blessed island from which the censor Patrick had banished the snakes. He smelt of them. He was coated with their slime. Far from the dry, redolent hazel woods where he had hunted the imbecilic nymph, Alfred was in the swamp studying life.

'Another custom they had,' said Jeff, 'should interest you, Kinnear, holder of medals, captain of victorious teams, beloved of women.'

Behind us in the dusk, hopping sideways and with great caution from jagged step to step, he was talking literally over our heads. The alpine alley shot down dizzily to the black dirt surface of Fountain Lane. On steps by dark doorways women sat and gossiped and screamed occasional admonitions to active children. From a stenchy hallway a young girl, glorious in imitation Hollywood finery, came stilted on high heels, met us, swept past in perfume, ascended perilously towards the old walls and the first evening stars. From one lighted room came sounds of singing and a melodeon.

'After the Zulu killed in battle he could have no social life, he couldn't even drink milk, until he had wiped the axe. The Zulu phrase if the two of you are interested was *sula izambe*.'

'Not interested,' James said.

'Ah, but James, you will be. To wipe the axe meant to have intercourse with a woman. Life after death. Do you follow me?'

'We follow.'

'The attractive aspect of the ritual was that any unmarried woman if (the book I read says) she was accosted by any warrior for this ceremony was morally bound to agree.'

'Morally,' said James, 'is good.'

'Any unmarried woman,' said Jeff. 'It opens up vistas.'

'Maggie Paterson, bless the girl,' he said, 'has in her time helped many a fusilier to wipe the axe. The phrase might be different for sailors.'

'The marlin spike,' said James.

There never was a woman who looked less like what she was than Maggie the Jennet. Yet, by the far-from-Paris ('Faraway is France,' said the doctor) standards of our city, she was our principal courtesan, supreme even above the beauties known to our *demi-monde* as the Bluebottle, Black Maddy and, because of unfettered opulence of bosom, Jingle Bells. Behind a black tin shed by the weighing bridge at the bottom of the city's cattle-market yard it was said she was at home every Saturday night to a dozen or two, one at a time and at threepence a head. A popular song of that halcyon, pre-inflation period went: 'We'll count the hours and kisses, and things that we may do, when I'm in the market for you.' It was publicity. It was her theme song. She greeted the derisive whistling of the melody or the singing of the words with a bony, vacuous smile, for when her own interests were not threatened (as they had been in the case of the rival who had tried to steal her fusilier) she could be as pacific as any shy village maiden. She was straw-haired, tall, fleshless, big-boned ('Strong scaffolding,' Jeff said. 'She needs it') and her freckled face and blue eyes gave her the lost, abstracted air of a middle-aged spinster of a schoolmistress who realized that all hope of a husband was past and that she might as well enter the convent. Her husband, in fact, had withdrawn from the unequal battle to the security of the mental hospital, where there was neither marrying nor giving in marriage, and had left his chair by the tiny, black-leaded kitchen range in her one-storeyed dwelling to be warmed by many a stranger. But not, as it happened on that evening of our quest, by Alfred Conway Chesney. Over the half-door she said: 'If you've money you're welcome. Even you, Jeff Macsorley.'

With a bow and a sweep our genius kissed her hand as we followed her into her kitchen-cum-boudoir, and Jeff was as easily at home with her as he had been with the Red boxer.

'No, it wasn't my luck,' she said, 'to catch Mr Chesney this time. He was grabbed before he got here by Josie across the lane.'

'By Josie the Bluebottle,' said Jeff, 'niece of the late lamented bell-ringer, our last city crier.'

Moving away from us into the past, rigid in a sandwich of wooden placards, moving to the sound of a handbell, as the captain to the sound of unseen pipes had vanished under the arch of the Guildhall Gate, went Andy Berney the last city crier. He had announced cataclysms, events dire by flood and field, the turning off for repairs of the city's water supply, the coming of a grand variety concert to the Guildhall, the raising of the Big Top high on barren slopes above the cathedral. In his leisure moments, it was said, he had set his blue-coated niece on the road to ruin.

'Call her Bluebottle to her face,' said Margaret, 'and she'd scratch eyes. She's a bad one. Such airs.'

'She's a beauty,' said Jeff, 'but she's not my Maggie.'

'She has legs,' said the Jennet, 'like elevenpence marked on a new bucket.'

'But she has Mr Chesney over there,' she said, 'picking his pocket and he as drunk as I ever saw a human being. I've nobody here but my sojer laddie.'

In her husband's chair, in socks and semmit and long woollen drawers, his head slung back, his mouth open and gently, blissfully snoring, was the bald, tattooed guardian of the boxing gym, the fusilier for whom Margaret had battled on the public street.

'Bless him,' Jeff said. 'He sleeps like a child. After life's fitful fever. On, men, to the rescue of Alfred.'

We stepped, two guardsmen in Cairo pursued by a talkative tout, across the black, dirt laneway. The air was stenchy in the close, warm dusk. Down deep in the swamp even the beautiful dragonfly is for one novitiate, underwater year a slimy, voracious, hideous monster.

'This Josie,' said the tout, 'was always formidable. Once when I was but a boy, satchel on shoulder, she met me on the Diamond

Hill, looked distastefully at my shining, morning face, and said: "Wee boy, did you pass many worms this morning?" Knowing nothing of the facts of life I tried to explain to her, although I was creeping like snail unwillingly to school, I could outdistance even the fastest worm. She didn't even laugh. She spat. She was no lady.'

So, since she was no lady we did not knock politely as we had knocked on Maggie's door but, led by the dauntless James, we strode into the dark little bower of bliss and lifted Alfred's half-inert body from the outshot bed. James inspected his wallet. Jeff and myself laced him into his boots and harnessed him wherever harnessing was necessary.

'Sweep him up and take him with you,' said a chisel of a woman's voice from the shadows.

'You did well for yourself, Josie,' Kinnear said.

'A miserable pound,' she said, 'and he owns half the country. I didn't invite him. I've the rent to pay.'

'Pay no attention,' said Jeff, 'to the lady's gentle tongue. She has her own troubles.'

'Adhesions,' he whispered. 'The semen of seven soldiers.'

'Bad for the digestion,' Kinnear said, 'if nothing else.'

'Would soldiers and sailors in embryo,' said Jeff, 'quarrel therein? Or would the phagocytes get them all?'

'If Owen had stuck to his medicine,' said Kinnear, 'he could have told us.'

'Get the tongs,' said Jeff. 'We'll move this fellow. To think that he was once in love. Oh, Mercury, my white and lovely mother.'

For that night brother and sister shared the hospitality of Grainger's hotel. She helped us to shovel Alfred into bed, then sat with us in my room and listened to our aimless talk, casual reminiscences of earlier times, deeds done in schooldays or in Dublin, memories of characters in the city, in the village, in the mountains beyond. I told my father's story of how Doran the wizard had provoked his pet gentleman goat to attack a Redemptorist father who had gone on safari into Segully with the high intent of weaning the wizard from his evil ways, and how the holy man was so forgetful of his Christian mission as to stun the buck with a spade. She laughed, but not as her sister laughed. Her laugh began quietly, then rose to a not unpleasant, hysterical note as if she were trying to keep something, not joy, not sorrow, under control. She rang Maeve at Bingen, but once, twice, thrice, Maeve was not yet at home and Greta, embarrassed, turned back to us. She was glad, I think, when in the fourth ringing she found her sister, told her where Alfred and herself were, and said to me, her lovely hand cupped over the mouthpiece: 'Do you want to speak, Owen?' Pouring tea for the four of us I pretended not to hear her. Later when Jeff, a little intoxicated, began to read poems aloud to us she fell asleep in her chair and Jeff, after a while said: 'A fine face. Good high cheekbones. Hair, as they used to say, like the raven's wing. But sad, boys, unspeakably sad.'

'All sleeping faces,' I said, 'are sad.'

'Nonsense,' he said. 'Did you ever see me asleep? Not that I ever did myself. But I'm sure I look comic when asleep. My sadness is to look comic.'

Red Molphy won his fight by a knock-out in the seventh round and brought honour to our city. His followers from the Fountain Lane grid-iron collected their winnings, redeemed their pledged belongings from the pawnshops and celebrated. He was a greater public benefactor than any library-founding millionaire.

He had merited a warm place in the common heart, wiped out bad debts, inspired the young.

Obliging the doctor, who wanted his boat back for repairs to the Guildhall dock, and simultaneously having our last day out together before Jeff and James returned to Dublin, the three of us made the journey from Tower Bay across the empty, mourning lake, by hummocks of green islands crowned with beech trees where the water close to the shore was dark and silent. Those beech trees, weaving spells, crackled skeleton fingers at us as we passed by, defying death and the voracious waters. The first bony rattle of autumn was in the leaves.

For me with my memories, the coloured walls of the bar in the Tower Hotel could have been draped with sable mourning-cloth. Luscious girls, wheat plains in Canada, temples in Tibet, The Rocky Mountains, Copacabana beach, Cologne Cathedral could have been discreet, sympathetic murals in an undertaker's waiting-room. My love was dead. The lake was dead.

'On that island over there,' James said, 'an old woman was burned alive that the kind, decent people said was a witch.'

Through Dr Grierson's magnificent binoculars we watched the island drifting backwards away from us across grey, Yeatsian water, and picked out, half-hidden by trunks of trees, the burnt-out shell of what had once been the solitary home of the old woman. Twice a year she had left the island, her hens and collie dog and three goats, and travelled to the mainland for Mass on Easter Sunday and Christmas Day. When her cabin went in flames she was not, it would seem, in bed, but sitting by the fire between the falling thatch and the concrete floor; and when the lakesiders who saw the flames had rowed across there were only smouldering ruins and one charred ankle. The dog and the rest of the woman had vanished. The hens complained with hunger. The three goats hid in terror in clumps of furze befouled with falling ashes. There, was the significant centre of the death that was over the doctor's lake.

'She vanished with her dog,' James said. 'So she was a witch. All but one ankle.'

Then with Geoffrey Austin Macsorley bombinating about the superstitions of lakesiders (navel superstitions, dark, lost in black blood, ringed by mountains) and the superstitions of sea-going people that could be touched and banished by brightness and free air, we left the lake for the river, saw the Alsatians and the Australian terriers on the green around the house of the Eel Queen.

'In that house,' said James, 'lived a dancing girl.'

'She vanished,' said Jeff. 'She was a witch. She vanished and left only her music. I remember her music.'

So does Alfred, I thought. He haunts the patriot's bridge like a man who had followed the fairies and heard unearthly harmonies under a green mound.

The last cobalt-and-crimson, spiny-backed, Japanese fish was dead, the girl in the bar told us.

We journeyed on. In the clear evening the city, hump-backed, horned with spires, rose up at us out of the water. Jeff, playing with the binoculars, picked out buildings: mills and stores, factories, churches, hospitals, schools, even his favourite tavern low down by the railway station.

'Never before have I stooped to play Peeping Tom,' he said. 'But there's a happy couple on the river bank by the station.'

'Covered with a raincoat,' he said, 'and working in unison. Team spirit is praiseworthy.'

'Let me look,' I said.

'I am Vicomte Voyeur,' he said. 'I am Lord Peeping Tom with the phallic telescope.'

'Let me look,' I said.

'They won't focus,' he said hastily.

He twiddled the screw.

'Let me try,' I said.

His pimply face was flushed. From his reluctant hands I took the binoculars. They were wonderful aids to vision. They were as illuminating as simple faith. They were better by far than the titled gentleman's telescope. They brought the green corner of Lovers' Bastion almost within reach of my right hand. They showed me the heaving, covering coat, the boxer's cropped head, almost even the expression on her face. Or did I imagine that: her glazed eyes, her open mouth?

'Training, Red, training,' said the tattooed fusilier. 'There's a time and place for everything.'

'He won his fight,' Jeff said. 'The great Zulu.'

For what it was worth, I told myself, I could have had my share of the gift that underneath the coat was being so generously bestowed. The trusting country boy had been diddled by fair-green tricksters. Then for a few moments I was possessed by a series of visions selected for me by the devil and radioed directly to me from the pit of hell. The great buttocks of the boxer strained their crimson covering as he pushed and butted in the sweating gym. Over the ripple and lap of water I imagined his grunting gasps for breath. Her mouth might be wet with his gumshield slaver. Then she was young and soft and new to life and running with Gortin Lass on the green before her house, limping slightly but with a peculiar grace because of that one stiff hip. Up in the wizard's Segully, crude people had once believed that the wildest, butting bull was afraid of the naked human form. A husband tested a wife for fidelity by pushing her naked into the bull's stall and if she emerged ungored she was a virtuous and also a lucky woman. Rather than follow that image through the mists in my brain I reversed the binoculars, looked through the large end, and Lovers' Bastion was so minute, so remote that my pain was lessened. The gyrations of diminutive comic puppets could not effect a grown man of flesh and blood. So many things have happened since then that apart from brown hair, squat hands and the deep base of her neck, I can scarcely recall what the Maeve of my dream looked like. Is it possible that I never saw her? She was the names of wines. She was beauty. She was swathed in her own light. Her image was lost in light and never defined itself. She dazzled all beholders. At any rate she dazzled Owen Rodgers before she returned under the great Zulu to the cave she came from.

Kinnear was never dazzled. Back at the tiller he made no comment. He didn't ask for the binoculars. He didn't need them. He had clear eyes of his own.

'Give those girls a chance,' he had said. 'You'll see wonders. Trust uncle who knows.'

Only then, in the boat, did it dawn on me that uncle had known all along, that certainly he had known since the night of the snow and the Christmas party and my lover's quarrel with Lucy.

After that my idyll was assuredly ended and the captain was alive again. In the bar in Grainger's, morosely drinking when the bewigged pious old fool who thought I was such a fine recruit for the hotel business couldn't notice me, I could hear the captain's neat steps descending from the Diamond to the Guildhall Gate as they had descended the morning he mocked myself and the medical man and invited me to the sheep-dog trials, or as they so often had tapped rhythmically down the stairs of Bingen when he went to deliver his perverted family the orders for the next day.

'How could she help herself?' the precise mocking voice said to me. 'She is my daughter, young Master Rodgers. My poison is in her veins. How could you, Owen, the son of a musical, kind father hope for trust and holiness in the woman I begot on the loins of a serving maid? How wise the wise Germans were, Owen, with that metal, medieval apparatus to ensure purity in the women of their choice. Did you see so much of me, Master Rodgers, admiring me in your ralcalcitrant half of a heart, and not learn from my example that the place for women is in the shadows and subjection, not high on hill and pedestal like the bronze Virgin Victory, enhaloed and surrounded by light? There are no virgins, Owen, except bronze ones with no entrails. All women, Owen, since they were born at all were born to be damned.

'She couldn't help herself, Owen. My curse was on her. She has the Conway Chesney predilection for monsters. She has lived too long in the shadows to be able ever again to take naturally to the light. Under the prone animal, the boxer, her eyes closed, her mouth open, panting, ejaculating, she was seeking only her native gloom.

'But the bottle is no refuge from truth, Master Rodgers, except for a sad, learned man like the Louvain doctor who can never solve even his own conundrums. Attenshun, Owen. Form fours. 'Eft right. Be courteous. Count the spoons.'

Counting spoons I sobered up, spent a holiday in London with, of all people, young Grainger. Old George who trusted me so much had asked me to take the young fellow under my wing. Afterwards I avoided Bingen. Petsie, suddenly a grown, sensible woman, consoled me a lot in those days and talked to me a lot about Lucy who, weary of the village, the mastiff, the shop with the dangling saws and axes, had gone away to Dublin to work in an office.

Gortin Lass vanished for ever the week-end Maeve ran away, and comically enough it was not with the monster, the boxer, but with young Beverley that in the autumn she left the land and fled to London. She left no note to say where she had gone or with whom, and after two days of mystery Edmund told the police who searched a week and found nothing. Coming to my father and myself in our silent home, Jim MacElhatton, his dungarees daubed with the dust of blasting operations in a road metal quarry, said, 'I know where she is, Owen. Drive down to Bingen and tell them.'

'Why should I?'

'They'll worry, won't they? That other poor dark girl. Even Alfred the Egg. That Maeve is a strap.'

'You've found out something?'

'Damned nearly blew herself and Beverley with the blind bat of a moustache into kingdom come. The charge was laid. The fuse was ready. There they were hand in hand on the rim of the quarry.'

'On the rim of eternity,' said my father.

He tested the strings of an old black violin that Barney Quigley had bought in Belfast and thought quite wrongly was a Stradivarius.

'"Run,"' said Jim. '"Run!" I roared. They ran. Two minutes later the ground they had been standing on was gone.'

'So were they,' I said.

'I saw them crossing the fields to the Beverley mansion. The old couple are off in France and the young fellow is cock of the walk and monarch of all he surveys.'

'It would seem,' said my father, 'that he takes his pleasures royally. He knows how to make himself comfortable.'

His grey eyes pitied me.

'Drive down to Magheracolton, Owen, to tell them,' he said. 'You know them better than anybody else.'

The river was loud and brown, the sea in fury; and yellow and black and pale and hectic red, the leaves of the great sycamores were yielding to the wind. Was it the autumnal day or my mood that made me feel the house resisted me because it was shabby and ashamed, because it had betrayed the reorganizing ambition of the captain. Once, so long ago, it had taken possession of me like a perverted love, but now I was the master, I was the captain, descending with metronomical steps to give to the children of shadow the ill news they had been unable to find out for themselves. In the conquering role of the captain, enthusiastic entomologist, authority on the sheep ked, sheep tick or sheep louse (*Melophagus Ovinus*), I looked into the lair between the serpent and the whatnot with the South Sea skull and saw there three specimens of the false caddis fly (*Acentropus Nivens*). Alfred, typical male, was a white creature without any markings; and a curious feature about the species, the book says, is that it has two types of female. One, slightly larger than the male, has wings like him and is able to fly about. She had flown away with Beverley, a fine specimen of the lecherous hopalong or jumping spider who has between his toes a pad of adhesive hairs (*Scopala*) to help him to climb perpendicular surfaces. The other female is smaller, has rudimentary stumps instead of wings and remains under water, crawling about the plants, rooted to the bottom. She opened the door to me. Together we struggled to close it against the following wind. Behind us invading wild air descended the stairs to moan imprisoned in hollows and cellars. The smaller female rises to mate, then goes underwater again to deposit its eggs which may number up to two hundred. On the impulse of that moment, struggling shoulder to shoulder with her against the furies of Magheracolton, and to show my captain's power over the life of this hidden female, I said: 'Greta, there is a job for you in the city.'

She was very pale. Her eyes were wide and hungry, and close to her, once the door was shut and the salt wind banished, the odour of blood was in the dead hallway. Her black, untidy skirt was contoured with stains and twisted awkwardly around her waist. Her strong dark hair was uncombed and unruly.

'But first things first,' I said. 'I know where Maeve is.'

'Edmund's here, Owen. With Alfred. They're drinking.'

Whatever Edmund was he was no false caddis fly. With brown beard and face flushed from brandy he looked more like a dyspeptic wasp. They listened to my news. Greta poured me a drink and Alfred sat in a low armchair, his glass on the carpet, his great hands protectively around it, his abnormally wide crown of short, curled, negroid hair down almost between his high, unshapely knees. Edmund paced smartly to and fro, door to wide window, window to open door.

'We'll follow them,' he shouted. 'We'll take the skin off his bones.'

'I'll be with you,' I said.

He scarcely heard me. I was another whatnot or at best a radio set that had delivered a news bulletin and could be silenced or set talking by one twist of a knob.

'She's disgraced us for ever,' moaned Alfred from the chair.

Greta said: 'You may talk.'

That was the first time I had ever heard her harden her voice in an angry word and she startled me so much that the warming brandy jabbled on our neighbouring hands as she reached me my glass. She wiped me dry with a small crumpled handkerchief. She knew I was there.

'They may talk, Owen,' she said, 'about disgrace.'

'Blame yourself, Alfred,' Edmund said. 'You've let this place go to wrack and ruin. The Macillions will soon own it. It needs a firm hand.'

'Be quiet,' said Alfred.

He stood up tumbling his glass, ignoring it and the spilt liquor. His clumsy body swung as erect as it could in four sections stiffly hinged at knees, hips and neck. As far as size went he seemed formidable and, fearful perhaps of a second disaster to his beard, Edmund was quiet.

'She's a disgrace,' Alfred said, 'to this house and our dead father. We'll pay her a visit she'll long remember.'

To nobody in particular he said: 'This couldn't have happened if our father had been alive. He never put a penny astray.'

They swept past me where I stood between the door and the serpent's baleful glass eyes. The drunken weight of Alfred set the floor vibrating. On the hearth under the snake's belly the fire was warm and high. In its flames, the brandy stirring my imagination, I could review strange stories read in newspapers of tyrannous parents and twisted children: a retarded boy child confined with the fowl in a three-foot-high henhouse and clucking instead of talking; a mother and two daughters so drilled by a father into a life of poverty and slavery, no outings, no male visitors, bread and water at his whim, that when he died they still abode by his rules and in sad, nostalgic pride burned the kind letters of neighbours inviting them out to life. 'This couldn't have happened,' said Slobber the Master, the weasel in the hazel woods, 'if our father had been alive.' 'This place,' said Edmund the hell-rider, 'needs a firm hand.' 'Owen doesn't

mind,' said the flying female false caddis fly, 'Owen's one of us.'
'You knew him well, Owen,' said the pale, lonely cleric, cold in
his faraway college, 'you listened to him, you saw him, we can
talk to you, you're one of us.' 'He generated contention,'
Hughie Heron said, 'but he was a decent man at heart.' 'I heard
so much about you, Owen,' said the wraith of a skivvy who had
peeped through the blind to see the troops march through the
town, 'you're a good friend to my children.' 'They may talk,
Owen,' said the female fly that clung to the underwater roots and
would rise only to mate, 'they may talk about disgrace.'

Faraway the wind moaned as the door slammed behind the
bright, avenging brothers who went out with spears to uphold
the honour of Bingen and the dead captain. The gale drowned
the noise of the engine. Greta was back in the room.

'They took your car, Owen,' she said. 'It was the first they
came to. You left the key in it.'

'They're welcome to it.'

'I'll make you food,' she said. 'It's as cold as winter.'

'Not here,' I said, sipping brandy.

She made food. We drank more brandy and waited and
listened to the wind and the first tentative cracks of great raindrops on the window and, in lulls, wailing noises that could
have been either the river or the sea.

'Tell me about the job,' she said. 'You're very good, Owen.'

Our hands came together as they had come together once in
the cinema by the Guildhall Gate. They were like people who
meet again after a lapse of years in a Victorian novel or in life
itself. Later she said: 'Should you have kissed me, Owen?'

'Why not?'

'It changes the relationship between people.'

'I suppose it does.'

'I only even held your hand once before.'

Glad to be able to remember, I said: 'In the cinema by the Guildhall Gate.'

'You remember,' she said. 'I hated Lucy that day because she had you and because she loaned me a shilling.

'And I kissed your cheek once,' she said.

'At the Christmas party. Lucy was leppin mad.'

Soft, foolish Lucy, faraway in Dublin, had known then by jealous instinct what was going to happen.

'But Maeve kissed your other cheek,' she said. 'Maeve could do things. She wasn't shut in and closed up. She could talk. She had an answer for everybody and cared for nobody.'

Then, gripping my right hand with both her hands, she said fiercely: 'Maeve has no part in you tonight. Maeve has no part in any of us.'

She said: 'It's growing late,' and, 'something must have gone wrong,' and, 'they won't be home tonight.'

Our hands were joined and cradled and swinging like the old, good hands of Kate and Hughie the day they sang the song about the moorcocks and the mountain streams, but it was lice-ridden Dublin Lass, oh darlint, darlint, had taught me what it was so necessary now to know. No fumbling, no stale preliminaries, we walked upstairs, the wind roaring around us, hand in hand like children. In all innocence she hid to undress behind a chair as Dublin Lass had hidden. High in triumph, conquering that crumbling house, Owen Rodgers knew it was better to be born and damned than never to be born at all. But the sheets were damp. The golden people in those story books in which every twenty-fourth page has an opulent copulation on an island in the sun compel my sceptical envy. For one moment their world is all giving and yielding and blood in the ears like organ music and afterwards, the books tell us, they lie happy and exhausted side by side. My ecstasy was vengeance on a night of loud wind and rain, between damp sheets, the baffled captain growling like a beast in a dark corner in an old house where decay had already set in. The woman's willingness was a rope knotted with pain and misery, with the dark knowledge that she possessed me because I had missed what I wanted.

Once she cried in moist, bloody darkness: 'It's not fair; it's not fair.'

Once she cried: 'I'm not clean for you, Owen.'

In the wet morning Alfred came home alone. The hell-rider had his shop to look after. They had invaded the Beverley stronghold to no purpose, for that night, favoured by a following south-westerly wind, the loving couple had sailed the Irish Sea. Without comment the Master accepted my presence at the breakfast-table: a whatnot complete with skeletal skull, a sinister, secretive bastard, one of themselves. There were dead leaves plastered by rain to his knee-boots. He chewed laboriously, drank sloppily. In the farmyard the fallen autumn leaves were drifted high in sheltered corners.

Seven

AMONG HIS MANY INTERESTS IN COURTESY, TOURISM, and the donating of stained-glass windows to new churches, George Grainger also owned the cinema at the Guildhall Gate. That was how Mr Rodgers was able to find the city job for Greta and the root-grubbing, female, false caddis fly was enabled to come, radiant for mating, to the surface. We developed a common interest in the catering business and, since Greta was the sister of the girl whose limbs he had once clothed with a dead woman's finery, George willingly agreed to her installation as manageress of the cinema restaurant. Food, steam, china, menus, coffee-urns, cutlery, customers and table cloths by the score became the links that bound us. Around her as she worked there were on the fake plaster of the restaurant's walls, gigantic portraits of film stars rigid with unnatural colour. Tall, in tight dark dress that outlined her strong figure, her upper teeth protruding slightly, her lips a little apart, a triple string of pearls on her neck, she moved between kitchen steam and the tables or sat sometimes sipping coffee with me, her watchful dark eyes on the waitresses, under a six-foot-high representation of Franchot Tone. It was part of her duty, too, to inspect before they went to their posts the ushers and usherettes lined up like soldiers and clutching torches as if they were atomic weapons. Nervously sometimes she watched my eyes to see if they fell, as any man's eyes might, on the crimson-covered usherettes. To the great delight of George she found some specific for eradicating steam-flies from the small, over-heated kitchen where they had always been a plague.

'A natural talent, Owen,' George said. 'A joy to introduce her to the business on the eve of my retirement. That new crimson costume she has for the usherettes and waitresses is good.'

'It catches the eye.'

'It does more. It enlivens the room. It says welcome as you enter. A pity her sister was so wild, Owen. She had talent too.'

'Any God's amount of it.'

'But Miss Greta has a quiet determination. She has changed this place.'

On every table she had placed small bowls of flowers heavy with Bingen earth. Touching it with my fingers recalled the captain, but how utterly impossible it would be to explain to old George that the work he so much admired was my work inspired by a dead man on a windy night of wickedness. Taking her, I had taken possession of the remote place by the estuary and under the white mountains where, for the time of Maeve's queenship, I had been only a pitiful, pleading shadow. Like her father, Maeve had been one of those people who reduce one, rebuke one's genius. When they are gone you can again take control of events, wipe the spilt sauce from the uniform, marry the girl, or do worse. Greta's mother had been the daughter of tall, unterrifying people. Greta could do me no harm.

Solving the problems of supply and demand—her father had been an authority on those problems—she seemed happy. But she cried bitterly the week-end we drove old George, wig-box and all, to his chosen place of retirement. Sixty miles west we drove to the seaside resort where Edmund and young Grainger had once wrecked a restaurant, then a farther five miles beyond the resort to a tower of a house where parkland sloped to the ocean and good grass fed a hundred Friesian cattle. Dr Grierson and Francis, home on Christmas holidays, came with us to stay for a while with George and the old couple, George's senile sister and her husband, who lived in the tower and owned the cream-scented Friesians. In another car Jeff and James, also on holiday, followed discreetly to meet Greta and myself in the resort on our return journey and to share with us a night of jollification. While old George gave me his final instructions, Greta in the background talked with or listened to the old woman. Then, seeing the doctor and Frank approaching us on the gravel before the house, George hurriedly clasped my hand and, unconscious of comedy, said: 'Owen, I can trust you as I'd trust my son. And Miss Chesney. There's a wise thoughtful head on those shoulders, Owen. You two would do well together.'

The five miles back to the resort I kept repeating that gem: 'He can trust me now as he would trust the son and heir.'

Greta's quietness to my left was as irrelevant to the joke as the green, undulating land, the short grass, bushes bent by sea-wind, the stone walls to my right, the rocks beyond and the grey, December sea.

In an hotel in the resort we celebrated with the happy abandon of respectable men fifty miles from home, drunk with companionship and wild talk that nobody could remember the next day. All I can remember, in truth, is that some time after midnight James decided to drive to a town ten miles away to see the female ex-hairdresser (Jeff called her Madame Gendarme), and Jeff decided to go with him, and they were so fuddled they went round and round their car vainly searching for a door. They leaned against each other and sang songs. They collapsed helpless in laughter over the car's bonnet and Jeff clambered aloft and sat on the roof. Owen Rodgers on the steps of the hotel laughed with them and behind him the night porter who had the car keys safely in his pocket also laughed, and Owen Rodgers, shaken and moist with good humour, turned back into the winy warmth, and the night porter said: 'Your wife has gone to bed, Mr Rodgers,' and I was by her bedside before I realized that I hadn't a wife but, at that moment, I was too full of merriment to care. But awakening in the morning with the woman untouched beside me was a different matter. Outside, the sea rattled like March hail and the useless wind whined as it does in a resort empty for the winter. The casement slowly grew a glimmering, modern oblong and in growing hurt my eyes. My ears were filled with wasps. She was awake. She could have been awake all night while, oblivious beside her, I slept the chaste sleep of the utterly intoxicated. All that remained of all the joy of the previous night were the fruitless circlings of Jeff and James and the instructions the night porter had given me at the door. Had he, or had he not, worn the face of a conspirator who had hoped for reward? Holding her two hands in one of mine, gently stroking her fingers to allay the asperity of his words, Owen Rodgers, hotelier, paladin of courtesy, remonstrated: 'Good God, Greta, we are in the hotel business. This isn't my room. You shouldn't have given the porter to understand we were husband and wife. You know what the hotel business is. We sink or swim together.'

'I could be listening,' she said, 'to George Grainger.'

'A man from Salthill,' I said, 'that I met at a catering conference in Dublin told me he didn't mind strangers cheating him like this but he wouldn't want a friend to put one over on him.'

'Go away, Owen,' she said, 'before you're caught.'

Because the tears were on her face, because it wasn't in me, ever since the enchanted morning before the sheep-dog trials, to turn away voluntarily from the captain or a person or place connected with him, I turned towards her and with my free hand touched her tears. She said: 'All day long that old woman kept asking me when we were married and how many children we had.'

'She was senile.'

'Did she have to be senile to imagine we could have children? Seven times at least she said: "You're both dark, he's a black-avised man, but I've seen the children of dark people come out as fair as scutched flax."'

My hand was drenched with her tears. She cried silently, no sobs, no movement of her body.

'The night that Maeve ran away, Owen, I was so lonely. I didn't want you to leave me. The wind was frightening. Night after night. Never quiet. That house. You could never keep the windows in repair. Even if the panes were small the winter gales always had one or two broken and the wind whistling through.

'I never knew what a virgin was,' she said, 'until I wasn't one any longer. I suppose that's funny.'

'The wind here,' I said, 'can't touch us.'

It whined up the long barren street where the crop of holiday-makers had long since been reaped and stooked. Owen Rodgers would have to bribe the night porter. Belatedly she said: 'Forgive me, Owen, sometimes I don't know what I'm doing.'

Every Thursday, from some undiscoverable source of industrial waste, the river turned green. To Dr Grierson I said: 'What is your grey French Gave to our green river?'

How red the brickwork of the houses was on the far shore when the seaward wind sent low clouds after the Glasgow boat.

How aery-faery and filigreed was the Virgin Victory visible on her hill and pedestal above roofs and old walls and against the last brightness of cold skies. Our pre-Christmas party that year was held in Grainger's: drink, song and supper in the upper room, Owen the host, Greta, who also lived on the premises, a capable hostess. Kinnear and Jeff were there, and Frank and Dr Grierson, and Petsie, and Edmund, for a while snatched from business, but Alfred not at all. My father came with Barney Quigley and Jim MacElhatton, and Hughie Heron and Lizzie met by my father in the Corn Market, entertained in seven pubs and brought, flushed and moist-eyed to the gathering.

'It does my heart good,' said Hughie at regular intervals.

Yet there was an air of loneliness about him. Or was it that I just imagined that he like myself had lost something. Once, speaking to Greta, he miscalled her by the name of her lost sister. Greta's face, set and pale even in the warm crowd, gave no hint that she had noticed the old man's mistake.

At the host's urging, Hughie sang: 'With my dog and gun o'er the moorland heather.'

'But it's never the same,' he said, 'without Kate Carr, the heavens be her bed. This winter and the nor'-easter were hard on the old people.'

From the Dublin poet, Jeff, bleary-eyed, quoted: 'A death wind, the flapping of defeated wings from meadows damned to eternal April.'

'Mortality, Hughie,' said my father. 'We'll all die.'

'You quote Higher Authority, John,' said the doctor. 'Higher Authority is also aware of mortality.'

Silent in a corner, Francis the student was restless and flushed, perhaps with concern for what the doctor might say, perhaps because the old illness had left a mark on his heart and breathing.

'Higher Authority,' said the doctor, 'dispatched me last week to the burial rites of the old man who had the donkeys for the children on the strand of Rossclara. Another day of rain, and off-shore wind beating the rain over the hedges in on the front of the little cottage where the old man lived with his sister.'

'He was fond of the children,' Hughie said.

My father asked: 'Did he send for your services? He never had a name for being gospel-greedy.'

'He lived without us,' said the doctor. 'God be with the poor simple soul, he died without us. Thirty years ago when he came home, contemporaneous with Captain Conway Chesney, from Spion Kop and the terraced ascent of Talana Hill, a nationalist priest spoke crossly to him in the confessional. He judged the rebuke sufficient grounds for dissociating himself from the church of Chrysostom, Augustine and Aquinas. He died in his bed un-attended by anyone but his sister who was trying to persuade him to sip punch from a teaspoon. He died without us.'

'At least,' said Francis, 'he had the prayers by the graveside read over his coffin.'

'And we collected the funeral offerings,' said the doctor. 'The coffin was in a little, whitewashed room. You could call it a parlour. There were family portraits on the walls that must have gone back to men who heeded Wellington and poured through the breach into Badajoz. The cottage was so small they had removed the lower half of the parlour window to allow the coffin in and out. The curtain blew out and in and was all wet with rain.'

'They recited the rosary in the kitchen,' said Francis. 'The old sister cried and knelt for Dr Grierson's blessing.'

'We're gloomy,' said the doctor, 'But this is a festivity. John, where's that fiddle?'

The phone rang. To evade the bedlam in my room I took the call in an empty bedroom down the corridor.

'Owen,' Alfred said, 'tell James Kinnear I'm in the railway station. The train's leaving this minute for Dublin.'

'You're not going away for Christmas?'

'There's a bit of trouble with the police, Owen. You'll hear all about it in due course.'

'Wait there,' I said. 'I'm coming.'

'The guard's whistling,' he said. 'You'll hear all about it in due course.'

The phone went dead. There was nothing else to do but go back to the party.

As red in the face as a beetroot, Francis, the neophyte, had given up all hope of calming his ecclesiastical superior into sober, discreet talk in the presence of the unconsecrated laity. His brown eyes burned reproachfully into mine as we shook hands and he thanked me for the party. All our life, it seemed to me, Frank's sad brown eyes would reproach me. All my life too, by perverse memory of light falling coloured through cheap continental glass stained in crude imitation of da Vinci, the doctor would be part of festivity in an upper room.

'Men,' said the doctor. 'This is uninspiring company. Bring on the girls. The fiddle, John.'

'In my will,' my father said sideways to me, 'I'll leave you Dr Grierson.'

'You have a staff of them, Owen,' called the doctor.

Far away at the sideboard he refilled his glass.

'Handmaidens of the Lord,' he said. 'Who also, Owen, had his faithful women.'

'In some dioceses,' my father said to me quietly, 'there's a tradition that if a priest drinks too much his clerical pals rally round to keep the sad truth from the eyes of the public and the knowledge of the bishop. In other dioceses the colleagues scatter and run from the black sheep in case they'd be dipped in the same wash. A matter of morale and the temper of the bishop. The doctor will always need a friend.'

With remote ironic irrelevance the doctor called to us across the room: 'Once I had a cousin who played cricket for the gentlemen of Ireland. John, the fiddle. Owen, the timeless houri as Chesterton says, from the cash and reception desks.'

The way he fingered the crown of his head made it clear that he was growing sensitive about his increasing baldness. My father, to quieten and please him, produced the fiddle that was not a Stradivarius, and, drawn by the enchantment of strings, came three temptations out of my glass boxes. One of them, with red hair, spiked heels, long silk legs, the rump of her dark dress—in the style of the year—somewhere at the backs of her knees, with white cuffs and collar, gold chain and cross, rimless octagonal spectacles and flashing teeth, sipped orange juice and stood shoulder to shoulder and proud of it with the celibate from Louvain. She was a pious girl and as far as I knew, a genuine handmaiden. Her name was Margaret. Watching her with interest I told my news of Alfred to Kinnear, keeper of secrets unknown even to Owen Rodgers who had thought he had known all about Bingen. Simply, lucidly, sadly Kinnear said: 'Something must have gone wrong, for I had those bastards of Brannigans fixed to settle for cash and keep away from the police.'

In due course Owen Rodgers and the world heard all about it. The developing contours of the juvenile Venus, the cheerful giver beloved by half the country, had first revealed the state of affairs to her parents and to her irate brother when he returned from sea.

'Damned well they knew,' said James Kinnear, 'she was public property. Her mother before her was no better. You never saw in your life such a houseful of cousins. Not one child resembling another.'

Circled by beeches that stood elegant and tall among the stunted hazels, the polyglot Brannigan house was a cream-washed cottage with a horseshoe for luck stuck fast to the gable and beehives busily receding among red and black currant bushes.

'The view over Bingen inspired them,' said Jeff. 'Virtue they valued not. But casting their eyes down they saw broad acres and money.'

To James Kinnear, legal consultant, Alfred admitted: 'I was there and back. I'm not one to deny it. So were seventy others and I'm as much the da as old Shannon of Ardstraw that was turned seventy. You see, James, I have the money. Without money you're nobody.'

The captain said: 'To the Uitlanders in the goldfields, Master Rodgers, Kruger said, "I have the guns."'

'That piece,' said James, 'Alfred spoke with pride. "You see, James, I have the money. Without money you're nobody."'

'For Alfred Conway Chesney,' I said, 'it was a fine piece of oratory.'

'Years ago,' said Kinnear, 'if his father had let him keep the girl he might have been normal.'

'Sainte-Beuve,' Jeff said, 'had a blocked urethra. And think of Ruskin.'

'Day and night I think of Ruskin,' James said. 'He is ever in my thoughts. For one hundred notes the Brannigans would have signed away the virtue, or what was left of it, of every female in the house, the mother included.'

It had taken Kinnear a long night of bargaining in the horse-shoe house of cousins to settle on the sum, to come away triumphant, to arrange to return with the money and exchange it for a signed paper exonerating Alfred Conway Chesney from hand, act or part in the rites of Sakti in among the mystic, nut-bearing hazels. That same night the talkative seaman Brannigan boasted in Lucy's father's pub that Chesney would pay through the pores and was overheard by a man who told the sergeant who had once, for some trivial neglect of duty, been reported to his superiors by that zealous citizen, the captain, and as a consequence penalized. He came with joy and speed to visit on the lumbering son the sins of the efficient father. But in panic and repentance young Brannigan got first to Bingen, warned Alfred, accepted ten pounds for his trouble. The sergeant found, as twice I had found, the front door swinging open. The big house was un-tenanted. Rain fell all round the days of Christmas and Greta and myself, visiting the place, found the wide hallway sodden and Fee the jockey drunk in the kitchen, the Macillions reticent and resentful at what they considered a disgraceful betrayal of the whole townland, the two old Herons sad and apathetic and Lizzie with a cough that set the yellow skin vibrating on her sapless, fleshless bones.

So at Greta's nervous, urgent request (that was the first time I remember her using sleeping tablets) James, Jeff and myself set off to Dublin to persuade the fleeing lover to return and face the music.

Separating by the dawn's early light the three searchers went by their various paths through the enchanted forest, asking questions of cottagers and wayfarers, roisterers in taverns, hermits in sylvan grots, or of bluff soldiery or halberd-bearing watch-men on the city walls.

Meeting again in the evening they conned the sum of the day's discoveries to find out, after a week, that even in a gossipy city like Dublin it was possible to mislay such a conspicuous object as an Austrian dog. Pubs and garden suburbs, presbyteries, cheap restaurants in back lanes where earnest working girls enticed sailors and where by night whiskey was secretively, illicitly consumed out of cracked teacups, football matches, dog-tracks, a day at the races, a night at the opera, careful scanning of all visible forms and faces produced never the face and form of the hunted satyr. A direct approach to the police we shunned.

Searching one day with eyes and ears I heard behind me in a bus the identical boo-hoo-hoo laugh he had. But when I looked around, the sound, I found, came from a buck-toothed fellow, bowler on his head, elaborately dressed and exerting himself to be pleasant to a handsome girl with a hockey-bag. The incident startled me and set me wondering about all the possible, grotesque consequences of and deductions from the basic, ineluctable truth that there was in the world one other man who laughed as Alfred laughed. It seemed to me to prove the existence of a sardonic god but to cast grave doubts on the theory of fingerprints and the infallibility of Scotland Yard.

Held up by traffic lights the bus throbbed impatiently, as if it too were a searcher, outside a greengrocer's shop. Beauty with the hockey-bag and Boo-Hoo-Hoo with the bowler walked away from us or, if you prefer it that way and since all shapes are in the mind and interchangeable, dissolved into another couple, also male and female. She seemed Italian but she was brown enough for Baghdad. Sandals, flat soles with no uppers, were tied by piebald strings around her strong, brown ankles. She wore tight blue denim slacks, a red jacket, and her deep blue-black hair was brief and crudely chopped. Her tanned features were regular and she had brown, thoughtful eyes. She carried an empty string shopping-bag and was attended by a male: tall, fair, Nordic, blue-eyed, wearing a navy, caped coat, stooping slightly to talk to her, possibly of an age with her but looking guileless enough to be her son. Before her remote, desirable passivity he had as much dignity as a man playing a tin whistle before the sphinx. She meditated before she entered the greengrocer's shop, then before my eyes melted away, or walked inside, to purchase in some other existence, sprouts or cabbage or french beans, green food for a brown body. All forms are interchangeable but that woman, I knew, could never be Alfred. The lights changed. The bus moved on. Big cities were all casual encounters with or glimpses of anonymous people who might or might not have some existence of their own.

It was a dark, windy day after a hurricane that the paper told me had sunk, two hundred miles off the Azores, one of the last of the four-masted, square-rigged windjammers and drowned seven blond sailors out of Bremerhaven.

Parallel with the bus she, the next image of my search, walked with quick, short steps along a crowded pavement, turned aside to enter a large hall above the door of which a red and white poster promised something so wonderful as ideal homes. She was doll-like, pretty, plump, with a bottom, as Hughie Heron would have said, like a pudding in a rag. With keen eyes, inherited from his father who from a moving car could spot a bird's nest in a June hedge, Owen Rodgers saw a beauty-spot on her left cheek, an inch from the corner of her coy mouth. In her lapel was a rosebud sleeping a baby-sleep in green, artificial leaves. Was she married or about to be married? Was she planning or did she already possess the ideal home? Then I knew I had seen her before in one of the windows of Lucy's father's shop, the artistic window with its fragile, ideal world of glossy china figurines and pictures on plates from which no man could eat without dyspeptic distraction. So, for old time's sake, I left the bus and followed that one plump, moving figurine. The city people around me were frail, happy figments from that remembered window: gipsy dancers, characters from Dickens, gnomes and fairies, old, silver-haired women at rose-entwined gateways, milkmaids and shepherdesses in charge of all the interchangeable forms of Noah's ark. This was the land of youth, the happy land of ideal homes, far away from a lonely, decaying house where sea wind wickedly persisted in shattering the small panes.

By busy gnomes of washing-machines, transparent bellies displaying the sudsy ardour of their toil, I went, by long corridors of deep carpet and discreet, built-in wardrobes, by all the willing genii of gadget kitchens and glistening chromium, by lotus islands of ideal drawing-rooms with low divans to lull the world to rest. No ship had ever sunk and drowned blond sailors. No scuffle of men in a country ditch had ever abused the imbecilic body of innocence. The air was pleasantly perfumed. The shaded lights simulated a spring day. Alfred the refugee would never be here.

Across an ideal garden with fountain and green plot, bird-table and swaying canvas seat, I tracked her to the model, life-size, modern house that was the ideal centre of all this happiness. In the carpeted hallway my feet following her were quiet as the pads of a tiger attentive to the succulent prey. By the time I had overtaken her at the rear of the house, in a Doré world of tubular fittings, the transformation had been accomplished. There she was, plump and soft, rosebud and green leaves, beauty-spot and careful fringe, fingering fabric and being, before my eyes, Lucy, my lost love. Bells of glossy china tinkled in the air around us. The figurines danced together. She said: 'Owen, I didn't know you were in Dublin.'

'Lucy,' I said, 'I didn't know I was in Dublin myself.'

'The man's astray,' she said.

'In an ideal, enchanted world,' I said, and kissed her beauty-spot, a tip-and-run touch of the lips, and held her hands.

'Owen Rodgers,' she said, 'the things you say.'

'The things I do,' I said, and kissed her gloved hand.

Far from the great Zulu wiping the axe in the cave, far from my night of storm and bloody vengeance, the world was normal and acceptable again. The voice of the captain could never be heard in this place. Her make-up, since, as the poet said, Dublin taught her to be wise, was applied with an expert hand. Her eyes glistened with witch hazel. For me, in a manner to gratify Casanova, they glistened again.

'To Dublin I came,' I said, 'to find Alfred Valentino Chesney.'

'I saw him,' she said, 'in the most curious place. The night before last.'

'My search then,' I said, 'is as good as ended.'

Her arm I hooked in mine. Around us the gadget genii waved happy chromium arms, washing-machines gurgled with delight. In one corner a trained nurse conjuring with a doll, a diaper and a tin of talcum, demonstrated baby-care. This was how ideal homes were made and maintained. Mimicking Eddie Cantor whose moon-eyed face was also on the fake walls of the cinema restaurant at the Guildhall Gate, I sang to her pink mouse's ear: 'We can build a little home, with a carpet on the floor made of buttercups and clover, all our troubles will be over when we build a little home.'

'Owen Rodgers,' she said. 'They should give you a job here.'

It was the next morning, a cold, sunny morning. Down full fathoms five the blond men of Bremerhaven swung like pendulum weights with the washing of giant tides. Across the street from me as I watched plump Lucy move away to her office was a shabby hotel, and if Lucy and the girl who worked in the cash desk in that hotel had not once walked together barefoot on the holy stones of Lough Derg the three searchers might never have found Alfred.

'By accident,' she said, 'I peeped into the lounge and saw him. The girl says it's an awful place to work in, a lost week-end place she says, people drinking night and morning. But what can she do? Bread and butter is bread and butter.'

Owen Rodgers agreed readily enough about the nature of bread and butter.

'He was stupid drunk,' she said. 'So I fled. The girl says he's that way since he came to Dublin. And rush I must now or I will be late for the office.'

The night porter, still on duty, had a stained waistcoat hanging open and a halo of tobacco juice around his mouth, and Mr Chesney was still abed, he said, would I walk right up. From a tooth-cleaning glass he sipped whiskey against the evil spirits that walk abroad in the morning. Over brass stair-rods that rolled and rattled, frayed carpet that slithered guiltily underfoot, I walked right up. George Grainger should see this place. Along a narrow corridor I made my way to number seventeen. Mr Chesney was, by God, abed in an apothecary's cavern of stained tumblers and bottles, empty, partially empty, and some still full. The tangled blankets swirled like the whirlpool of Corrievreckan. A vast foot and a calf in long woollen drawers protruded as if asking a startled question. The wide, flabby face was as white as a ghost and when, after a while, he recognized me, he moved his lips, displayed bare gums, and sibilated, spraying saliva. With a lax left hand he indicated some region under the bed. On cross-examination he re-sibilated. The words proved to be: 'False teeth, my teeth on the floor.'

On the floor, by God, I found his false teeth, close to a huge discarded boot, a pathetic little pile of fragments and white and brown powder. While I scraped them into the cup of my left hand he hoisted himself to a sitting position, shivered, pulled the clothes around him, surveyed the damage with slowly comprehending eyes, again sibilated. The words proved to be: 'Jasus, I'm ruined all out without my teeth.'

Then he shook my hand and, as if this latest disaster had reduced all disasters, previous and to come, to comedy, he laughed until he choked and coughed. Without my help he got to his feet and dressed, pulling clothes on skew-wise, pausing to mop sweat from his face, to sniff hopefully at tumblers. He hissed: 'No brandy, that blasted night porter swiped it, I'm ruined all out, Owen, without my teeth.'

He dry-retched until tears fell from his eyes into the soiled hand-basin and, gasping for breath, he said: 'You wouldn't tell me a lie, Owen.'

'No, Alfred.'

'You'd tell me the truth if I asked you a straight question?'

'Yes, Alfred.'

He mopped his eyes and chin with the corner of an abominable towel. He said: 'What bloody day of the week is it?'

The information seemed to brace him up. He reacted even more favourably to my suggestion that a little brandy and soda might settle his stomach and, he leaning on the shoulder of his dark sister's lover, we went down the shifty stairs, along an unpleasantly odorous tiled passage to a small dispense bar where the night porter, his good vigil done, was surrendering his keys and his tally of the night's drinking to the day porter. The air was grey with stale debauch.

'This is an old friend,' lisped Alfred, 'encountered unexpectedly.'

He didn't mean me. He meant the sallow-faced day porter, a sullen man with a thin moustache and a brown, calculating eye. Unlike the tobacco-haloed watcher of the night he was clean and sober.

'We met,' said the day porter, 'in a pub on the quays.'

'He brought me here,' said Alfred.

'People meet, but the mountains never,' said Hughie Heron, repeating an old proverb and studying the white hills around Bingen.

'You were a chauffeur once,' I said, 'up in our part of the country.'

'I gave that up.'

'It gave him up,' said Alfred. 'The old lady met a preacher.'

His boo-hoo-hoo was horrible to listen to.

'Gilbert knows they're after me. But Gilbert's not talking. That's the sort Gilbert is.'

'There's no money on your head,' said the chauffeur.

'I'm partly guilty you might say,' said poor, toothless Slobber. 'I'm blamed. I'm on the run.'

'Sooner or later,' I suggested, 'you'll have to face the music.'

'It's not the first time I was the cause of trouble,' he boasted.

He gulped brandy and soda, coughed and before my eyes was, gums and all, the most amazing parody of a dashing blade.

'There was wee Rose,' he said, 'who had to leave the country. Did I ever tell you that, Owen?'

I said he never told me that.

'I didn't even tell Kinnear, the up-and-coming lawyer. She had a child in a Salvation Army home. I never said a word.'

Serving more drinks, the chauffeur twisted his wry lips and never said a word. Before me in that sordid place I could see and smell the most gigantic, most fetid Austrian dog and I knew for ever that everything human rots and rots.

'But I'm ruined all out,' he said, 'with no teeth.'

'Only now he's noticing,' said the chauffeur, 'he has no teeth.'

'My spare set's at home,' Alfred said.

'We'll get you home,' I said.

'You'll have teeth in the dock,' said the chauffeur.

So to put an end to it I told the yellow man the party was over, and rang an old medical friend to come and relieve Alfred's case of the jigs, and rang James and Jeff. It was no job for a man alone.

Behind the blank, indifferent back of the taximan I recalled with guilt how that day on the Diamond Hill I had half-laughed, half-sneered at her peahen thoughts, had obscenely shaped her in the image of a Reeperbahn waitress with bare breasts and tail. She was innocent and that was a great thing. Her little, weepy fits of sadness never went deeper than the corners of her eyes. She was fragrant, plump, comfortable, a doll for an ideal room in a furniture display. But underneath all that she would be exactitude and clockwork, as practical about pennies as her parent in his pub and hardware store. There was no gloom in her, no waste places and she had a tender heart: 'Owen, I won't go into the station. Poor Alfred would be terribly embarrassed. What will happen to him?'

'Twelve months will happen to him.'

'How perfectly horrible. Poor Greta.'

Our taxi stopped fifty yards from the station. Ahead of us, like a captured criminal between two detectives, Alfred shambled up the station steps, Kinnear to the right, Jeff to the left.

'Owen, it was lovely meeting you again.'

'It was lovely meeting you, Lucy.'

'I can come home again now.'

'Never say I kept you away, Lucy.'

'But you did, Owen. You wouldn't even talk to me. That night years ago, you left me as if I was garbage.'

'You told me to go.'

'I didn't really mean you to go. I'm stupid.'

'You're not stupid, Lucy. I'll miss my train.'

She dabbed her eyes with, inevitably, the tiniest of handkerchiefs. She would never do anything strange or unexpected.

'Soon,' she sobbed, 'we'll meet again.'

'Soon,' I said.

'And everything will be, Owen, just as it was?'

'Just as it was, Lucy.'

She risked her lipstick and we kissed and that was that. In the station bar the three men were drinking, Jeff talkative, Kinnear morose, Alfred lisping pitiably in response to Jeff.

'You've dismissed the scent bottle,' Kinnear said. 'Now we can take him home.'

We took him home. Twelve months happened to him.

The case, unlike the escapade of Edmund the hell-rider, was kept out of the local papers and, since in Ireland the national papers are decent enough to deprive their readers of spicy reading, the story went on the spike automatically in every office in Dublin, Cork and Belfast. But newspapers are not really necessary for the dissemination of news, especially in a kindly land like Ireland where every man takes such a genuine interest in his neighbour's welfare. Angel whispers bore the glad tidings to the ears of the bishops and the big men in Saint Patrick's College, Maynooth. In the old Gaelic days a man could not become chieftain of his clan if he had physical blemish. Nowadays moral blemish in a relative may stand as a bar between a man and the sacerdotal chieftaincy. Far away at Lisieux, Francis must, like James the Less, have contracted calf's knees from constant prayer.

'After discussion on the highest level,' said Dr Grierson, 'they, the Lord Bishops, have decided to let Francis go forward. Let us hope for the best.

'They debated about me,' he said. 'Did you ever know, Owen, that my one sister had the misfortune to have a child born out of wedlock shortly before I prostrated myself for ordination?'

'I was a devout neophyte,' he said. 'I was an assiduous student. Because of that they put no bar in my way in spite of the fact that my sister whom I loved was human.

'I never forgot their forgiveness,' he said. 'The knowledge of it was in my heart like a hot coal when I lay down with bound hands and they told me I was *sacerdos in aeternum.*

'I was marked for Louvain,' he said, 'to walk among the learned. But I was handsome, Owen. In Dublin, in Belgium, in France, every woman I saw was my frail sister.

'I was a grown man of twenty-six,' he said, 'and from Latin books I knew in theory how men and women made love. This (he held up the bottle) was the golden road to Samarkand and forgetfulness.'

That was the great era of Edmund the showman. The passion his father had for drilling his sons, a passion common in many small men for uniforms, medals, badges, bugles, all the military trappings, had passed on to him. He worked it off in showmanship and in speed.

Aping the efforts of a great showman in some English city

he had visited, he rented the largest football ground our city had, collected from local enthusiasts money for the laying of an up-to-date cinder track, inaugurated the new stadium with an event that was part sports meeting, part circus, part military tattoo. Prancing at the head of the inaugural parade went a silver band from an American warship that had lain for a week in the estuary, just barely visible from the windows of my upper room. The young bandsmen had bent the military music to the rhythms of the deep South. They were jaunty. Their march was half a dance. Their two cymbalists were jugglers that children or poets would have followed for miles. They made Edmund the most popular man in our city since the glorious day of the Red boxer. They fascinated Jim MacElhatton. Behind them came a solid array of trustworthy English policemen playing Colonel Bogey, dock policemen from Liverpool leading Alsatians that could do everything but talk, then seven kilted bands of pipers from our own part of the country, the band from our own village, trick cyclists and trick motor-cyclists who were an ironical recall to the routed hell-riders, step-dancers, gymnasts, jumpers, runners, weight-lifters and hammer-throwers, six girls in tights on piebald circus ponies, everything except Nubian eunuchs and Circassian slave-girls, then the trumpet, then the tucket, and Edmund himself in his brave beard curled, young Grainger (torn away from alcohol by the more lunatic intoxication of speed and the machine) and A. N. Other—all three in helmets, goggles, spacesuits and low-slung racing motor-cars. It was a long way back to the sultry day when he had trotted naked with two naked Macillions by the bank of the Bingen river. It was better by far, according to Hughie Heron, than the valley of Jehoshaphat would ever be.

He swept ahead to greater glories. Contusion hazarding of neck and spine, he brought back racing trophies to lay at the prim feet of the Maiden City and the Virgin Victory, to display in his shops, he had three of them now, and thus attract custom. The walls of the shops with photographs and newspaper clippings on every free space, and his own talk with anecdote and factual detail, added up to a fantastic muddled montage. His favourite stories were all about men who had risked lives to break records.

'When men like these,' he would say, 'shake hands at the pits and say good-bye, they mean good-bye. You may never see them alive again. Look at this now.'

This was a news picture of a bearded Australian photographed with his pretty wife a few minutes before he, twelve miles away, was to make violent and final contact with a stone wall. Edmund gloated.

'Speed, Owen. Then wham. Tragedy. Out like a light. The wife went to the pits when the race began, to watch the indicator clock to see how the husband was doing. The clock never moved. When the officials took her out behind the stand to tell her, all she said was: "I had an idea this would happen."'

'They can take it,' young Grainger said. 'It's all in the game.'

From another paper Grainger read with glee how an Italian ace had broken four ribs at Rouen and how four racing cars and an ambulance had also been involved in the smash.

'An ambulance,' Edmund said with unction. 'A bloody ambulance.'

Grainger read: 'Rocketing round his fourth lap of the Senior T.T. course at the Isle of Man here today, one of Britain's greatest riders had to leap for his life from his blazing motor-cycle.'

'Motor-cycles,' said Edmund. 'Okay, but small stuff. Give me the big birds with four wheels.'

'Our picture,' Grainger read, 'shows the destruction of his

one-thousand-pound Italian machine. "I felt the heat on my legs," he told our reporter, "but I got the shock of my life when I saw the flames licking me."'

'The man,' James suggested, 'could have been badly burnt.'

'All in the game,' said Grainger.

He read: 'His team-mate challenged the leader but on the last killer lap he tried too hard and crashed. He is in hospital with a fractured elbow.'

'Do you know,' said Edmund, 'that for the big race in the Argentine a million wireless sets tune to the one station, ten million evening papers with their headlines scream forth the names of the winners of the day's lap.'

He and Grainger were men in a frenzy.

'We'll have our own circuit soon,' he said. 'I'll organize it. From Redmond's Bridge to your village, Owen, to the Big Tree, out to the coast, back along the coast, inland again to Redmond's Bridge.'

Grainger said: 'Not a better circuit in the British Isles.'

'Made for it,' said Edmund. 'Specially designed. All it needs is organization. What the whole country needs.'

He made noises in imitation of a high-powered engine. His hands were on an invisible wheel. He vibrated by proxy with the power the machine fused into him. Roaring, swaying, skidding monsters terrified the countryside.

'Wait and see, boys,' he said. 'Wait and see.'

'It should be good for the hotel business,' Owen said.

'Not to mention the undertakers,' said Jeff.

'Wait and see,' said Grainger. 'Wait and see.'

There were no swans that year on Thread the Needle. The triumvirate of Hughie, Fee and Black Macillion, running

Bingen in the regrettable absence of the master, were as sullen and resentful before every visitor as mud-eating Guaharibos in the Amazon jungle. They and the earth they trod had turned mean and sour. The house, outhouses and fields had an unkempt, unshaven appearance.

In mid-May, in the cinema restaurant, before a glowing, gigantic picture of Clark Gable, Greta collapsed at her work and was carried away to hospital with a burst appendix. In those pre-penicillin times she lay for three weeks swinging wearily between life and death. The hospital, a new building high on a hill on the fringe of the city and above the widening estuary, was the best we could boast. To have it run to his wishes, the bishop of the diocese had imported a community of French nuns and, touched by some kindness, had transferred Dr Grierson from our village to a city parish where part of his duties was to hear, in the most civilized of languages, the confessions of the foreign nuns. Greta, more remote than ever from me in her convalescence, must also have confided in him her spiritual distresses, to be guarded by that grave man under the seal of holy silence.

All round the hospital, on young grass on newly-levelled slopes, nun-like sheep grazed. In cool, antiseptic corridors the nursing sisters, whiter and more quiet than the sheep, moved legless about their duties. During her convalescence we walked in the corridor outside her room because it was easier to talk there than in the presence of her room-mates, three matrons, wives of merchants, and all with prolapsed wombs. They remembered past pregnancies and deplored the insatiability of man.

'They're swathed in this medal and that ribbon,' she said. 'They belong to more religious confraternities and orders than I ever thought existed. The stout lady with the black hair is so proud that the bishop established this hospital especially for the middle classes.'

In heelless slippers and a silk, flowered dressing-gown she was fragile and small by my side.

'But I feel out of everything,' she said. 'I envy them.'

'You envy what, Greta? Their husbands are never heartbroken when the duty visits are over. They race back like antelopes to the commercial clubs.'

'But, Owen, they have husbands. And homes. And children. They've somebody who's bound in duty to them.'

'If that's what you want.'

'I don't know what I want. But I know what you don't want.'

'Greta, do we have to have this all over again?'

'I'm sorry, Owen. It's just that this place gets on my nerves. I feel like an outlaw. A pariah. I feel, if those women only knew about me, what a tribunal there'd be.'

As startling as a maenad in the middle of all the nuns, one lay-nurse, unconsecrated and unvowed, passed along the corridor. To defy the whole cloistral, suffocating air of the place, Owen Rodgers would have liked to touch her. She was grass and stone and young streams. She was free and unfettered. My greedy eyes followed the fine haunches, clad in blue skirt and white linen apron. Greta's hand, tight and quivering, gripped my elbow.

'What's wrong with us, Owen? Why did we have to come together if there was to be no peace for us? I thought at last I was at the beginning of something good.'

'That's silly talk, Greta. You're weak after your illness.'

'Couldn't I have stayed an old maid like old Mary of Segully mountain who spent every Sunday of her life siphoning bees' wine and porter into her bachelor lover with the long nose? No matter how old I grow now, I'll never be a maid.'

'Greta, if you disturb yourself like this I'll stop coming to see you. You're supposed to rest.'

The thought of her white skin, scarred by knife and stitches, still swathed in surgical dressings, filled me with revulsion. Once again, cheerful and as free from bonds and vows as a circus procession, the jaunty nurse passed along the corridor. Far away, Dr Grierson emerged, to my relief, from a ward and approached, head bent, stepping with slow gravity, talking his fluent French to the reverend mother and to Francis Conway Chesney.

Greta said: 'I suppose you owe me something, Owen. But I can't ask you to pay a debt you don't want to pay.'

'We won't talk about debts, Greta. It's a bad word.'

She could only be fully alive for me when the wind blew around us where the river bent and thrust into the sea and the black horses ran wild. Owen Rodgers was older and more weary. Bingen was a broken place. The enchantment of a morning far away in boyhood was dead and gone. What had been between us was not love but necromancy, a vengeful spell evoked out of empty mist by whispering false words, love runes read backwards, and practising evil rites on the body of a woman. The memory of the captain had for a while salted and kept from corruption our embraces, but here, in this place of nun-like sheep and sheep-like nuns, of wealthy merchants' wives, protected by all the charms and medals of all the confraternities and perpetually bemoaning the fact that they had ever lived or aped life, the captain's dark daughter drifted farther and farther away from me and I knew no charm to help her or keep her.

'When Maeve went,' she said, 'I had a hope that everything would be alright . . .'

The doctor raised his hand in salutation as he approached. Whatever he had heard from Greta he, because of his duty, kept to himself. He knew too, as Greta did not know, that Lucy had returned, but neither of them knew that at that moment the sweet smell of Lucy's perfume was about my wrists. With Lucy —and this was odd, because she too might one day be a pro- lapsed and wailing matron—I had no sense of obligation or bondage.

'Come again to see me, Owen,' she said. 'I'll try to be more cheerful.'

'You're tired,' I said. 'Just tired. You need rest. You've had a bad time.'

If she hadn't suddenly departed from her pleading mood and laughed bitterly it might just have been possible that I would then have known myself as I really was.

In slow, considerate English the doctor said: 'This, reverend mother, is Owen Rodgers, a power in the hotel business in this city.'

Greta's mood and state of health being as they were, there seemed little point in my telling her of the welcome-home party I had organized for Lucy. The participants were Lucy and my- self, Kinnear and Madame Gendarme, whose policeman was absent on a special training course, Jeff and Petsie to keep the talk going, young Grainger and Edmund and a stout, dull girl of the better sort of people, who had fallen in love, as girls of her class are liable to do, with Edmund's daredevil tendencies. In the course of the night she showed me proudly a newspaper clipping, a photograph of herself along with a bearded, helmeted monster described in the caption as: 'Edmund Conway Chesney whose driving thrilled the crowd.'

Since some discretion was called for, because of the presence of Madame Gendarme, we met in the Tower Hotel in a private room with a wide window that looked out over the evening lake and the dark, homecoming boats of the mayfly colonels.

Now that the repellent avoirdupois of her early development had gone, Lucy's china-doll prettiness fascinated me. Her arms, of course, I had always loved. Now they were round and smooth and, because both of lotion and the sun, edibly brown. She sang in a sweet voice, easy to listen to and soothing to the nerves, conventional old-fashioned songs of sentiment: vowing to return to some beloved when the roses bloomed again down by yon river and the robin redbreast sang his sweet refrain, asserting that there was nothing half so sweet in life as love's young dream, or complaining of the silence of Kathleen Mavourneen, the voice of her heart. Her choice of songs gave her a delightful flavour of the antique, of a lost, chiming world of shepherdesses and winsome boys seated, against all the laws of gravity, on golden stooks of corn: mantelpiece ornaments as unlike the Bingen snake as day from night. Her presence, her conversation raised no questions that could not be settled for ever with something so trite and purchaseable as a wedding ring. She was, moreover, as lawyer Kinnear pointed out to businessman Owen Rodgers, an only child and extremely well off.

'For a man in trade like yourself,' Jeff said, 'the fair Lucy would be a sound investment. For an artist like Geoffrey Austin Macsorley . . . why, she'd drive me mad in a fortnight.'

'There's money in it,' my father had said. 'Dress to kill. Chat to people. Manage the whimsies of the female staff. Count spoons.'

From Tower Bay to the Big Tree I drove my fragrant Lucy home. We made love on the way like two elegant film-stars in a comedy about rich, eligible socialites who never approach each other except in evening dress and, because of the sus-ceptibilities of a general audience, are unaware of animal im-pulses.

Her father and mother had separated. The mother remained

above the hardware shop. The father and the mastiff, now decrepit, had removed to the flat above the lounge bar which was on the first floor of the Big Tree. Lucy varied her loyalty and her residence as the mood moved her. We sat in the lounge. It was after closing time and the customers had long gone home. Above us the mastiff slept, the father read paper-backed books. But by the illustrations on the walls of the lounge it would seem, Jeff reckoned, that the old man's taste had moved on from tales of the great Wild West. Lucy and Owen, still on the respectable fringe of the forest, had their good-night cuddle and cup and cosset while, on the wall behind us, a jocular poster said: If you sleep, let it be by yourself. If you lie, let it be by a pretty lady.

A companion poster joked with an undertone of grave meaning: Poor Trust! Bad Pay Killed Him.

An even more business-like companion stated bluntly: No Cheques Cashed.

Behind the bar a radiant calendar showed a pretty girl with her arms full of parcels. Some defect of hook or elastic had delivered her skimpy, flimsy panties down to her ankles. She turned a pneumatic tail and an appealing but unintellectual face towards the public. Away from the dominance of Lucy's mother, did the old man at night burn candles before that Yoni image?

'What will Higher Authority say,' my father asked the doctor, 'about that odd manifestation of autumn fire in one of his best-paying parishioners?'

'Higher Authority,' said the doctor (he was now as close to France as the tongues of foreign nuns could bring him), 'knows about bullocks. A harmless knowledge for a cleric. He also possesses the invaluable gift of knowing when his bread is buttered on both sides. A hundred-pound note for the church building fund covers all the calendars from here to China and is as welcome, if not more so, than the Paraclete.'

In the presence of the debagged damsel we gently kissed. The curtains were drawn around the big bay window. Here was comfort. No seawind, breaking panes, blew around us.

'From that window,' said Lucy, 'will be the very best place to see Edmund's race.'

From that window by daylight you could see along the crescent street the sweep of the traffic advancing towards the giant, isolated oak that gave the pub its name. As far as Edmund's great race was concerned, Lucy never said a truer word.

One of the nuns, dressed in nursing white, came from Malaya. Another, in the black habit of a teaching nun, was a negress from Uganda.

'Among those solid Frenchwomen,' I said, 'they look like children's toys.'

'More warriors than toys,' Frank said rigidly. 'They do great work on the missions. They fulfil a great aim of the Holy Father. Native priests and nuns.'

We walked down the slope between the sheep to the place where I had parked my car. That year, with study and worry, Frank was thinner and more pimpled than ever. He looked straight ahead and spoke to me coldly. He said: 'This illness has done Greta good. It has turned her thoughts more to God.'

'For God's sake,' I said. 'I never heard that peritonitis and a slash through the stomach nerves ever did anybody any good.'

'There are worse things, Owen, than peritonitis.'

'Cholera morbus,' I said. 'Bubonic plague. Poison gas.'

His idiotic solemnity, after that whole ordeal of still corridor and white nuns, enraged me.

'Greta will be well,' the doctor said uneasily. 'She needs rest. She needs a change.'

'She's worked too hard,' I said.

'She worries a great deal,' Frank said. 'She always did. She even talked to me about a religious vocation. But I doubt if community life would suit her.'

His distant, holy stiffness relaxed as we climbed into the car. From the balcony at the end of the corridor Greta watched us and I waved, but there was no answering wave. He gripped me by the elbow. His brown eyes were as soft as ever. He said: 'Owen, you'll see she gets the change. She's very much on her own now when I'm away.'

We drove to Grainger's. In the entrance hall I invited them both for drinks to the upper room, and Frank, if he cared to, and because Bingen was a desolate, homeless place, to stay for the night.

'No thanks, Owen,' he said. 'No whiskey for me.'

'Who mentioned the vile stuff?' said the doctor.

The brown eyes were almost tearful. The college barber had butchered him. He said: 'Not now, Owen. I can't afford to drink now, doctor.'

He shook hands with us and, as clumsily almost as Alfred, stumbled out through the revolving door to spend the night, he said, in the flat of his brother Edmund. Going up in the lift the doctor pitied him.

'The only prop, Owen, of a falling house. The sins of the fathers. Alfred in prison, a weak mind in prison in a clumsy body. Maeve adrift and rudderless on the waves of the world. The only one in that sad house that the sun ever shone on.'

'Edmund,' said I, 'has his place in the sun.'

'Edmund's a bumptious fool. Edmund's the selfish coward he always was. A fast car is only a quicker means of running away. And Greta, Owen, Greta's not well. You know she's not well.'

To my relief we were joined at the next floor by Margaret,

the handmaiden, who came with us, sat on the arm of his chair while he talked and we drank. A handmaiden and a perfect employee, Margaret did not drink.

'Like Higher Authority himself,' he said, 'Frank flees from whiskey. Bedew your lips, my dear Margaret, with one sweet sip.'

Simpering she said: 'No, thank you, doctor, you know it would break my total abstinence pledge.'

'A pledge,' he said, 'a pledge to bright eyes.'

He raised his glass.

'Higher Authority,' he said, 'among his other vices eschews drink. No vice in you, my dear, but a patent weakness in a grown man.'

'Once,' he said, 'we journeyed together to the city of Dublin by way of Portadown. One cold winter, and the hot whiskey steaming, while we waited to change trains, in the railway station buffet in that noble town, Higher Authority elected to drink cold juice of grapefruit.'

Margaret said: 'I much prefer orange.'

'Orange it shall be, then. Owen, some orange for Margaret.'

'The girl in the buffet,' he said, 'came from my own part of the country. A sonsy, strong woman. "Where are you bound for, doctor?" she says. "For Alaska," said I, "for the Alaskan mission. I'll bring you back a polar bear." A fantasy, Owen, you understand. Like the poet, James Stephens: "The slow, sad murmur of far-distant seas, whipped by an icy breeze upon a shore windswept and desolate, a sunless strand, the frightened croon, smitten to whimper, of the dreary wind".'

Her spectacles shining, her moist lips apart, Margaret, entranced, listened. She was a poetic girl.

'It's beautiful, doctor,' she said. ''Tis like the flight of little birds.'

'Then a cattleman in the buffet, one of those demigods who

carry rolls of five-pound notes inside their hats, said: "Doctor, a drink for the road, it's a long, cold way to Alaska." And with that, Higher Authority stamps out into the night and spends the rest of the waiting time on the windy platform.'

'The cattleman,' I said, 'should have appealed to him.'

'He had, you see, to exert his authority from which, providentially, I am now released. I had to join him on the platform. He didn't freeze me. He thawed me. He dissolved my Alaskan fantasy.'

'The selfish beast,' said Margaret.

'Speak well of the Lord's anointed, child,' he said.

Kate Carr's old face was before me, and for a second it was once again a windy, showery spring day. We refilled our glasses.

'Poor Higher Authority,' he said, 'means well. He's a symbol of the Irish church. He's a great builder now, even if his taste is execrable. Taking his part in the national mania: church-building. Raising above your father's lovely old village a gazebo of a modern church that would shock the aesthetic sensibilities of Al Capone if he saw it in one of the uglier corners of Chicago. And to raise money for that horrific edifice he will stoop to the most bestial practices. Not an old man or woman dying that has money in the bank but Higher Authority will be by their bedside night and day. On Segully mountain, Owen, they tell that he spent a week consoling an old fellow who, *in articulo* himself, was worried about the Pope's health. "John," says Higher Authority, "one Pope dies, another takes his place, the church is immortal. I'm building below in the village a house of God will outlast the pyramids." But aged John was not consoled, so Higher Authority—fill up once more, Owen, we'll drink a toast to comrades far away and another toast to Margaret's bright eyes, Margarita, pearl among women . . .'

'Oh, doctor,' Margaret simpered.

'So Higher Authority, for once himself indulging in fantasy, said: "To prove my point, John, I can tell you that just the other day we ordained a thousand young priests in Maynooth college." And old John who was then at death's door sat bolt upright in bed and said: "Mother of Jasus, they'll rob the country."'

'Oh, doctor,' said Margaret, 'the naughtiest stories about the clergy are always told by the clergy themselves.'

'The same is said,' he said, 'of the Aberdonians. "They'll rob the country," old John said. "Black locusts."'

'You'll stay the night, doctor,' I said.

'I'll help you to your room,' said the handmaiden.

'Black locusts,' he said. 'Black locusts.'

It rained on the great day of the first race on Edmund's circuit: heavily in the early morning until the world was sodden, then in a steady mizzle that gave the roads the surface of a skating rink. The lounge bar of the Big Tree was closed for the occasion to all but a select group: Lucy and myself, and Greta sitting also by my side as once she had sat in the cinema at the Guildhall Gate, the doctor, Lucy's father, Kinnear, Jeff, my own father and Jim MacElhatton.

Now, as you approached our village at the Big Tree there was a bridge over the narrow-gauge railway that serviced in summer the wide sands of Rossclara. There are humpy bridges like it all over Ireland. Edmund hit it like a rocket, rose in the air, touched the greasy road surface again, skidded, finished up in a heap of scrap-metal against the sand-bagged bole of the Big Tree—the tree, not the tavern. Edmund was never a success at running away.

Lucy screamed. Greta made no sound. But as I reached blindly for her hand and as the first-aid men came running across the street and Dr Grierson, reaching for his stole, was fumbling with the handle of the door, she fell limply from the chair by my side.

Edmund didn't die. He simply went out cold for six weeks, emerged from his coma with a head that would never harden, married his nurse, a free-and-easy cow of a girl from the County Roscommon. Since he was no longer a hero whose driving could thrill crowds, he no longer appealed to the stout girl of the better sort of people.

'With all his cleverness,' said Jim MacElhatton, 'the poor devil was destined to marry the town bump.'

'When he tottered down the aisle on her elbow,' said Barney the big drum, 'there were seventeen heroes at the back of the church who had fingered her or worse.'

'It is common knowledge,' said Jeff, 'that the nurses are the worst.'

Be that as it may, she was a good nurse and a good manager for Edmund's shops. She mothered him, guarded him and bore his children. He settled down to whittling sticks and watching his children play in the sun. He was an odd parody on a father who had managed things until he fell.

She should have gone away from Grainger's, from that city, from the mean man who had stolen her on a stormy night.

At the window of the upper room she sat looking out at the ebb and flow of the estuary, the far mud bank revealing itself with the ebb and vanishing again at high tide, the coming and going of the few dilatory ships. Just so her mother had sat at the closed window of the room in Bingen watching the rising and falling of the sea, the gigantic, monotonous dance of wind and water.

She said: 'I'm an affliction to you, Owen. You don't want me here.'

Her thin hands clutched each other protectively and one day I discovered that behind my back she had become a heavy brandy drinker, but what right or power had I to stop her?

She said: 'I get so bored, Owen. So depressed. Everybody out there is going somewhere. I have nowhere to go. I'm no good to you. I can't even work any more.'

She said: 'Edmund's accident was a dreadful shock. I have a horror of road accidents. I never told you about the accident that happened to me one day driving back from Dublin. I couldn't tell you because I was afraid and sick and I didn't want to remember it. I couldn't help it. The accident, I mean. I read somewhere in a war book that a battle isn't ever what you would expect it to be. You can have fighting here and there and in between a girl milking a cow or a man putting an edge on a scythe. An accident's like that, too. Just a ring of people standing as if they were playing pitch-and-toss or watching a newt that had crawled up out of a drain. But there was this child lying in the middle of the road.'

'Greta, what on earth are you talking about?'

Fiercely she said to me, turning towards me her dark, dark-rimmed eyes: 'About the accident I had once on the road from Dublin. It's why I don't like accidents. There was this child. From shoulders to heels it was wrapped in a man's overcoat. It cried like a lost, bleating lamb. I kept thinking I had killed somebody's child. The little head was resting on a pile of handkerchiefs and towels all sopping with blood. There was this woman crying. In apron and blouse. She was a labourer's wife from some roadside cottage. She said to me: "I don't blame you, ma'am, children'll always be running across roads looking neither right nor left." There was a big, rough man who said:

"Let him lie flat, Jesus only knows what's broken inside." The sergeant wrote all down in his book. I hadn't seen the child until he darted out like a rabbit, yet every time the woman cried I felt like a murderer. It was an awful thing to happen on a lovely morning.'

'Why didn't you tell me about this before now?'

'The child didn't die. It wasn't necessary to tell you. It wasn't even in the papers. I sent money to the mother. I never could tell you anything. Not long ago when you were happy with Maeve. Not that day in the cinema with Lucy. I could only hold your hand when I thought nobody was looking. You didn't want me to hold your hand. You never wanted me. You only wanted Maeve. Even if now you think you want Lucy.'

To all this, the only possible answer was the one Owen Rodgers could not make, and the morning that Margaret, the handmaiden, told me Greta was not in her room, nor in the upper room, nor anywhere in the hotel, my first feeling was genuine relief. The house was no longer haunted. A woman in the creeps of nerves was no asset in the hotel business. She was a ghost from a lost day when the sheep and dogs had been on the green by the river, the rude rams in their pens, the captain's men sweeping the water for salmon. A day passed and Edmund told me she was not with him, and Frank and Dr Grierson were away for the week-end at the miracle shrine of Knock in the County Mayo, and Lucy was in Belfast buying the latest creations; and, drinking alone, panic and remorse came over me like uncontrollable nausea. She could only have gone to one place: back to the shadows where she once had stood mutely in the great kitchen while her father read the orders of the day and the legs of horse and man in the yard outside passed and re-passed the barred window.

*   *   *

The footbridge was broken. One third of it still stood, clutching to the far bank. The water, high and brown after rain, swirled around the piles, cluttering them with driftwood and broken branches. The centre sagged wearily and swayed and creaked at the will of the river. There were no thrawn, black-faced mountain sheep on the grass, no crowds, no dogs, no drink, no laughter, and the great space that had once been soft and green and a running ground for Maeve and Gortin Lass was, even in summer, grey, damp, cold, uninviting. The house beyond it was a broken, blind giant, but when I pulled up on the rusted cowgate at the beginning of the neglected, grass-grown avenue there were, far away along the sands, a man and horse and cart, seemingly motionless, the life drained out of them by distance. They could have been there since that first morning. Because I was afraid of what I might find in that house, nervously remembering what I had once discovered by playing Peeping Tom from the loft above the stables, I walked on the damp land by the edge of the water and waited, for company, until it was clear that the man and horse and cart were moving towards me. It was Hughie Heron. He stood up tall, legs wide apart, the reins taut, slightly inclining backwards on a load of sea-sand. He called to me across the water: 'She's in the house, Owen. She has Lizzie with her. She's in a bad way.'

'I'll be after you,' he said. 'I have to go upstream to the stone bridge to cross.'

Avoiding the front door—it might be opened to me by the dead captain, or behind its blistering, peeling surface I might hear the creak of a foot on the stairway or a whispered word and feel once again that somebody was watching me—I drove into the untidy, littered yard. Hughie was no longer able to keep the place in order. The Macillions, who were planning a total emigration, had lost all interest. Fee the jockey was where he always was, sprawled drunk by the kitchen fire. Around him farmyard fowl fed on grain and crusts and potato peelings or flapped up to table and dresser to peck at unclean crockery. She was wrapped in rugs in the captain's chair, facing the snake, facing an untasted glass of warm milk and a half-full glass of brandy, and Lizzie, handful of brown skin and bones as she had come to be, had done her best for her. Lizzie whispered: 'Drink your milk, Miss Greta. It'll give you strength. She wandered out, Mr Rodgers, and got drenched with rain.'

Then she left us. I said: 'Greta, I've come to help you home.'

Through the dry, unhealthy hair on the crown of her head I could see the white, porous scalp.

She said: 'I have no home.'

'Then I've come to help you back to the city. You'll be more comfortable there.'

'You were always a great one to help, Owen. You caught Edmund from falling the day Fee booted him in the farmyard. I was looking out of the window. You found me a job in the city. You found Alfred when he was lost. You couldn't keep Maeve, though, but then she wasn't worth keeping. You weren't there to catch your friend, my father, the day he fell. But he was dead before he hit the water.'

'Greta, you're raving,' I said.

'For fun and games, Owen, I offered myself this morning to wee Fee in the kitchen. Why not? He's a man, too, even if he has no nose. That's what I told him. You don't need a nose to be a man. But he didn't know what I was talking about. He was too drunk or he thought I was mad.'

From the door I called: 'Lizzie, Lizzie.'

The wind blew cold up the stairs and along the hallway, rattling the front door.

From the captain's chair she said: 'Don't run, young Master

Rodgers. A clever young man like you, Master Rodgers. Is it better to be born and damned than not to be born at all? Oh, we saw you, Owen. Afraid of my father. Six of us afraid in this house. He was twisted and he twisted us. But you could have escaped, Owen. You had no excuse. You wanted to be afraid.'

When I tried to take the brandy from her she struck me in the face. The rugs falling aside showed her half-naked. She screamed when I held her flailing hands, and behind me Hughie whispered: 'I found her in the stream hanging to the timbers of the bridge. She didn't realize the bridge was broken.'

He soothed her and nursed her as Owen Rodgers never could have done. Two days later, when Dr Grierson and Frank returned, we took her back to the city. Never again did I intend to touch Lucy.

'It was time,' my father once said, 'somebody saved something from that wreck.'

Then one dark afternoon, after rain, when lonely women conspicuously pull down windows, lean out, look up and down the street, when pavements are quagmires and all houses prisons in a Siberian marsh, she flung herself out of a window of the upper room. For some odd reason she had torn chair covers and piled furniture against the wall, not, as one would have thought, against the door which wasn't even locked. The traffic was desultory at the time and only a few people saw her fall, but young Grainger, who was taking an increasing interest in the possibilities of his father's business, was one of them. An old woman on the steep streets beyond the river saw the falling body and fainted. Grainger, white in the face and ill, told me again and again how Greta had come down in a dressing-gown in a sitting position and flattened as she hit the pavement, how her head burst in halves and a dock-labourer with the help of a young priest put it together again.

'In O'Connell Street in Dublin,' said the captain, 'between the Nelson Pillar and the monument to Parnell I counted on the footwalk, on one side of the street only, seventeen priests and two nuns.'

The young priest gave what was left of her conditional absolution. For night after night I sweated in hideous nightmares in which moustached, Montenegrin princes on windy towers clove the skulls of vampires and screams descended and descended. Greta had gone down quietly without cry or complaint.

'This diary of hers,' said the doctor, 'Frank found among her papers. I don't know if he read it. You may want it, Owen.'

Maeve didn't come back for the funeral, nor did Alfred, although he could have had parole. The occasion, perhaps, was too painful. Or perhaps it was simply that the Conway Chesneys were never good at attending funerals.

Never again was the diary mentioned. It spoke only to Owen Rodgers and ever since then I have had a horror of diaries. The trouble is, I told myself stubbornly, that no matter how reasonable you are yourself you can't expect other people to act reasonably. Owen Rodgers had never considered himself a Don Juan, never thought himself essential to anybody. How was he to know that Greta Conway Chesney, darkly walking away for ever from him under bright chestnut candles, valued him more than sanity and life?

'A tragic capacity,' she wrote, 'for making people love him.'

'Betrayed,' she wrote, 'the love he inspired. Persuaded the betrayed to accept betrayal. Persuaded himself he was honest.'

Such testimony before violent and self-willed death might have convinced a worm he was Casanova. For me it only meant that never again could I sleep in the room beside the upper room. She had left cold shadows behind her. Grainger's hotel day by day was a cheerless, meaningless prison.

'What could I have done?' I asked myself.

I told myself: 'I did my best.'

Since it would have caused talk to leave too abruptly, I endured the place for a few years.

'Hand it over and get out,' said my father. 'Hand it over to the son of old George. It's his business anyway. He's a changed, steady man since Edmund hit the tree and that poor girl took her own life.'

He came with me to the station the day I left. We sent my baggage ahead and walked, my eyes looking at the ground, because that way I could see the whole place for the last time, and absolve myself from memories, desires and regrets. In a little city, as I had known in better times, you become familiar with everything and know where everything is: the press button for the fire alarm, the sparse accommodation for gents, the corners where lovers can be alone, the old creaking wooden quays, Lovers' Bastion.

'There,' said my father, 'sits the Scion.'

It was Edmund sitting on the courthouse steps. His beard was unkempt. He was one of the Robinson Crusoe derelicts that the strayed reveller sees in the chill, repentant dawn in one of those corners of a big city where the wind drives dust and torn papers. In the telephone kiosk by his side his first toddling infant was corralled, secure from the traffic.

'I would go to live in Dublin,' my father said, 'only it's a long way from your mother's grave. Besides, Jim MacElhatton would miss me. But you'll come back often. Your own place is your own place no matter how far away you go.'

I said I would come back often.

The train moved. The wide estuary diminished. It became a sleek, black snake writing its name for ever on my land, or on what I had thought foolishly was my land. In high ground far beyond the great lake it diminished suddenly to tributary streams.

Then the gradient ascends, descends. You are across the watershed and in a new world.

Eight

A CHANCE ENCOUNTER THE OTHER DAY BROUGHT THE whole story back to me. It was not with the image of an impassive Italianate woman, brown enough for Baghdad, nor yet with the image of a glossy, china figurine from a tinkling, ideal world. She came, accompanied by a seven-year-old boychild, along the canal bank, by a pounding lockgate, a soiled, city relative of a waterfall, to stand by my side at a bus-stop. She said: 'Owen, I didn't know you were in Dublin.'

Owen had been notoriously in Dublin for years but the light, meaningless phrase or sentence always came easily to her. Behind us as we waited children like limpets on a low wall watched the slow approach along a dying weed-grown waterway of one of the last of the chugging, asthmatic barges. The boychild tugged his hand free and went to join them. Her eyes followed him anxiously. She spoke a few words about the dangers of deep water. She's thinner, I thought, or taller, and noticed as her mouth opened and closed, her eyes away from me and still following the boy, that one of her top front teeth was dark with decay.

'You're taller,' I said. 'I didn't know you were in Dublin.'

She said: 'High heels. We came back from England a month ago. I really did hear you were living in this part of the city.'

Somebody, Petsie perhaps, had once told me, against my

blank wall of indifference, that she was married to somebody, certainly not to Molphy the boxer nor to young Beverley who, six months after the runaway, had been killed in a car accident in Luton. Somebody would be the father of the boychild. She opened her mouth again to speak. She had two black teeth. How gladly would one record that, like the wilful, unbiddable girl in a Victorian romance, she had ended up as an abandoned woman, that, as in East Lynne, no luck had attended the runaway match or the decamping to Gretna Green. She said: 'Have you been anywhere yet?'

I said: 'What?'

She said: 'Holidays.'

I said: 'This year I haven't taken my holidays yet.'

'My husband has taken a week of his,' she said. 'I don't know where we'll go for the other fortnight.'

Owen Rodgers, hotelier, who should have known about holidays, was devoid of suggestions but he thought, remotely and far away from the unreal canal water: Go back to Bingen, to the Gortin river, to Magheracolton, to Segully where the fleas ate the man, to the old creaking quays, to Lovers' Bastion, to sunlight through stained glass, to childhood, to the dark cave.

She said: 'How many children have you now?'

I said: 'Three.'

'This is my only one,' she said. 'He takes after my husband.'

'My sons,' said the captain. 'My daughters.'

Her son and herself walked ahead of me to the bus and covertly I noticed that her walk was still young but there was no sign of that slightly stiff hip that, walking or running, had once made her body so attractive. She sat beside her son and, awkwardly turning around in the seat in front, I bought two fares and one half fare and she said: 'I heard your wife died.'

'Yes,' I said. 'Lucy's dead.'

There was no point in telling her, for would she be interested and anyway half the bus would overhear, that I intended to marry again, that my children had grown up around me and hated the woman I wanted to marry, that that woman came from another land and Bingen to her might be portion of a remote, Icelandic legend.

She said: 'Do you see many people from our place?'

'Jeff Macsorley. He works on a newspaper. He wrote three books.'

He had never written The Book: a deep south novel, suh, *the Book of Bingen* or *the Monster of Magheracolton* by Geoffrey Austin Macsorley.

She said: 'He always wanted to be a writer.'

Once at school Jeff had written, as an admonition, on the fly-leaf of Owen's *Golden Treasury*, Kipling's wisdom about the Himalayan peasant, the he-bear, the she-bear and the dangerous female of the species. The book, oddly enough, was preserved, among ledgers and tourist guides, in my office in the more exclusive of my two hotels.

'We see a lot of each other,' I said. 'We go for long walks. Out into the country and along the canal bank. He would never consent to play golf. We drink in a pub called the Red Bear. He's a widower too.'

She said: 'I heard he had a daughter running wild. Your grey hair suits you,' she said. 'You went grey early.'

'Like my father before me. And I go now and again to see Dr Grierson,' I said.

'Dr Grierson. I heard he was locked up.'

Then, startled, she looked tenderly at her boychild as if unwittingly she had exposed him to some dreadful suggestion.

'No. Not locked up. He's in a rest home.'

'You were always thick with the doctor, Owen.'

'My father left him to me in his will.'

In the captain's will, too, the doctor had been remembered. I saw green lawns behind high walls and a benevolently-closed gateway, a corkscrew drive, an artificial lake with seven mallards unhappy because their wings were clipped and they could never fly away. The expert attendants wore white coats. The supervising brothers wore black robes. There was billiard chalk on the shoulders of the doctor's faded coat. He was a bald, quiet man who prayed for his beloved sister and no longer needed the golden sublimation of whiskey, who rested, oars shipped, far from his wide lake, in a lulled backwater where broken men, mostly clerics, would rest until death.

'Fear of loneliness, Owen,' he said. 'The need of community. We're all gregarious, Owen. The day I put on this collar I joined a regiment. No longer can I ignore the mess rules and try to live alone. Yourself and myself, Owen, in spite of some accidental, biological resemblances, are animals of a different species.

'The captain had his masses,' he said. 'The hundred pounds I sent to a home in the midlands. A home for unmarried mothers in the middle of a prosperous rural area of selfish, unmarried farmers. The captain, God have mercy on him, used to talk a great deal about supply and demand.'

'The Macillions;' she said, 'lock stock and barrel, went off to Canada.'

'So I heard. James Kinnear writes to me.'

'You were always thick with James Kinnear.'

'We were always friendly,' I said.

She wondered: 'Did the Macillions have their hair cut before they crossed the wide Atlantic?'

'Crew cuts should settle them,' I said.

'Hughie Heron's in Dublin,' she said. 'He works in a timber yard. He lives near the docks.'

'I didn't know he was in Dublin,' I said. 'He never came to see me.'

She laughed at that, an old laugh I had never heard before. She said: 'Your grandeur would frighten him away. But fancy you not knowing. Fancy you being out of touch.'

Then after a while she said: 'What are you thinking of, Owen?'

There was no good reason, apart from the sound of my own name, why I should have told her.

'Of a man used to travel with me in a surburban bus,' I said. 'He had a tiny white terrier that perched like a pigeon on his shoulder. A young man. He was killed in a road accident. Off an auto-cycle. I always wondered what happened to the terrier. Where it found a new shoulder to perch on.'

'You're as odd, Owen, as you ever were,' she said. 'The world is full of shoulders.'

'What happened to the red setter?'

'What red setter?'

'You remember the red setter you had.'

I couldn't say the red setter I brought you, or the red setter we had, or the red setter that came out of mystery and vanished for ever the night you ran away. Her forehead corrugated. She was genuinely trying to remember. She said: 'But I never had a red setter.'

Following the golden body of Gortin Lass I walked again into the lost, wet valley. There was only that abandoned cabin now used for cattle, and the sound of a faraway waterfall. In all my days on those mountains, that was the only time I saw the valley of the golden dog. Trying to look back to it from the top of a city bus was a doomed, hopeless effort. The mountain mist, the wizard's mist from Segully, came all around me. The torrent moaned over drear, green stones. Perhaps, like the dog, the valley had never existed. Nothing existed except somebody's faceless son.

'Who made me? That's in the catechism. God made me. A priest made me, a scholar, a drunkard, a soldier, a monster, a kindly musical man, a wizard from wet mountains: God the father in seven mystical shapes.'

'Owen,' said Petsie (my more select manageress for my more select hotel), 'we'll fix a bed for you in forty-two. Why did you have to meet that strap? This was one day you should have been sober. Those Bingen women were never any good for you.'

'Who was good for whom? Who was bad for whom?'
I began again: 'Who made me . . .'

'What about your wife?' Petsie said.

'Dead, Petsie. Unreal. No part of the story. Children who grow away from me. This place. Deep carpet. That ornamental copper warming-pan. That phoney hearth. That false bellows. Kate Carr would laugh. That hardwood buddha. That trick card-table, roulette wheel and chessboard I brought back from Italy. The plaster images of the seven dwarfs coyly half-concealed in the shrubs in the enclosed garden. Come one and all and pay your bills, this desk shall fly from its firm base as soon as I.'

'Bow once again like that,' she said, 'and you'll topple.'

'At your service. Owen Rodgers who couldn't be a healer but is now a *maître d'hôtel*. Courtesy combined with culture. Neat but by no means cheap, or shall we say inexpensive. Stop with me when you come to friendly Ireland. Today, Petsie, I saw a boy with no face. I saw beauty with two black teeth. Only the Gortin river was real and the captain and the music of the village band. My father was good and grey, kind and melodious. The captain was a certifiable monster. The doctor was a learned man twisted by celibacy and sustained by drink. It took the three of them to make a man, me, the child of kindness and music, burnt-out hopes and whiskey, and compressed malevolence. That's me. That's man.'

'There's a letter there for you,' she said, 'from James Kinnear.'

So when I had slept and sobered I read the letter.

'Your old friend, Alfred,' Kinnear wrote, 'is going from bad to worse or from conquest to conquest like Alexander. He came into me the other day and threw on the table a piece of paper that looked as if it had wiped the rumps of half Ireland and he says, says he, "I want advice." It was a letter from a woman from up near Segully and what it said in brief was: "Mr Chesney, you have my daughter Minnie in trouble and pay up or I'll leave the baby on your doorstep." Minnie had been a maid in Magheracolton. Tell Jeff that. Minnie the maid of Magheracolton. Went in a maid but didn't come out a maid. You see, I remember my Shakespeare. Old Mrs Brannigan who housekeeps now for him was off patrol for one night and on that night the damage was done. Incidentally, the sailor Brannigan who made money mysteriously in Cairo has, they say, his eye on Bingen and, in a fractional way, I suppose, they have a family claim on the place. Alfred, says I, your family motto should be *age viriliter*, and it's a good thing that farming prices are as high as they are because I declare to God he has more progeny here and there than the Grand Turk. You'll be as bad, says I to him, as the man in Connacht who named his illegitimates after the points of the compass until he ran out of directions.

Then he looked at me out of the big, bleary eyes with the red rims under them and, says he, there wouldn't have been a word about it if it hadn't been for the sister. It seems that Minnie's sister, Marianne, came the next night, a night too late, to sleep with Minnie and didn't she waken up in the middle of the night to find Alfred with his hand under the bedclothes. "What do you want, Mr Chesney?" says she. Where was the girl reared to ask such unmannerly, unnecessary questions? "Socks," says Alfred, "dry socks. Mrs Brannigan says she left them somewhere." Socks, I ask you. It was Marianne who told the mother and the mother wrote the letter. I settled it out of court and Abraham, father of many, bestowing his image lavishly, is now paying for another part of Ireland.'

'Socks,' wrote Kinnear. 'That's better by far than Austrian dogs.'

No bugle blew it would seem the night Minnie was left alone to be dishonoured. Had the girl known the past, could she have invoked the spirit of the place: 'Oh, captain, my captain, come to my aid, in my battle take part.' Or was the bugle silent and the echo of the Boer War guns faint beyond illimitable veldts because the captain, enigmatic and possibly still bewhiskered in the grave, fiendishly allowed his misshapen son to slobber deeper and deeper into absurd responsibility? Dead or alive (who knows better than Owen Rodgers?) he could make them remember him. Alfred, rummaging under rustic petticoats, might pause in the night's occupation, a tinker caught rifling eggs in henhouses, look around fearfully, shake his head to dislodge the brazen echo, as a dripping bather might shake his head to burst a bubble in his ear. Frank, the levite, could conquer the captain by praying for him as we should pray for all tyrants when they're safely dead. Edmund might stir uneasily in his daze in the Diamond, blink painfully at the descending sweep of the Diamond Hill, squint ferret-wise over his shoulder to see was his infant son still closed in the telephone kiosk and safe from the traffic.

'One day,' wrote Kinnear, 'he fell asleep in a wheelbarrow outside the farm machinery depot and some japer wheeled him home and parked the wheelbarrow outside his own door. . . .'

'I shudder away from their story,' Jeff said.

But Jeff was never part of their story. The story of Peeping Tom Rodgers was all about other people.

Over our heads cranes swung red barrels of porter to the holds of ships. Ahead of us, like a line of slag, scrap-iron was deposited for the roaring belly of a foundry. The day's tumult had temporarily banished the gulls. We walked eastwards towards the evening and along the South Wall.

'Irish novels,' he said, 'are all mud and misery, all bejasus, all parish priests, all girls having babies. I want an idyll for my next book. I want a novel in which every man and woman's a virgin and nobody, not even a cow in a byre, has a baby.'

'Alfred's Caliban in a cave,' he said. 'The mountains around him would no more take pity on him and cover him up than the mountains that refused to answer the call of the children of Jerusalem. Outside the earthquake belt there's no point even in hoping unreasonably for such a merciful release. And there's no end to any story, Owen, even to this one that may have had a beginning when the servants stood in line to hear the music box. Alfred will see to it that there's no end to this story. Scattering the captain's image broadcast throughout the land so that monsters can spring up right and left and nobody even know where they came from. Neat, little, anonymous monsters. Illegitimates all over the place. Working in England. Emigrat-

276

ing to Canada, wedding female Eskimoes, carrying something of the captain's blood to the frozen frontiers of Russia and, for all we know, beyond.

'Caliban in his granite cave,' he said. 'A shambling monster. An ogre from a child's tale.'

'Alfred,' I said, 'wouldn't be the ogre in this tale.'

'He wouldn't be the fortunate third son. There's no fortunate son in this story. The captain left his curse in those old, damp rooms, surrounded by relics of wild animals. The great winds blow, bending sycamores and hazels, the mountains glitter. Alfred gnaws bones, broods on young love lost, brown hair, dancing and the sound of mouth-organ music.'

'Even now,' I said, 'I doubt if the captain was the monster.'

'The image of life,' he said, 'that would come out of their story would be one of the blank stone images of Easter Island. Nobody's sure where they came from. Their story would be a ghost story from a dying island.'

Across the scum-coated Liffey preparatory steam hissed from the Liverpool boat. A plane went south towards Paris. To the screaming of some factory hooter, dockers were slipping on jackets, ending the day, leaving the river wall quiet for the foraging, returning gulls.

'The sadness of the land we live in,' said Jeff, 'is no longer the melancholy Celtic sadness of low skies, soft rain and birds crying on the bog. It's the exhausted sadness, the slough following in the wake of exasperation, of the little man who missed the train. We were too late for everything. We were too late even to be free.

'The great Victorian steamroller,' he said. . . .

'Here we go,' I said. 'Master, I listen.'

'The great Victorian steamroller, rusty and discarded by its inventors when they got rid of dewlaps and mutton-chop whiskers, still functions well enough to flatten the fair hills and squeeze into pulp the young people of Ireland. The agile ones run East and West. We bought the steamroller second-hand. Duly we had it vetted and blest by the clergy.

'We thank Blessed Oliver Plunket,' he said, 'for keeping us out of the war. If you were a Christian and saw a man bloated with dropsy would you thank Blessed Oliver because you, child of exceptional grace, were not dropsical? Would you thank him that it wasn't your fate, as it was his, to be hanged, disembowelled and chopped into pieces?'

'There's hope for us, Jeff. Cleanliness and courtesy. Saying darlint, darlint to every tourist stranger.'

'The weather,' he said.

'We can beat our bad weather.'

'But we can't beat our latter-day Victorians. Didn't you yourself tell me of the plight of the visiting astronomer who thought, God look to his wit, that he'd find in Dublin some place like the amusement area in Hamburg?'

Meditating on the guileless astronomer's comic plight we came in the evening on the edge of Ireland to the dockside home of Hughie Heron.

He was gaunt and shrunk in his clothes and, like Jeff and myself, he was a widower. The great gently-drooping moustache was grey. His long swinging stride was too elastic by far for unyielding pavements. He was a great scyamore withering far from its native earth in Magheracolton. But his voice was clear and melodious as it ever was, when he left his neat little cottage with us and walked where a canal burst out between bulwarks to join the main, sea-going stream. Two city fishermen stood fifty yards from the junction, one of them inexpertly spinning, raking up a truss of foul weeds.

'It's not what we we're used to, Owen,' he said. 'You'd take pity on them. They never, I doubt, dropped a fly over a clear water.'

His voice was as loud as if he was hailing a neighbour across seven fields but the two fishermen laughed good-naturedly, waved to him, called him by name.

Swans were arranged in a lethargic row on a black mudbank. Behind them rose a huge oblong of workers' flats, a few windows brightening the dusk. One cargo-ship headed out to sea and from somewhere came the pip-pip-pip of a small motor craft. An idle barge rested on mud. From a shabby pub paid-off dockers sang a melancholy porter-and-coaldust chorus. Far upstream, behind a stately eighteenth-century dome, the sky was red. We leaned on an iron railing and recalled the people, all except one, who were dead.

'It's not bad here,' he said. 'The neighbours are kind. My niece Rosie looks after me, my brother's daughter that was killed with the Inniskillings in the first big war. She worked in the house at Redmond's bridge years ago until she had a bit of misfortune when she was foolish, as maybe you heard, Owen. But she kept the child and everything went well with her afterwards.'

We walked inland, breathing the odour of a gasworks, by foul slums and canal docks, by two fishery-protection corvettes, by two student wardsmaids fresh from the country, free for a while from servitude in a neighbouring hospital, pointing down the lane towards the gasworks and asking innocently where does that go. All rust, dust and desolation in one corner of the dock was an old passenger boat slave-sold for breaking to the foundry.

'The sights you see,' he said. 'I travelled on her when I went first to the potato fields in Ayrshire. That was long before your day, Owen. Long before the captain came to Magheracolton and Lizzie and myself made a home in Drumard, God rest them both.'

Ahead of us then we viewed green trees, tufted and painted along the sky, wispy clouds above them and a crowd on a canal bridge by a lock, watching a rich man's white pleasure-boat beginning a journey westwards to the Shannon. We were within barking distance of a home where injections were ultimately given to homeless, unwanted dogs, within sight of a place where cattle were impounded on the silent premises of a derelict meat factory.

'Whatever it is, it's Ireland,' Hughie said. 'Paddy and all his fine sons are faraway in Canada.'

Jeff asked: 'You never thought of emigrating, Hughie?'

'Once I did,' he said, 'when I was young. I had the money put by for my fare. I was touring down by the river in the townland of Lislap saying farewell to the people when the priest rode down to ask me to stand godfather to a child that was born. I took it as an omen and I stayed.'

The pub that we drank in was in a swarming area, half slum, half new suburb. Seven members of the Legion of Mary, fervent after a meeting, chatted in a church porch. Children carried away, wrapped up in newspaper, two bottles of black stout for me daddy's supper. His voice, when we tempted him to sing, was all memories of the first sudden spring day when cows are milked in the field and scraping hens do gavottes in straw and dung at stable doors.

'With my dog and gun,' he sang.

City people who knew him and had taken to him and his songs, listened. Then, nailed boots prancing, he sang in a randy voice about some long-forgotten, rural house of ill fame.

'My father he keeps a long staff and a ferrule, a spike on the end to hold fast by the floor. I trusted too much to the old fellow's halberd. A mortification I got, to be sure.

'My mother began for to reel and to rattle, and swore that her house I would not enter in. Says I: "My good woman, don't fly in a passion, for sure I'll get lodgings with Nora MacGlynn."

'Here's to Nora keeps a jar without licence, and keeps the one bed, too, behind the skew wall. Of all the houses I know in my calling, sure Nora MacGlynn keeps the best house of call.'

They were with him now. The black and yellow drink was flowing. Closing time was not far away.

'So Nora,' they sang, 'keeps the best bed of all.'

'Farewell Segully,' he sang, 'and Magheracolton, where rural pastimes did once abound; and in each cottage, a home for strangers, a hearty welcome was always found.'

'A hearty welcome,' they agreed, 'was always found.'

'For William Moore,' he sang, 'and his brother Arthur, two loyal comrades will sail with me. Likewise their sisters, three handsome fair maids, possessed of wisdom and chastitee.'

To the chorused, repeated praise of those three paragons among women they gave all the benefit of the irony of a shabby trollop of a city.

'And when in Quebec,' he sang, 'we're safely landed, kind friends will greet us upon the shore. But the hills that stand above Magheracolton and the Gap of Gortin we will see no more.'

Voices of Dublin people who had never seen Magheracolton, never heard of the captain, chorused plaintively: 'And the Gap of Gortin we will see no more.'

In the lull that followed I could hear the wash of the Gortin river, the bird voice of the ocarina, and my grey, dead father said kindly out of eternal silence: 'He was a re-organizer, that's a destroyer. He changed the name of Magheracolton to Bingen. There was a good song once about the hills that stand above Magheracolton. Would that be a sufficient reason for hating a man like the captain?'

Afterword

Benedict Kiely has a particular kind of reputation and, like a lot of public perception, it doesn't tell the full story. It's based upon the much-loved image of the man as a leisurely, sonorous story-teller, a latter-day *seanachai* or Gaelic reciter of tales out of the rich repository of the folk. However rich this vein of folklore may be in Kiely's work, there is more to his writing than this, as *The Captain with the Whiskers* beautifully illustrates.

The great German critic Walter Benjamin once described, in an essay on the Russian short-story-writer Leskov, the process whereby an oral folk tradition is subsumed into the literary short story. The movement is from a pre-literary form to a literary one, from a pre-modern imagination to a modern one. And no matter how sophisticated the writer, such writing will always carry something of the traditional in its narrative flow, its easy-going tone, the natural exuberance of the oral story-teller before his peasant audience.

Benjamin might be describing the roots of any number of modern Irish writers of fiction, including Benedict Kiely. In Kiely's case, it is a view further advanced by the personality of the man himself, particularly in his radio broadcasts. That amber voice has delighted many listeners over the years with abundant anecdotes, songs and poems out of a repertoire which seemed inexhaustible.

Kiely is also a master of several other skills crucial to a living folk tradition of oral story-telling. He has a memory which seems on constant alert. He has a detailed knowledge of landscape and all the associations of a particular place. This sense of place permeates his work, what he himself once called 'the interweaving of love and imagination with locality'.

He possesses as well a large fund of what might be called the work of amateur authorship. This too is a legacy of the oral folk tradition. Once so common in rural Ireland, it is a fund of rhymes, poems, ballads, sayings and all the mish-mash of interchanging, oral entertainment among the people in simpler days, before the invention of modern media.

This generous, story-telling personality is best illustrated at a literary level in the magisterial volume *The Collected Stories of Benedict Kiely*, one of the great contemporary collections in that genre. But it is also there in the novels – sometimes, as in a book like *Cards of the Gambler*, giving the novel its peculiar, narrative force.

There are, however, several other sides to Kiely the writer. For one thing, he is an astute critic of fiction and has written one of the best studies of early-twentieth-century Irish novels, *Modern Irish Fiction*. This intelligence and mastery of literary form lie as a basis of his own best novels, including *The Captain with the Whiskers*.

He is also a man of passionately held convictions. Yet many of his readers have been surprised by the ferocity with which he engaged the mindless slaughter in his native Ulster in books like *Proxopera* and *Nothing Happens in Carmincross*. How could such an apolitical writer, it was asked, be so engaged?

No one should have been surprised. There is a moral indignation in most of Kiely's work and much of it is directed at the social and political absurdities of his native land. Sometimes this sharpness is hidden beneath that rare virtue, a genuine affection for and tolerance of most human frailties. But in Kiely's fiction this moral discrimination still sees beneath the surface. When it faces the truly monstrous, as in the legacy of Captain Chesney in this novel, the effect is both chilling and tolerant – unflinching in its depiction of waste but never losing that generosity of spirit.

There is a particular pleasure in revisiting a book that one enjoyed a long time ago. I must have read *The Captain with the Whiskers* shortly after it was first published, over forty years ago. Of course, I was not simply going back to the book again. I was also going back to the kind of reader that I was, myself, back then. We read books in the present moment of our lives. Tomorrow we will read them differently.

The Captain with the Whiskers is a story told by Owen Rodgers of his involvement with the satanic Captain Conway Chesney and his five children – three boys and two girls; in particular with the two girls – the beautiful, seductive Maeve and the cramped, unhappy Gretta. Owen loves Maeve in one of those disastrous affairs that young men tend to get into, falling in love, as they are wont to do, with images rather than real people. But Owen beds Gretta and that too is a disaster.

Outlined like this, the book may appear grim but it is nothing of the kind. Partly this is due to the fact that everything Kiely touches in the novel is filled with vivacity, with the spring of natural life. And the story in the foreground is set against a fully realised community and landscape that brims with energy and loving background detail. Kiely is a splendid writer about Irish social life.

When I first read the book I was fascinated by the captain, obviously. He is one of the more memorable monsters in Irish fiction. But I also read the book as a growing-up story, a *Bildungsroman*, the story of a boy of about my own age. Indeed, his story even reflected some of my own problems with young women! All this was happening in an Ireland that was utterly familiar to me but is now part of history. Here is one description of the captain talking. His speech is set securely in that Ireland of the immediate past, an Ireland incomprehensible to the young of today:

> The captain was a wit. With all his suavity and pseudo-politeness he was well known to be a man of strong mind and advanced opinions.
>
> 'In O'Connell Street in Dublin between Nelson Pillar and the monument to Parnell I counted on the footwalk on one side of the street only, seventeen priests and two nuns. What would Nelson and Parnell have said?'

I remember, too, being enraptured by the musical tone of the narrative, which perfectly captures an engaging speaking voice, that oral tradition again. I had just come through the Irish school system and its seven years of Latin and Greek, so that I responded with delight to the easy learning of this narrator.

Kiely is a writer who can transpose Ovid's *Metamorphoses* into his native landscape without the slightest pretension and in the most natural fashion possible. If, on one level, *The Captain with the Whiskers* is a version of the expulsion from Eden, complete with snake and bitter fall, there are other, pagan myths swirling about in the narrative as well. Following one particularly lovely flourish, he offers us this aside:

> That, as you can see, is a slightly altered passage from one of the books of Ovid they never gave me to read in school, that diverting book about animals turning to stone, men and women to trees or animals or stones or stars, seduced Io to a sleek heifer, and of genial Jove trying his luck with a Grecian nymph every time Juno turned her broad back; and it's my way of introducing you to the sheep-dog trials on the greensward before the captain's house in Bingen.

This time round, however, I found a harder, more sharp-edged book than before. It still celebrated conviviality and humour in that fully realised community. The exchanges were still laced with music and song and generous rounds of drink. The great heart was still beating there in the writing. But, with age, perhaps, I was able to see a more penetrating, more demanding writer at work. Certainly I had become more aware of how the writing stares into an abyss of suffering, loss and failure and how it comes to terms with the harsh compromises of life.

There were two details that I had forgotten about completely from my early reading and I think they had a significant effect upon the way I read the book the second time round.

One is the fact that the monstrous captain is dead and buried just short of a third of the way through the novel. He is such a dominant presence that you feel when you put the book down that he has been there from beginning to end. And in a curious way this is, indeed, true. He may be dead by page ninety-two but he dominates the following, nearly two hundred pages. This is because one of the things that Kiely is writing about is the genetic transmission of character, the passing on of evil from father to child. Of the three boys, the dog-like bumbling Alfred is, perhaps, the most tragic, a compulsive, demented seducer of girls. There is even a surreal, grimly comic vision in the book, of Alfred spreading the seed of the captain throughout the length and breadth of the land.

The other detail of the novel that I had totally forgotten over the years had to do with the ending. The final chapter is a kind of projection into the future. Here Owen is made to look back on the story he has just told us from the perspective of a troubled maturity. It is as if we, as readers, are being asked to go back over that story afresh but from an entirely new perspective. It makes for a memorable ending and is one of several sophisticated techniques in the book involving time. Incidentally, the ending also includes a kind of early-post-modernist discourse on Irish fiction, since one of Owen's pals is an aspiring novelist.

When other writers admire Kiely's writing they often talk about the variety that he brings to the narrative voice. One of the technical virtuosities of this book is its use of multiple voices. This is some distance, indeed, from the simple structure of the oral folk tale. But we are reminded again of Kiely's origins in a culture obsessed with the anecdote.

In addition to Owen's narration, there are these other, choric voices inserted into the storyline. The effect of this is to enlist the community in the telling of the story. The community becomes, as it were, part of the most intimate exchanges, a loss of privacy which was part of the cost of living in rural Ireland in those days. One wonderful, comic example of this is the chorus of the local band, where each instrument provides its own sly, gossipy comment on the proceedings.

There is another, quite brilliant use of voice in the case of Owen Rodgers himself. He speaks to us directly but he also speaks of himself in the third person. This is a kind of double narrative which is entirely in keeping with his character: self-ironical, sensitive to his own passion and the damage it causes. But he is additionally the carrier of that Kiely moral discrimination which I've already mentioned and which gives this book so much of its moral substance. That moral discrimination emerges through the self-reflection of Owen.

It is the narrative which keeps the dead captain alive long after he's dead, a ghost at every feast and every tryst, a shadow that actually shapes events long after his death. There is one extraordinary scene where this ghostly presence takes hold of the three sons, possesses them 'like a diabolized Ariel' and Owen collects a wallop or two in the mêlée. This is a very powerful portrayal of personality and the way it can impress itself on everyone and everything within its ambit, even from beyond the grave.

The Captain with the Whiskers is, however, essentially about young love and why it cannot survive in the hero and heroine that Kiely has created. The young man has to learn about the flaw in beauty, the very disfigurement which made that beauty so attractive in the first place. In the process he learns something of the dangerous gift of desire. The young woman is, quite simply, a child of the captain and, as such, is both victim and transgressor.

There is, however, one constant in all of this human flux which brings us back again to place, to locality. The novel gives a vivid sense of the student life of the Dublin of its day. But its real centre is elsewhere, in the natural beauty of the Irish countryside of Kiely's Ulster.

This is the Eden of the book from which the young lovers are driven out. Its rich, well-watered landscape is evoked throughout as a way of measuring, even taming the antics of human beings. It is never merely decorative background, although Kiely's lyrical writing is a joy in itself. This is, after all, the same land taken by the captain with something of the brute intrusion of any planter, imposing his own, foreign name, Bingen, on the ancient Irish one, Magheracolton.

Through the eyes of disillusionment at the end, the landscape itself eventually takes on the shading of loss. When the older Owen looks back on the story he has told to us, he remembers the countryside through an elegiac mist, through the memory of an essentially decent but damaged man on the top of a Dublin bus.

In his mind's eye, Owen walks through mountains again with the red setter dog, Gortin Lass. The dog was his gift to Maeve, but like much else now, including their love, it might never have existed.

Following the golden body of Gortin Lass I walked again through the lost, wet valley. There was only that abandoned cabin now used for cattle, and the sound of a faraway waterfall. In all my days on those mountains, that was the only time I saw the valley of the golden dog. Trying to look back to it from the top of a city bus was a doomed, hopeless effort. The mountain mist, the wizard's mist from Segully, came all around me.

Thomas Kilroy
2003